DELUSIONAL TRAITS

David George Clarke

The Rare Traits Trilogy
Book II

To Linda

Very Best Wishes

David Clarke

Feb 2014 .

This is a work of fiction. Any resemblance of any of the characters or places to real persons living or dead or to real places is purely coincidental.

Other books by David George Clarke

Fiction

Rare Traits

Non-fiction

Hong Kong Under The Microscope
– A History of the Hong Kong Government Laboratory, 1879 – 2004

For my wife, Gail, my family and many friends,
with grateful thanks for all your support in so many ways

Part I
1970

Chapter 1

Sheriff Mort Bachman prised his three-hundred-pound frame from his patrol car. It was early July, the hottest time of year, and tonight a ferocious thunderstorm had developed out of nowhere. Bachman took it personally. He'd driven all the way to Colorado Springs for a stupid meeting that the state's chief of police cancelled at the last minute, and then all the way back. Seven hours in a car with no AC and his shirt had been drenched in sweat the whole time. Now the rain was coming down in torrents as he waddled to the motel entrance, the darkness broken with the flashing blue and red of police and ambulance lights and the more erratic, staccato flashing of a motel sign that had seen too many summers.

"Jimmy!" he barked at a police officer standing in the small reception area. Deputy Lance 'Jimmy' Winslate turned his pencil-thin, six-foot-four body to face his boss. He would have been even taller but for a pronounced spinal curvature in his neck that pushed his head well forward of his body. This and a long and very cleft chin gave him a more than passing resemblance to a crowbar.

The normally relaxed Jimmy's face was taut, his eyes haunted. "Sheriff," he drawled in little more than a whisper. "Glad you could make it so quick. This is a bad one. I never seen so much blood."

Bachman raised a quizzical eyebrow. Jimmy very seldom called him 'sheriff', preferring just 'boss'. He must be spooked.

"Tell me what you got, Jimmy, 'fore I take a look," he said, removing his hat and shaking the rainwater from it.

"Three people, sheriff: two dead – one male, one female; and one unconscious – the female that killed them. Covered in blood, but she don't seem badly injured, just knocked around a little."

"How d'you know she did it?"

"Witnesses, two of 'em. Seen her knifing the male in the back while he was crouched on the floor. Brutally, they said." He paused, his eyes squinting in distaste at the memory as he pictured the scene. "And you should see his face. It's like his mouth's been through a shredder."

"Where's this woman now?"

"In the ambulance. Doc said she ain't in no danger. Gave her a shot of something to knock her out. She's still unconscious, far's I know, but anyway, she ain't goin' nowhere. She's all strapped down; nice and secure."

"OK, let's take a look."

"Mind if I don't go back in there, sheriff? I ain't too good with this stuff."

Bachman cast a reproachful glance at the deputy, thought about giving him a lecture, and then decided against it. Jimmy had his limitations and there was nothing he could do about it.

"Stay outside, son. Don't want you throwing up and contaminating the scene, now."

"It's number four, boss," said Jimmy, pointing to a side door labelled 'Rooms 1-12', relaxing now he thought he wasn't going to see the bodies again.

Bachman opened the door and grunted as he looked up to see the corrugated metal roof of the covered walkway leaking freely through its joints. He fixed his hat firmly back on his head.

Several people stood on the walkway, blocking the sheriff's path, their own path blocked by another police officer.

"Gangway, folks!" yelled Bachman, trying to exude a politeness he didn't feel. His wet clothes were sticking to his body and he didn't relish the thought of what was waiting for him in the room. The police officer, Deputy Will 'Sweet' Praline jumped to attention and tried to assist in clearing a way for his boss.

"Sweet," said Bachman, "why don't you find an empty room for these folks rather than have them standing out here? Which of you two folks were witnesses to what went on?"

"Those two are with Tracey-Ann down the way in another room, sheriff," explained Praline. "These folks just heard a lot of shouting."

"In that case," said Bachman, turning to the group, "why don't you all just return to your rooms and we'll call on you later? But don't go checkin' out before we got your statements."

He fixed his eyes on them, his imposing if sodden figure asserting an authority that saw them reluctantly shuffle away.

Bachman walked past the deputy, now lurking back in the shadows, and stopped outside room four. He glanced around. Further down the walkway, he could see light streaming through the partly open door of another room and hear Tracey-Ann's voice, muffled by the noise of the rain. He took a deep breath and turned the door handle to room four.

Inside, Doctor James Truman, pathologist and head of surgery at the local hospital in nearby Del Norte, was jotting notes into a small leather-bound notebook.

"Doc," said Bachman in greeting.

"Mort," replied Truman. "Careful where you stand; there's a lot of blood around and your boys haven't finished with their photos yet. I couldn't wait for them since I got an emergency back in town – the living needing more urgent attention than the dead, you understand."

"Busy night, huh, Doc?" said Bachman, the distraction evident in his voice as his eyes took in the extent of the horror laid out before him.

A young woman was lying face up on the double bed, her head tilted unnaturally to one side to reveal a huge gash in her throat. Her sleeveless top and denim miniskirt were soaked in blood, as were her matted blond hair and the sheet and pillow beneath her. Her eyes were wide open, the terror of her final moments frozen in her lifeless face.

Between the woman and the body of a shirtless man lying face down on the floor was more blood than Bachman thought a human body could contain. It covered the floor around the man and had soaked into the bedding at the foot of the bed. The spray had reached as far as the ceiling. A knife was buried to the hilt in the man's back and next to it, Bachman could see other torn and jagged wounds.

"Jimmy said something about the man's face," muttered Bachman, still transfixed by the silent aftermath of the extreme violence that must have exploded in the drab motel room.

Truman stooped to pull the man onto his side. "I turned him back to the position he was in so you could see for yourself how he was found," he explained.

"Jeeze," whispered Bachman when he saw the ragged remains of the man's mouth and cheeks. "What in hell was that all about?"

Below the man's lifeless eyes, his face was cut to ribbons, his cheeks and mouth a series of ragged tears. Strips of flesh hung loosely, exposing several teeth. With blood soaked into and matting the man's full, black beard, his features were now almost unrecognisable.

"Looks more like mangled roadkill than a man," muttered the sheriff.

"There's a wound to the chest as well," said Truman, "but it's wide of the mark. It won't have punctured his heart. I think it was probably the ones to the back that did that. Whatever; it was a vicious and frenzied attack."

"You ain't wrong there, Doc. What about the unconscious woman?"

"She was lying across him. Collapsed that way after she'd stabbed him, according to your witnesses," replied Truman. "She's covered in blood, most of which will be his and perhaps the girl's." He nodded towards the body on the bed.

"The woman's injured," he continued, "but it's all fairly superficial. Taken a few heavy blows to the body and one eye's black and half-closed. She came around when she was moved and it seemed like she was a threat even though your boys had cuffed her, so I sedated her. She'll be out for a while."

"Was she high on something?"

"Hard to say. Her pupils were pretty normal, but the look on her face was like a crazed animal. I've taken a blood sample for testing."

"Reckon she did them both?"

"Hard to say if she killed the woman; she certainly had the knife."

"DA'll be wanting the death penalty for something this vicious. Do we know who they are?"

"Only the man at the moment, I believe. There's a billfold with a driver's license. Ty Donnington. Does that mean anything?"

"Rings a little bell, but I can't think where."

Truman nodded. "OK, Mort, now you've seen the bodies, I'll bag this knife." He reached out a gloved hand and carefully removed the weapon from the man's back, placing it in a brown paper bag. After handing the bag to the sheriff, he picked up his case. "I gotta rush. I reckon the woman won't be much use to you for a few hours. As for the autopsies, I should be able to start them in the morning."

"OK, Doc. Thanks. We'll get the bodies to the morgue in Del Norte. I guess I'll have to wait till tomorrow before I get more from Lizzie Borden out there."

Chapter 2

Annie Carr awoke the following morning and immediately panicked: she couldn't move her arms and legs. As she struggled against whatever was holding her down, a sharp pain shot through her ribs and a hammer pounded in her head. She strained to look down the length of her body. Although her vision was blurred, she could see her wrists and ankles were constrained by leather straps attached to the bed on which she was lying. A larger belt was pulled tightly around her stomach. Her throat constricted as her pulse started to race.

She looked around in confusion. She was in a cream-coloured room that smelled of antiseptic. A large window to her right had bars on it. She frowned, wincing as the movement of the muscles in her face sent a spasm of pain through her eyes. Was this a hospital room? Had she had an accident? If she had, why was she constrained?

Through the fog in her mind, images of the previous day drifted slowly into focus – images of Petra, Ty and Seth; images etched with violence and screaming. She closed her eyes and tried to remember. Drop City. They had been to the artists' community of Drop City, south of Trinidad in southern Colorado, the first time the two women had been allowed out of the commune in years. It had been a great disappointment to her. She had expected a group of creative spirits, people to whom she could relate and interact with artistically, although Ty wouldn't have let her get too close. However, if Drop City had been like that at one stage, it wasn't now. Politics and infighting had taken over and no one was interested in her work. Worse still, Ty had argued with the two men who ran the place and had been virtually thrown out. She'd had no choice but leave with him and the others.

She remembered Ty being very bad-tempered in the truck on the way back, smoking one joint after another and yelling at them to shut up. As ever, his music was so loud they could hardly think, let alone talk. After some hours, it was starting to get dark and Ty decided to stop for the night at a motel. He'd calmed down and it was clear what he now wanted: there was that arrogant glint in his eye as he looked at Petra, a sneer lifting one side of his nose. Annie remembered stealing a glance at Seth, only to catch him leering at her in the same way. She hated Seth almost as much as she hated Ty but she remembered feeling pleased that they were stopping; that it might be an opportunity.

What had happened? She went to scratch her head and the restraints tightened once more against her wrists, rattling the bed. She frowned.

In her mind's eye she suddenly saw the cardinal advancing on her across his bedchamber to where she was lying on his bed, her wrists tied to a rail behind her head. Cardinal Alvaro! She struggled harder against the restraints as he started to unbutton his cassock, a victorious, dominant smile on his cynical lips. She pulled again with all her strength and the rail broke, weakened by a century or more of woodworm. Her hands now free, she grabbed a length of the rail and swung it as hard as she could, connecting firmly with the cardinal's left temple. He staggered and sank to his knees. In a flash she was on him, crashing the rail across his head a second time, then a third. She knew he kept a knife under his cassock; she felt for it; found it; removed it. With hardly a pause for thought, she plunged it into his back as he crouched on all fours, dizzy from the beating. She continued stabbing him, time and again, until he sagged to the floor. Even then, she stabbed him several more times. Finally she sat back on her heels, her mouth foaming, her heart pounding.

The hospital bed rattled loudly as she tried to move. Her thoughts came back to the present. Why had she thought of the cardinal? That desperate scene had been acted out nearly four hundred years before in Naples, following her subjection to the scheming cleric in the

1570s and '80s. It had been centuries since she'd fought off Cardinal Alvaro's advances and left him dead on his bedroom floor in the Inquisitional Chambers; centuries since she'd fled Naples with Luigi, her son.

She heard a door open and looked up to see a figure in white framed in the doorway.

"No use fighting against them straps, honey," she heard the figure say as it walked up to the bed. "They're only there for your own good. Don't want you hurting yourself, now, do we?"

The nurse reached out to Annie's wrist to take her pulse and then checked her forehead and pupils. "How are you feeling?"

"I need some water," croaked Annie, "and I need to use the bathroom." She winced, aware again of a throbbing in one eye. "I can't see properly. Why am I tied down?"

"One thing at a time," said the nurse as she lifted Annie's head and pressed a cup of water to her parched lips.

As her head was raised, Annie saw a dark, hazy shadow fill the doorway. She recoiled in horror, spilling the water.

Father Bonsanto! The bloated, ugly little priest from Padua who had discovered her secret and threatened to expose her! She'd let him have his way with her in return for his silence. Fat chance; all he'd wanted was more. She still vividly remembered his foul breath and fouler body, his fleshy lips caressing her limbs, her neck and her face. She shuddered. She'd smashed a glass goblet and thrust it repeatedly into his face, tearing at his flesh. Then she'd run from the room, leaving him bleeding to death on the bed, his hands clutching at his shredded face in agony. That escape in the early seventeen hundreds had been a close-run thing. She'd fled Italy, never to return there to live again.

Now he was back and she couldn't escape.

The nurse turned to the man.

"Sheriff Bachman!" she scolded him crossly. "You can't just come in here without asking, even if it is a custodial ward. I've got to monitor the patient first."

"Then monitor her please, nurse," said Bachman, not taking his eyes off Annie. "I need to talk to this little lady urgently."

The nurse grunted in annoyance. "Then you can help me by calling in your watchdog from outside. This lady needs to use the facilities."

Bachman went out and returned with a female police officer.

"Deputy Bachman will help you, nurse." The one-hundred-and-ninety-pound Elvira Bachman was the sheriff's niece.

Ten minutes later, Annie was sitting up in bed, her right wrist now attached by handcuffs to a rail that ran along one side. Her left wrist was free, so she could at least help herself to water. Elvira Bachman stood by the door frowning at her charge, her sturdy arms folded. The prisoner wasn't going anywhere on her watch.

Once the nurse was satisfied, she called to the sheriff in the corridor outside where she'd banished him. He ambled in, drew up a chair and sat next to the bed.

"OK," he said, getting out a notebook and taking in Annie's bruised face and purple, swollen right eye. "Let's make a start. What's your name, young lady?"

Annie glared at him, still disturbed by his resemblance to Father Bonsanto, although this man was far taller and even fatter.

"Can you tell me why I'm here, sheriff, and why I'm handcuffed?" she snapped.

"I'll ask the questions, little lady, and we'll get on a whole lot better if you answer them in a nice, civil tone. Now, name, please."

Annie sighed. "It's Carr. Annie Carr."

"That's better," replied the sheriff, writing her name in his notebook. "Wasn't too difficult, now, was it? Where do you live, Annie Carr?"

"At Ty'sland."

The sheriff puckered his lips. "Ty'sland? That's where I've heard the name. That's that camp of weirdos up in the hills north of Durango, isn't it?"

"We're not weirdos, sheriff," replied Annie dismissively. "It's just an alternative way of living–"

"–And dying, Annie Carr? You and your kind quite happy about cutting each other up, are you?"

"I don't know what you mean. We don't mean anyone any harm. We just ask to be left alone."

The sheriff gave her a long, hard look. "You don't know what I mean," he mimicked. He'd noticed Annie's accent was quite cultured. "Care to tell me about last night and why you were in the motel?"

Annie's eyes flashed wildly. Visions of the Cardinal and the priest appeared again in her mind. Then an image of Petra lying dead on the bed crashed into her consciousness. The motel.

There was so much blood. Ty was just standing there, shirtless; he hadn't even locked the door. He turned towards her in surprise, although that sneer was still on his face. There was a gutting knife in his hand, its blade dripping blood. Annie didn't pause for thought: she launched herself at him, grabbing at his hand. He stumbled, falling backwards onto the end of the bed, Annie falling on top of him. His wrist smashed against a chair back and the knife fell from his hand. He threw a punch at her face with his other hand, his fist pounding into her right eye, knocking her from the bed. He was up in an instant, kicking at her viciously. She yelled in pain as his boot cap crunched against her ribs, once, twice, then a third time. She rolled away, screaming at him to stop. He stood back and laughed, that sneer taunting her, feeding her with strength. Suddenly she felt the knife beneath her and her hand instinctively closed around its hilt. She was good with a knife, but she needed an advantage. She pulled her legs under her and as Ty bore down on her again, she sprang at him, the knife flashing forward. But he saw it and twisted, the blade sinking into his chest below his shoulder, rather than into his heart where Annie had intended. He grunted in pain as she twisted the knife and pulled it back, spinning away from him and then kicking out at his crotch. He doubled up and sagged to his knees. He scowled up at her, his eyes pure hatred, but still that sneer was there, that Bonsanto sneer that continued to haunt her after more than two hundred and fifty years. She was determined he would never sneer again. She lashed out, slashing at his face, cutting and tearing as she screamed at him. Her rage was all-consuming as he finally fell forward, clutching at the remains of his mouth and cheeks. Now it was Annie who was sneering, joyous in her victory over this monster who'd killed her friend, this monster who had controlled their lives and taken her daughter from her. She let out a full-throated screech and sunk the gutting knife into his back, pulled it out and then stabbed him again and again.

She slowly became aware of two men standing at the doorway, their faces white with the horror of what they'd just witnessed, their instincts telling them to run at the first sign that this feral vision might turn on them. But Annie didn't move. The world around her starting spinning violently as her mind imploded with the pressure of the past few crazed seconds. She groaned loudly as her strength left her and she collapsed onto Ty's motionless body.

Annie's thoughts returned to the hospital room as her eyes slowly focussed on the sheriff's vastly overweight body crammed into the chair. She wondered absently whether the chair's tortured frame would collapse. She took a couple of deep breaths.

"We'd … we'd been over to Drop City and on the way back we stopped at a motel because it was getting late. I don't … I don't really remember anything else."

"Like what you took and what you did? And who is 'we'? How many of you were there?"

She stared at the sheriff, her mind spinning with the events from the motel. How much did the sheriff know? Did he know about Seth? She remembered that Seth stayed in the truck while she'd gone with Ty and Petra to the desk. Ty just tossed some cash at the bored creep behind the desk and snatched two keys. There had been no discussion and no mention of Seth. Then Ty sent Annie and Seth off to buy some food from the nearby town. Another violent scene flashed in her head, the crunch of rock on bone, but it faded. However, she was now sure they didn't know about Seth.

"There was just Ty, Petra and me. And sheriff, I wasn't on anything; I don't do drugs."

Bachman scribbled something and looked up.

"Petra? Petra who?"

"Petra Bozark. She's my friend. Where is she? Has something happened to her? Is she OK? Can I speak with her?"

"Petra Bozark, if that's her name, won't be speaking to anyone ever again, Annie Carr. She's dead. Her throat cut. Her head was almost severed, and I'm guessing by you."

"Dead?" she whispered. Then she realised what he'd said.

"By me?" she yelled indignantly as her wrist pulled hard against the restraint, rocking the bed. "What the hell do you mean? Are you suggesting I killed Petra?"

She pounded her free hand onto the bed.

"Keep your hair on, little lady," said the sheriff, trying to appear unmoved by this display of wild behaviour, but inwardly concerned that what both Jimmy and Sweet voiced the previous night might be true. "The woman's nuts, boss," they'd both said to him independently of each other. "A total crazy," Jimmy had added.

"Well, there ain't no doubt you killed this Ty Donnington, Annie Carr. Who's to say you didn't kill Miss Petra Bozark?"

"I say it! I wasn't even there. I'd gone into the nearby town to buy some food. Ty sent me."

"We'll see about that, Annie Carr. But I got two good witnesses who saw you stabbing Ty Donnington. 'Viciously and repeatedly' they said. Their exact words."

"I stabbed him? That's crazy. Why would I do that? I admit I have many reasons not to like him. Ty for tyrant; that's how Petra and I talk about him. But stab him? I'm not a murderer."

She paused as the cardinal's image flashed across her mind once again, followed by the priest's.

"We'll see about that," snorted Bachman derisively. "OK, Annie Carr, I'll ask you again. Just what do you remember?"

Annie suddenly realised she was in serious trouble. She studied the sheriff's face as her mind raced, trying to decide on a plan. She needed to gain some control over her situation. She'd always been thought crazy if she tried to explain about herself. Right now, crazy might not be a bad thing. Then she thought about her actions the previous night, and her behaviour that morning when confronted by the sheriff. Maybe crazy wasn't too far from the truth. In any event, she decided to sow some more seeds.

"I remember the cardinal."

"The cardinal?"

"Yes, Cardinal Alvaro. You wouldn't know about him; he was before your time. And Father Bonsanto; I remember him too. You wouldn't know about him either. He had the most revolting fleshy lips."

"Got a thing about lips, have you, Annie Carr?"

"What do you mean?"

"Simply that before you stabbed Ty Donnington to death, you stabbed him repeatedly in the mouth, shredding his lips and cheeks to ribbons."

There was a noise from behind him. He turned to see Elvira leaning against the wall and looking very pale.

"Think I need to go to the bathroom, Uncle Mort, if that's OK." Not waiting for an answer, she ran from the room, a hand clasped over her mouth.

"I seem to be surrounded by squeamish deputies," muttered the sheriff to himself as he watched the door swing shut.

He pursed his lips in resignation and returned his attention to Annie. "Well, little lady, what do you say to that?"

Annie gave him a calculated smile. "They deserved to die," she said.

"That so?" said the sheriff triumphantly. "So you admit killing them both?"

"Of course, and I got away with it. You can't prosecute me now; it was too long ago."

"It was only last night, little lady."

Annie frowned. "I wasn't talking about last night. I was talking about 1582."

The sheriff's eyes widened. "1582? What's that got to do with the price of anything?"

"That's when I killed the cardinal."

The sheriff scratched at a fold of flesh on the back of his head. "You killed the cardinal in 1582," he repeated incredulously.

"Yes, I stabbed him in the heart. I also killed Father Bonsanto," smiled Annie matter-of-factly. "But that was much later, in 1712."

Bachman scribbled something in his notebook and looked up. "Well, it's 1970 now and you just killed two more."

Annie shook her head. "I might have killed Ty in self-defence, especially if you have witnesses who say so, but I certainly didn't kill Petra. She was my friend. Now, sheriff, if you'll just release these handcuffs; I need to find my daughter. They've taken her away from me."

Bachman snorted a laugh. "You're not goin' anywhere, Annie Carr."

"Sheriff, my daughter's only four," protested Annie. "I don't want Zelda and Pete to keep her. She doesn't like them."

"What's this daughter's name?" asked Bachman.

"Serena, sheriff. Serena Peace."

The corners of the sheriff's mouth twitched in amusement. "Serena Peace," he repeated, pronouncing the words slowly.

"And where is young Miss Peace?" he added.

"I told you. At the commune with Zelda and Pete. They're an older couple without kids of their own. She doesn't like them. I need to get her back."

"You don't seem to understand the trouble you're in, Miss Carr. I'm about to charge you with murder. If I know the DA, with the witnesses we have and the vicious nature of the killings, he'll make that first-degree and want the gas chamber for you."

Annie knew she had to hide the panic that slammed into her gut with the sheriff's words. She swallowed hard, trying her best to smile guilelessly. "Oh, my," she said, putting her hand to her mouth and leaning forward. "Looks like it might be a few more days until this is all sorted out. Sheriff, could I ask a favour then? Could you get someone to check on Serena for me? They might take her somewhere else. They've been keeping her from me."

The following day, Mort Bachman was wedged into his long-suffering office chair in the Del Norte Sheriff's Office staring accusingly at the huge hamburger clutched in his pudgy hands. He winced as he heard the slam of a telephone handset crashing onto its cradle in the outer office.

"That was Durango, Uncle Mort," Deputy Elvira Bachman yelled through to him. "Young Annie's lying her pretty little head off. Sheriff Brewster's boys just got back and they're sayin' that Annie Carr don't have no daughter."

"That right, Elvira?" said Bachman through a mouthful of meat, bun and ketchup.

"Just so, Uncle Mort. 'Parently she's always tryin' to claim that different kids are hers. Said she's crazy and not only that, gets wild when they tell her she can't have one of the kids. The commune elders even showed Brewster's boys a couple of kids called Serena, but they ain't four and they ain't hers."

She heard Bachman grunt as he absorbed the news.

"And there's somethin' else, Uncle Mort," yelled Elvira.

"Elvira!" Bachman was at his office doorway.

The deputy looked up, shocked at her uncle's tone.

"Elvira, you may be my niece but you're also my deputy. I'd appreciate it if instead of just yelling, you'd get off your backside once in a while and walk to my office to give me a message. Way you do it, the whole town gets to hear. Now what was the something else?"

Elvira was stunned; the case must be getting to him.

"Sorry, Uncle Mort. It was just that Durango said there were four of them that went to Drop City."

"Four?"

"Yes, somebody called Seth Short. Don't remember Annie making any mention of him."

"You're right, Elvira. Annie Carr said there were just the three of them. Guess I'd better ask her."

Half an hour later, Mort Bachman was back in his office taking solace in a huge jelly doughnut. He stared at the wall as he chewed, thinking over the conversation he'd just had with Annie Carr. When the wall failed to oblige with inspiration, he lifted the phone and dialled District Attorney Kal Kallings' personal line. The DA was on a diet and Mort knew he would be resisting the temptations of the nearby diner by staying in his office at lunchtime. The downside was that he'd probably be in a bad mood.

He relayed the information from Ty'sland about Annie Carr. "Looks like she's one crazy lady, Kal. I tell you, the way she was talking yesterday in the hospital, she weren't on this planet."

He heard Kallings' fist hit his desk and pictured the red flush of anger climbing his thick neck.

"I don't want her found not competent to stand trial, Mort. I want her in the courtroom before a jury and then I want her in the gas chamber. I don't care if the creep she killed was some hippy, or the one she nearly decapitated. The law's the law and we gotta show folks that we mean business. Who've we got that can get us the right assessment?"

"You know it's not our call; it's up to the court to appoint the shrink," replied Bachman. "Although they don't have a lot of choice: they're bound to use one from Sawpine Ridge. The director's a reasonable man. Reckon he'll give you what you want."

"Let's hope you're right," snarled Kallings.

"Listen, Kal," continued Bachman, "there's something else."

As he told the DA about Seth Short, he heard grunts of discontent coming down the line.

"So she says Short and Donnington had a fight and they left Short in Del Norte before they got to the motel," echoed the DA. "Then where is he now?"

"Carr reckons once he's cooled down, he'll hitch a ride from someone back to the commune. Says it wasn't the first time they'd had a fight."

"I don't like it, Mort," replied Kallings. "I think you need to find this Seth Short."

Bachman glared at the remains of the jelly doughnut for a few seconds, then crammed it into his mouth. This case was getting too complicated for his liking.

Chapter 3

Nancy Wright pulled her Buick Riviera into a parking space outside the Del Norte Sheriff's Office. She checked her make-up in the mirror and touched at her dark brown, backcombed hair. Satisfied, she picked up her briefcase from the front passenger seat and got out of the car, narrowly avoiding stepping into a puddle from yet another summer storm the previous evening.

She locked the car, straightened the midnight blue skirt of her suit and peered myopically through her black-rimmed glasses at the building to locate the main entrance.

Nancy was one of three resident psychiatrists at the Sawpine Ridge Custodial Psychiatric Institution, a high-security facility for women near Sagauche, and, at thirty-two, the youngest and most junior, having been appointed just three months before. This was her first professional foray into the towns served by Sawpine Ridge; the new girl awarded her first big case. Her director, Hector Higgins, would normally have taken the 'competency to stand trial' assessment of a murder suspect, but he had no time for hippies and anyway, the case seemed straightforward enough on paper. Assistant director, Martha Blunt, was away dealing with her ailing mother in Denver.

Elvira Bachman looked up as the young woman walked into the untidy reception area that doubled as desk space for the deputies.

"Help yuh?" she drawled, scowling as she surveyed Nancy's trim figure with some jealousy.

"I'm looking for Sheriff Bachman," said Nancy, ignoring the overweight deputy's hostile tone. "My name is Dr Nancy Wright. I'm from Sawpine Ridge."

Elvira continued to observe her with some suspicion, noting in particular the cultured accent. She didn't look old enough to be a shrink. Without taking her eyes off her, she yelled out to the office in the far corner. "Uncle Mort! Shrink's here!"

There was a crash from the office as the sheriff attempted to hide the evidence of his mid-morning snack in a desk drawer. In his enthusiasm, he had pulled it out too far, spilling its contents on the floor.

Nancy turned in the direction of the sound to see, a few moments later, the sheriff's huge frame filling his office door as he brushed crumbs from his uniform shirt.

Bachman cocked his head to one side as he looked Nancy up and down. "My, my, I must be gettin' old. Or Sawpine's recruitin' youngsters fresh outta school."

He held out his hand. "Sheriff Mort Bachman at your service, ma'am."

Nancy took his hand. "Dr Nancy Wright. I'm pleased to meet you sheriff. I came as quickly as I could. The DA indicated to my director that there was some urgency."

"S'just that Kal wants to be able to tell the judge this girl ain't crazy before any proceedings start. He figured the court'd appoint you anyway, so why not begin now? Can't do no harm."

"It's a little unusual," replied Nancy. "However, I can see that a preliminary assessment might speed up the whole process. Seeing your suspect here rather than in the county jail will certainly be less formal, so she might be more inclined to relax and tell me the truth."

"Just what Kal said, Doc," beamed Bachman. "He had a feeling you'd see straight through the little lady's BS, if you'll pardon the expression."

"I shouldn't make any assumptions, sheriff. My assessment will be entirely objective and take no account of the fact that this woman might face execution, however much I might be against it."

A cloud passed over the sheriff's face. Nancy could see that he was confused. She smiled and touched his arm. "You can rest assured, sheriff, that if I think she's competent, I'll say so with no hesitation."

The cloud evaporated and the sheriff relaxed. "Then let's get to it. Like a coffee before you start?"

"No, thank you, I had one earlier. Do I need to see her in her cell or is there somewhere more comfortable we can chat? Somewhere secure, of course."

"There's a room at the back of the station where you can interview her, doc. No need to worry; I'll post Elvira right outside the door."

"Sounds good, sheriff. As you say, let's get to it!"

Five minutes later, Nancy had set out her file on the table in the small interview room together with her notepad and pencils. She looked up as the door opened and Bachman escorted Annie Carr into the room. She was handcuffed and her legs were constrained by chains attached to metal bands round her ankles. Her clothing had been taken for examination so she was wearing beige prison drabs with the words 'Rio Grande County Jail' printed on them in large black letters.

Nancy made the rapid assessment of a fellow female. Slim, good-looking, olive skin and faultless complexion; aged around thirty. Her luxuriant jet-black hair was a mess but that didn't detract from her beauty. However, what caught Nancy's attention more than anything were the young woman's pale grey eyes observing her with suspicion.

Bachman sat Annie down and fastened her leg chains to a ring set in the floor. "I'll leave you then," he said, hovering.

"Thank you, sheriff," said Nancy as she continued to study the wary Annie's face.

"Elvira's right outside the door, don't forget," said Bachman as he left, more for Annie's sake than Nancy's. He didn't want her trying anything.

The door closed and Nancy smiled at Annie.

"Hello, Annie. I'm Dr Nancy Wright and I'm a psychiatrist. I've been asked to interview you about what happened three nights ago. Do you understand?"

Annie sat back, her eyes fixed on Nancy's, her expression neutral.

"I'm not stupid, Dr Wright, and neither am I a child. I know you're trying to assess my mental state, and I know the DA will want you to find me competent to stand trial and be found guilty of murder so that he and his cronies can dance in glee outside the gas chamber as they watch me die in agony."

Nancy was taken aback. Annie Carr was lucid, intelligent and, at first sight, rational. She had expected an act to try to convince her she was insane, something rambling and only partly coherent. Perhaps this wouldn't take long.

She smiled again. "Shall we start by talking about the events of Tuesday night, Annie?"

"No," replied Annie, surprising Nancy again. "I want to tell you my worries about my daughter. She's only four years old, Dr Wright, and she's been taken from me and put in the so-called care of a couple in the commune. I've not been allowed near her for months and before that I was allowed only supervised access. I'm afraid they are going to take her somewhere else. They're already treating her like a drudge. Another couple of years she'll effectively be a slave."

"This is Serena, is it?" said Nancy. "I saw her name when I read the report. You know the police visited the commune and were told that she doesn't exist?"

"Of course I know," snapped Annie, her voice rising. "They are bound to say that. They are lying, Dr Wright, and your police officers are too stupid or too uncaring to take it further."

Her breathing was faster and her eyes angry. She lifted her arms to wipe them with her sleeve, her handcuffs rattling loudly.

Nancy said nothing, trying to decide if this sudden show of emotion was genuine or merely for her benefit.

Annie took a breath. She had decided to tell this psychiatrist the absolute and total truth about herself. There was no chance she would be believed – how could she be? It was not a strategy she would normally use: normally the last thing she wanted was to be thought crazy. But in the circumstances …

"I have had a number of children throughout the years, Dr Wright. However, Serena is special. She's like me, you see."

"The others weren't like you?" asked Nancy.

"No, only Serena. She has the same eyes and she's never ill. She'll live forever. Like me."

"We all want our children to live forever, which, because a child normally outlives a parent, means, for the parent, they do." Nancy smiled, pleased with her explanation.

Annie looked askance at her interviewer.

"You're not listening, Dr Wright. I said like *me*, she'll live forever. We both will." She paused to let the psychiatrist absorb her words before she continued. "Well, maybe not forever, but for a long, long time. Until we are killed. That's the only way we can die."

Nancy's smile faded. She didn't understand where this conversation was going.

"You said you'd had other children, Annie. Are they at the commune too?"

Annie's eyes had a tinge of sadness.

"No, Dr Wright, they're not. They came and went long before I was at the commune. They are all long dead."

Nancy glanced at the file. "Annie, you are thirty years of age and you have been at the Ty'sland Community for six years. Since you were twenty-four. Are you telling me you had children before you went there who have died for some reason? How, Annie? How did they die? Was it an accident?"

Annie looked down, gathering her thoughts.

"It's going to be difficult for you to understand, Dr Wright. Perhaps I should start at the beginning."

She paused, and then she raised her pale grey eyes to Nancy. "No, perhaps it would be better to start at the end."

Nancy sat back, waiting.

Annie took a breath. "I suppose the first thing I should tell you is I am not Annie Carr." She noted the immediate look of scepticism on Nancy's face. "Oh, don't worry, I'm not saying the police have replaced the real one with me. I don't deny I was at the motel where Ty and Petra were killed, nor even, perhaps, that I killed Ty. No, it's nothing to do with that. You see, although I've been Annie Carr for six years now, I'm not the real Annie Carr. She died of a drug overdose in San Francisco in 1964. She was Petra's friend. She looked something like me, so when she died, I took her ID and left mine on her. My name was Mali Whittaker. Petra thought it was cool to swap identities. She didn't understand, you see, that I more or less had to."

"I'm afraid I don't understand either, Annie. Why did you need to take her ID? Were you in trouble with the law?"

Annie laughed dismissively. "Only peripherally. No, it wasn't that. It was because I was getting a little old. I had been Mali Whittaker for twenty-four years."

"You mean you were really Mali Whittaker, aged twenty-four, which you were in 1964 – it says so here in your file, says you were born in 1940 – and then you decided to change?"

"It says in the file that Annie Carr was born in 1940, not Mali Whittaker, Dr Wright. No, Mali Whittaker was born in 1920, so by 1964 she, that is, I, was forty-four. OK, it was a bit early to change, but the opportunity happened along and I jumped at it, in the circumstances."

Nancy was now totally confused. She thought through the conversation, computing the numbers.

"So you're saying, Annie, that you are really Mali Whittaker and you were born in 1920. Do you realise that would make you now fifty!" She laughed. "If I look like you do when I'm fifty, I'll be very pleased! No, I'm sorry, it doesn't make any sense. No one of fifty can possibly look as youthful as you. Look at you; you're not even wearing any make-up. Your skin is perfect; your hair is lustrous and very dark; and your figure, well, it's the full and firm figure of a thirty-year-old."

Annie shrugged. "I told you it would be difficult to understand, Dr Wright."

Nancy frowned. "You said the real Annie Carr died of a drug overdose in San Francisco. Do you know the date and where it happened?"

Annie smiled to herself. The good doctor was picking up the clues.

"I can't remember the exact date. It was summer, July. In the Haight."

Nancy wrote it all down and reviewed her notes.

"Tell me more about your daughter Serena, the one in Ty'sland."

"I told you, she's four years old. She's a happy, loving child, full of energy." Her face darkened and she became agitated again. "I'm very worried about her, Dr Wright." She started to raise her voice. "Ty was determined to take her from me because he wasn't her father. He's the father of many of the children in the commune, you see, but not Serena."

Nancy reached out to touch Annie's arm. "It's OK, Annie, let's remain calm. Who was the father?"

"His name was Johnny. Johnny Quinn. He was a lovely young man. Ty disliked him as soon as he turned up at the commune; saw him as a threat. We hit it off pretty quickly and I was hoping he would be a way for me to get away. However, although he saw through Ty, he wanted to stay. I got pregnant, which, as I say, infuriated Ty. He hit me hard in the stomach when he found out; I thought I'd lose the baby. Then, about two months before Serena was born, Johnny was killed. They said it was an accident. He and some of the others were in the woods cutting trees. One fell on him and he was crushed. They were very secretive about it. I think they killed him. I never saw his body. He's buried, like everyone else who dies there, at the burial ground in a glade in the woods."

Annie looked imploringly into Nancy's eyes. "Can't you help me, Dr Wright? Ty imposed his will so strongly that they relied on him completely. If they think I killed him, they might harm Serena."

She paused, breathing heavily again as her eyes danced wildly.

"If they hurt my daughter, I'll … I'll …"

Nancy sat back, assessing her behaviour. "I'll see what I can do, Annie. However, I think that's enough for today. I can see that these questions are upsetting for you."

Chapter 4

"**Y**ou think she's what?" snapped Kal Kallings rather too loudly as he pushed his chair back and sprang to his feet.

It was the morning after Nancy's first interview with Annie. Nancy had returned to Sawpine Ridge after the short session, written up her notes and mulled over her preliminary diagnosis. Although there was still some way to go, she was quietly confident. However, she knew it wouldn't be well received.

Kallings marched round the desk to where Nancy was sitting in the visitor's chair. Sheriff Bachman was spread across a sofa near the DA's office door.

"You gotta be kiddin' me," Kallings continued, his chin sticking out aggressively. "There's no way she's delusional. It's an act for your benefit. She's conning you, Dr Wright; taking you for a sucker."

Nancy was not impressed by this pugnacious man and she certainly wasn't going to be swayed by his prejudices.

"Have you even met with Annie Carr yet, Mr Kallings?" She was almost certain he hadn't.

Kallings faltered. "I'm saving that pleasure until my assistant, Abby, gets back from Springs tomorrow. Been in court there. I want her to appeal to Carr's better nature, woman to woman, assuming she's got one. We can do the good cop, bad cop thing."

"Very productive, I'm sure," replied Nancy not even trying to hide the sarcasm in her voice.

"Hey, you got your job to do and I've got mine," snarled Kallings.

"You're right, Mr Kallings, I do. And like you, I don't appreciate being told how to do it." Nancy's eyes were angry. She took a deep breath and pushed her glasses back to the top of her nose. This man was bringing out the worst in her.

She continued more calmly. "I only said that my preliminary assessment is that there's a possibility Annie Carr is delusional. I have not, as yet, come to any conclusions as to whether I think she is competent to stand trial. I need to interview her further, but before I do that, as I explained to Sheriff Bachman on the way here, there are some points in her story that need checking up on. Then, later, we'll go over the same ground. It's a good way of assessing the validity of a story. If she's making it up as she goes along, there will be inconsistencies that very quickly show up. If, on the other hand, she's prepared it well in advance, there will be a strong element of repetition and she won't want to go into territory she hasn't planned. She'll keep it superficial."

She paused, noticing she was starting to make sense to the DA.

"If she is delusional, then I need to determine the extent of it and how much it affects her own world and her perception of the world around her. I also need to know whether it's connected to any drugs she might have been taking. There are many levels of delusion, Mr Kallings, and only a few would result in someone not being competent to stand trial."

"That's good to hear, Dr Wright, because I go in front of the judge in the morning." He turned to the sheriff. "Mort. Did your boys find anything in the way of drugs at the motel?"

"Just some marijuana, Kal. Joints and loose stuff. It was in Donnington's pocket and there was some in the glove box in the truck. No sign of nothin' with the other victim's things or Carr's."

Nancy nodded. "So Annie Carr could have been telling the truth when she said she doesn't use drugs. That's interesting. Has anything been done about a lawyer for her, Mr Kallings?"

The DA shook his head.

"Not yet. Thanks for reminding me. I believe Carr told the sheriff she hasn't got one, which is no surprise, so we'll get one appointed. It'll be someone local so he won't be a problem. Certainly there isn't a chance of bail. I guess I'll be ready to interview her tomorrow afternoon."

"I'll wait until we hear something from the San Francisco police before I see her again," said Nancy. She turned to Bachman. "If that request could be expedited as soon as possible, I shall be able to continue my interviews. I also really think it would be worth pursuing this story of a child at the commune, regardless of what the Durango police have been told."

The sheriff grunted, muttering the word 'expedited' to himself as he shifted his bulk to torture another section of the sofa.

Two days later, Nancy Wright was back in the DA's office with Bachman. The sheriff had heard from the San Francisco police and he wanted to relay the information to both the DA and Nancy at the same time. He chose to stand since he was not convinced the sofa was strong enough to take his weight a second time and certainly none of the office chairs looked man enough for the job.

"Seems Carr's not making it all up," he said with a cough as he consulted his notebook. "SFPD say they found a record of a Mali Whittaker being found dead in some backstreet apartment back on July 10, 1964. Seems she was an artist of some sort."

Nancy nodded, taking notes. "Did they say how old she was?"

"Yeah, forty-four years of age. Born April 17, 1920"

"Well, well," said Nancy, raising her eyebrows. "Very interesting. Do they have a record of her fingerprints?"

The sheriff shook his head. "Seems not. Apparently it was a busy time with a number of murders that weekend. There was nothing suspicious about her death; it was a simple OD. They were overlooked."

"Pity," replied Nancy. "Although I don't think for one second that Annie is this Mali Whittaker, it would have been good to be able to prove it scientifically. What about the commune, sheriff, have you given any more thought to my request?"

"I'm meeting Sheriff Brewster over in Durango tomorrow and we're headed up there. He's none too happy about it; thinks it's a waste of time. Kinda the way I feel too."

"I'm sure someone with your experience will be able to tell if they seem to be hiding something, sheriff," said Nancy, giving him her most winning smile.

The sheriff grunted.

Nancy turned back to the DA. "How did your interview with Annie Carr go, Mr Kallings?"

Kallings propped his chin on his hand and pursed his lips, pondering his answer.

"The bitch is nuts, Dr Wright, and dangerous."

Nancy raised her eyebrows in surprise. "You've changed your tune."

"Obviously I need to know if she's faking it, which is your job," Kallings replied pointedly. "But if she is, she's damned good."

"What happened?"

"She was in the interview room when Abby and me arrived. All chained and secure. We walked in and sat down; introduced ourselves. Carr said nothing, just fixed her eyes on Abby. She's got the weirdest pale eyes I've ever seen. They just seemed to bore into Abby's eyes. I tell you, the look on Carr's face was pure evil."

He paused to rub a ruminative hand across his mouth.

"I spoke to her but she ignored me. Just kept on staring at Abby. Now, Abby's no greenhorn; she's seen plenty of nasty types, but after a few minutes she was completely spooked by Carr. Couldn't take it. She suddenly stood up, said she couldn't stay, and walked out."

"I haven't seen that side of her," said Nancy, frowning. "So you were left alone with her?"

"Yes, although I didn't stay long. She turned her eyes to me and gave me the same look. I told her she wasn't fooling no one; that she was … as sane as me and she'd answer for what she's done. But she just kept staring at me. I tell you, Dr Wright, I felt like she was cutting into me with those eyes. She didn't say a word. Just stared. I tried more questions but it was like she wasn't even hearing them. So I left. Abby was still shaking when I got outside; told me she didn't ever want to be alone with Carr, even if she was shackled."

"Shouldn't her court-appointed lawyer have been present?"

"Technically, yes, but I asked her and she ignored that too. So I took that as her accepting the situation."

"I'll explain her rights to her again," said Nancy.

Two hours later, Nancy walked into the interview room at the county courthouse, where Annie Carr was now being held in a cellblock for prisoners awaiting trial.

Annie seemed pleased to see her and showed none of the behaviour Kallings had described.

"Would you mind telling me what happened with the DA, Annie?" said Nancy as she sat down. "From what he's told me, you weren't very cooperative."

Annie shrugged. "Nothing happened except he called me a murdering bitch and said he'd make sure that I go to the gas chamber. I figured there was no point in talking to him after that, so I didn't."

"What about his assistant? Kallings said you intimidated her."

Annie shook her head. "I simply looked at her, Dr Wright. She's quite a pretty girl; young. I was trying to look into her; see what was behind her reserve – the mask of her face."

Annie smiled to herself. She'd learned the art of quiet intimidation from an old gypsy woman in a forest in Germany in the early 1700s, soon after she'd fled Italy following the death of Father Bonsanto. The old woman was impressed by Annie's eyes, knowing that Annie could use them to her advantage. There was no such thing as witchcraft, she'd explained, just suggestion and exploitation of what a person assumed in their mind.

It didn't always work – Ty had been impervious to her stares – but when it did the effect could be profound. As with Kallings' assistant, Abby.

Annie had been thinking very carefully about her strategy. With the likes of the DA, she had to appear crazy, sometimes threatening, needing to be constrained. The combination of her seeming to put a hex on people and the murder they knew she'd committed would ease them towards thinking she was either insane or at least deranged. To convince Dr Wright, her approach was very different: she would simply tell the truth about her life. Not all at once, but little by little, each new episode reinforcing the doctor's diagnosis of serious and dangerous delusion. At least telling the truth was easy, although it wasn't something to which she was accustomed.

"I think you did more than look at her, Annie," said Nancy. "According to the DA, she was extremely upset."

"I can't think why," replied Annie, her face a mask of innocence.

Nancy caught Annie's eyes, but they were calm, in no way threatening. She decided to move on.

"OK, what about Kallings?" she continued.

"I told you. After the young woman left the room, he got angry and called me a murdering bitch. There was no point in talking to him. After a few minutes he was so red with frustration I thought he might have a seizure. I certainly thought he was going to hit me. However, in the end, he did neither. He just stormed out."

"I'll talk to him," sighed Nancy, "but, in the meantime, you shouldn't agree to see him unless your court-appointed defense lawyer is present. There should also be a female officer from the courthouse present as well."

"No!" Annie thumped the table with her fist, making Nancy jump. "I don't see the point of having some court-appointed lawyer. He's in Kallings' pocket. How could I trust him?" She was almost shouting.

Her sudden change of mood surprised Nancy. For Annie's part, she thought a little instability with Dr Wright from time to time wouldn't go amiss.

"It's OK, Annie, you don't have to see him. However, I'm concerned that there should be a third party present if Kallings comes to interview you again, which he has a perfect right to do."

"Can't you be the third party?"

"It's not my job, Annie. I'm not a lawyer or a police officer. I'm not representing you; I'm appointed by the court to … assess you."

"I'll think about it," muttered Annie.

"Good. Now, I'd like for us to continue our conversation of the other day. I want you to tell me more about Mali Whittaker and why you think you are her."

Annie studied Nancy's eyes. "You've found out something, haven't you, Dr Wright?" she said, her own eyes now sparkling in amusement. She'd let her mood change again. "You know I'm telling the truth."

"Hardly the truth, Annie. How could your tale possibly be true? But, yes, I have found out something. Tell me, when was the incident you described to me? Can you remember the date?"

"No, not exactly. I do remember it was early July. It wasn't long after Independence Day."

"Tell me what happened."

Annie paused to gather her thoughts.

"I had known Petra for a few months. She was a very young artist, while I was becoming quite well established. I was forty-four, don't forget, and my sculptures – did I say I was a sculptress? – were finally selling. I'd been featured in *Art Aspects* magazine some years before – check it out if you want. 'Up-and-coming sculptress' was how I was described. A colour feature – quite unusual in those days. It really helped. Anyway, Petra came to see me in my studio. She showed me her work; it was good. I said she could put a few pieces there to display. But, you know, she was starting to get into drugs. She thought they would 'free her soul from the shackles of urbanity and the constraints of repressive thought. Help her achieve her true creative persona'. She never accepted that everything she produced when she was high was junk."

Nancy laughed.

Annie continued. "Petra met Annie Carr, the real Annie Carr that is, at some party about two months before Annie OD'd. I never met her, although Petra had shown me some of her work. Now, she really did have talent, but she wasted it. She was, apparently, more interested in getting high. The night Annie died, Petra called me in panic to tell me that she couldn't rouse Annie; that she'd had a really bad trip. They both had, but only Petra woke up. I went round to where they were – I was pretty panicky myself, although Petra didn't know that."

She paused, remembering something. "It was a Friday; it must have been: I always went to the jazz club on a Friday and I'll never forget that particular visit." A half-smile flitted across her face and then she continued.

"When I got to the apartment where Petra was, it was clear Annie was dead and Petra was in a bad way. It was then that I studied Annie's features and noticed just how like mine they were. She had very dark hair and olive skin. I couldn't believe my luck. She even had pale eyes, although not quite my colour, or lack of it. You see, I also had a problem."

"Problem?" echoed Nancy, her voice very quiet. She'd stopped scribbling notes; it was all getting too confusing and she'd decided just to listen.

"Yes. As I said, I was becoming quite successful. However, I was now forty-four and people were starting to notice how young I looked. It doesn't normally happen so early, but this time it had and it was beginning to spook me. Then that night at the jazz club, the problem got worse. The one thing I always dread will happen actually did happen: I was recognised."

She paused and looked up to see the puzzled expression on Nancy's face.

"Something you don't understand, Dr Wright?"

"What do you mean by it doesn't normally happen so early and that you were recognised?"

"Well, it normally happens when people think I'm in my fifties. That's what happened with Mali Whittaker."

"You just said you swapped identities to make Mali Whittaker into Annie Carr."

"No, Dr Wright, I meant when I became Mali Whittaker in 1940, not when I moved on. At that time I was thought to be fifty-five but, of course, I didn't look it. Things were getting more and more awkward and I was fed up with constantly having to look older."

"You've completely lost me, Annie," said Nancy, the exasperation sounding in her voice. She was increasingly convinced that the person sitting opposite her was living in an entirely different world.

"Don't you go to the movies, Dr Wright? Maybe you don't like the oldies from the silent era. Rather before your time, perhaps. You see, Dr Wright, before I was Mali Whittaker, I was a silent movie star. I was Dolores di Napoli."

Nancy sat back, incredulous. "As it happens, I do go to the movies – I love them – and I enjoy the oldies as well. Annie, Dolores di Napoli was a star in the very early years of silent movies. Her star had faded by the late-1920s. She was born in the last century–"

"In 1885," interrupted Annie.

"Exactly. Heavens, she would be, let me see, she'd be eighty-five if she were still alive. As it is, I think she died quite a while ago."

"Precisely, Dr Wright. Dolores died in 1940. I know that for a fact. You see, I killed her off."

"You did what?"

"Well, not literally, of course. However, I really needed to change."

Nancy stared across the table at this young woman who was quietly and very lucidly recounting a tale that could only be the ramblings of a seriously confused mind. Her first suspicions of Annie Carr being delusional were becoming firmer. She'd studied the subject in depth and was intending to specialise in it. As a resident, she'd seen a number of delusional patients in psychiatric facilities in and around Boston, although none of them had been accused of murder. However, that aside, Annie fitted the bill so far, but Nancy needed much more information.

She sat back and took a deep breath.

"Annie, let's stick with the night of what you are calling Annie Carr's death. You were saying you were someone called Mali Whittaker, aged forty-four, and you had just been recognised. Recognised by whom?"

"His name was Manny Goldstein. He was an ancient theatrical agent who should have been long dead – the way he abused his body with cigars and whisky. But there he was, as large as life and sitting in the jazz club. He must have been ninety and he had a girl of no more than twenty on his arm. I didn't see him at first. However, he saw me and I think I nearly gave him a heart attack."

She stopped and laughed as she remembered it.

The ancient agent was chewing on his ever-present cigar and regaling the small group of people around his table with tales of jazz clubs of sixty or more years before; places where white people seldom went – dark, smoke-filled basements where the musicians played such tender jazz it broke your heart, and then jazz so wild and carefree you fell in love with everyone in the room. He was in full swing, his piping but still-strong voice dominating the corner of the room, whistling over the top of the notes from the saxophone playing soothingly a few feet from him. His eyes never stopped sweeping the room as he spoke, the habit of a lifetime, still looking for the perfect face for the silver screen. Suddenly he bit right through his cigar, a three-inch piece falling into his whisky and splashing one of the young things next to him.

"Jeeze, Manny, are you losing it? You paid a fortune for this dress."

Manny wasn't listening. His mouth had dropped open as his face changed colour from its normal yellow-white to something resembling wet clay. His mouth moved as he tried to speak, but nothing came out.

The assembled company was shocked. Was this finally it for the old man?

"Manny, say something. Are you in pain?" said one.

"Dolores," the old man whispered.

Then something stirred in him and his jaw clenched. "You!" he yelled. "You! Broad! Who are you? What are you doing made up to look like Dolores? She was special; you shouldn't be so disrespectful. Come here this minute!"

Mali Whittaker stopped in her tracks and turned her head towards him. The room had hushed; even the musicians had stopped. All eyes were on her.

She took a couple of steps towards the old man, still not understanding what had happened. Then she looked into his eyes and recognised him. It had been fifty-nine years. Nineteen hundred and five. Manny Goldstein, the son of the agent who'd put her on the road to success, the young man who'd become an agent himself and who'd fallen in love with her. The young man she'd rejected and left behind as her star ascended.

Their eyes locked on one another. "Manny," she said, without thinking of the consequences.

Manny's mouth was working but again nothing would come out. He finally managed a croak. "Dolores. How can it possibly be you? You been dead for more than twenty years. You look like you did when you was young. Are you a ghost? Is my time up and you've come for me?"

He tried to get up but his strength had deserted him.

"Dolores!"

Mali went to speak but then regained her senses. She had to get out of there. She turned on her heel and ran for the door.

As she pushed through, ignoring a group of people making their way in, she heard the old man's voice again. "Dolores! I'm here. Take me with you." Then to one of the men in his party: "Stop her, you jerk! Whoever she is, I need to talk to her."

Mali ran outside and along the alley to the busy main road. She heard someone running behind her, heard a shout, but she ran on and merged into the crowded street, not stopping until she was sure she'd lost her pursuer.

"Annie?"

Nancy's voice brought Annie back from her thoughts. She focussed on her interviewer's puzzled face.

"What did you do with Annie Carr's body?"

It was Annie's turn to be puzzled. "What do you mean?"

"Well, did you just leave it there?"

"Oh, I see. Well, yes, we did. I told Petra I had a problem; that I needed to leave San Francisco. I also said I wanted to swap papers with Annie, so that when she was found the authorities would think she was Mali Whittaker. Petra didn't ask why, she just said that the papers wouldn't be enough; that the police'd want a formal ID. I thought about it and decided I'd go back to my apartment and wait there until the police turned up. I'd tell them I was Annie Carr – show ID that was convincing enough and offer, as a close friend, to ID Mali Whittaker. And that's exactly what happened. The police had no interest in the death of some drug addict; they'd far more important things to do. They willingly accepted what I told them. In the meantime, I'd put Petra on a Greyhound bus to Colorado where she said she had a friend. I told her I'd join her as soon as I could. I caught up with her four days later. Her friend turned out to be Ty Donnington's current woman and we moved into his commune. Once there, it was OK for a while, but eventually I was more or less imprisoned. We both were, even though Petra became Ty's main woman."

"What happened to her predecessor? Is she still there?"

"In a manner of speaking, yes. She died rather suddenly. I never knew why. She's buried in the woods in the burial ground."

"Burial ground?"

"Yes, I've already told you about it. It's where anyone who dies in the commune is placed."

"Have there been many deaths?"

"More than you'd imagine for a community of relatively young people. Of course, many of them were fairly heavy drug users."

"Where did the drugs come from?"

"Ty. It was always Ty. He controlled it all and what people took."

Nancy looked down at her notepad. There was hardly anything on it. She needed to stop and write up the conversation before she forgot the details. The problem was that in trying to follow Annie's account, she was finding it difficult to make notes at the same time.

"Annie, I need to stop for today."

"Have you heard any more about Serena, Dr Wright? I'm very worried about her."

"The Del Norte sheriff is going to Ty'sland tomorrow with the sheriff from Durango. I'm sure they'll get to the bottom of it."

"Tell them to be sure to see Zelda and Pete and to talk to all the four-year-old girls. There aren't that many."

Chapter 5

The following day, while the two sheriffs were reluctantly driving up into the woods miles north of Durango on what they regarded as a fool's errand, Nancy was back in her office at Sawpine Ridge writing up her notes and pondering over Annie's story.

On returning to Sawpine Ridge the previous evening, she had gone immediately to assistant director Martha Blunt's apartment, which was situated next to her own in the main administration building of the complex.

Martha was an obsessive collector of glossy magazines, among which were complete sets of *Life* and *The New Yorker* dating back to their respective first editions. However, they weren't the ones that interested Nancy. Martha also collected numerous art magazines, including *Art Aspects*, an influential publication for more than fifty years. Although Martha was still away in Denver, Nancy knew she wouldn't object to her rifling through her vast collection and extracting all issues of *Art Aspects* from the 1950s. The neatly stacked pile of magazines was now sitting on the corner of Nancy's desk.

Nancy was a methodical worker and she'd intended to complete her notes before searching the magazines. But her eyes kept straying to the pile and eventually curiosity got the better of her. Annie had said there was an article about Mali Whittaker written some years before the overdose incident she'd described. Nancy decided to start with the issues for 1955 and work back to 1950.

Fifteen minutes later, she reached the issue for October 1952 and as she ran her finger down the contents list, there it was: 'Up-and-Coming West Coast Sculptress with a Rare Talent', just as Annie had described. She turned to the article and her mouth dropped open. Not only did it praise Mali Whittaker's work enthusiastically, but also among the colour photographs of her work was one of the sculptress holding up a bronze of a fish eagle, its talons extended as it was about to capture its prey. However, it wasn't the quality of the bronze that shocked Nancy; it was Mali Whittaker. Although the photograph was full body and therefore the face quite small, the likeness to Annie Carr was uncanny.

Nancy retrieved a magnifying glass from her desk and held it over the photo. The hairstyle was different and part of the face was in shadow, but enlarged, the similarity was beyond question.

No wonder she couldn't believe her luck, thought Nancy: Annie and Mali Whittaker could have been sisters, identical twins even. Then she laughed and shook her head. She realised she had found herself believing Annie's story about Mali Whittaker taking on the real Annie Carr's identity. She tapped a finger absently on the magazine. That couldn't possibly be right. The photograph had been taken nearly twenty years before and the woman in it looked like Annie did now in 1970: a woman of around thirty. Not the fifty that Mali Whittaker would now be.

As she continued to study the photograph of the young sculptress, Nancy considered the nature of Annie's delusional condition. She clearly wasn't just making up a story; she'd researched it thoroughly. She must have found this article somewhere and noticed the similarity between her own features and Mali Whittaker's. Nancy wondered how she'd had the opportunity to do that since it seemed unlikely a reclusive commune would have an extensive collection of art magazines.

As an idea about Annie's delusion started to form in her mind, she remembered Annie's mention of the silent era actress, Dolores di Napoli. Although Nancy knew of her and had even seen some of the movies she'd been in, she couldn't remember what she looked like. However, she was fairly sure that Martha Blunt's collection included movie magazines. There must be one with a photo of Dolores di Napoli.

Half an hour later she pushed open her office door with her shoulder, staggering as she did under the weight of the huge pile of issues of *Motion Picture Magazine* she was carrying. She set them down on the desk, picked up the top one and started to leaf through it.

It was ten minutes before she found a photograph of the silent screen star. There were several brief articles without photos, some commenting on the flop of two movies in the mid-1920s, some praising her talents. When she turned the page and saw the photo of Dolores di Napoli, once again Nancy couldn't believe her eyes. It could be Annie dressed in the increasingly liberated fashions of the years leading up to the 1920s. She was wearing a floor-length, high-waisted, silk evening dress with a short, gathered, chiffon overskirt cut away at the front. The dress's beaded bodice was held in place with beaded shoestring straps. Her shingled hair was adorned with a feathered headband. However, despite the heavy make-up and different fashions, the face was Annie's and, even though it was a black-and-white image, Nancy could see that the eyes were very pale and distinctive.

She stared at the photograph in disbelief. How could Annie look so much like the long-dead movie actress? Energised now, she set about scanning through the other movie magazines for all the information she could find about Dolores di Napoli. Had she ever married? Had there been any children? She was thinking that perhaps Annie could be a granddaughter. Maybe that was it: Mali Whittaker was the movie star's daughter and Annie was Mali's daughter. That could explain how alike they all were and why Annie would know all about them. Not so much delusional as living in the past.

However, this theory failed at the first hurdle. There was no mention of any marriage or family for Dolores di Napoli. Just the opposite. She had artfully moved from competing with rising young starlets in the mid-1920s to playing supporting roles cast as older women. By the time the talkies came in, she was in her forties and although her talent was recognised, she was seldom cast with any prominence. There were reports in some of the magazines from the '30s of increasing rifts between Dolores and the studios. Then in a magazine dated 1940, there was an obituary stating simply that she had died in a private nursing home in Switzerland of an unnamed illness. There was no marriage and no child.

Nancy spread the various photos of Dolores over her desk. The consistently strange thing about them was that although the clothing and make-up became more severe as the years passed, when she studied just the face in each of the shots, she could see that it remained very youthful. It was almost as if Dolores were trying to dress older than she looked.

She took off her glasses and rubbed her eyes as she puzzled over the information. Though there was much she couldn't explain, she thought she could see a pattern. Having noticed that she bore a strong resemblance to Dolores di Napoli, Annie must have studied her in great detail. That wouldn't be difficult given her name was all over the Hollywood magazines. In her delusional mind, she had convinced herself that she was not just like the actress; she was her. The stories she had invented about Dolores could not be proven or disproven, and in Annie's mind they were the truth. The same applied to her tales of being Mali Whittaker. It would all be harmless enough but clearly Annie had a violent side to her character, a side that emerged unpredictably with fatal consequences.

Chapter 6

Nancy Wright prepared her third interview with Annie Carr very carefully. She reviewed all her notes, summarised them and listed a set of bullet points to remind herself of all the aspects she wanted to cover. While she wanted the entire tale in Annie's own words, she wanted to ensure that she missed nothing; that they didn't shoot off at a tangent and overlook important areas.

Inside the increasingly bulky file on the table in front of her was a selection of the magazines with the photographs of Mali Whittaker and Dolores di Napoli. Nancy intended to show these to Annie later in the interview.

However, things did not get off to a good start. When Nancy entered the interview room, Annie was already there. She looked preoccupied.

"Something up, Annie?"

"I still haven't had any satisfactory news about Serena," replied Annie, her face tense.

"I'm sorry," said Nancy, "but it's as you've been told. Sheriff Bachman said that he and Sheriff Brewster made a thorough check of the commune. They spoke to many of the people there and even took some of the children aside to talk to them without the adults knowing. The DA didn't like that, but Bachman's a pragmatic sort who knows when and how to bend the rules to reach his goal. The fact is that no one there, including the children, agreed that you have a daughter. They said you were often trying to claim one or other of the children was yours; that you had to be watched all the time since they were afraid you might frighten the children with what they called your strange ways. The sheriffs came back quite convinced that there is no Serena Peace and, incidentally, no Johnny Quinn. No one had heard of him."

Annie chewed her lip as her eyes roamed the room and her breathing became heavier. Then suddenly she thumped her fists on the tabletop. "They're lying, all of them. Ty completely twisted their minds and they are still coming up with his nonsense even though he's dead."

"That was another thing, Annie," said Nancy, deliberately keeping her voice quiet in an attempt to calm Annie. "Sheriff Bachman said they could hardly disguise their dislike for you. They blame you for the deaths of both Ty Donnington and Petra, as well as the disappearance of Seth Short. Several of the women were still in tears about Petra as well as Donnington. They talked of her being inspirational, said she was a key figure in the commune and that she radiated happiness to them all. They also all said they would go against their normal refusal to participate in regular society and happily give evidence against you in a trial."

Annie shook her head and laughed drily.

"They are all hypocrites. I would never have hurt Petra. Never. Ty killed her. As for Petra being inspirational, most of them didn't have the time of day for her. They were jealous of the fact that Ty took her as his main woman, even though she hated him. So much for Sheriff Bachman's detective skills. He's had the wool pulled well and truly over his piggy eyes."

"I don't know what else we can do," said Nancy.

"Take me up to the commune; that's what you can do. I'll show you where they are hiding Serena. I'll take you to Zelda and Pete's. They won't find it so easy to lie directly to my face."

"You know that can't happen," replied Nancy, shaking her head. "Annie, they told the sheriff there's no couple called Zelda and Pete in their community and that there never has been."

"It's a conspiracy, Dr Wright, a conspiracy." Annie wiped her eyes on her sleeve, the chains of her cuffs rattling loudly.

Nancy gave her a few moments to calm down and then continued.

"Look, Annie, I know it's disappointing but can we lay that to one side, just for now. I really need to spend some time going over your story again. It's very important. For your future."

Annie closed hers eyes in an apparent attempt to regain her composure. When she reopened them, she shifted her focus to Nancy's face. "What is it you want to know?"

"All of it, Annie, all of it. I want you to start at the beginning and cover all the ground you've covered before."

"OK," sighed Annie, "where shall I start?"

Annie talked to Nancy for the following hour, mostly without interruption. Nancy only occasionally brought her back if she seemed to be digressing or if she felt that Annie had glossed over something. When she'd finished, Annie shrugged and said, "Anything else?"

Nancy was laughing. Annie had just retold her the tale of Manny Goldstein, embellishing the night in the jazz club more than the first time.

"No, Annie," said Nancy, wiping her eyes. Then she decided to take a risk. "You know, it's amazing. You make it all sound very believable."

Annie frowned. "What do you mean by that? I make it sound believable because it's the truth. You don't think I'm making it up, do you?"

Nancy looked into Annie's pale grey eyes and tried to read her, but she couldn't. Annie saw the confusion in her interviewer and smiled to herself. Her campaign appeared to be working.

Nancy opened the file. "Annie, I've got a couple of photos I want to show you."

She pulled out the magazines and spread them across the table, the pages open at the single picture of Mali Whittaker and the several of Dolores di Napoli.

Annie picked up the first. "I remember that eagle," she said, pointing to the picture of Mali Whittaker. "It was one of my most successful pieces. I sold it to a rich collector from Texas. The cash kept me going for six months."

Nancy shook her head. Detail, detail, she thought, there is so much detail.

"Do you like the dress?" Annie had picked up the magazine with the photo of Dolores di Napoli in the evening dress.

"I do, Annie, yes."

"I had it made for the premiere of *Magical Nights*. It was very like one that I wore in the movie, but this one," she tapped the photo, "was much better quality. My, look at that hair." She absently brushed a hand through her hair. "They were fun times, for a while."

Nancy closed the file and put the cap on her fountain pen.

"Annie," she said, sitting back in her chair. "There's one point we haven't really discussed very much. I wanted to wait until I knew more about you; knew you better."

"What's that, Dr Wright?"

"You have been arrested for the murder of two people and the DA, at least, is convinced you're involved in the disappearance of a third. Now, you've said you didn't kill Petra, and I tend to believe you. As for Seth Short, well, there's no trace of him. However, for Ty Donnington, you've agreed that you killed him, given there were two witnesses who were standing only a few feet away when you stabbed him. You've killed a man, Annie. How do you feel about that?"

The corners of Annie's mouth lifted in a half smile.

"I'm pleased you said 'killed', Dr Wright, and not 'murdered', because I certainly didn't murder him. I have to accept that I killed him even if it was in self-defence."

She shrugged. "How do I feel about it? He's not the first man I've killed, as I've told you, so the experience wasn't new to me. What can I say? He didn't necessarily deserve to die, although in my experience, some people do. Some people are manifestly evil, inflicting hardship and pain on others, ruining their lives and making their existence a living hell. I don't really see why such people deserve to live. I've met a number during my life and I can say that when they die, the world is always a better place without them."

"Was Ty like that?" asked Nancy.

"Not completely, no. I mean, he wasn't pure evil, although close. He could be charming when he wanted; he was very charismatic. But he was also totally controlling. Once he'd lured people into his special community, he was their leader and they were his disciples. They weren't quite his slaves, but close. People think Ty'sland is some sort of hippy community and Ty is … was … happy to maintain that illusion. The reality is very different. You see, hippies are generally laid-back people doing their own thing, advocating peace and the freedom to choose. At Ty'sland, Ty dictated everything that happened."

"How did he achieve that? Surely there must have been some resistance to him?"

"Well, first of all, he was a big, powerful man; very strong, which made him physically extremely intimidating. Second, he chose his followers carefully. They were all weak people; lost; people looking for purpose; needing and wanting to be controlled. He gave them that purpose by convincing them they were special, by placing himself and therefore them above the rest of the human race, who, according to Ty, are to be pitied for their shallowness, their lack of enlightenment.

"Then he drugged them – he was very skilful with drugs, particularly herbal drugs. I know that because I've studied them myself, been taught by some very good practitioners. You see, Ty worked hard for his control. He could never have been accused of being lazy. He supervised every aspect of life in the commune and he had control over the food, which is how he drugged people."

"Why did you stay?"

"Escape was an option, although very difficult, given he made everyone watch me constantly. I was never alone. It was a deliberate policy on his part to wear me down. You see, he realised I wasn't like the others; that I saw through him. I was, therefore, a challenge. Yes, I could have escaped – I even tried once with Serena when she was very small. But they caught me; dragged me back. After that, although for a while I was allowed to be with her, the supervision was always, always there. It's so cruel: Serena knows I'm her mother but at the same time she is taught that all the women are her mother; that she is part of a community where everything is shared. It's rubbish of course. The only thing that is shared is Ty, who drugs the other men to make them impotent and takes most of the women as his own. Although, as I've said, for some reason Petra was a special favourite. Not that she encouraged him; she didn't like him. However, she didn't say no and she was, apparently, an accomplished lover.

"Lately, in the past few months, I've been allowed to see Serena less and less. It's as if Ty knew I might be plotting to escape again and would try to take Serena with me. I think his reasoning was that Serena would resist being taken since she now regards all the other women as her mother; that I'm no different from them in her eyes. I would never have left without Serena and he knew it."

Nancy nodded. "So when the four of you went to Drop City, Ty would have been sure you wouldn't try to escape since he'd got Serena back at the commune. Didn't you think of slipping away and going to the authorities?"

Annie snorted derisively. "That wouldn't have done me much good. Look how the commune people have closed ranks and denied Serena's existence, even without Ty there to guide them. They are programmed, you see. No, if I'd snuck away, I'd have lost any chance of seeing Serena again."

"So, can you answer my question, Annie, in a nutshell?"

Annie thought about it. "If you want me to say I feel remorse, I can tell you I don't. However, I do feel regret. Not over his death, to be honest, but because I have now lost any chance I had of escaping with Serena. Whatever happens, I'm going to be incarcerated with no way of having any contact with the commune. I'm the loser here, Dr Wright. Ty may have lost his life, but I've lost Serena."

A short while later, Nancy went to the DA's courthouse office to discuss her findings with Kallings and Abby Shaw, his assistant.

"Well, Dr Wright, have you come to any formal conclusions? Is the lady nuts?" taunted Kallings as she walked through the office door.

Nancy put her bag on the floor and sat in one of the guest chairs.

"That's not a term I'm familiar with, Mr Kallings. However, if you are asking if she is competent to plead, I'd say the answer's no."

The DA's neck flushed slightly, but he held his tongue.

Nancy continued. "The interview I conducted with Annie Carr in the past hour was quite remarkable and has convinced me my preliminary assessment was correct, although my diagnosis can now be more specific."

"What was so profound about it, Dr Wright?" said the DA, a cynical sneer on his face. "Did you get the beady eye treatment as well? Has she hypnotised you?"

"Not at all, Mr Kallings." Nancy straightened in the chair and pushed up her glasses. "No, what was so profound, as you put it, was that I asked Annie to go over all the ground we have covered before. Which she did. However, rather than her tale being a very similar repetition of her previous account, she told it quite differently. Obviously there was a degree of similarity in some places but, for the most part, she certainly didn't use the same words and there was no attempt at glossing over anything. When I asked for even more detail, I got it. This was not a well-prepared and well-rehearsed story rehashed to order. This was spontaneous and free-flowing. If I didn't know better, I could be forgiven for thinking she was telling the truth."

"So we have Dolores di Napoli sitting downstairs?" asked the DA, his voice heavy with sarcasm.

"No, Mr Kallings, we don't. What we have downstairs is a severely delusional woman who cannot distinguish fact from fiction. She somehow has a remarkable knowledge of real facts from both Mali Whittaker's life and Dolores di Napoli's. I simply don't know how she has acquired that information. As well as that, since much of what she says cannot be substantiated – the story of her being recognised in a jazz club, for example – then clearly a great deal of what she says is also complete fabrication. But it's clever fabrication, very clever.

"She is also totally convinced she has a daughter at the commune, something we know isn't true – I simply don't believe that all the members of that community could put up such a consistently convincing story if there had been a child. Someone would have given the game away. However, there's no denying that Carr has a vivid imagination. If I didn't know the truth, I could have been completely taken in by her.

"All that in itself wouldn't be too much of a problem if she were functioning normally: she could lead a normal life and perhaps just be regarded as rather eccentric. However, as we know, she is prone to extreme violence. She has killed a man viciously in front of witnesses and at various times since, she has appeared to lose control. I should add that while she accepts that she killed Donnington, she says it was self-defence. If she would agree to speak to the court-appointed counsel, he could probably make a good case for manslaughter, even if he is very young and inexperienced. But she won't even agree to see him."

Kallings was contemptuous. "She murdered 'em both, Dr Wright, and the People will prove it. Maybe she somehow murdered the other man, Seth Short, as well, the one who's conveniently disappeared."

Nancy shook her head vigorously. "There's absolutely no evidence of that, Mr Kallings. For all we know, Short just decided to move on. You don't even know he's dead."

Kallings shrugged his shoulders. "Well, whatever has happened to Short, I shall certainly be raising objections to your report, even though I think the woman's nuts. She's a danger to society and society will sleep easier at night knowing she's out of the way, even if I don't get her to the gas chamber."

"Then we'll leave it to the judge, Mr Kallings. Whatever happens, I guess you'll be getting your wish. It'll be the county jail or Sawpine Ridge."

Chapter 7

Judge Lorna McPhee looked over her glasses at the assembled gathering in her courthouse. She was surprised that a routine Competency to Stand Trial hearing should have attracted such an audience. However, the faces were all familiar, apart from some humourless-looking men and women from the Ty'sland commune whom she considered having thrown out on the grounds they probably needed a good wash.

She'd been angry with Kal Kallings for calling in a psychiatrist from Sawpine Ridge before she'd had a chance to review the case, especially once she'd realised his motives were aimed at a quick opinion that would make the trial go ahead. Fortunately, the new, young psychiatrist, Dr Wright, had proved sufficiently professional to ignore Kallings and carry out her task with all due diligence. The judge was impressed by her report – it was very convincing – and she was willing to be persuaded by it. There were just a couple of points about which she wanted clarification. She looked again at the crowd and hoped there wasn't going to be trouble. If there was, at least the town's police force was at hand. She let her eyes fall somewhat ruefully on them.

Crammed into the first row behind the prosecutor's table were Sheriff Mort Bachman; his niece, Elvira, who was heading down the same voluminous route as her uncle; the stickman, deputy Jimmy Winslate; and the guileless third deputy, Sweet Praline.

Good day to commit crime in the County of Rio Grande, thought the judge. With almost the entire police force in the courthouse, there's just Tracey-Ann back at the sheriff's office, keeping the forces of evil at bay.

The judge shifted her gaze to the front benches. Sitting at the prosecutor's table were the objectionable Kal Kallings and his assistant Abby Shaw. Judge McPhee noticed that, as ever, Kallings had a superior sneer on his face and was sprawling rather than sitting; acting for all the world as if he owned the courthouse.

Across from the prosecution team at the defendant's table was the timid-looking, court-appointed defense counsel Byron Spelling, who appeared to be about twelve years old. Next to him and ignoring him completely sat the defendant, Annie Carr, who, it seemed, had no clothes of her own since she was still in the County Jail garb. Judge McPhee's eyes stopped with interest on Annie, who was in turn staring unblinkingly straight back at her. Even across the twenty feet or so of the courtroom, the judge couldn't fail to notice Annie's striking, pale grey eyes. Despite her no-nonsense character, she found them unnerving.

Sitting primly behind Annie in the first public row was Nancy Wright, looking rather nervous.

The District Attorney cleared his throat noisily to announce he was ready.

"Yes, Mr Kallings," said the judge, knowing the DA would not have dared to start without her invitation.

Kallings stood. "Your Honour, as you know, the defendant stands accused of two vicious and brutal murders and today's proceedings are simply to determine her competency to stand trial. I'd like to inform the court that the People are ready to begin presenting evidence for these wicked crimes at the–"

He was interrupted by a nervous cough from Byron Spelling, who had lifted a limp hand towards the bench. Unable to suppress a smile, the judge said, "Mr Spelling, you can't really raise an objection at this point in the proceedings."

Then the smile disappeared. "But I can. Mr Kallings, you know as well as I do that if the defendant is not found competent, there will be no trial. So stop grandstanding. If you want to make a statement to the press, do it in your own time."

The DA blushed, more with annoyance than embarrassment. "I apologise, Your Honour. I had no intention of …" His words faded away as the judge gave him another withering look. He looked down angrily at his papers. "Your Honour, I should like to inform the court that the psychiatrist from Sawpine Ridge appointed to make the assessment of the defendant, Dr Nancy Wright, has written up her findings and is ready to present them."

"Thank you, counsel." The judge turned to the defense counsel. "Mr Spelling, before I ask Dr Wright to explain her findings, would you be so kind as to inform me whether in your opinion the defendant understands these proceedings?"

Spelling jumped to his feet on mention of his name. He blushed. "Er, I'm afraid I have no idea, Your Honour."

The judge frowned. "How can you have no idea, Mr Spelling? Have you not spoken with your client?"

"No, Your Honour, I have not."

"What! Mr Spelling, you are here to represent your client. How can you do that if you don't speak with her?"

"I have tried, Your Honour, but she refuses to speak to me."

"What do you mean, she refuses to speak to you? She's your client."

"I know that, Your Honour. I have tried on several occasions; she just ignores me."

Judge McPhee massaged her forehead with her left hand.

"Will the defendant please stand?"

All eyes turned to Annie, who remained seated while continuing to stare directly at the judge. There was an embarrassed silence and then Nancy Wright leaned forward to whisper to Annie.

"Annie, do what the judge says. It's for your own good."

Nothing.

"Go on, Annie."

Annie slowly put her hands on the table in front of her and started to push herself up. This was the first time outside of her cell she'd been free of handcuffs and chains since the morning after the killings. She wanted to savour it. She stood up straight and waited.

"Right, young lady. I take it you can understand what I am saying?"

Annie took a deep breath. "Perfectly," she said.

The judge looked relieved. "Then tell me, if you will, why you won't speak to your counsel."

Annie shrugged. "He's not my counsel. He was appointed by the court. He's the court's counsel. How do I know I can trust him? He might be in league with that fat man." She pointed to Kallings, who grunted. "Or that one." Annie moved her finger to point at the sheriff, who wriggled uncomfortably in his seat as a titter of laughter rippled around the room.

"That's enough!" said the judge sternly, banging her gavel.

"The defendant will sit. You clearly understand the language of the court even if you don't understand what's going on. I'll hear the psychiatrist and come back to you."

The judge welcomed Nancy to the stand and thanked her for her report, telling her that she'd read it with great interest.

"There are just a few points I'd like you to clarify, Dr Wright, if you please. Now, when you say that the defendant claims to have been other people, are you saying she has a split personality?"

"Not at all, Your Honour," replied Nancy. "She is most definitely not oscillating between one personality and another, as would be the case in a split or multiple personality disorder. She just claims to have been these people in the past. Not only that, she can give an incredibly detailed account of their lives, some of which is verifiable, but of course, most isn't."

"You mean she could just be making the whole thing up?"

"That's what I expected, Your Honour, yes. However, people who do that tend to have a fixed story and are unlikely to stray outside its borders, that is, the borders of their knowledge or what they have prepared. If they do, they will quickly contradict themselves. Annie Carr's accounts are not like that. I've had her repeat them to me on a number of occasions and each time there is a different version of the same story, as you would expect from somebody who is relating an event that has actually happened to them. There is no evidence of the stories being rehearsed or that she is speaking from a learned script. I have never come across a case like it, Your Honour, nor can I find anything similar in the literature. In both the previous personas she has described to me in great depth, the detail is quite remarkable. It's as if she really has lived those lives. In the case of the actress, Dolores di Napoli, I found–"

The judge interrupted. "Yes, that's an interesting one. You made mention in your report of how similar the defendant's features are to those in photographs of that actress. My father, the late Judge Callum McPhee, God rest his soul, was an ardent fan of silent movies as a young man. He used to collect photographs from movie magazines and paste them in a scrapbook. He had a huge collection and I remember one particular favourite was Dolores di Napoli. You know what, doctor, I agree with you: the defendant bears an uncanny resemblance to the pictures I remember from my childhood."

There was a rustling from the public seats as people strained to check Annie's face more closely. One reporter rushed out of the courtroom.

Judge McPhee realised she was digressing. Personal reminiscences from the bench had little place in her normally tightly run court.

"Could you summarise your conclusions for the court, please, Dr Wright?"

"Yes, Your Honour. I find that the defendant is suffering from a severe personality disorder in the form of delusion. She is under the impression that she is considerably older than she really is and that she has lived other lives as other people prior to her present life. The reality, Your Honour, is that this is a young woman of thirty years old in perfect health and fitness. She claims to have had a number of children, some of them many years ago. A medical examination has shown that she has indeed borne at least one child, although it is difficult to determine exactly when. In addition to her delusional state, she is subject to violent mood swings and an unpredictable onset of either aggressive or threatening behaviour. She has admitted to me that as well as killing one of the victims in the present case, she has also killed several people in the past. However, since she claims to have killed these people hundreds of years ago, they must be figments of her imagination."

There was a derisive laugh from Annie. "They certainly aren't," she said quietly, but clearly enough for everyone in the courtroom to hear. There was a buzz of comment which stopped abruptly as the judge again banged her gavel.

"Please continue, doctor," said the judge, glowering at Annie.

"My conclusion, Your Honour, is that this woman is unable to distinguish between the real world and a sort of parallel world that exists in her mind and which she confuses with reality. With her unpredictable episodes of violence, she is, in my opinion, a potential danger to herself and others. She is also, in my opinion, incapable of understanding the significance of what she has done."

The judge sat back. "Thank you, Dr Wright. Could you tell the court if there is any treatment that could return the defendant to the real world? Are there drugs that can be used?"

"There are, Your Honour, yes. However, I should recommend intensive counselling in the first instance, rather than attempt any drug interventions, apart from sedatives to control any violent episodes. The approach would be symptomatic."

Judge McPhee nodded and turned to the court.

"Before I give my decision, I should like to hear more from the defendant. Miss Carr, will you please stand."

Annie did not move.

"Miss Carr!"

Nancy, who was returning to her seat, walked up to where Annie was sitting and bent over to whisper in her ear.

"Annie, this isn't helping. Do what she says. Let me help you up."

She offered her arm but Annie just stood up, ignoring it.

"Thank you, doctor," said the judge. "Now, Miss Carr, I–"

"I am not Annie Carr."

The judge looked at Annie.

"I beg your pardon."

"I said I am not Annie Carr."

"Young woman, we have heard about your other personalities from Dr Wright. Are you claiming to be one of them? Are you–" Judge McPhee referred to her notes, "–Mali Whittaker? Or Dolores di Napoli?"

Her tone was patronising and there was a ripple of laughter from the courtroom.

Annie ignored them.

"I am neither of them, and I am not Annie Carr. I have been all three and suppose you could say I am Annie Carr at the moment. But I am not really her. Annie Carr died in 1964."

Nancy Wright frowned; she was worried by this turn of events.

"Well," continued the judge, "if you are not any of those three, would you be kind enough to tell the court your real name?"

"My name – my real name, that is – is Paola Santini."

"Paola Santini," repeated the judge. "Tell me, Miss Santini, where and when were you born?"

Annie let her eyes focus sharply on Judge McPhee's, the judge feeling the strength of them.

"I was born in Naples, in Italy, although at the time it wasn't really in Italy: it was in the Kingdom of Naples. I was born in 1518."

This time the buzz of comment around the courtroom was loud, mixed in with some laughter. Lorna McPhee banged her gavel several times.

"Now listen here, young lady, I've accommodated your behaviour in order to let you be heard; I do not expect you to show this court disrespect by coming out with complete nonsense."

Nancy Wright closed her eyes. This was not the way to speak to someone with Annie's problems.

Annie raised her chin and fired her reply back to the judge.

"I am showing no disrespect to the court. I fully recognise and respect its duty, its functions and its authority. In return, I do not think I am asking too much to expect the court to show me an equal amount of respect. I am simply telling you the truth. My name is Paola Santini and I am four hundred and fifty-two years old."

Judge McPhee stared back at Annie.

"Dr Wright," she called out.

"Yes, Your Honour," replied Nancy hesitantly as she stood up.

"Why did you fail to mention any of this in your report?"

"Given the need for verification, I have limited my interviews to an exploration of the recent past, Your Honour. I realised that there was more to be heard from Miss Carr from the violent episodes she described to Sheriff Bachman. However, since these were supposed to have occurred so long ago, I felt that verification would take longer. So the reason I made no mention of it in my report is simply because the defendant made no mention of it to me, Your Honour. This is the first time I have heard it."

Lorna McPhee banged her gavel with an air of finality as she glared around the courtroom.

"Right," she growled, the exasperation strong in her voice, "I've heard enough. I accept Dr Wright's report and I find the defendant, Annie Carr, or whatever her name is, is not competent to stand trial at the present time. I order that she be detained indefinitely in the custodial psychiatric institution at Sawpine Ridge. I also order that this court be provided with psychiatric reports every six months and that if the defendant is ever deemed to have overcome her delusions and can reasonably answer to the court, she will be required to stand trial."

Chapter 8

Annie Carr sat sketching at the small desk in her cell. She had been at Sawpine Ridge Psychiatric Institution for a little over three months and, on the whole, things were going her way.

She was well aware that life in Sawpine Ridge, although rigid and restrictive, was immensely better than it would have been had she been found competent to stand trial. Even if she'd only been found guilty of manslaughter and not first-degree murder, she would have been in the state prison with hundreds of other hard-bitten lifers for who knew how many years, and with no hope of escape.

No, Sawpine Ridge was by far the better option.

Her first victory had been to show Nancy Wright that the strong medication normally given to someone with Annie's diagnosis was best avoided.

"The problem I've found," Annie cautioned Nancy at their first meeting after Annie arrived, "is that most drugs have a very negative effect on me; far stronger in most cases than expected. I seem to have some sort of built-in sensitivity to medication; for some reason my body reacts against it. Most of the time at the commune when the others smoked pot or used other drugs, I pretended. I tried them but not only do I not like being out of control, I also found my mood often became very negative and heavy, or I'd just go to sleep. And the hangover was always horrible. Of course, I experimented with various remedies to try to counteract their effects, but they didn't always work."

Nancy was puzzled. "What do you mean by 'experimented'?"

"Well, I'm very knowledgeable in herbal medicines from way

back when I was relatively young – soon after I escaped from Italy after killing the priest. There are many potions and preparations, you know, that can prevent a medicine or poison from having its desired effect. However, the problem at Ty'sland was that the Colorado flora are different from the European plants I know so well, and many of the species I sought weren't there."

"Annie, I'm sorry, I can't go against the protocol. We have a number of drug combinations that are prescribed to patients here, and I am obliged to use the one appropriate for your condition."

"Presumably many of these drugs are not mainstream," said Annie perceptively, "not yet anyway. The inmates of this place must be the perfect guinea pigs for trying out new formulations. We're not in a position to complain and if they kill us, who cares?"

"That's extremely cynical of you, Annie. It's not like that at all. I agree that sometimes you might get the benefit of a new drug before it is more widely prescribed, but that is all to the good."

"If it works, yes," retorted Annie. "However, be warned, Dr Wright, I can assure you that whatever you give me might not produce the result you expect."

Nancy took no notice of Annie's warning and went ahead with the standard set of sedatives, antidepressants and antipsychotics normally tried on delusional patients. The antipsychotic was exactly as Annie predicted: an experimental drug under development by a pharmaceutical company hoping to produce enough human data to demonstrate the drug's worth while quietly ignoring any negative results. Annie's reaction was too extreme to ignore – on taking what should have been a mild dose, she slept for three days continuously, her breathing becoming so shallow that she was rushed to the infirmary for constant monitoring.

When she eventually woke up and worked out where she was, she smiled to herself in satisfaction. Unbeknown to Nancy, she had grabbed a handful of leaves from a potted plant in a guard's office, a plant she knew had a strong sedative effect. With that and what she knew would be a powerful synthetic sedative in the mix, she could guarantee she would be getting a long sleep.

Nancy was horrified and immediately stopped all medication for Annie, prescribing instead close monitoring for signs of any violent episodes. Annie kept her outbursts to what she considered an acceptable minimum.

Able to remain mentally sharp, Annie started her campaign to achieve more freedoms than would normally be granted, along with her continued indoctrination of Nancy Wright. Her plan was to steer the psychiatrist to the position where she finally believed her and would help her get away from Sawpine Ridge. She had no idea that her plan was doomed to failure for the simplest of reasons.

At their first meeting after Annie was released from the infirmary, she asked Nancy if she would mind if she sketched while they talked.

"I don't like my hands to be idle, Dr Wright; it's not in my nature."

Nancy agreed, regarding anything that potentially relaxed Annie as a bonus. She fetched a drawing pad and a selection of pencils.

Nancy was still obsessed with finding a chink in Annie's armour, the one point where her complex tale would fall apart and she'd finally admit she was simply inventing her life.

"Could you tell me more about your early days in Los Angeles, Annie," she said as she watched her patient's hands moving rapidly around the sketchpad with total confidence. "I'm intrigued by how you got into the movie business. Was it through Manny?"

Annie stopped sketching, lifted her eyes to Nancy and smiled.

"No, the first agent I dealt with was Manny's father. I'd arrived in LA in 1912 using my proper name: Paola Santini."

"Where had you come from?"

"New York City – I'll tell you about that later. I met a couple of girls on the train. They were younger than I was – I mean, the age I was saying I was – but they were great fun. They were coming to LA with the prime intention of getting into the movies. It was all incredibly primitive back then, before the industry really got going big time, but they knew what they wanted. They'd even got some interviews lined up and persuaded me to come along.

"Sadly for them, at all four agencies we went to, the agents were more interested in me. I think it was the Mediterranean complexion.

Manny's father – his name was Saul – was the nicest and more or less thrust a contract into my hands. I remember his words: he didn't like my name."

"Paola," said Saul Goldstein, his eyes running over her body. "Don't have much of a buzz. Hard to say. Me, I like Dolores. Beautiful name, gotta great ring to it. And we got too many Santanas."

"It's Santini, my surname, Mr Goldstein, not Santana."

"Yeah, of course. Where d'you say you was from?"

"Naples."

"That Naples, Italy? They got a different name for it?"

"It's called Napoli."

"That's it, kid! You can be Dolores di Napoli. You gonna be famous. I can see it now," he said, his arms spreading to embrace an imaginary movie theatre sign.

"Well," smiled Annie, "I did become famous, although not as famous as I could have. You see, I wasn't prepared to bow to the off-set demands of all the producers and directors – I turned down too many golden opportunities of nights in their bedrooms and so I was often sidelined. But Manny, Saul's son, worked hard for my cause. He always carried a torch for me and although he was a good-looking young man in those days, there was no spark for me. Through Manny, I got a number of leading roles for the next ten years or so, but, by then, there was a glut of younger, more compliant talent. Being already skilful at making myself look older, I readily accepted the offers of smaller parts for older characters. I liked it because I could use some acting skills and not just flutter my eyelashes. Of course it wouldn't have been sensible to be too much in the limelight as I grew older. I had to think ahead, as always.

"By 1940, I was claiming to be fifty-five and it really was time to move on. I wanted to leave this artificial world. So I let it be known I'd developed an incurable illness and that I was going to a sanitarium in Switzerland for treatment. You know, the agent I was using by then hardly looked up when I told him, the heartless bastard. It was announced that I was off but no one followed up on what happened to me. As far as they were concerned, I simply ceased to exist. Which, in fact, suited me very well since I didn't go to

Switzerland at all. I went to San Francisco and became Mali Whittaker."

Annie paused and Nancy looked up from the notes she'd been scribbling furiously. Annie was holding out the beautifully intricate sketch she'd been working on. Nancy was incredulous: it was clearly a self-portrait, but the costume and hairstyle were pure sixteenth century.

"Heavens, Annie, it's incredible. Tell me, why have you chosen to draw yourself like that?"

Annie smiled. "I told you, Dr Wright, my name isn't Annie; it's Paola. Paola Santini. This is how I was as a truly young woman in Naples. I would have looked like this around 1540. Would you like it?"

"I'd love it, thank you, but you know it doesn't prove anything, drawing yourself in the costume of another century."

Annie laughed and spoke in the rapid-fire Neapolitan language of her youth.

"What was that, Annie?" said Nancy with a frown of incomprehension. "It sounded vaguely Italian."

"Vaguely is right," laughed Annie. "There are few who would understand it now, even in Naples. It was the language I grew up speaking, though it's not much use to me in the modern world."

Nancy glanced again at the drawing and then her notes. She was feeling increasingly confused. She'd heard of speaking in tongues, but Annie's little speech sounded very convincing. She felt Annie's eyes boring into her and raised hers to meet the stare.

"Annie, you seem to have the ability to drift from this century to another quite effortlessly. Tell me, why have you chosen the sixteenth century? Was there a specific reason? Why not the twelfth or tenth? Or the eighteenth?"

Annie smiled softly. "I didn't choose the sixteenth century, Dr Wright. It chose me. You haven't been listening carefully enough. The sixteenth century is when I was born. Fifteen eighteen, as I told the judge. I can tell you plenty about the times since then, and I will, if you want to hear it. But I can no more give you a first-hand account of, say, the thirteenth century than you can. Like you, I wasn't born then either."

"Annie, 1518 was hundreds of years ago. You can't possibly be that old."

"It was hard for me to believe at first, Dr Wright, but it's true. You see, I don't seem to age. I haven't since I was about thirty. I haven't aged and I have never been ill. Not once in all those four hundred and fifty-two years."

Chapter 9

Nancy Wright was beginning to doubt her own sanity. The more she read over Annie Carr's story in her now extensive notes, the more convinced she became of its truth. But that was ridiculous. There was no way that anyone could be as old as Annie was claiming; it simply defied all logic. She decided it was time for some more detailed research. The library at Sawpine Ridge was limited; she needed the resources of a prestigious university. What better seat of learning than her old Alma Mater, Harvard University?

Nancy's supervising tutor throughout her postgraduate studies in psychiatry was Professor Martin Smythe-Richardson, an old-school Brit who'd left England in the early nineteen thirties for what he thought would be more enlightened halls of academia. Having talked his way into a post as a junior lecturer in the department of psychiatry that was part of Harvard University's medical faculty, now, nearly forty years later, he occupied one of the several chairs of psychiatry, his specialty being psychotic and anxiety disorders.

"Nancy! How delightful! How are the mountains?" enthused the professor when he answered Nancy's telephone call.

"Don't you mean 'How do I feel about the mountains?'" laughed Nancy, reprising the banter they often exchanged about patient consultation approaches.

"Now, now, Nancy, only if you are lying on the couch, which I doubt."

After more exchanges of pleasantries, Nancy described Annie Carr's case and her desire to delve into the literature.

"Fascinating case, Nancy," said the professor reflectively once she'd finished. "From what you say, I'd agree one hundred per cent with your diagnosis and recommendations. An individual such as you describe cannot be allowed to be loose in society. There are normally strong paranoid tendencies associated with such delusions and if she already has a track record of violent behaviour, she could become dangerously provoked by an innocent remark, let alone by the sorts of rebuff that her tales would generate."

"The problem, Martin, is that she is so incredibly convincing. The detail she comes out with is staggering and if I push her further, there's always more. When she's describing her other identities, I feel transported into a bygone era."

"Clearly a very vivid imagination."

"Yes, but somehow it's more than that. Which is why I want to come up to Harvard for the weekend to dig in the library. I want to research other cases of this type of delusion. I'd also like to know if her strange response to drugs is in any way related to her specific condition."

"I don't really see why it should be, Nancy, although it's well worth looking at. All very intriguing. I tell you what, if you're arriving on Thursday for a long weekend in the library, then I'll do some foraging myself; see if I can come up with anything. Now, while you're here, you must come to dinner. We have a few of the faculty members coming to the house on Saturday evening. Just a barbecue, all very informal. I know Marie would be thrilled to see you and hear all your news."

"Thanks, Martin, that all sounds wonderful."

Nancy felt a surge of confidence as she put down the phone. She was sure that she was about to gain some excellent insight into Annie's condition.

On the return flight from Boston to Colorado Springs the following Monday morning, Nancy sat staring at her elevated view of the world with the enthusiasm of a deflated balloon. The past three days had been an exercise in frustration.

She'd spent most of the weekend trawling through dozens of textbooks, journals and research publications. Delusional behaviour was well documented, but the deeper she went, the less she found that mirrored Annie's case. Sure, there were plenty of recorded cases of individuals convinced they came from all sorts of eras, from prehistoric times onwards. There were reborn prophets from Ur; Inca priests; Mayan temple acolytes; ladies-in-waiting to pre-Reformation English royalty; witnesses to the birth of Christ. They were all there and they all had one thing in common: the past lives they claimed were anything but ordinary. There were no farmers' wives living out routine existences with little happening except the changes of season, the births and deaths of their family and a few minor crises in otherwise inconsequential lives. No one was just an average person. While Nancy found this observation potentially heartening – Annie was claiming to have been a movie star – it was also confusing. The other persona Annie had related in detail, Mali Whittaker, was just another artist. Certainly not famous or notable.

However, the most perplexing difference between Annie and every single one of the delusional people recorded in the material she'd read was that Annie's stories contained so much consistent material. In the cases Nancy had read about, initially detailed stories of some past life or other were eventually found by the interviewing psychiatrists to be full of inconsistencies and contradictions. When challenged, the patients normally became angry or they withdrew into their shells, waiting out the storm of their detractors, and then with an innocent smile, recounting the same flawed stories all over again. Nothing in Annie's account remotely resembled this behaviour. She appeared to be unique.

Nancy resolved to take Annie back to the time she claimed she was born; to record each and every story through her claimed long existence. There must be a pattern, and there must be inconsistencies.

The morning after her return to Sawpine Ridge, Nancy set up an interview with Annie. As usual, Annie was ready and waiting, having been escorted by a guard from her cell in the high-security wing. The guard unlocked the cell door to admit Nancy and then left, locking Nancy in. At Nancy's insistence, Annie was not restrained, so the bored guard was obliged to wait outside the cell. There was no viewing window, but there were three panic buttons strategically placed in the cell in case of emergency.

Annie had brought a large folder with her and placed it on the table. Nancy was about to ask about it when Annie tilted her head quizzically, a wry smile on her face.

"You look uncomfortable, Dr Wright. Is that skirt too tight?"

Nancy pulled a face. "Yes, as a matter of fact, it is. It's been let out once, but the tailor didn't do a very good job. You know what I mean – it pulls in odd places creating wrinkles where I don't want them and the seams and darts are really not very straight."

Annie cast her eye on the offending skirt. "I can do something about it, if you want."

Nancy's face registered her surprise. "Another one of your skills, Annie? Dressmaking?"

"Yes," replied Annie simply. "I was a seamstress for many years, both in Germany where I was taught the skills and later in Trinidad."

"Trinidad? Do you mean the one south of Colorado Springs?"

"No," laughed Annie, "I mean Trinidad in the Caribbean. I lived there for thirty years."

Nancy smiled inwardly. Another tale. With Annie's expanding story, there must be facts Nancy would be able to check.

"Thirty years?"

"Yes," replied Annie. "From, let me see, the mid-1830s to, yes, 1867. Before I moved to America."

"Annie, that's–"

"If you fetch me a needle and thread, I can fix it in a jiffy. I really don't think you should be uncomfortable while we're talking. You'll be distracted."

Nancy thought about it. If Annie were concentrating on her stitching, she might lose track of her thoughts and produce the inconsistencies that must be there. Anything was worth a try.

"OK, Annie, I won't be long," she said, standing up.

Ten minutes later she was back, wearing what seemed to Annie to be another equally ill-fitting skirt. Nancy placed her first skirt on the table along with a small sewing basket. Annie lifted the lid and peered inside.

"Just one needle, Dr Wright? And no scissors? Don't you trust me?"

"It's not that, Annie, I–"

"It's OK, Dr Wright, I understand," said Annie smiling. She picked up the skirt and examined the stitching. "Can you stand up, please?" she said, retrieving a tape measure from the basket.

Nancy stood while Annie measured her. "I'll do that one after," said Annie, nodding to the skirt Nancy was wearing as she sat down.

"Now, where would you like me to start?"

Thinking Annie was referring to the skirt, Nancy frowned. Then she remembered why she was there.

"Trinidad?" she said, opening her notepad and unscrewing the top of her fountain pen.

With a deft flick of her wrists, Annie ripped apart the skirt seams and began removing the unwanted threads.

"I needed to get away from Europe. I'd been either on the run or imprisoned for too long and I was fed up with it. I wanted a new start."

"Imprisoned?"

"Effectively, yes, although not like this." She waved a hand around the room. "Not locked up in a cell for who knows how long." She smiled. "Interesting thought, Dr Wright, don't you think? Most of the people here, your 'patients', will very likely spend the rest of their lives in this institution. Is that what you have in mind for me?" She glanced around the room. "What's the life expectancy of this building? Because I'm sure I'll outlive it."

Nancy avoided Annie's eyes by concentrating on her notes.

Annie chuckled. "Don't worry, Dr Wright, I'm not digging a tunnel. Now, where was I? Yes, Rivolo."

"Rivolo?"

"It was a city state, a principality in the Western Alps. A tiny place, just a hill town really, but its independence went back many centuries. You might have heard of San Marino, in Italy."

Nancy nodded.

"Well," continued Annie, "it was a bit like that. There were many of them in those days – in the eighteenth and nineteenth centuries. Most have been absorbed into modern-day Italy now. I think San Marino is the only one left, probably because it has no strategic value – it was simply not worth fighting over.

"But Rivolo, that was different. I escaped there from the French Revolution. It was an incredibly dangerous time to be in France. I was in the Toulouse area where I'd set up as a travelling herbalist about twenty-five years previously. I could pass for a Frenchwoman, of course – do you speak French, Dr Wright?"

Nancy was taken aback. "Um, yes, a little. From school. I had something of an aptitude."

Annie pursed her lips. "Let's continue in French then," she laughed and broke into a dialect that was very different from anything Nancy had ever heard. Nancy put up her hand to stop her. "Sorry, Annie, I got none of that."

"I'd be surprised if you did, Dr Wright. That was the Toulouse dialect from the mid-seventeen hundreds."

"It was very different from the one you spoke previously," noted Nancy.

"Of course, that was Neapolitan, a variety of Italian, loosely speaking. It hasn't much to do with French. Anyway, as I was saying, although I could pass for a Frenchwoman, we were vulnerable and we had to leave. We had no desire for our heads to be separated from our bodies by a blunt and rusty travelling guillotine."

"We?"

"Yes, there were two men with me. One, Yves, had been with me for over twenty years. I'd cured him of various ailments with my herbal medicines, but I couldn't cure his failing eyesight. He was huge, and like a faithful dog. He could handle the horses and the cart I travelled in and carry massive loads. His general presence was enough to protect me from unwanted advances and because he didn't see well, he didn't notice I wasn't getting any older.

"The other was a youth, Armand, who joined us a couple of years before the Revolution. He was quick, strong and good with a knife. Saved our skins on more than one occasion."

Nancy shuddered.

"We made our way into the Alps. When we arrived at Rivolo, the place was in uproar because the duke's young daughter was dying. None of his physicians or healers had been able to cure her. I made it known I was a herbalist and offered my help. I was summoned to examine the girl and recognised the problem immediately: she'd been bitten by a venomous spider. However, the puncture was under the hairline and no one had found it. I treated her – calmed her raging fever and gave her a herbal concoction I knew would counteract the poison in her system. Of course, I told no one about finding the place where she'd been bitten.

"From then on, I was treated with great reverence and became the chief herbalist in Rivolo. This was all fine for some years but then Yves died and Armand wanted to return to France now it was safe again under Napoleon. That was when we realised we were effectively imprisoned: we weren't allowed to leave.

"The duke was indebted to me, but he was wily. He knew I was in a position to drug him and anyone else. Send them all to sleep if I wanted to escape. So every time I compounded a medicine for him or anyone connected with the palace, I had to give it to Armand as well.

"The years passed and eventually the old duke died, as did Armand. The duke's son, Alfonso, became the new duke. He was evil and he hated me for the preferential treatment I'd received from his father. By then, in the 1830s, I was thought to be in my early seventies. I kept myself well shrouded in voluminous clothing, hoods, and wild long hair I coloured grey."

Annie stopped and cackled harshly as she lifted her arms in the air and bent her fingers into claws. "I was like some old hag out of a fairy tale. But this fairy tale had a dark side. Alfonso was well known for taking his pleasure from any woman he chose, regardless of age. Every female in Rivolo lived in fear of him. Late one night, one of his guards arrived at my lodgings to escort me to the palace. Alfonso was ill, apparently, and needed my help. I was immediately suspicious but I had no choice. When I arrived at his rooms, I was pushed inside and the door slammed behind me. He called to me from his bedchamber."

"Come here, you old witch, there's something you can do for me."

Paola walked warily into the duke's bedchamber where she saw him lounging in a large deerskin-covered chair by a raging fire. He was wearing just tight-fitting leggings and a flowing white blouse, open to the waist. One leg was draped over the chair arm.

"Closer, hag, let me take a look at the brilliant healer, so favoured by my fool of a father. I want to see your dried-out husk of a body before I treat it to some long-forgotten pleasures." He took a swig from a jug of wine and belched.

Paola backed slowly away but the duke sprung to his feet, surprising her.

"Shy, are we, hag? Don't want to show off that wrinkled mess of a body?"

He jumped at her but she had anticipated it. Her hands clawed at his face, drawing blood.

Alfonso took a step back, and they faced each other, Paola half crouching, a cat waiting to spring. The duke shifted his weight from one foot to the other, snarling as he leered at her.

"I've waited for this for years. It's going to be an entertaining evening."

In a flash, his hand shot out, grabbing the folds of Paola's dress and ripping the seams. As the material came away in his hand, he slapped her face with his other hand. He spun her round, took the collar of the tattered dress in both hands and wrenched it downwards. Another vicious slap followed and she was spun around again as the remains of her clothing were torn from her.

The duke's eyes fell on her body and he stopped in his tracks. Paola was trying to cover her nakedness with her arms as she crouched on the floor near the fire. She glanced down and grabbed at a portion of her torn clothing, pulling it up in front of her.

The duke continued to stare at her in disbelief. "You scheming witch! You have the curvaceous body of a young woman and now I look closely at that evil face, you have no more wrinkles than one of the maids I normally summon here."

His eyes roamed from her breasts to her hips and his confidence returned. "You really must be a witch!" he bellowed, and then he burst out laughing. "You don't have your potions with you now, do you, hag. I'll take my pleasure of that fine body before I have you trussed up and burned in the town square. All these years you've had your way – you must have cast your foul magic on my father. But you won't on me."

He took a step towards Paola, reaching out to pull the clothing from her grasp. However, still crouching, she'd backed closer to the hearth and surreptitiously wrapped a torn shred of her dress round her hand. She reached out, grabbed a burning log from the fire and launched herself at Alfonso, ramming the flaming wood into his bare chest. He screamed in agony, but the sound was stifled when she drew *her arms back and then thrust the red-hot weapon at his wide-open mouth.*

The cloth fell away from Paola's body as she stood back and grimly surveyed the duke's charred face. The last thing he saw as his eyes bulged in fear and pain was her slightly crouched and naked figure, her mouth snarling and hair wild as she wound up her arms to smash the still-burning log across his head.

Alfonso collapsed in front of Paola. She stood in shock, surveying his blistered and blackened face and chest, and the blood oozing from the gaping wound to his head. She had to finish it. She looked around and saw his sheathed sword lying on a low table at the end of his bed. She picked it up, withdrew the sword and lifted it high above her head. With her two hands firmly grasping the hilt, she plunged the blade into Alfonso's chest, pinning him to the wooden floor.

Annie sat back and laughed at Nancy's horror-struck expression. "I told you Ty Donnington wasn't the first man I'd killed, Dr Wright."

"How … how did you get away?" stammered Nancy. "You were standing naked in the duke's bedroom, his body in front of you."

"I'd always planned an escape and I had saddlebags ready and packed in my lodgings. My problem was getting back there. My clothes were in shreds. However, I knew the palace well from years of treating the various family members. There were many secret passages so I had no need to go out past the guards. I knew the duke would have killed any guard who interrupted him while he was raping his latest victim. I had a few hours.

"I grabbed a thick cover from the bed and wrapped it around myself. Before I left, I was determined to take payment for all the years of captivity. It was rumoured that the duke kept a hoard of precious stones in his rooms, so I hunted until I found them. As it turned out, their value was hugely more than I imagined. I was rich!

"Back in my lodgings, I quickly dressed, added my newfound wealth to my saddlebags and made my way carefully to the town walls where there were stables. The guards were lazy; nothing had challenged them for years. There was a woman I knew, a cook, who brought them food at midnight. She'd suffered at the hands of the duke so she made no objection when I intercepted her and added a few drops of something to what she'd prepared. Half an hour later the guards were all sleeping like babies. I took the fastest horse and quietly walked away from Rivolo, mounting up only when well out of earshot."

"That's quite a tale, Annie," said Nancy as she finished scribbling her notes. "Could you tell it to me again?"

"What?"

"Could you go over it again? It's fascinating and I want to make sure that I've missed nothing."

Annie shrugged. She knew exactly what Nancy was doing and she knew that in the story's retelling, she'd embellish here, add detail there and answer any of her interviewer's questions on the way. She smiled to herself when she thought of how even more confused Nancy would be when she wrote up her notes.

"So why Trinidad?" asked Nancy when Annie finished retelling her tale.

"I'd escaped from Rivolo and on the way transformed myself back into a young woman. Even if the guards from Rivolo had caught up with me, they were looking for an old woman, so I was effectively invisible to them. However, I thought it better to leave Europe. I now had wealth and I wanted to start again elsewhere. I made my way to Marseille where I boarded a boat out of Genoa bound for the West Indies. On the way I made a plan and prepared some papers." She stopped and smiled.

"You look pleased with yourself, Annie; the plan was obviously a successful one," said Nancy, realising as she did that, once again, she was accepting everything Annie told her, believing it more and more.

"Yes, Dr Wright, it was," nodded Annie. "I enjoyed my time in Trinidad. I was there for over thirty years. Of course, I had to have a reason for going. Young women in the eighteen thirties didn't just get on a boat and sail for thousands of miles on their own. So I invented a scoundrel of a husband."

"A scoundrel?"

"Oh yes, an absolute bounder, as they said in those times."

"My dear Mrs Lethrington, I regret to inform you that these letters are completely fictitious."

"Fictitious, governor?" Paola Lethrington fanned herself rapidly, her reply a whisper of incredulity. "That cannot possibly be so. They are in my husband's hand. Personally delivered by his manservant from the docks in London."

"That may well be the case, madam; however, I can assure you that the plantation referred to, the one your husband claims to have bought, simply does not exist. I know that for a fact, since, as it happens, I, myself, own the land on which it purports to be situated."

Paola gasped, letting the governor know that the truth was slowly dawning on her.

"And my husband?"

"No one of his name or description has landed at this island in the past year. In fact, ever, according to the harbour captain."

Paola let a tear form at the corner of her eye and she dabbed gently at it with a lace handkerchief.

"Do you mean to tell me, governor, that my husband has tricked me?"

The governor of Trinidad, Sir Julian Critchley, looked lost. He wasn't used to attractive young women turning up at his island with tales of non-existent sugar plantations and erring husbands. He was quite convinced that the beautiful Mrs Lethrington had been duped, stripped of her fortune by a devious scheme and left destitute. She might not be English, but he had no doubt about the truth of her story.

He coughed delicately.

"I believe that may be the case, Mrs Lethrington." He paused. "Ahem, I, er, do not wish to embarrass you by touching on a delicate matter, but if your, er, husband has left you destitute, I could arrange for a loan … a suitable sum such that a lady of your standing could return to England, or if you prefer, to your native Sardinia."

He looked nervously at her. His wife would not be impressed by his generosity.

Paola looked up coyly through her softly fluttering eyelashes.

"Oh, governor, how kind of you to consider me so. However, I can assure you that I am not destitute. Although it appears that my husband has indeed stolen away with a considerable part of my fortune, I took the precaution of not revealing it to him in its entirety. I *have brought a sufficiency of funds with me from England, for the time being, at least. I find myself quite enchanted by this beautiful island, even after a few hours. Would it be possible for me to remain? With the funds I have, I could purchase a property, a small business perhaps. My mother was a practical woman. Even though I had no need of any trade, she insisted that I should not be idle like so many of our class and she instructed me in the arts of sewing and dressmaking. I am a skilled seamstress and I should be delighted to offer my skills to the European ladies of this island. I am familiar with all the latest English and European fashions."*

"That is extremely enterprising, madam, and, may I say, very brave. Few are the young women who would consider such a move under these distressing circumstances."

Annie broke the thread to separate the needle from her handiwork and tossed the skirt onto the table.

"Would you like to try it now, Dr Wright? If it's fine, I'll do the one you're wearing. It looks equally uncomfortable."

Nancy stood, slipped off her skirt and put on the one Annie had adjusted. She zipped it up and smoothed down the material.

"Annie, that's amazing. It fits perfectly and is wonderfully comfortable. You really are very talented with your needle and thread."

"I've had years of practice, Dr Wright," laughed Annie. "Let me fix the other one for you."

As Annie picked up the skirt from the table, Nancy noticed the folder she'd meant to ask about.

"More drawings?" she said, nodding at the folder.

"Take a look," said Annie as she dismantled the second skirt.

Nancy picked up the file and separated the contents. On top were two very detailed pencil drawings – both self-portraits. One was the modern-day woman sitting opposite Nancy, engrossed in her stitching. The other showed the same woman sitting demurely by a window in a tropical setting. She was wearing a high-neck blouse and her hair was drawn back in a bun. The period appeared to be early Victorian.

"This is you, Annie?"

"Yes, of course," said Annie. "At least, it's me when I was Paola

Lethrington. That's a copy of a beautiful painting of me by an artist who was prolific during my time in Trinidad: Michel-Jean Cazabon. He had a steady business drawing and painting the colonial wives and daughters. He also painted wonderful scenes of island life, some of which might still adorn houses down there. I got to know him quite well and once he discovered I too could draw, we spent many sessions together. It was an interesting distraction from my dressmaking. The colonial ladies loved it. They could visit my shop and leave with a dress *and* a portrait."

"It's so detailed, Annie," replied Nancy, taking in all the nuances of the drawing. "Do you know where the original is?"

"No, I've no idea. I left it behind when I left Trinidad in the sixties." She paused and laughed. "That's the 1860s, of course. It's possibly still there. Have you seen the painting underneath those drawings, Dr Wright?"

Nancy lifted the drawings and saw that under them was a full painting some twenty inches by twelve. It was a portrait of her.

She gasped; she had never seen anything like it.

"Annie, this is exquisite. Where did you learn to paint like this?"

Annie shrugged. "I've always been able to draw, from the time I was a little girl. My mother discouraged it, saying she didn't want me to be like my father, but you can't stifle creativity forever and slowly, over many years, I developed and honed my skills. Whenever I got the opportunity to study other artists' work, I would pore over the details, examining the brush strokes and techniques. I learned a lot from that and slowly applied it to my own work. However, as I say, most of it was innate."

"I look so ... so animated, as if I'm talking to the viewer, to myself!"

Annie laughed. "It's for you, Dr Wright. A gift."

"I shall treasure it, Annie, thank you."

"It comes with a request, Dr Wright," said Annie with an artful smile.

Nancy waited.

"I'd like to do more drawing and painting but my cell is hardly the most comfortable place to work. Would it be possible to use one of the rooms near the library? I'd be pleased to produce portraits of any or all of the guards and other staff. I'm not asking for special treatment; just a place to work. Perhaps you might think it would be good therapy for me ...?"

Nancy nodded, a knowing smile flickering in the corners of her mouth. She increasingly felt she was being played like a violin, but for the time being she would allow it. The more Annie relaxed, the greater the likelihood of holes appearing in her story.

"It would be excellent therapy, Annie. I'll discuss it with the director."

Chapter 10

Four-year-old Serena Peace awoke hugging her one rag doll whose name, for no reason anyone knew, was Klondike. She instinctively called out for her mother in the hope that this time she would appear at the door. But she didn't. Instead, it was Zelda. It was always Zelda.

Serena pulled the blanket over her face. She didn't like Zelda and she didn't want to see her.

"Come out from under that blanket, kid. It's time you were up. There's chores to be done. Jus' coz we're away here in the woods don't mean the chores don't get done."

"I want my mommy."

"I told you a hundred times, kid, your mommy's gone. She don't want you. She's been taken away coz she's a crazy woman. She killed our leader Ty and your Aunt Petra. They won't ever let her go from where they've taken her."

"She does want me. Where is she?"

"She's in a place where they keep crazy people. So's they can't hurt no one else."

"I want to see her."

"Well, you can't kid and that's it. You might as well get used to it. Now get up out of that bed before I have to pull you out of it."

Zelda roughly pulled the blanket back, snatching it out of Serena's hands.

Serena hugged Klondike to her chest and stared up at Zelda from under her eyebrows, her lips pouting. Then they quivered.

"I want my mommy!"

Zelda reached out for Serena's arm but the child wriggled to avoid her. More firmly now, Zelda took hold of her arm and pulled her to the edge of the bed.

"Do we have to have this performance every morning? Now get over to that door so I can shift your rope."

Serena reluctantly stood and shuffled over to the door. The end of a rope was knotted around her ankle, the other end attached to a ring too high up the wall for her to reach. The rope was about twenty feet long, enabling her to carry out whatever chores she was ordered to do without Zelda having to keep an eye on her every moment. There were several points inside and outside the cabin where it could be attached so that she could work in a number of places. Sometimes, when Serena had been particularly bothersome in her constant wailing for Annie, Zelda and her man, Pete, were sorely tempted to tie the rope to the ring on the porch and leave her outside all night along with Zac, their dog, but the nights were too cold; the child would freeze.

Serena worked long and hard at trying to undo the rope at her ankle but her small hands weren't strong enough to loosen the knots, and Pete checked and retightened them every night, just in case.

Zelda took the end of the rope, walked out onto the porch and refastened it to the ring there.

"Get yourself washed kid, and go use the potty. I'll get you some breakfast."

"I don't want any breakfast. I want my mommy," wailed Serena.

Under her strict exterior, Zelda was secretly worried about the kid. She wasn't eating and she had visibly lost weight during the three weeks they'd been living in the cabin deep in the woods while the police were snooping around the commune. The others in the commune had completely closed ranks and no one had given the nosey cops any indication that Serena, Zelda or Pete even existed. It was the best way. Annie had been trouble since she arrived in the commune almost six years ago. She'd got herself pregnant with young Johnny Quinn almost immediately. When Ty found out, he had exploded with rage. He was the father of the commune and the other men accepted it. They were no use that way anyway. They either couldn't get it up or if they could, no one ever got pregnant, not until Annie Carr did. Johnny paid the ultimate price, as he well deserved. This was Ty'sland and Ty's word was the law. Or at least it had been. Zelda didn't quite know what was going to happen now that Ty was dead. Killed by that stupid bitch Annie. Who was going to look after them now? She didn't know and neither did Pete. They'd been told to lie low in the woods with Annie's kid, the brat with the same strange eyes as her mother, the brat who never, ever got a cold or cough or any kind of illness. Nothing.

Time and again, before the murders, it had been explained to Serena that she didn't just have one mommy; she had lots. All the women were her mommy, even the older ones like Zelda. The other kids bought it and lived together under one big roof. It worked so well that most of the kids didn't now know who their real mommies were. But not the brat. Not Serena. She knew she was different, knew she was like Annie and no amount of telling her otherwise or keeping her from Annie seemed to make any difference. Her resistance to their brainwashing would upset the other kids, cause them to question the adults' wisdom. It was clear that Serena was going to have to be kept apart from the others as she got older, like she was at the moment. Hell, she was four now, and strong enough. She certainly had a temper on her and would fight like a cat. She would be given more chores to do when it was safe for them all to go back to the commune, kept busy while the other kids had their lessons. No point in teaching Serena anything. The less she learned the better. All she needed to learn was how to do her chores.

Serena was even more wary of Pete than she was of Zelda. Men hadn't featured much in her life. She knew Pete could be a daddy, although Zelda didn't have any children, but she wasn't really sure what a daddy did. Mommy had told her that her daddy died before she was born. She'd asked Annie if all the children's daddies had died since all the other children stayed together in one large group with the mommies; the men didn't have much to do with them. Mommy said that Ty was the daddy to all the other children but he was too busy to look after so many.

Most of the time Serena had to be with the other children from the commune, although they didn't have much to do with her. She only had a couple of friends who let her play with them. However, Serena was only really happy when she was with her mommy. Together they would laugh a lot, her mommy would sing her songs and draw wonderful pictures for her, and they would play games, run around the commune and even sometimes into the woods. But whenever they did that, one of the men would always appear from behind a tree and tell them to go back to the main commune area. Then other mommies started telling Serena that Annie was busy; that she would come to her the next day, and then the next, and the next.

Eventually they said her mommy had gone away and wouldn't be coming back. She had run to her cot with Klondike and cried inconsolably. Then they took her into the forest – for her own safety, they'd said. Bad men were coming who would hurt her. If they found her, they would also hurt her mommy. So she went with Zelda and Pete, but she didn't like them.

She would talk to Klondike, find scraps of paper to draw pictures for him, and, so that he didn't worry, she would tell him Mommy would soon be coming home.

Every night in her bed, safe under the blankets, Serena would remember her mommy's words.

"We're different, you and I, my darling Serena, very different. We're not like these people and one day we'll leave this place. We'll leave them behind in their silly commune; leave them to their silly lives. We have very different lives to live. Very, very long lives. We're going to live forever, Serena, you and I. Forever. We can do anything we want, go anywhere we want and we'll never worry about getting sick or being ill. Never. We're different, my sweet angel."

Chapter 11

It took Nancy Wright two weeks of hard bargaining with director Hector Higgins to persuade him to allow Annie Carr space in the old library block for use as a studio. Martha Blunt had returned from Denver and hadn't helped matters by siding with her boss.

On the morning Higgins finally relented, he began his argument as he had every day. The three of them were sitting in his office with Blunt nodding in agreement.

"It's very unorthodox, Nancy," said the director. "This patient has only been here a short time. You still haven't completed your full assessment. As a rule, we don't allow such privileges until we are very sure the patient is stable enough not to cause trouble, and normally under medication, I might add."

Nancy's insistence that Annie take no medication was still a major point of disagreement between her and the director.

"This young woman is, I should remind you, a murderess, a fact that was not only witnessed, but which she herself readily admits to you, and she is subject to well-documented violent episodes."

"I appreciate that, Hector. Nevertheless, I really do feel it would be so beneficial to her mental state. She's very calm when she's working, and she is incredibly talented. Perhaps you'd be more convinced if you let her paint your portrait. It would look very fine adorning this office, don't you think?"

Not immune to vanity, Higgins adjusted how he was sitting, unconsciously turning his head slightly to one side, straightening his back and lifting his chin.

"A guard would have to be present at all times, Nancy. If there's any sign of trouble, the privilege will be cancelled."

"Thank you so much, Hector. I'm sure this will help Annie no end and it will certainly help my assessment. The detail she has given me so far about her imagined former lives is impressive. She must have studied history in depth at some stage, or read and absorbed many passages from the Encyclopaedia Britannica. I've checked up on the artist she mentioned, Cazabon, and he really did exist, living in Trinidad at the time she claimed. There was also a Duke Alfonso of Rivolo murdered in 1832 by a female assassin who was never caught."

"Well, Nancy, if you can find these snippets of information in the encyclopaedia, I'm sure she could have as well. However, to create whole lives around such people demonstrates a wandering and unstable mental state."

The director was very old school.

The portrait of Hector Higgins was a great success. Once it was hung in his office, the director strutted around peacock fashion for days, taking every opportunity to invite people to show off the work.

Annie chuckled when Nancy told her about his behaviour. "Men are like putty, Dr Wright. Remember that as you live your life and you'll get what you want. You must develop your skills as a sculptress."

Nancy laughed. "I've certainly seen a side of the director I hadn't seen before. He's like a dog with two tails."

They were sitting in the room Nancy had commandeered for Annie's studio. The guard who would normally be present while Annie was working had locked them in and, with Nancy's agreement, was taking a coffee break – there had been fewer and fewer episodes of irrational and potentially violent behaviour from Annie during the past weeks.

Nancy opened her file.

"I'd like to recommence our talks, Annie, from where we left off three weeks ago. I needed time to verify a few things and I also wanted to give you more time to settle into the routine of this place."

"I appreciate it, Dr Wright, although I would say that the routine of this place is stultifyingly boring. I think I'd go mad if you hadn't arranged this room for me."

She laughed. "Of course, you think I'm mad already, but you know what I mean. Now, tell me about your verifications. What have you found?"

Nancy sighed to herself. Whenever Annie adopted this tone, it was like she was the interviewer and Nancy the patient. However, she was prepared to play along with it, especially since she thought she'd hit upon a potential inconsistency in Annie's story.

"Well, there is one particular point I'd like you to clarify."

Annie wondered what was coming.

"How many languages do you speak, Annie?"

"How many? Well, I've never really thought about it. You see, it's not so much how many languages as how many dialects. Languages change over the centuries, so for me to say I speak French would be misleading. In fact, if I were to speak to a Frenchman or woman now, they would be puzzled by my archaic use of language since I haven't really used it for well over a hundred years. The same with my German. For that it's been even longer. As for my Italian, well, I know many dialects since I lived in several parts of Italy over my first almost two hundred years and I adapted my language accordingly."

It was not the answer Nancy was expecting, but it sounded so plausible.

"What about your English, Annie? You speak English like any other American, although I would say your accent is quite refined and not very strongly American. However, according to what you've told me, you have never lived in England and you would not have been speaking English until you went to Trinidad. Even there, with Cazabon at least, you might still have used French. How come your English is so good?"

Annie eyes creased in pleasure as she recalled a settled period in her past.

"You haven't heard the whole of my story yet, Dr Wright," she said, tilting her head to one side and smiling softly.

"You're right; I've never been to England. However, I did have an English lover. In Paris, for nearly thirty years. It was before I took up my wandering life in the Toulouse area. He was a lovely man and a very rare one. An aristocrat with a heart, a man with a soul who truly loved me. We had a good life and during those years he resolved that I should learn his native tongue. He regarded English as the most refined and literary language in the world, more sophisticated than any other, and he made it his mission that I should be able to speak it as well as any aristocratic English lady."

As she was speaking, Annie's gaze was elsewhere, reliving fragments in her memory. When she brought her focus back to Nancy, she stopped, puzzled.

"What is it, Dr Wright? You're looking at me very strangely."

"Annie, do you realise what you were doing just then? While you were telling me that?"

"I was seeing it all in my mind's eye, if that's what you mean."

"Yes, I'm sure you were but it was more than that. As you started talking, your American accent disappeared and was replaced by a very cultured English one, though not a modern day one, I'm almost sure."

Annie scratched her forehead absently. "Was I really? Well, well, how strange. He had a powerful effect on me. It was one of the happiest times of my life, one of the few oases of light in otherwise vast deserts of darkness. We had three children, you know: two daughters and a son. One daughter died very young, but the other two lived to be adults. Neither of them was like me; Serena's the only one who's been like me."

"Like you?"

"Yes, I told you. I am never ill and I don't get older. Marie and Charles were both strong, like their father, but they had their fair share of illness. It was an epidemic of cholera in Paris that killed Marie. She was only twenty, about to be married. It broke Richard's heart."

"Richard?"

"My husband, Sir Richard Barrow. He was one of the few people in my life who believed my story unreservedly. It worried him, poor man, since he knew I should have to leave Paris eventually. He tried to make every provision but soon after he died, I was robbed when I was heading south and I was left destitute. By then, Charles was in England and I had no way of contacting him. He didn't know about my secret – he was rather starchy and Richard thought it best not to challenge his faith. He was also very religious, you see.

"So I went from speaking the smattering of English I'd picked up from two nuns in separate convents to the delicate and sophisticated language of a refined lady who, for all the world, was a member of the English aristocracy, and without ever setting foot in their country." She laughed. "You're looking puzzled again, Dr Wright."

"Convents?"

"Yes, convents. When I think of it now, it seems absurd. But way back before all that happened, back in 1582 when I escaped from Naples, I was desperate. After my escape, I lived in a total of six convents, one after the other, for over a hundred years."

"What?"

"Sounds ridiculous, doesn't it? However, you must understand that I was very frightened and confused. You see, I was over sixty years old and, even though I felt young and strong and only looked thirty, I was convinced I was possessed and about to die. When I was younger, my mother had told me repeatedly that my father had a pact with the Devil; that he too hadn't aged. She seldom mentioned his name, but when she did, it was in a hushed tone with much crossing of herself. And now I was on the run, a fugitive – I had been branded a murderer because I'd killed Cardinal Alvaro by stabbing him in the chest as he tried to rape me and, according to the Church in Naples, I was a she-devil–"

"What was his name, your father?" interrupted Nancy.

"Stefano Crispi. He was a brilliant artist. My mother wanted to hide that from me as well but my Aunt Anna, who as an old woman confided in me that she'd been married to my father's grandson, had secretly kept a few of his works. They were incredible.

"Apparently, months before I was born, my father had escaped by the skin of his teeth when my mother discovered his secret and reported him to the Church. When I was forced to escape over sixty years later, it was more difficult because I was a woman – it was infinitely harder for a woman to break away in those times. Women did as they were told. Fortunately, I had a son, Luigi, who by then was about forty, who came with me. He was a very quick thinking man; it was thanks to him I escaped at all.

"Hidden away in the forest, we talked long and hard about what I might do. As I said, I truly thought I was getting old. I told Luigi I wanted to die in peace rather than be burnt as a servant of the Devil.

We decided the safest ploy would be to hide within the Church, not try to run from it. Since I could pass for a young woman, I could turn up at a convent and persuade them to take me in as a novitiate. Luigi provided letters of guarantee for me that we forged together. It worked well.

"Of course, I didn't die and I didn't age, although it took me a long time to accept how different I was from other people. In that first convent I watched the old mother superior drift into her dotage and my fellow nuns get older, fatter and slower. I padded out my habit, shuffled around like the rest of them and no one suspected a thing – a nun's habit is a good disguise and no one in the convent ever sees you in any state of undress. But as time went on, it all became increasingly difficult. Almost forty years after joining the first convent, I simply ran away; disappeared. I travelled to another part of Italy, found another convent whose doctrine wasn't too strict and started all over again. Luigi, who was an old man by then, helped me on that occasion, but by the next time I did it, he was dead."

"And you did that for over a hundred years?" Nancy was incredulous.

"Yes, until the early seventeen hundreds. When I killed Father Bonsanto. That was up in the north of Italy, near Padua. The man was a sex maniac. He got away with so much under the protection of his Church: abuse of young girls, nuns, boys, everything. You see, he had power and the ears of the right people. He was above any law. Even I gave into him once because he'd discovered my secret. However, the second time, I resisted, stabbed him in the neck and face with a broken wine glass and left him bleeding to death on his bedchamber floor. I stole a horse and rode and rode and rode. Into the mountains, all the way through Switzerland and on into the forests of southern Germany and a new life, my first outside the confining, suffocating constraints of the Church since I'd lived in Naples. I was nearly two hundred years old and I'd been drowning in the dogma of the Church for most of it; a victim, an enigma too threatening for acceptance."

Back in her apartment, Nancy Wright stood at a window that faced onto the mountains, staring blankly. Although the scenery was stunning, she hardly noticed it. On the table behind her was the file containing the most perplexing case study she had ever encountered. There would be a very important academic paper to be written if she could put her finger on the source of Annie's delusional behaviour, if she could show that everything Annie said was made up, as she knew in her heart it must be.

As it was, she now felt further from the truth than when she started. With every new tale from Annie, every new twist, she became more confused. There were plenty of verifiable facts scattered among the detail of Annie's supposed lives and Nancy had checked out many of them. She had even found reference to Stefano Crispi in her encyclopaedia, but no examples of his work. What staggered her was that there were no contradictions. Everything that could be cross-checked turned out to have happened. How was it possible for someone with Annie's youth and background to have unearthed so many facts and then woven them into a tale about herself?

It occurred to Nancy that the ultimate test would be time. Annie was locked up in Sawpine Ridge without hope of release and would die there, or in some similar institution, of old age. She was now thirty years old. In ten, fifteen, twenty years, there must be some change. Since Nancy was just two years older, she could use herself as a control against Annie.

An idea began to form in her head. One of the problems she'd had initially was cross-referencing any photographs of Annie when she was younger, simply because there were none. But that didn't mean there couldn't be in the future. She would take a series of detailed, close-up photographs, not just of Annie's face but also of her hands and arms. Surely as time went by there would be wrinkles forming; signs of her very good musculature going; hair greying – some change that would show up when in years to come Annie compared herself with Annie in the photographs. Then perhaps she would see through her own delusion. Because it would only be once she accepted that she was not all the things she claimed – when there was irrefutable proof of her ageing in the same way as everyone else – that she would be able to get beyond her fantasy world and gain some chance of being cured.

Part II

Chapter 12
1975

Nancy Wright sat in her large, comfortable office in an ageing brownstone off Broadway in New York City's Upper West Side and shivered. The building's heating was acting up again and an unusually early November cold spell was creeping in. The partners in her practice had often suggested she join them in the more modern main offices further down Manhattan but she continued to resist a move. She liked her building despite its shortcomings and many of her patients lived in the area. They might have been intimidated by the downtown glass-and-steel extravaganza.

Nancy checked the time. It was shortly after nine in the evening and she really wanted to get home, although it was now way too late to see Connie before she went to bed. Wednesday evening consultations were the one concession she made towards juggling the balance of the needs of certain patients against the desire to spend time at home with her nine-month-old daughter. She shrugged and decided she would finish the notes on the difficult patient she'd spent the last hour counselling.

Sitting back in her chair as she gathered her thoughts, her eyes fell onto the wall opposite and the portrait Annie Carr had painted of her five years before. She constantly marvelled at the intricacy of the piece; the subtle detail imbuing it with a dynamism that never failed to be noticed and envied by the many visitors to her office: patients, family and friends. More than a few insisted that if she ever thought of selling it, they were to be the first in line no matter what the price. However, Nancy had no intention of selling her masterpiece. It was part of her life and a constant reminder of Annie.

Nancy had resigned her post at Sawpine Ridge with mixed feelings in October 1972. Despite loving the mountains, she increasingly missed the East Coast and when the offer of a lucrative partnership in a New York City practice came up she knew she would be foolish not to accept it. However, there had been Annie to consider.

Although their relationship was a professional one – that of psychiatrist and a dangerously delusional patient – their two years together, with its hundreds of hours of interviews and discussions, had created a strong bond between them. Annie regarded Nancy as her only real friend, the one person at Sawpine Ridge with whom she could communicate. The other psychiatrists were too formal and inflexible, while the inmates mostly lived in their own fantasy worlds from where they seldom emerged. Annie still peppered her life with seemingly irrational outbursts, displays of temper and fury she calculated very carefully, just in case Nancy should consider recommending her for external reassessment. She mistakenly thought she was slowly getting through to Nancy; that one day Nancy would accept her for what she was and agree to help her escape. She thought of little else, spurred on by thoughts of her daughter, Serena, whom she assumed was still confined in Ty'sland. The reality was that no one, Nancy included, believed her story of a daughter: Serena was regarded simply as one more figment of Annie's weird and complex imagination.

When Nancy dropped the bombshell of her departure, Annie was devastated and, for once, her wild reaction was far more fact than fiction.

"You can't leave me, Dr Wright; you simply can't!" she shouted as she stood to pace the studio, her special privilege. *"No one else here understands me like you do, no one! I'll lose this"* – she swept her arm to indicate the studio – *"I'll be herded into the stockade with all the*

others, injected with sedatives and left to rot. Is that what you want?"
she yelled.

"Of course it isn't, Annie. I can give you my word that nothing like that will happen. I shall be leaving explicit instructions on how you are to be treated and what medication is acceptable for your strange metabolism. My replacement, Dr Clifford Johnson, is a very capable young man who is extremely interested in your case. I have told him that I want to remain in overall charge of your case, informally, that is, since I will no longer be working for the State of Colorado. He understands that your treatment is very long-term and your case one that will require years of study. He has agreed to keep me fully informed of all significant developments. In addition, I shall be returning every two years without fail for our photographic sessions. They are of supreme importance to me, Annie, and nothing, I repeat, nothing, will keep me from continuing them."

Annie calmed at the mention of their photographic sessions. There had been just three so far but they'd not only been fun, they had also further cemented the bond between the two women. Nancy remembered the time in 1970 when she first raised the idea.

"I didn't know you were a photographer, Dr Wright. You are a dark horse."

Nancy laughed. "There's quite a lot about me that you don't know, Annie. I have a life outside psychiatry, you know."

"But photography?"

"Why not? Is it beyond your imagination that I could be artistic?"

"Not at all, but is photography art? You forget, Dr Wright, that I witnessed its earliest days. I have seen it grow from the arcane pursuit of eccentric inventors to a mainstream multimillion-dollar business. However, only occasionally would I equate it with art. For me, it's too easy, too random. I know you have to understand all the science and the settings, but it seems to me it's quite easy to produce something that is regarded as 'brilliant' almost by chance."

"Much the way I regard abstract painting," rejoined Nancy.

Annie threw her head back and laughed. "Touché, Dr Wright, I am being elitist! Tell me, how come you are skilled in photography?"

"I wouldn't say I am skilled; I just have a good working knowledge. The truth is that at Harvard I had a boyfriend for over two years who was crazy about photography. He never went anywhere without a camera and he did all his own developing and printing."

She paused and pursed her lips into a suggestive pout. "We spent many happy hours in the darkroom, some of which were spent in the pursuit of photography."

"Dr Wright, you shock me!" laughed Annie.

"You'd be surprised how liberated I can be when I remove the barrier of these glasses," replied Nancy.

"What happened to the boyfriend?"

"Eventually we drifted apart. I realised he was more interested in posing my body than in my body itself. I was like a clay model to be draped here and positioned there. I think he stopped seeing me, the woman, altogether. He was very upset when I insisted on claiming all the negatives and prints of our sessions – at least the ones where I was identifiable – I didn't want to find myself pinned up in locker rooms around the campus. But I did walk away with a working knowledge of how to use a camera and how to arrange lights. All I need to do is make the long drive into Colorado Springs and buy a new camera."

Annie cocked her head to one side. "Well, Dr Wright, I think your proposal is an excellent one," she said with a playful smile. "It will serve to prove to you that I am not making anything up. It will take time, but one day you will be convinced."

Her smile broadened. "You know, your 'Darkroom Tales' make me think that you wouldn't be averse to approaching this whole project with an extra dimension you perhaps haven't considered."

Nancy frowned, puzzled.

"Don't you think," Annie continued, a twinkle in her eye, "that it would be far better for you to include yourself in your photos, as a sort of control? Then as time goes by we can compare our relative rates of decay!"

"I'm glad you thought of that too, Annie. I was going to suggest it myself."

"But were you intending to go as far as I am thinking, Dr Wright? You see, with your darkroom knowledge, you are in a position to process all the films and make all the prints yourself. That way, we can take the study to a whole new level. Why stop with our faces and hands? Don't you think that a record of us side by side and from top to toe would be far more valuable? After all, if what you are still convinced about me is correct, then my decline into old age should match yours. There should come a time when our boobs and butts sag, our skin changes from its baby's bottom smoothness to elephant hide and our jowls compete with a turkey."

She shook her head briskly to wobble her cheeks.

"On the other hand, if I'm telling the truth, all of that will only happen to you!"

Nancy looked over her glasses. "I hope you're not suggesting we strip off, Annie. I think that would be stretching limits of the doctor-patient relationship."

Annie laughed. "No, not completely, of course not, but I should think that some shots in our underwear, discreetly posed, that show the general tone of our bodies would be acceptable. I'm certainly game if you are. I think it would be fun. In years to come we can compare notes and have a good laugh at ourselves at the same time; see whose bits and pieces are heading south faster."

Nancy nodded as the idea began to appeal. "I think it's a brilliant idea, Annie."

"The only question I have," continued Annie, "is that if we're both in the photos, would we need a third party to press the button on the camera?"

"Oh, we certainly don't want that," replied Nancy. "This project will remain strictly for our eyes only. I have no intention of appearing in my lingerie in front of some third party and run the risk that our curves might be peddled to all and sundry. Think of the scandal if it got out that one of the resident psychiatrists had been partly undressed alongside one of her patients. However, don't worry, it's not a problem. I can get a cable to attach to the shutter release that allows me to press the button from afar, so I can take the pictures and be in them at the same time."

She chuckled. "This is going to be fun, Annie!"

And, she thought, oh so valuable for your long-term treatment. There must eventually come a time when you have no choice but see the effects of the passing years on that presently perfect body.

The first session three weeks later went by in gales of laughter. It started with Nancy arriving proudly clutching her new Rolleiflex SL66, the latest model with interchangeable lenses that could be reversed for detailed close-ups.

Annie raised her eyebrows. "Which bits do you have in mind for your close-ups, Dr Wright?" she said in mock horror.

"Your eyes, Annie, your eyes! And your mouth! I'll be looking for crow's feet."

Annie laughed. "I hope you've got plenty of patience."

With an initial slight embarrassment, they both removed their outer clothing, having made sure that the studio door was securely locked, the curtains closed and the guard under strict instructions not to disturb them.

The first few shots were coy as they got used to the idea of the intimacy of their situation. However, once they started posing together for full body shots, the barriers fell and the only problem they faced was stopping giggling for long enough for the pictures to be taken.

Standing back to back – they were similar in height – they rested the backs of their heads against each other and turned their faces to the camera.

"Chest out, buttocks under, Dr Wright!" said Annie, giving Nancy a playful prod with her backside. Nancy pressed the shutter release in the hand partly hidden from the camera, then they turned to try another pose.

Six rolls of film later and fully dressed again, they collapsed onto the sofa Nancy had imported into the studio.

"I haven't had such fun in years, Annie," laughed Nancy. "This is going to be one hell of a project."

"I can't wait to see the pictures, Dr Wright. I hope you've got plenty of brown envelopes to hide them in."

"Plenty, Annie, don't worry. However, there is one thing that I'd like to say. After all, you can't get much more informal than frolicking scantily dressed with someone. Don't you think it's time you started calling me Nancy? Many psychiatrists these days prefer the informality of first names anyway, you know."

Annie turned her head to Nancy and surprised her by kissing her on the cheek. "Dr Wright, we may have had the most wonderful time behaving like a couple of crazy sisters, but I must insist on my own piece of formality until I am convinced that you truly believe my story. Only then will I feel comfortable calling you Nancy."

The photographs were very successful, both as the type of documentation Nancy wanted and as a brilliant record of their relationship.

"Wow, some of these would make very good pin-ups," commented Annie a few days later when Nancy spread them out in front of her. "I hope you've got a decent lock on your filing cabinet."

"I have," laughed Nancy, "and it's the filing cabinet in my apartment, not in the office."

"Pity you don't run to colour," said Annie.

"A bridge too far, I'm afraid, Annie. However, these black and whites have given me everything I wanted and more."

The session in 1972 was two months before Nancy's announcement that she was leaving, so there was no cloud hanging over it. Now they were fully relaxed about the project, the session was even more punctuated with uproarious laughter than the first. When Nancy produced the prints, they pored over them together looking for signs of change in each other's faces. But there was nothing; no discernible change in either of them.

"Next time," said Nancy.

"We'll see," replied Annie with a knowing smile.

When Nancy returned to Sawpine Ridge in the summer of 1974, her circumstances had changed. Soon after arriving in New York City, she met Chris Hawesley, a neurosurgeon. Their mutual attraction was immediate and they were married within a year. Nancy told Annie all about Chris in her regular letters; what she didn't tell her before they met was that she was pregnant.

"Dr Wright, how wonderful, I am thrilled for you. I wondered how long it would be."

A beaming Nancy took Annie's hands. "I'm so excited, Annie; it's what I've always wanted. It's almost five months and I'm starting to show, as you can see. But I'm still up for the photos, although everything is slightly different in shape from the last time. Next time I imagine there will be stretch marks."

"Not necessarily, Dr Wright. I don't have any and I've had several children, as I've told you."

Nancy was still thinking back to their photographic sessions when the phone rang in the outer office followed by a click from her phone as the call automatically switched through – her secretary, Jennifer, had long since gone home.

"Nancy Wright."

"Nancy, it's Peg Cooke."

Nancy smiled, snapping back to the present. Peg was a friend from her time at Sawpine Ridge, a family medical practitioner in Alamosa.

"Peg, how lovely! I've been meaning to call you. How are you?"

"I'm really well, thanks, Nancy. More importantly, how are you? And how's that little bundle of joy? I was surprised to find you were back at work. I called the house first and Chris told me."

"Yes, I've been back at work for three months now. I didn't really want to but I have a number of patients who are high maintenance. I simply have to see them on a regular basis. I'm not taking on any new ones at present, so I'm only part time. Connie's such a delight that I hate being away from her, but looking at it sensibly, she's still at an age when she sleeps a lot, so I don't feel too bad about the time in the office. Anyway, it's only Wednesdays I work late."

"That's my girl; ever practical."

Despite the words, Nancy detected a flatness in Peg's voice, an edge that wasn't normally there.

"Peg, is something wrong? You sound preoccupied."

"I see your analyst's antennae are as sensitive as ever, Nancy," Peg replied, but there was no humour in her words. "You're right, there is something up and I thought I should call you immediately rather than have you hear about it on the news tonight or tomorrow. There's been a fire at Sawpine Ridge. Earlier this afternoon."

Nancy felt her whole body tighten. "A fire?" she whispered. "How bad?"

"I haven't gotten the details, just a third-hand tale, but the word is that it's bad."

"I'll call Chief Jefford. Do you know if anyone has been hurt?"

"There was talk of fatalities, but I'm sorry, Nancy, I really don't know any more. I only just found out myself and I thought you should know."

"Thanks, Peg. Look, I'll call you back."

Nancy put down the phone and chewed on her bottom lip. She felt her heart thumping. Reaching for the phone again, she punched in the number for Sawpine Ridge, but all she got was the unavailable tone. Grabbing her bag, she hunted for her address book. When it wasn't immediately to hand, she impatiently up-ended the bag, tipping the contents onto her desk. She picked out the address book from the pile and turned to the Alamosa police department's number.

Her fingers drummed on the desk as she waited for the call to connect.

"Alamosa police."

"Hello, this is Dr Nancy Wright; I used to work at Sawpine Ridge as a psychiatrist. Could you put me through to Chief Jefford, please?"

"'Fraid the chief's a little busy at the moment, Dr Wright. I can connect you to one of the sergeants."

"That's fine, thank you."

There was a click and then another dialling tone.

"Sergeant Cartwright."

"Sergeant Cartwright, I don't know if you remember me. I'm Nancy Wright, I was–"

"Of course I remember you, Doc," the sergeant interrupted. "I expect you're calling about the fire."

"I am. I just heard about it from a friend in Alamosa. How bad is it– it's Kevin, isn't it?"

"Yes, ma'am, on the button. I'm afraid it's pretty bad. I just got off the phone from Chief Jefford who's at the scene. It's still too hot for the fire department to have a good look around, and of course it's dark, but there appear to be quite a number of fatalities. We don't know how many yet but we think maybe a dozen or more including a number of the staff, since they haven't been accounted for."

"A dozen or more?" gasped Nancy. "It must have been very extensive."

"Yes, ma'am. Chief says it's gutted the main administration building and a number of outbuildings including the old house that I think was the library."

Nancy grasped the edge of her desk; she thought she was going to faint. Annie's studio was in the same building as the library.

"What time did it happen?"

"Just a coupla hours ago, Doc, just before five."

Nancy frowned, then she remembered the two-hour time difference.

The sergeant's next piece of information increased her agitation further.

"The chief did say one of the fatalities is thought to be the director."

"Hector?"

"Yes, ma'am, Dr Higgins. He was seen running into the main building holding a fire extinguisher. He hasn't been seen since. However, by all accounts, it's fairly chaotic up there. It was already getting dark when the fire started and then the electricity failed. When the guards opened the gates for the fire department, several of the inmates escaped; ran off into the woods."

Nancy could hardly talk. Learning of Hector Higgins' possible death was shocking enough; the thought that Annie might have been hurt was devastating.

"Thank you, Kevin," she finally managed to stutter. "I'm sure you're very busy so I won't keep you. I'll call back in the morning to see if you have any more news."

"Why don't you give me your number, Doc? Once I hear some more, I'll call you direct. How's that?"

Nancy gave the sergeant her direct line number, thanked him again and rang off.

Staring at her painting, her mind raced with thoughts, worries and possible scenarios. Although she had been thrilled to get a studio set up for Annie, one of the on-going problems was that the director wanted Annie to produce paintings of not only all his staff, but also of all the patients at Sawpine Ridge. Higgins had a vision of an administration building overflowing with high-quality portraits of his charges.

The problems arose when Annie started her portraits of the patients. Some of them were sufficiently lucid to understand they needed to sit still for long enough for Annie to at least be able to sketch them. Whether they complied depended on their condition and potential for violence. Annie had told Nancy only the previous year that even for many of the comparatively calm patients, there were several who were prone to sudden outbursts of anger. For some, seeing themselves on canvas was enough to produce a violent reaction – when the scheme first started, a number of paintings were immediately destroyed or damaged when patients took offence at Annie's interpretation of their looks and charged at their portraits. Later, in order not to make the whole project a waste of time, every patient, regardless of her condition, was shackled and at least one guard would remain in the studio at all times.

Despite this, Nancy feared that one devious patient might have managed to run amok, maybe spilling solvents that Annie was now allowed to use and setting them on fire.

It was with these thoughts that Nancy locked up her office and headed home. Connie was a placid baby, sleeping through the night from just a few weeks old. However, Nancy thought this particular night was going to be a long one as she waited anxiously for news.

Chapter 13
1975

Nancy called her practice early the following morning to tell her secretary to cancel all her appointments for the day. She knew she would not be able to concentrate on her patients, which simply wouldn't be fair to them.

"When Sergeant Cartwright, or anyone else from the Alamosa police calls, please give them my home number, Jennifer."

"Certainly, Dr Wright."

Nancy passed a difficult morning trying to distract herself with Connie, but the baby picked up on Nancy's mood and began to cry inconsolably, only adding to Nancy's anguish.

Finally, at three in the afternoon, Sergeant Cartwright called.

"Sorry to take so long, Doc, but once it got light, it was clear things were even worse than we thought first off. It's quite a scene of devastation up there, so it seems, and, I'm sorry to say, a lot more fatalities than we thought last night."

Nancy found she couldn't speak, so she just waited for Cartwright to continue.

"Fire boys reckon the whole thing started in the old library block, almost definitely in the library itself. There was that patient you'd got special privileges for–"

"Annie Carr," Nancy managed to croak.

"That's the one. She had a painting studio in one of the rooms near the library and a storeroom where she locked stuff away, including her pictures, so I'm told."

"Yes," said Nancy hoarsely, "I arranged everything with the director. The guards supervised it thoroughly and Annie never kept the keys herself. Also any potentially dangerous materials, such as thinners, were stored out of harm's way."

"Yes, well, Carr herself isn't a suspect since one of the surviving guards saw her in her studio minutes before the fire started. She wouldn't have had access to the library at that stage since it was locked. The fire boys are working on the theory that somehow someone got hold of something flammable, hid in the library and set the fire. There are a couple of bodies in the library but they are too far gone for recognition."

"You said there were even more fatalities than you'd thought. How many, Sergeant Cartwright?"

"Present count is thirty, ma'am."

Annie Carr was just putting the finishing touches to her portrait of Tory Bevan, a long-term, middle-aged detainee at Sawpine Ridge, when she thought she could smell something burning. Tory's presence had not been necessary for a week, but it had become normal practice for patients sitting for a portrait to remain in the studio while their portraits were completed. Tory herself was permanently sedated and appeared to float in her own benign dream world.

Annie turned to the guard, a large and miserable half-Mexican woman of about forty. "Can you smell something burning, Juanita?"

The guard's face remained impassive as Annie spoke, only reacting a few seconds later when there was a scream from somewhere outside followed by the deafening siren of the general alarm sounding.

Tory Bevan jumped up, then immediately sat again as her body pulled against the chains. She giggled in embarrassment.

The guard opened the door to the corridor and dark-grey smoke billowed in.

"I think you'd better release her," said Annie nodding towards Tory. "We've all got to get out of here."

Not waiting for a reply, Annie ran to the door at the back of the room, opened it and went in. Inside was a small, windowless storeroom with floor-to-ceiling shelving lining three walls. She grabbed an armful of paintings from a shelf and returned to the studio. The guard was trying to push the now unshackled Tory out of the door, but the overweight fifty-year-old was resisting.

"Tory!" shouted Annie. "Come on, we've got to go!"

Tory turned to Annie, a nonchalant expression of incomprehension on her face.

Alongside her now, Annie tried to guide her with her elbow down the corridor and past the main door to the library. It was shut but dense smoke was forcing its way through gaps at the top and bottom.

They pushed through the double exit doors into a scene of total chaos. Detainees were running around wailing while a number of guards, unused to physical exertion, were trying to intercept them. Annie felt intense heat on her back and turned towards it. It was then she saw the full fury of the fire. Flames were belching out of several of the library windows, fanned by a strong breeze blowing them in the direction of the administration building. Bushes and trees in the thirty-yard strip between the two buildings were burning and on the nearest wall of the administration building, wooden shutters were in flames.

There was a boom and a whoosh as another window in the library block blew.

"Tory!" yelled Annie. "Take these!" She held up her arms to indicate the paintings. Tory turned in Annie's direction, a frown on her face as she tried in vain to understand what was going on.

Just then the main lights went out, leaving the area in an eerie half darkness as a few emergency lights switched on.

"Take them," insisted Annie, "and keep them safe. That's very important. I need to go back in to get some more."

Still saying nothing, Tory lifted her arms and took the paintings. "I'll just be a few seconds," said Annie, then she turned and ran back in the direction of the library building.

She heard one of the guards call out. "Carr, don't go in there!"

Hearing the shout and seeing Annie ignore it, some of the nearby detainees seemed to be suddenly energised, perceiving a chance to disobey the guards. They ran after Annie, laughing when the guard called again, and followed her into the burning building. Feeling they had no choice, two guards ran after them and disappeared into the smoke.

Tory Bevan stood stock still, clutching the paintings and humming quietly to herself. Suddenly there was an explosion from the library building and flames burst out of the main door. She felt the blast roll over her, staggered slightly under its impact and then turned to walk away. As she did, she was almost knocked over by a man clutching a fire extinguisher who was running in the direction of the main building. She recognised Director Higgins and, ever-trusting of the psychiatrist, she trotted after him.

While the main administration building was by now well alight, the entrance door was still free of flame. Tory saw the director disappear through it and she followed him. Once inside, although she could hardly see through the thick smoke filling the large entrance hall, she walked on, ignoring the increasing heat on her face. There was an explosion to her right as a door blew out and flames jumped in her direction. She continued on towards where she remembered the stairs were, although she could hardly breathe. She knew this was the right way because the director had come here. She stumbled over a bookcase lying in her path, blown down in the blast. Loose papers were scattered across the floor, some of them burning slowly, but they were made of some sort of glossy paper that didn't burn well. Tory thought she would help. She peeled off the top painting from the pile in her arms and tossed it onto the burning papers. Nothing happened for a few seconds. Then with a whoosh, the painting ignited. That's better, thought Tory, and tossed another. She lost consciousness wondering where the director had gone, collapsing onto the fire now spreading around her and still holding the rest of Annie's paintings.

The following day, Nancy flew to Denver and picked up a shuttle to San Luis Valley Regional Airport, two miles south of Alamosa, arriving late morning. The drive in her rental from the airport to Sawpine Ridge was another hour and fifteen minutes. As she rounded the final corner and the institution came into view, she couldn't believe her eyes. The high-security fence was still there but the gates were wide open. At the top of the main drive, she could see a blackened and roofless shell – all that was left of the grand mansion where she'd lived and worked for over two years. Nearby, the library building was burned to the ground, just the charred remnants of some wooden uprights remaining. In a state of shock, she parked her car next to a number of police vehicles.

Another sergeant she knew from her time there, Todd Morrison, saw her arrive and walked over. "Doc," he said, the grim expression on his face telling Nancy there must be more bad news on top of what she'd heard the previous day.

"Just tell me the worst, Todd," she said.

The sergeant leaned against her car, trying to control his emotions.

Nancy looked around and saw two garden chairs under a tree about fifty feet away. They appeared to be undamaged.

"Let's go and sit over there," she said, nodding towards them.

The sergeant was a tall man, well-built but lean, a man who looked after himself. As he sat in one of the chairs, his whole frame seemed to shrink; he was suddenly far older than his years.

"It's not just the fire, is it, Todd? It's something personal."

Morrison lifted his eyes to hers and nodded slowly.

"It's my kid sister, Doc. She worked here as one of the senior guards. She was always saying how the place weren't suitable for a high-security detention facility. Old, largely timber-framed buildings converted. She said the State skimped on the cost, just threw a fancy wall around it all, installed a pile of lights and alarms. Thought they could save money. She said it was an accident waiting to happen. Always has."

"Yes," agreed Nancy. "I was critical of it myself when I worked here. It certainly didn't match up to similar institutions back east, but the director was happy to simply toe the State's line; he thought nothing could happen up here in this beautiful area."

Morrison nodded. "Well, he was wrong and you were right, Doc. And so was my sister."

He paused and then his voice dropped to a whisper. "I just identified her body."

"Oh, Todd, I'm so sorry. Where ...?"

"In the main building. Seems she saw Higgins running in there and she went to pull him out. There was a big explosion ..."

Nancy put a hand on the sergeant's arm and let him sit with his thoughts. After a few minutes, she said, "Todd, how many staff ...?"

Morrison sighed. "Six. We've found the bodies of six staff, including the director and the young psych who replaced you."

"Clifford? Oh my God, it just gets worse."

"He was upstairs somewhere, conducting some patient counselling. Got trapped."

"What about the patients?"

"Thirty-one bodies identified, but there's a shortfall of six from the total count compared with those we've rounded up and now bussed to Alamosa. We know some escaped through the gates in the confusion when the fire department arrived. There's a party out in the woods now searching for them. I doubt they'll get far. Probably more scared than anything else."

Nancy shivered involuntarily as Annie's face flashed across her mind.

"Have the bodies been identified?"

Morrison slowly shook his head.

"Only some; most are burnt beyond recognition. Chief says it's going to be a real problem since the skin's gone and there won't be fingerprints for many of them. All the records, including dental, which would normally be the fallback position, were kept in the records office in the main building. Seems there's no duplicates and they've all gone in the fire. So it's gonna be pretty gruesome identifying them. A matter of elimination mostly."

"Todd, do you happen to know if Annie Carr is among those surviving? She was a patient I … I spent many hours counselling."

"Sorry, Doc, we're pretty sure she perished in the fire. She was seen to run back into the library just before there was an explosion. There are four bodies from in there that haven't been identified – the chances are she's one of those."

Nancy left the sergeant to his thoughts and wandered over to the fire scene, images from the past tumbling through her head, memories of Annie and their many conversations. How could she be dead? Nancy knew Annie would have been desperate to save her work and it seemed that in trying to do that, she had perished. It was so unfair. Annie had had a vitality, a vibrancy that was very special. Nancy knew she shouldn't get emotionally involved, but with Annie there was a bond far stronger than any she'd experienced with her other patients. She was sure that Annie's case would have been resolvable once they had a few more years of photographs, convinced she could have proven to her that she would grow old and die like everyone else. She had so wanted to bring Annie back from wherever it was she went to in the recesses of her mind and establish her firmly in the real world. Now that could never be.

There was nothing Nancy could do that day beyond stand and watch as the fire investigators carried out their painstaking work. All the bodies had been shipped to Alamosa where the grim process of identification would commence. She felt useless, in the way. She decided she would return to New York City and come back in a week. By then, the authorities would know more.

Eight days later, she was once again driving up from Alamosa to what remained of Sawpine Ridge. She'd arrived the previous evening and spent that morning in the Chief's office talking to Chief Jefford. Todd Morrison's sister had been buried the day before and the sergeant had taken time off to be with his family.

"The docs've had a real time of it trying to identify the bodies, Dr Wright," Jefford told her, "but they think they've sorted it all out now. Some of them had clothing that was marked with their names; some had bits of jewellery that could be identified. In the end, it was just a couple in the library block that they couldn't be certain about one hundred per cent."

"Is one of those Annie Carr?"

"No, they're fairly certain about a body from the library area they've ID'd as Carr's. OK, there was nothing on the clothing and the dental was no good, but the body size and shape agreed with Carr's. We know from witnesses that Carr went into that general area and she didn't certainly come out. So with all that, we're satisfied we've got her body."

Nancy swallowed, trying to contain her emotions. She knew she was being stupid; she just didn't want to give up hope.

"What about the ones that escaped?"

"We got them all except one the day after the fire. In fact three gave themselves up and the other two offered no resistance once the boys caught up with them."

"And the sixth?"

"She's disappeared, but we know who she is and I've no doubt she'll turn up somewhere. They always do. Can't live alone in them woods for too long. Either starve to death or get caught by a bear. If she does make it down to a town, there's an APB on her and she'll soon be identified."

"What's her name?"

"Cheryl Lepri. Italian origin. Murdered her two young children. Dangerous lady, by all accounts. She was seen near the library block around the time your Annie Carr led everyone to their death."

"That's hardly fair, chief. I doubt she had any intention of leading anyone," snapped Nancy. "She was just desperate to save her work."

"Whatever you say, Doc, but the fact remains that if she hadn't gone into that building, a lot more folks would be alive now."

Nancy bristled but let it pass.

"How come this Cheryl Lepri escaped when she was seen near the library?"

"She must have taken her opportunity and slipped away. It was night-time and the main lights had blown."

This time when Nancy arrived at Sawpine Ridge, there were just two cars parked by the trees, both marked with the insignia of the fire department. She introduced herself to the officer-in-charge, who knew of her but they had never met.

"I just want to look around the remains of the library building, if that's OK, Officer Brandt."

"It's safe enough now, Dr Wright, just mind your step."

"I've got hiking boots in the car and I'm well-padded," she said, pointing to the thick jacket she'd brought with her, knowing the November air was cold in the foothills of the mountains. The first snow was forecast within days.

"I'll leave you to it, ma'am, if you're sure you know your way round the site."

"Yes, I know the library building very well. Thanks."

"Anything you need, just holler," said the fire officer.

Nancy made her way to the remains of the library building. When she saw that it was little more than a few charred posts protruding from debris strewn around the blackened floor, she felt less confident about locating the various rooms. However, parts of the stout timbers that had comprised the main doorframe were still there and they acted as her point of reference.

She stood in the doorway and looked along what had been the corridor leading to the library on the left and, further along, Annie's studio and storeroom on the right. She tested the floor timbers – they seemed sound. Officer Brandt was right; it was safe enough.

Nevertheless, not wanting to fall through any holes or trip up on something, she very carefully traced the familiar course to Annie's studio door. She stood in the doorway and looked around. There was little recognisable from the studio she knew, just the remains, in part, of the walls, burnt down to within inches of the floor. The room looked smaller now she could see its floor plan in relation to others near it.

She kicked around a few of the remaining pieces of debris on the studio floor. Something resisted. She stooped and found a charred piece of rolled, folded cloth. Studying it closely, she realised it was a brush holder, the one in which Annie kept her more precious brushes.

As she stood there, the wind picked up and disturbed the debris. The smell of the fire returned and suddenly, in her mind's eye, Nancy could see Annie, bent over her easel. The image faded and she walked over to where the storeroom had been, but there was nothing, not a shred of anything identifiable. She walked back to the doorway. Why had she come?

The wind gusted again and the smell of fire became stronger. She thought she heard a shout. She looked up towards where the main door had been and she was aware of smoke billowing and swirling. A lot of smoke.

There was a cough and Annie was there, one hand clutching a scarf to her mouth, the other reaching out, as if she couldn't see.

"Annie!" cried Nancy. "It's OK; I'm over here." She reached out a hand but Annie ignored it and rushed straight past her into the studio. Nancy turned to watch her. Annie's body shook as she coughed hard. She bent to pick up a portfolio that must contain some paintings. Nancy frowned. Why hadn't she seen that? Annie placed the portfolio on a chair and staggered towards the storeroom where many of the completed pieces that Director Higgins hadn't yet had framed were kept. But before she could reach it, she wobbled and fell to her knees. Nancy reached out and tried to speak, but no words came. Annie was on all fours now, her body convulsed with coughing, her head down. Nancy tried to run to her but her feet were stuck to the ground. She could only watch as Annie tried to crawl towards the storeroom, the flames now playing round her body. Suddenly Nancy was seeing with Annie's eyes, experiencing the horror of the blaze. She could hear the terrifying whoosh and beat of the flames, smell the tars as they released from the wood and, more than anything, she could feel the intense, suffocating heat. She couldn't breathe. She had become Annie.

A timber cracked loudly as it fractured in the fire and came crashing down on her back. At first it didn't affect her, but then, slowly, her arms buckled and she pitched forward onto the burning floor. She opened her eyes for one last time and, tantalisingly close, she could see the storeroom that contained all her precious work. Nothing would remain. Her eyes rolled back as the room began to revolve around her. All she was aware of now was unbearable heat and a black, endless tunnel that she was spinning down, faster and faster.

"Dr Wright! Dr Wright! Are you OK?"

Nancy's eyes flickered. She could taste something burnt in her mouth.

"Dr Wright. Let me help you up."

She let her eyes focus and tried to work out where she was. Then she remembered. She pushed herself up to a sitting position and buried her head in her hands, knocking off her glasses. Her body started to shake uncontrollably as she gulped for air, the tears stinging her eyes.

"No!" she screamed. "No! It can't be!"

The fire officer knelt beside her and gently wrapped his arms round her, easing her head into the shelter of his chest.

"It's OK, Dr Wright," he said gently. "It's OK."

Slowly the shuddering in Nancy's body subsided and her breathing became more controlled.

"It's not OK," she spluttered, shaking her head wildly. "It'll never be OK again."

"What happened? What did you see?"

"She's gone," she said, the desperation burning in her eyes as she pulled back from his hold, her face and hair streaked with soot, black tears flooding her cheeks.

"Who's gone, Dr Wright?"

"Annie. Annie's gone. I know now for certain. Annie Carr died in the fire."

Chapter 14
1980

Zelda Pannic leaned on her walking stick and shuffled stiffly to the door of her cabin. Jabs of pain in her right knee reminded her it was time to take her medicine and to rub some cream into the skin around the swollen joint. But first she needed to check the lanterns on the porch – she liked to keep at least two burning all night; it helped keep the dense blackness of the forest at arm's length as the lonely autumn nights grew longer.

Her foot caught the edge of a floorboard that had loosened over the summer and she stumbled. She threw out an arm and managed to grab the nearby tabletop, the sudden movement sending a further fusillade of needles into the raw nerve endings of her knee. She gasped at the wave of pain. It was at times like this she missed Pete, times when little chores carried out so easily when she was younger and able-bodied became major tasks.

Dammit, she thought, I'm only checking the lanterns. Jaw clenched, she hobbled on, grabbing the doorknob and pulling open the door. Reaching up, she removed the first lantern from the hook over the doorway and placed it on the low table to the left of the door. Lowering herself into a chair, she removed the glass and set about trimming the wick. Once she'd relit the lantern and adjusted the flame, she hung it on its hook and shuffled across the porch to trim the second.

Satisfied with her work, she hobbled back inside the cabin and closed the door. There was no lock – no one ever came to the commune uninvited, while those that remained kept themselves largely to themselves: a disparate collection of waifs and strays without direction. So different from when Ty was in charge, she thought wistfully.

Leaning heavily on her stick, she moved to the small kitchen area beyond the two battered sofas that served as a sitting room. She was hungry and it was time to cook her evening meal. At least there was gas these days, one of the few good things Pete achieved before he abandoned her. She reached for her small transistor radio and switched it to a country station she liked. With no electricity, television was unknown to her. Not that she would have been interested: she still had her principles and the last thing she wanted to witness was a parade of smooth-talking politicians in their expensive suits spewing out their lies.

As she hummed along to Dolly Parton, she didn't hear the cabin door quietly opening and closing. Nor did she hear the faintest of creaks as the floorboards yielded to the light footfall. She was aware of nothing until out of nowhere an arm encircled her throat and a hand was clamped firmly over her mouth.

"Drop the walking stick!" her assailant hissed in a sharp whisper.

Zelda ignored the order, thinking about the best moment to swing the stick.

"Now!" her assailant repeated and her head was wrenched sharply to one side. She dropped the stick and was immediately pulled towards the table.

"Sit and don't even think about screaming. There's no one who will hear you."

Zelda felt a shiver go down her spine, not from fear but from the voice. She knew that voice; remembered it so well. Hated it.

"Annie Carr!" she gasped.

Annie released her hold on Zelda and moved back out of arm's reach.

"Don't think about moving, Zelda," she spat.

Zelda turned her head to her intruder, an arrogant sneer turning to wide-eyed shock when she saw the light on Annie's face.

Her eyes narrowed and her lips tightened. "Annie Carr," she repeated. "So they were right; you really are a witch. You haven't changed one jot in the last ten years and you certainly haven't been burned to a crisp like they said you had. More's the pity. You're pure evil, Annie Carr; always have been."

Annie was surprised that Zelda showed no signs of fear; she was not the coward she had thought.

"What do you want, Annie Carr? Why have you come back? Isn't it enough that you destroyed this place when you killed Ty? It's never been the same. None of the men had any spine."

"I thought that was the point," said Annie quietly. "The last thing Ty wanted was men who might answer back, question his great wisdom."

"Maybe, but we're still a commune; we still have our principles. We still want peace."

Annie laughed sarcastically. "Peace! Ty didn't know the meaning of the word. He just wanted control. Look what happened to anyone who dared to answer back. Look what happened to Johnny Quinn. I know they killed him. Where's Pete, Zelda? I know he's not here, not about to rush in and save you. I've been watching you for two days. You and the others."

Annie's words struck a nerve. "He's gone," replied Zelda bitterly. "Gone almost a year now. The bastard left just when I needed him." She looked angrily at her knees and flexed the swollen knuckles in her hands. "He went out one day and never came back. And he ain't dead in the woods – we searched. He's gone."

As she was speaking, Zelda was watching Annie's face carefully. There was uncertainty in her eyes. Perhaps she didn't know about Serena, didn't know she'd finally escaped more than a year before. If she didn't know, she, Zelda, wasn't going to tell her.

"Well, Annie Carr, what is it you want? I'm sure you're not here to ask after my health, or Pete's for that matter."

She looked into Annie's eyes and waited for her question, waited for the reason she was there. The corners of her mouth lifted in a cold smile of anticipation.

Annie dropped her eyes to the table. She'd waited for so long but now she was here and ready for answers, she was suddenly no longer sure she wanted to hear them. When she spoke, it was little more than a whisper.

"Where's my daughter? Where's Serena? She's why I'm here."

The sneer on Zelda's face was pure evil. She had her. The bitch had suffered all these years and she was going to continue to suffer. For the rest of her life.

She threw her head back and laughed, the sound brittle and coarse.

"You're too late, Annie Carr. More than a year too late."

"Too late?"

"Yes, far too late for your little menace of a daughter. She's dead, Annie Carr! Serena's dead!"

The words hit Annie like an avalanche. She felt she was suffocating. She sat down in a chair opposite the elated Zelda. "What do you mean, dead?" she whispered. "How can she be dead?"

"People die, Annie Carr, hadn't you noticed? They grow old and they die. Or they're stabbed to death brutally, like when you killed Ty and Petra. Probably Seth as well, although he was never found. Stabbed, with no mercy. Or they fall out of trees. Like Serena did."

"Fell out of a tree? How-?"

"Yes, fell out of a tree where she was collecting eggs. Stupid child. Broke her neck. Shouldn't think she felt much." She grinned with a satisfied malevolence. "Just heard a sound, I expect. A snap; and she was gone."

Annie was stunned. She had hoped to find Serena still at the commune but there had been no sign of her during the past two days while Annie had been quietly watching from the woods. She'd begun to think that her daughter had escaped or perhaps left with someone, a possibility that worried her – Serena was still only fourteen. What she hadn't considered was that Serena was dead. Annie was convinced that her daughter was like her – she had her eyes and certainly up to the age of four, she'd never been sick – so she wasn't going to catch anything. But to be killed; the thought simply hadn't crossed her mind.

Zelda could see the conflict in Annie's face. She knew she couldn't outwit her for the moment – her walking stick was out of reach, as were any knives, while her tortured joints prevented her from making any sudden moves. She would try to gain the mental advantage. Rub salt into the wound.

"Not much of a life for your little brat. Slaving for anyone who demanded it; at everyone's beck and call."

"I thought you people believed in peace and freedom. Slavery's still an option for you, is it?"

"There's always someone needed to shovel the shit, Annie Carr. Your precious baby was not exactly loved. She was the daughter of the mad woman who killed our leader; had the same rebellious behaviour – I shouldn't be surprised if someone pushed her out of that tree. Yes, we enjoyed paying you back through her."

She paused, threw back her head and cackled.

"Do you know what the best thing was?"

Annie waited, tense with anticipation over what this hag was going to say next.

"Best thing, Annie Carr, was that she died not even knowing your name."

"I don't understand," said Annie.

"It's simple enough. When you killed Ty and Petra and we heard from the police just how vicious it was, before Pete and me hid in the woods with your brat, we all agreed your name would never be mentioned again in the commune. Never. We agreed you were evil: a monster. We told the kids that if they ever even said your name, they would be cursed."

"What did you tell her?" Annie was horrified. "She must have asked what my name was?"

"Evil Bitch. Everyone called you the Evil Bitch. That was your name. I doubt your real name has been said out loud in this place in ten years, not until tonight when I recognised you. I'll have to go and wash my mouth with carbolic when you've gone, just to get the foul taste of your name out of it." She spat the words venomously.

Annie gripped the arms of the chair. She thought she might faint as the thoughts cascading through her head threatened to overwhelm her. How could Serena not have known her name? She thought back to their all-too-brief times together. She had simply been 'Mommy'. Ty called her 'woman' and the others hardly ever addressed her by name. Serena had only been four; she would almost definitely have forgotten.

She should have come back earlier. The past five years since she escaped the fire had been hard. She'd been constantly on the move, stealing identities as she went, never remaining in one place as one person for long. She'd been lucky to escape from the fire, lucky to be running in a different direction from the first squad hunting the forest for her, lucky to be picked up by a truck driver whose radio was broken so he hadn't hear the news of the fire and escaped lunatics on the run, lucky to be taken all the way to Florida. She'd stolen and lied her way for two months before she broke into a smart condo unit belonging to a woman she'd followed from a mall, taken some fancy clothes and then visited the intensive care unit of a nearby large hospital. There she found the names of two no-hope patients, women in vegetative states from traffic accidents. She discovered the relatives of both women had long since given up visiting more than every few months, so when she claimed to be a distant cousin of one of them, the nurse was pleased to welcome her.

Left alone, she rummaged through her new cousin's nightstand, but found nothing useful. Moving quietly to the patient in the next room, she struck gold when in that woman's drawer was a document pouch with not only a driver's license but also a passport. The woman was thirty-three, with an olive complexion and features close enough to Annie's not to be questioned. Still feeling the pressure of being on the run, Annie knew the best thing was to leave the country. Some sleight of hand in another couple of shopping malls gave her enough cash to take a flight to Dallas and from there she flew to Mexico as Maureen Finnegan. She made her way to Cancún and joined a loosely knit artists' colony where any questions asked could be easily brushed aside with generalities.

However, the need to return never diminished; she had to rescue Serena. Nevertheless, she wanted to construct a plan that would put neither of them at risk. The last thing she wanted was to be recaptured, stand trial for Ty's murder and lose Serena forever. So she waited for the right opportunity to arise, the possibility of going back into the US with two identities, one for each of them, finding Serena and then leaving the country for good. The wait took longer than she wanted but finally it happened: a thirty-something, guileless mother and her fourteen-year-old daughter on holiday in Rio, where Annie in her latest identity was now living. With the right hairstyle and carefully applied make-up, Annie was very like the passport photo of the woman, and she knew she could easily adjust Serena's looks to match the daughter.

The two passports were safely stowed in Annie's backpack as she sat trying to absorb the destruction of her plans.

She slowly controlled her breathing and looked up at the still exultant Zelda.

"Where is she?"

"Buried."

"Buried where?"

"At the burial site of course, where we all end up. Those of us who stay true to our beliefs."

Zelda smiled to herself at the lie. The reality was that the burial site had plots not only for members of the commune who died in whatever circumstances but also for anyone who left or ran away. Ty Donnington's belief in his own dogma had been so strong that, as far as he was concerned, anyone who left the commune had effectively died, so a plot and headstone were prepared for them. The practice continued after his death, with the commune members slavishly adhering to their dead leader's rituals. During Annie's six years at the commune, no one left, so she was unaware of it.

"Take me there."

Zelda laughed and pointed to her knees. "Too far for me. You'll have to find it for yourself."

Annie jumped to her feet, the chair falling over behind her.

"You'll take me there if I have to drag you. Now get up!"

She reached out and grabbed Zelda's arm.

"Hey, watch out," cried Zelda, trying to shrug her off. "Give me my stick and I'll do it. We'll have to go slowly."

"You'll take my arm. You're not having any stick, Zelda. I don't trust you."

Annie pulled Zelda to her feet and half dragged her to the door.

"Careful," grumbled Zelda, "I told you, we must go slow."

"We'll go at my pace," said Annie through clenched teeth.

The burial ground was deep in the woods in a natural glade about half a mile from Zelda's cabin. Annie took a flashlight from her belt to light the rough path and together they stumbled their way through the overhanging brush and branches, with Zelda resisting as much as she could. After fifteen minutes – Zelda had insisted on two pauses to rest – they arrived at the burial ground. Annie shone the light around it and was surprised to see so many headstones.

"There must be thirty stones here," she said, turning to Zelda.

"Life can be hard in these hills," grunted Zelda, knowing perfectly well that about half the stones were for people who were probably still very much alive, the ones who in the early days had escaped, and latterly, simply walked out.

"Where is it?" demanded Annie. "Where's Serena's grave?"

"How do I know?" shrugged Zelda. "You'll have to find it for yourself."

Annie pulled Zelda closer to the headstones and sat her down on a low earth mound. "Stay there while I find my daughter," she ordered.

She turned her attention to the headstones. One, slightly apart from the others, was considerably larger. She walked towards it, shining the light on the crudely carved inscription.

"Touch that and I'll kill you, Evil Bitch," screeched Zelda, taking Annie by surprise.

Annie read the name: 'Ty Donnington 1970' was all that was written. Nearby, in a row with others, she saw Petra's name and the same year.

She sighed and walked on, flashing the beam from one stone to another. Then she saw it. 'Serena Peace 1966 – 1979'.

Annie fell to her knees and reached out to touch the stone, tears flowing freely down her face.

"Oh my baby, I'm so sorry. I was too late. Can you ever forgive me?"

She leaned forward and embraced the stone with her arms, hugging it to her and sobbing as she kissed her daughter's name.

Suddenly, through her tears, she heard shouting. "Help me, someone! Get over here! The Evil Bitch has returned!"

She looked up to see Zelda hobbling away towards the edge of the glade using a broken branch as a walking stick and screeching loudly.

Annie leapt to her feet and ran towards the old woman. She was there in a few strides but as she reached out to grab her, Zelda swung the branch round, aiming at Annie's head. Annie saw it coming and snatched it from her. Overbalancing, Zelda fell to her knees. But there was fight in her. She snarled and with great effort, stood up and immediately threw herself at Annie.

The move surprised Annie. She dropped the branch and lifted her arms to fend off Zelda's head-first charge. Her hands fumbled and then firmly grasped Zelda's head as she fell backwards, her body twisting as her left foot stumbled down a hole in the uneven ground. They tumbled over, falling heavily as Zelda's head followed Annie's unexpected twist. There was a snap, like a branch breaking, and Annie felt Zelda's body slump. As they rolled over, Annie's grip on Zelda's head had twisted it in a different direction from her body and her brittle neck bones had broken.

Annie lay winded on the ground with Zelda's body sprawled across her. She pushed the body away and sat up. Zelda's open and staring eyes told Annie all she needed to know but to be sure, she felt for a pulse in her neck. Nothing.

The glade and forest were suddenly very quiet. All Annie could hear was her own breathing. She listened carefully in case Zelda's screams had aroused anyone. There was nothing.

She had to get away. If the other members of the commune found her, they would probably kill her. If not, they would hold her and alert the authorities. If she were caught, there would be another death to be held against her and although Colorado had never executed a woman, there could always be a first time. Even if not executed, she would doubtless be sentenced to life imprisonment with few privileges, given her track record. She smiled grimly to herself: life imprisonment was a concept too awful to contemplate.

She stood and looked down at Zelda's body. There were no injuries apart from the broken neck, nothing to indicate there had been a struggle. She hadn't let Zelda bring her stick with her, but if it were here, alongside her and broken, it would look as if Zelda had fallen and landed on her head. Given the commune members were very secretive, they would probably accept that rather than alert the authorities. She ran quietly in the direction of the cabin, her senses alert for sounds of anyone coming.

Fifteen minutes later, she'd repositioned Zelda's body by an exposed root she could easily have stumbled over, broken the walking stick and laid it alongside her. There was nothing else she could do. She now needed to get out of the area.

She walked over to the headstone with Serena's name and knelt in front of it one final time. This was not the outcome she'd expected. Serena had been in her life for four short years, but in the ten years since, Annie had never stopped hoping they would be reunited. Now that would never be.

Her vision blurred with tears that were now flowing freely, she stood and slowly walked away. Then, shaking her head in frustration and anger, she started to run, her pace increasing through the trees until she was running flat out, not stopping until she reached the car she'd hidden two days previously.

Part III
2012

Chapter 15

On the evening of his forty-ninth birthday, Pete Farsley pulled open the door to the Ristorante dell'Ottocento in downtown Boston and stepped aside to allow his wife, Sara, to walk past him. Sara looked up at him and smiled. "Thank you, kind sir."

"Always your honourable servant, my lady," replied Pete, tilting his head deferentially.

Sara stopped and rested her head on her husband's shoulder.

"Always my knight in shining armour," she said coyly. Then she poked him playfully in the ribs with a finger. "Come, my liege, the kids are waiting."

Pete bent and kissed her on the forehead, marveling, as he always did, at this woman who'd been his wife for the past twenty-two years and the love of his life for even longer. She was only two and a half years younger than he was and yet miraculously, he thought, she looked no different from when he'd first met her almost twenty-five years before. He knew Sara worked at it, like the wives in all the couples they knew. She went to the gym, ran along the pathways by the Charles River, and rubbed a number of creams and lotions into her skin. The difference was that for Sara it seemed to work.

They made their way through to the rear of the restaurant where their daughter, Julie, a twenty-year-old, pre-law student, and seventeen-year-old son, Matt, in his final year at high school, were waiting for them in the booth they always reserved for special occasions. It had been a tradition since Pete first took Sara there, more than fifteen years before, to celebrate his becoming a partner in the law firm where they both worked.

As they approached the table, the restaurant manager, Mario, intercepted them, greeting them warmly.

"Signor e Signora Farsley. Un piacere, come sempre," he said as he bowed his head of tight, black curls to them. "Prego," he added, indicating their table. "Your daughter, the bellissima Giulia, and your son and-a hair, Matteo, are-a halready 'ere," he said, his dazzling white teeth sparkling like a toothpaste advert. Pete smiled to himself. He had known Mario forever and he knew the Italian-American's English was as good as his own and his Boston accent as strong. However, he always played along with the little theatre.

Julie and Matt stood to greet their parents with hugs all round while Mario hovered, picking up napkins for Sara and Pete and ensuring they were comfortable. He reached over to the ice bucket to retrieve and open the bottle of Prosecco Pete had ordered in advance and poured two glasses.

"Many 'appy returns, Signor Farsley," he beamed, bowing his head again.

"Thanks, Mario, we'll order in just a minute," said Pete.

He turned to see the others raising their glasses – the fizz in Julie and Matt's being sparkling water.

"Happy birthday, darling," said Sara.

"Yeah, many of 'em, Pop," grinned Matt. "Hey, it's the big one next year!"

"It's only fifty, no big deal!" admonished Julie, running to her father's defence, as always.

"*Only* fifty," said Matt, raising his eyebrows. "Since when have you been an expert on middle age, Big Sis?"

"It's a female thing, *Little* Bro, and remember to be polite to your older and wiser sibling. I *am* twenty to your mere seventeen."

"Now, now, you two," laughed Sara, "leave your squabbling for the nursery; you're out with the grown-ups now. Anyway, it's your pop's forty-ninth. Fifty is a whole year away."

Matt leaned over the table and peered into his mother's eyes. "Are you sure you're my mom?" he frowned in mock confusion. "No, I don't think so. I think my pop traded her in for a younger model. I think you're my long-lost older sister, the one my folks put up for adoption when they were too busy and too poor to raise you."

"Same happened to my younger brother," Julie chimed in as she gave Matt a disdainful toss of the head. "When Mom and Pop claimed him back, they were given the wrong one and got you by mistake. Please, Mom, can't we go down to social services and find the real Matt?"

Pete laughed as he watched them go through the same performance they had acted out for over ten years. However, in the last couple of years as the kids matured into adults, Sara really could be their older sister, especially Julie's. The only differences in the two women were their skin colour and their eyes: Sara's olive skin contrasted with Julie's far fairer complexion, while her eyes were the palest of pale grey. Julie's eyes were dark brown like her father's.

A waitress handed them the menus.

"Let me see," said Pete, opening his, "I think I'll have–"

"–The bruschette della casa for starters and spaghetti alle vongole for the main?" interrupted Matt, cocking his head at his father.

They all laughed. Pete had ordered the same meal at Ottocento for longer than any of them could remember.

While they were enjoying the meal, Pete regaled them with his favourite stories of how the Farsley family had settled in 'Bah-stin' many generations ago, soon after the Revolutionary War. The original Farsleys were all sea captains on trading ships until Augustus Farsley broke the mould and studied medicine in the 1850s. Pete's elder brother and sister had continued in that now long family tradition, but Pete chose a different path: he had studied law. Now he'd started his own tradition, with not only his wife working in the same practice where he was a partner, but also with his daughter fully intending to follow suit. Matt still claimed to be undecided on his future, although Pete was sure his son's intended undergraduate option of history would also lead him to law school. He was quietly confident that sooner or later there would be not one but two more Farsleys on the company name plate.

As they indulged their father in his birthday monologue, Matt and Julie occasionally exchanged glances and secret smiles: they'd heard it all so many times that they knew it by heart. As Pete paused to top up the glasses while they waited for their desserts – "Let me guess, Pop. Pannacotta?" Matt laughed – Julie decided it was time to move the conversation elsewhere.

"Pop, I feel I could write several volumes on the Farsley history, and I'd be proud to do so. Maybe I even will someday. But Mom's half my history too, and Matt's, and I don't think I could write more than a few lines about her."

She turned to Sara. "You've told us so little, Mom. Surely you know more. Now we're all cozy after that wonderful meal, couldn't you tell us?"

"Yes, Mom," added Matt, theatrically half closing his eyes to give them an air of mystery. "You've been so secretive over the years; I reckon there must be some skeletons in the family closet. What dark tales are there that you won't let see the light of day? We're not kids anymore, Mom, don't you think we should know whatever there is to know? You've only ever said that Grand and Gramma are your foster parents. Do you really know nothing about your real parents?"

Looking uncomfortable, Pete shifted in his seat and put a protective hand on Sara's arm as he started to speak. But Sara placed her other hand on his. "No, Pete, they're right; it is time they knew what there is to know. However," she added, turning to her children, "I warn you, there's not a whole lot."

Julie and Matt leaned forward in anticipation. They'd often speculated to each other over what their mother's history might be, but it seemed always to have been a room to which the door was locked. Now, at last, the door was ajar.

Sara played with an earring as she gathered her thoughts. "I don't quite know where to start," she said. Then she took a deep breath.

"As you know, Grand and Gramma, the Patersons, are not my birth parents. They agreed to foster me when I was thirteen years old."

"Thirteen!" exclaimed Julie. "I thought you'd grown up with them; that you'd been with them since you were tiny."

"No, you just assumed that from the vague information I gave you and it was easier to let you keep on thinking it."

"Where were you before?"

"I was in Colorado."

"Colorado!" interrupted Matt. "Is that where you were born?"

Sara laughed. "You sound as if you think Colorado is some

foreign country, Mr East Coast. There are other parts of the US besides Boston and Cape Cod, you know. But yes, to answer your question, I was born in Colorado. In a commune."

"A commune?" said Julie in disbelief. "Were you a hippy?"

"Yes, a commune, but no, I was anything but a hippy."

"Wow!" added Matt. "A commune. This is getting good."

"Be quiet, Matt!" said Julie. "Let Mom continue."

"I'm not the one who keeps interrupting."

Sara waited for a couple of seconds. "Finished?"

"Sorry," they both said together.

"OK," smiled Sara. "I was born in the commune in 1966 and my name wasn't Sara. It was the Patersons who decided to change it; they thought it would help me to get a new start. My original name, which I assume was given to me by my mother, was Serena; Serena Peace."

Julie raised her eyebrows. "Serena Peace? That sure sounds very hippy."

"Yes, well, perhaps my mother was a hippy, although I don't think so; it wasn't that sort of commune. You see, I don't really remember much about her. I last saw her when I was four."

"Oh, Mom," said Julie, reaching out and taking Sara's hand. "Four! That's terrible. What happened to her?"

Sara picked up her wine glass and took a large gulp.

"Well, that's the thing, the difficult part. The reason, really, why I didn't want you to know when you were younger. You see, she killed someone. Two people, in fact."

"Killed them?" said Matt. "Who? How?"

"One of them was the leader of the commune, someone called Ty, although I don't remember him at all. Apparently he was very charismatic and totally in control of the place. It was never the same after he died and the people there hated my mother for it. They just kept telling me she was evil, possessed."

"Who was the other?" asked Julie.

"Her name was Petra. She was Ty's partner, I think, although I don't remember her either."

"How did she kill them?"

"She stabbed them. In a motel somewhere, not in the commune. I don't know any details."

"So is she in prison?" asked Matt.

"No, she isn't. This is the other difficult part, the much more difficult part, in fact. You see, she was found to be not competent to stand trial. She was incarcerated in a custodial psychiatric institution. I don't know where or even what it was called. They would never tell me."

"Oh my God!" whispered Julie, almost inaudibly, and then she added, "What was she called, Mom? What was her name?"

Sara bit her lip and looked from her husband to her daughter and son. Her eyes briefly showed such deep sadness that Julie moved closer and put an arm round her.

"I don't know," continued Sara, "they would never tell me. They said she was evil and that just saying her name would bring a curse on whoever said it. They referred to her only as the Evil Bitch. No one in the commune was ever allowed to repeat her name and so I never knew."

She paused and gently leaned her head on Julie's shoulder. "I don't know my mother's name."

There was a silence at the table that was finally broken by Matt.

"Mom. Pop. I'm sorry. We're sorry, Julie and I. Sorry we brought it up and have spoiled the evening. We didn't think Mom's past would contain such unhappy memories."

"No, Matt, no. Don't be sorry. You have a right to know. In fact, my telling you both is long overdue and anyway, no matter what happened in the past, it's what we have now that's important."

Matt put a hand on her arm. "You said that … that you don't know her name. Presumably it wasn't Peace."

"No, it wasn't. I really have no idea what it was. I was so young, you see."

"Is she still there?" said Julie suddenly. "In the psychiatric institution?"

Sara shook her head. "No, I'm afraid not. She's not there and nor is the institution. There was a fire, in 1975, I think – I remember I was about nine. It was a very bad fire, apparently. Many people died, including my mother."

Matt looked puzzled. "How did you find out?"

"From the people in the commune. They must have been told. They were ecstatic, jubilant. They were normally so serious and humourless, to me at least. They were whooping and dancing around. It was disgusting."

"Is that when you left?" asked Julie.

"No, it wasn't. I couldn't leave. I was effectively a prisoner. Remember, I was still only nine years old and I'd had no education because they refused to allow me into the classes they held for the other commune children. Ty's children."

"I don't understand," said Julie.

"As far as I know, Ty was the father of most of the children in the commune, although he wasn't mine. I think he regarded all the women as his own – certainly the other men weren't up to much; they were a fairly weak bunch, as I remember. There were other kids who weren't Ty's, older ones born before their parents came to the commune. Apparently Ty grudgingly accepted them, but I was treated as the drudge, little more than a slave used for all the menial jobs around the place. At nine and on my own, it was hard to get away. It wasn't until four years later that I escaped."

"Do you know anything about your father?" asked Julie.

"No, nothing at all. I was told he died before I was born."

"You said you don't remember much about your mother," persisted Matt. "What little do you remember?"

"Only that she was very kind and peaceful. I didn't spend a lot of time with her even when she was there, I don't think they allowed it. But when she was with me, she'd talk to me gently all the time. I don't remember what about, except that she'd tell me I was different, special. Of course, all mothers tell their children that." She laughed. "There's no such thing as a normal child, is there? I remember her saying it about both of us; that we were both special and different."

"Different?"

"Yes, different from the others. She told me we'd live forever and that we'd never be ill. Well, it obviously wasn't true because she died. However, she was certainly right about my health: I've never been ill in my life. I think the commune people thought it was all part of her being evil; that somehow she'd fed me with something or bewitched me. They thought that if I was removed from her influence, I'd become normal, as they put it. But nothing changed; I remained totally healthy. I think it angered them since they just made me do more and more work."

"You know," said Julie, "it's interesting what your mother said about your being healthy. You're never ill, are you? My friends' mothers always seem to have something: colds, headaches, sore joints, plus sometimes more serious things, but you never have anything. Don't you think that's odd? What do you think, Pop?"

Pete Farsley reached out and stroked his wife's hair.

"I'm not sure that odd is the right word. Unique is perhaps better. If everyone were like your mom, there'd be no need for doctors, hospitals or health care plans. Imagine how much money it would save."

They all laughed.

"I'm also sure," he continued, "that the fact that Mom hasn't changed in appearance – doesn't seem to have aged – is all connected to it as well."

Sara looked uncomfortable.

"Yes," she nodded, "in my thirties it was great; I just felt and looked young. However, now I'm in my forties, people are starting to think I'm secretly having work done, which I'm not, as you all know. And yet I don't have a grey hair in my head; my skin doesn't really seem to need the creams I rub into it and the only time I ache is when I work out too hard in the gym."

"How's the hearing?" whispered Matt very quietly, a mischievous sparkle in his eyes.

"Perfect!" laughed Sara and poked her tongue out at him. "My eyesight, too. Twenty-twenty."

"The guys at the tennis club have started to suggest I have a trophy wife," laughed Pete, "that I cradle-snatched you."

"Well, enjoy it while you can," said Sara matter-of-factly, "because I'm convinced that time will soon be catching up with me and my face will collapse into a crater of wrinkles. Then I'll be the one with a trophy – a trophy husband."

Pete brushed his hand through his hair.

"A toy-boy with greying hair. I'm not sure that works," he laughed.

Julie wanted to get back to the conversation.

"Tell us about your escape, Mom. You said you were thirteen?"

"Yes, I was. At thirteen, all the normal things were starting to happen to my body and I was aware that a number of the men were looking at me differently. In particular, the male half of the couple I lived with. Their names were Zelda and Pete – a Pete who couldn't have been more different from the one sitting here," she added taking her husband's arm.

"That Pete was a brutish sort, very un-bright, and I knew he had forced himself on several of the girls who were a bit older than I was. So I quietly gathered a few things together and slipped away one night. By then they'd ceased to tether me like they did when I was younger."

"Tether you!" cried Matt and Julie together.

"Yes, by the ankle, with a rope. As I got older, I could undo the knots and when I made no attempt to run, they seemed to think I'd accepted my lot. But I hadn't.

"The commune was in the foothills of the mountains and around it were thousands of square miles of forest. Living there, I developed a number of skills, particularly tracking and covering my tracks. I'd practised this quietly for a long time, knowing it could prove useful one day. And it did. After I escaped, rather than run and run, I set a false trail and then doubled back, covering my tracks as I did. I hid for days not very far from the commune. After about ten days I was running out of food, so one night I left my hiding place and ran deep into the forest, miles from the commune. It was summer so it wasn't cold. I stayed there for three months, living off fish and small animals I caught."

"Wow!" said Matt. "That's so cool. I've always wondered why you made us go on all those camping trips when we were young: you wanted us to improve our survival skills. Now I know why you were so brilliant at tying knots."

"Yes," laughed Sara, "but when I was up against a true professional, I was soon discovered. It was early September 1979 when a forest ranger patrolling the forest looking for an escaped criminal found my trail and surprised me. I told him everything – there wasn't much choice – but I was terrified he'd send me back. However, by then the commune had come under investigation and he, or his boss, decided to put me in the care of the social services. My caseworker decided it would be better for me to be somewhere else entirely. She had contacts here in Boston and I was moved, firstly to a home in Middleton, but then, very quickly, to be fostered with the Patersons."

She held out her hands, palms upwards. "And the rest, as they say, is history."

"Yes," added Pete, "the Patersons were incredible. They realised that Mom was very bright; she'd just had no education. They soon rectified the situation with intensive schooling that she soaked up. I remember Jim Paterson telling me how amazed he was at her capacity for learning and then later how proud he was when she studied law and he could take her on in his firm, just three years after I joined him."

"A fairy-tale ending," said Sara, nestling her head against his shoulder.

Matt wasn't satisfied. "Don't you think it would be an even cooler story if you could find out a bit more? Have you never tried going through the newspapers for the period, trying to find your mother's name, at least?"

"It's not such an easy prospect here in Boston, Matt," said Sara. "The City Library is unlikely to carry the Colorado newspapers and anyway, that part of my life is over; finished. I hardly knew my mother and she has been dead for a long time. There really doesn't seem much point in going there."

"But, Mom," objected Matt, "these days everything is available on the Internet, particularly things like newspaper archives. Would you mind if I had a look? I should at least be able to find the name of the institution and details of the fire." He sat up and tucked his thumbs under an imaginary waistcoat, adding in a pompous voice. "I should be neglecting my duty as an historian not to research my own family."

Sara laughed. "If you want to, Matt, go ahead, but you mustn't spend too long on it. You've exams coming up and I don't want you to be distracted by something that's really of no great importance."

"No time like the present, Mom. It's exciting to know more about your background, which is our history too, Julie's and mine. I'm sure I'll be able to find something without too much effort."

Chapter 16

Sara, Pete and Julie were tucking into their bacon and fried eggs the following morning when a bleary-eyed Matt shuffled through the door to the large family kitchen.

"Morning," he yawned as he slumped onto a stool by the breakfast bar and picked up Julie's glass of fresh orange juice.

"Hey, get your own!" objected Julie, reaching across her brother, but Matt extended his arm to put the orange out of reach.

"I'll get you some more momentarily," he said, suppressing another yawn.

Sara eyed him sceptically. "I trust your walking-dead appearance is because you've been studying for your exams."

Matt smiled sheepishly, the smile turning into a grin as the cool of the juice revived him and the fruits of his labours in the small hours came flooding back into his mind.

"No, not really, in fact, not at all. What I've been reading is far more exciting. I've been on the Internet–"

"–For way too long, I would guess," chided his mother. "You need your sleep, you know, otherwise when you come to take your exams, your head will be a mess."

Matt shrugged. "And you never stayed up all night working for your papers, Mom? Anyway, once I got going, I couldn't stop."

He stood and shuffled over to the fridge to pour himself some more juice, which he gulped down in one.

Deliberately avoiding their eyes, he surveyed the breakfast bar to decide what to have.

Julie drummed her fingers next to her plate. "Well, come on then, super sleuth, tell us what you've found," she said in frustration.

"I thought you were more interested in your orange juice," replied Matt nonchalantly. He reached out for berries but his sister blocked the way.

"Spill the beans, buster," she snarled, "or I'll feed you to the dog."

Matt grinned smugly at her as he sat down again on the stool.

"Well," he said, "it took a while and a lot of digging, but in the end I got some very interesting information. You said, Mom, that there was a big fire in 1975 at the psychiatric facility where your mother was being held. I found the Colorado newspapers online and there was only one incident like it that year. It was at a place called Sawpine Ridge Custodial Psychiatric Institution, which was out in the sticks – the nearest town of any size was a place called Alamosa. The fire was in November 1975 and you were right: a lot of people died – thirty-one of the inmates and six staff including the director of the place and one of the psychiatrists. It was classified as arson and it must have been an inferno."

"Did they find out who started the fire and why?" asked Pete.

"No, Pop, they didn't. They narrowed down where it started to a library in an outbuilding and they think whoever started it died in the blaze. The fire also spread to the main building and gutted the place. According to the reports, it happened at dusk. By the time the fire department got there it was dark and there was chaos. In fact, six of the inmates escaped into the forest."

"Escaped?" asked Sara. "Were they recaptured?"

"Five of them yes, but one got away completely."

"Interesting," mused Julie. "Did they give a name?"

"Cheryl Lepri. I followed her up – she's never been seen again. There was speculation in the newspaper reports that she got lost in the forest and might have been killed by a bear or a mountain lion. However, according to some state records I unearthed that are now public, no body was ever found."

"Did they say anything about her?"

"Yes. There was a police wanted notice issued; seems she was quite a nasty lady. Killed her two young kids. She was a paranoid schizo."

"Oh," said Sara quietly, not able to hide her disappointment.

"Did they identify everyone who died?" asked Julie.

"No, not completely. That was one of the interesting things. The bodies were badly burned and most of their records – dental, fingerprints and so on – were in the administration building that was destroyed. So it was done by a process of elimination using anything recognisable, like jewellery, remaining on the bodies. There was no DNA in those days."

"They kept all the records at the institution?" Pete was incredulous.

"It was 1975, Pop. Things were different," shrugged Matt.

"1975 was hardly the dark ages," objected his father.

"There were no computers to speak of, Pop. It was pretty dark."

"What about the names of the inmates?" asked Julie.

"There's a list of them but no other details, like the crimes they committed and so on."

"Nevertheless, our grandmother's name must be on that list. Do you think it might jog your memory if you saw it, Mom?"

"I very much doubt it, but there's no harm in looking," shrugged Sara.

Julie's mind was still ticking away, processing everything she could think of. "I wonder if the shrink who was killed was the one who dealt with our grandmother, or if it was another," she speculated.

"I wondered that too, so I checked," said Matt. "He wasn't, at least not for the whole time. The shrink who died started at the place in 1972, whereas our grandmother was sent there in 1970, I think you said, Mom."

Sara nodded.

"I found some more state records – it's all there if you look," continued Matt. "Apart from the director, there were two other shrinks. One was killed in a car crash in the eighties; the other left in 1972 and moved to private practice in New York City. Her name is Dr Nancy Wright."

"And thanks to the wonders of the Internet, you have her life history?" smiled Sara, raising a quizzical eyebrow.

"Well, yes, actually, I do," replied Matt gleefully. "She went on to become quite eminent in her field. She's getting on a bit now – she's seventy-four – but still works part time. She's also written a number of books with weird titles, but most recent one sounds interesting. It's called '*The Delusional Mind. Forty years of case studies*'."

"Riveting stuff, I'm sure," laughed Sara.

"We'll find out," replied Matt. "I've ordered a copy."

"You know," said Julie as she thought through what Matt had been saying, "this Dr Wright could well be worth speaking to. Even if she didn't treat our grandmother, she might have known enough about her to identify which of the people on the list she was. She might be able to give us a name."

Sara's thoughts were going in another direction.

"I wonder what happened to the commune," she said as memories of her childhood flashed across her mind.

"I'd forgotten about your hippy days," said Matt. "Do you know where it was?"

"Not really," said Sara, "although when you mentioned Alamosa, it sounded sort of familiar. I think it might have been in the forests around there."

"Let's have a look," said Matt standing up. "I'll fetch my laptop and the list of the inmates who died in the fire. Any chance of some eggs, Mom?"

"Oh, sorry, Matt, I forgot you hadn't eaten. I'll do some now."

"Great," he said as he ambled off to his bedroom.

Ten minutes later, Matt was tucking into his food while Julie scrutinised the printout of the Sawpine Ridge fire victims' names. Sara leaned over her shoulder and ran her eye down it. She shook her head. "None of those names means anything to me, I'm sorry to say."

"Really, Mom?" Julie was surprised. "You must have heard her name."

"I know, Julie, but I was only four."

She read the list again. "Audrey McCluskey, Maureen Cooper, Anne Carr, Laurel Corrigan, Joan Klein."

She puckered her lips, frustrated.

"What about diminutives?" suggested Julie.

"You mean like Laurie or Annie? Audie? Could be, but I'm really not certain."

140

"OK," said Matt, wiping his mouth on a piece of kitchen roll, "let's hit the keys and see what Mr Google has to say for himself."

He typed in some search parameters including the names 'Ty' and 'Alamosa', along with 'hippy communes' and a range of dates.

Microseconds later, the top page of a few million references appeared on his screen. He started to scroll down them as he chewed his lip in thought.

"Mmm," he mused after clicking on a few of the references. "Not much of use there. It says that hippy communes didn't really get going until the seventies, although there was a sort of artist's colony at a place called Drop City in Colorado that dates from earlier."

"Mom said it wasn't a hippy commune," countered Julie. "Is there anything on communes in general? You know, odd religious groups and so on. Maybe we should look at a map."

"A map?" echoed Matt.

"Yes, nerdy little brother, a map. It's a sort of book, if you know what that is. It has printed pages with geographical details."

"You mean the sort of thing a man won't look at when he's driving, no matter how lost he is?" said Sara, half-closing her eyes in her husband's direction, a cat-like smile spreading across her face.

"Highly amusing," harrumphed Pete as he disappeared into the den. A few moments later he was back and slapped a US atlas on the counter.

Julie grabbed it and opened it to Colorado.

"Here's Alamosa," she said. "It's really close to the Rockies, must be beautiful there. Cool names; it's like the Wild West: South Fork, Saguache, Grand Junction, Durango…"

"Durango?" interrupted Sara. "You know, that really does sound familiar. Try that in your search, Matt."

"OK," said Matt, his fingers on the keyboard. "Let's try Durango and commune…"

He hit the return key.

"Let's see, there's a housing community… no, that looks fairly new… what about, yes, there's a place called Rocky Mountain View Organic Farm and Wilderness Retreat."

He clicked on the link and scanned the information.

"Well?" said Julie impatiently.

"Hold on, Big Sis, this could be something. Mom, it says it's a community of organic growers providing the neighbouring towns with genuinely pesticide-free vegetables grown the way nature intended."

"You mean full of holes where the bugs eat them," said Pete as he spread butter on some toast he'd just made.

"Probably," laughed Julie as she peered over Matt's shoulder. "Look! They offer 'Vacation experiences for people seeking to return to the natural stress-free life of yesteryear. Join the community of organic farmers to rekindle your karma'."

"Where is it?" asked Sara.

"Let's see, er, it's in the foothills about an hour's drive from Durango," replied Matt as he clicked around various links. "It's been going for quite a while. Says it was established in 1982 when a group of people bought an existing commune plot that had been abandoned by most of its original inhabitants."

He scanned some more links. "It seems to be the only place that might fit the bill. What do you think, Mom?"

"Sounds like the right sort of area," nodded Sara. "I think it was around there that I was picked up after I escaped. I wonder if there's anyone there from the seventies."

"Even if there isn't, they might know something about the history and know some names," said Julie excitedly.

"If it's not the right place, they might know of the one we're looking for," mused Pete. "There's a long weekend coming up. Why don't we go? Pass me the map, Julie. It's a bit of a way, but we could easily drive there, I'm sure."

Matt was stunned. "Pop, you're joking, right? It must be more than fifteen hundred miles. Have you never heard of airplanes? What's wrong with flying there?"

"I suppose it is a bit far, even for a long weekend," conceded Pete. "Where's the nearest airport to them?"

"I'll check it out for you, and the schedules," said Matt. "They've got all the information on the site."

Sara was hesitant: the memories from her childhood were suddenly very strong; she was no longer sure she wanted to rekindle them further.

"You know, I don't think it's such a good idea. Maybe it would be better not to rake over the ashes of somewhere I left behind a long time ago; in another lifetime, really."

She had been staring through the window as she spoke, her mind elsewhere. Suddenly she realised there was complete silence in the room and she turned her head to her family. They were all looking at her with such utter disappointment in their faces that she burst out laughing, knowing immediately she had to go through with it.

"OK," she said, holding up her hands in resignation. "Let's do it!"

Chapter 17

Early the following Friday morning, Sara, Pete and Julie took a flight to Denver and then picked up a shuttle across to Durango where their rental car was waiting for them. Pete had brought an armful of maps, but the agent insisted on providing them with even more once they told him where they were going.

"Great little community they've got up there," he informed them. "People drive for miles for some of their produce and folks come from all over to spend time there. Very different from what my ma said it was like forty years ago."

"Forty years ago? Do you know what it was called at that time?" asked Sara hopefully.

The agent shook his head. "Can't help you there, and now that my ma has passed, she can't either. You folks planning on staying there?" he added, noting their lack of luggage.

"Just checking it out for the future," replied Sara as she breathed in the sweet country air.

She turned to Pete. "It's such a pity Matt had to miss this; I think he'd love the scenery. But exams are exams."

"I don't know, Mom," said Julie, "it's not Cape Cod. There are no boats."

"I guess we are a long way from the sea," laughed Sara, "but the fishing's good in the mountain streams. I should know – it kept me alive for three months."

The drive to the farm took an hour and a half, the last ten miles on a single-track but well-maintained, gravel road. At the end of the track, they were greeted by an arched wooden gateway with the words *Rocky Mountain View Organic Farm and Wilderness Retreat* carved in large letters around the curve of the arch. Sara peered at the sign and the neat fencing running into the distance on either side of it.

"Look familiar?" asked Pete.

She shook her head. "The forest does, sort of, but then again, forest is forest. This gateway and fence seem fairly new. It certainly appears to be welcoming enough; let's check out what they've got."

"It has an air of success about it," said Pete as they approached a large cabin that was the reception and farm shop. "Everything is neat and tidy; looks well cared for."

"And like I said, fairly new," added Sara. "I wonder if there's much left of the old commune."

They parked and walked into the reception where they were met by a smiling girl of Julie's age wearing a name badge that announced her to be Holly. Her olive-green T-shirt bore the farm logo and the legend 'Nature's Way is the Best Way.'

"How can I help you folks today?" she asked.

Sara smiled back at her, wondering how to start. Her eyes fell on some posters on a wall to the left of the reception desk that showed photographs and plans of the farm.

"We were wondering about how long you'd been here, but the photos probably answer that question. It all looks pretty new. Quite a project!"

The girl pushed a hand through some loose strands of her long, strawberry-blonde hair. "Well, I've been here all my life, born and raised on the farm, but I don't think that's what you meant." She gestured to the buildings. "All this is new; you're right about that. My pa and his folks and the other owners developed it slowly, and once city folks started coming for holidays and stuff, Pa decided most of the old buildings had to go, 'part from a few of the more interesting ones. So he invested what he'd saved in new cabins, workshops and a coupla classrooms. We've got schools interested now, so there'll be more next year."

Sara walked over to the posters and studied them, but nothing in the photos looked familiar.

Holly followed her and continued with her patter. "We like to think we're making a difference, reaching out to city folks and helping them develop healthier lifestyles by eating natural food. Nothing we use or sell here has ever been near any industrial pesticide. We use nature's way: no additives, no chemicals; just pure good products."

Sara smiled at her. "That's a great message. I've always said we're slowly being poisoned by food manufacturers who brainwash us into believing the chemical rubbish they peddle as nourishment is better and healthier than anything you might grow in your garden. God forbid that any of it should have touched any dirt!"

There was a loud laugh of agreement from behind them.

"You're on the nose there, ma'am, and then to make matters worse they are in cahoots with the drug companies who push their patent medicines to cure the ills brought on by the unhealthy food."

Sara turned to the owner of the booming voice, a large man of about her age who had walked into the reception from an adjacent office.

He held out his hand. "Clay Pritchard, at your service – please call me Clay. Welcome to Rocky Mountain View. I see my daughter here has been filling you in, not that you sound like you need convincin'."

Sara took his hand. "Sara Farsley. My husband, Pete, and daughter, Julie, are just over there reading your brochures. You're right, Clay; we follow a fairly healthy lifestyle, even though we are city slickers. However, I wouldn't use the word 'cure' for what the drug companies are doing. The last thing they want is to cure anyone since healthy people don't buy drugs. They just want to relieve you of your symptoms for long enough to convince you that you need their rubbish long term."

Pritchard threw his head back and laughed. "Exactly my message, ma'am. It always surprises me just how many folks don't get it, don't realise that even though they don't use heroin or coke, they are still drug addicts, totally dependent on their chemical foods and pills."

"Not to mention sugar," added Sara, "it's the worst of the lot."

She decided it was time to get off her soapbox. "This is quite a place, Clay, how long have you lived here?"

146

"I came here as a teenager with my parents in the early eighties. They'd had enough of town living and wanted something different. The place wasn't like this then. It had been a sort of commune originally, – not a hippy one; it pre-dated those – and it certainly wasn't very enlightened, by all accounts. However, my folks and a few of their friends convinced those few people that remained here that with a bit of hard work they could make a difference. To be honest, I don't think many of them cared. They were an old community by then and there had been a lot of problems, plus I think their brains were addled by too much drug use. And I mean hard drug use, not just smoking stuff. Eventually they either drifted away or grew old and died. There's none of the original folk left now."

"Do you know what it was called, the original community?" asked Sara.

Pritchard narrowed his eyes at her. "Why would you want to know that, Mrs Farsley?" he asked, his face serious.

"It's Sara," she replied with a smile she hoped would reassure him. "You might be surprised to know, Clay, that I think I might predate you here, if I've got the right place. You see, I grew up in a commune in this area that was like the one you've described. I'm trying to trace my roots."

"Well, well," said Pritchard, stroking his bushy beard. "How interestin'. It was called Ty'sland. Is that the name you're looking for?"

"Ty'sland," repeated Sara quietly, nodding to herself. "Of course, it has to be."

She turned to Pete and Julie, who had walked over to listen to Pritchard. "Did you hear that?" she said, the excitement clear in her voice as she hugged on Pete's arm. "Ty'sland. This has to be the place."

"Was it named after the founder of the commune?" Pete asked Clay.

"Sure was," said Clay. "Apparently he ran it as his own little kingdom; a very alternative lifestyle, you might say. His name was Ty. Ty Donnington. A tad egocentric, I think, using his name for the place, but I suppose a lot of companies have the names of their founders. Not that Donnington had much to brag about to the outside world. Anyway, the place had a bad reputation and we didn't want to be associated with that, so it became Rocky Mountain View as soon as we bought it. Tell me, Sara, when were you here?"

"I was here from when I was born in 1966 until I was thirteen. That's when I escaped."

"Escaped?" Pritchard raised his eyebrows, although he didn't appear surprised.

"Wow!" added Holly, who'd been following the conversation with great interest.

"Yes, escaped," smiled Sara. "Ty'sland was certainly a very different place then, even if it was long after Ty himself died."

She paused, reflecting on their conversation.

"I don't know if I'm really disappointed to hear that no one remains from those days or if I'm relieved. It's been a long time and they'd be pretty old by now anyway. Tell me, Clay, do you remember anyone by the name of Zelda from when you were young? She would have been around sixty then, I suppose."

"Zelda?" replied Pritchard. "There's only one Zelda I ever heard of who lived here, and it was only a story I was told some years later. Apparently she was found dead in the woods a coupla years before me and my folks came here. Would've been around 1980."

"That's the year after I escaped. How did she die?"

"Apparently she fell and broke her neck. All a bit strange since it seems it happened at night. No one could understand why she'd be there after dark."

"Where?"

"It was up by the old burial ground."

"Burial ground?"

"Yes, the original commune members were into the spirit world. They had their own natural burial ground where they placed anyone who passed. It hasn't been used for years now since my folks established a small church here with a graveyard. It's still there, although it's fairly overgrown."

Sara suddenly felt an urgent need to see it; that it might have some answers.

"Could I go there?"

"Why not? Holly here can take you. It's about half a mile along some trails."

Sara turned to Julie and Pete, who had joined them.

"Coming?"

"Sure," said Julie.

"I think I'd like to talk to Clay about some of his farming methods, if that's OK," said Pete. "We should seriously think about developing a proper garden in our yard. I'd like to do it right."

Sara sighed. Whenever Pete took on a new project, everything had to be done according to the book. She hoped he wasn't thinking of growing a bushy beard.

Fifteen minutes later they walked into a clearing in the forest. They'd made their way from the main farm and cabin area along a number of trails that were increasingly overgrown. As they were walking through the farm site, Sara had looked in vain for something that might jog a memory, but there was nothing.

"Don't often come this way these days," said Holly as they stopped to survey the clearing. "Most of the development has been in the other direction."

She nodded. "We used to come out here as kids to look for spooks. We knew there were graves and we made up all sorts of tales about the place being haunted."

She led them towards the centre of the clearing where large prickly bushes and tangles of creepers had established themselves in the natural break in the trees. Sara saw a number of stones among the creepers and suddenly realised they were headstones.

Looking closer, she was surprised by how many there were.

"Seems to have been an unhealthy community," she commented.

"There are a lot of tales of people dying young. OD-ing and stuff," nodded Holly. "Particularly in the early days of the commune. Not so many as time went on."

She bent to pull the creepers from in front of a stone.

"Some of them just have a single name; some a name and a date, which is presumably when they died. It always struck me as being sad that there isn't more about them. They were people and all that remains of them is a name badly carved on a stone."

Sara walked among the stones looking at the names. She turned to Holly. "You're right, it does seem sad. I can't see one with a surname."

"There are a few," said Holly, pulling away some more creeper. "There's a Molly Turner here. 1968. And another one here. Serena Peace."

"What!" exclaimed Sara and Julie together as they rushed over to where Holly was standing.

Sara bent down to clear the area around the stone.

"It's got two dates on," she gasped.

"Yes," said Holly, not registering the potential significance of the dates. "'1966 to 1979'. Hey, she was just a kid."

Then she thought about it. "You must have known her," she said to Sara. "Did you? Do you remember her?"

Sara was temporarily speechless as she stared at her name on the stone. She glanced up at Julie, noting the shock frozen in her face; then she stood and turned to Holly.

She took a deep breath to regain her composure. "Yes, I do," she said quietly, "I didn't know she'd died. It must have happened after I escaped."

Julie felt in her bag for her phone. "I know it might sound a bit macabre, Holly," she said, her eyes still fixed on the stone, "but would you mind if I took some shots of these? They're kind of unusual."

"Go ahead," said Holly. "Perhaps you'd like one of Ty himself. I mean his stone, of course."

"He's buried here too?" asked Sara, surprised.

"Yes, over here. His stone's quite a bit larger than the others."

When they returned to the reception area, Pete was still deep in organic conversation with Clay Pritchard.

"I can see what Pop's going to be busy with for the next few months," whispered Julie to Sara behind her hand.

Clay saw them enter the room.

"Did you find Zelda's stone?" he asked.

"Er, no, we didn't," replied Sara, with an embarrassed smile. "We became rather distracted looking at the names."

"Yes," nodded Pritchard, "it's certainly quite a collection. There are no other records of them, just those stones."

"I was wondering," said Sara. "There seem to be an awful lot of graves for what I think was a fairly small community. Holly said there were drug deaths, but still, it seems out of proportion."

"Well spotted," said Pritchard, "it's an interesting point. It's rumoured – and we've never done anything to investigate it – that not all the graves actually contain bodies."

"Really?"

"Yes. Apparently once Donnington took over, he regarded this commune as a place of true enlightenment, different and more special than anywhere. It was beyond his comprehension that anyone would want to leave. If they did, he regarded their return to the outside world as like dying. So he insisted on a headstone being placed for anyone who left the commune. In his eyes, they had died."

"Weird," said Julie. "You'd think having a headstone would have honoured them."

"You'd think so, yes," agreed Pritchard, "but the truth is more sinister, according to rumour my father heard from the old-timers. It seems that since they were dead in Donnington's eyes, if someone changed their mind and returned, Donnington would ignore them completely as if they were a ghost, and then the person would suddenly disappear again. It's said that Donnington lured them out to the burial ground, showed them their stone and then killed them, burying them where there was already a headstone."

"Have the police ever been involved in any of this?" asked Pete.

"Not to my knowledge, no," said Pritchard shaking his head. "It's only rumour and since Donnington is dead, along with anyone else that might have been involved, it doesn't seem worth creating what would be a lot of disruption that could be potentially damaging to us now."

He looked at them, wondering if he'd said too much.

"Of course, if it is true about Donnington, it stopped after he died, although I do know the practice of marking a grave for anyone who left continued until the early eighties. His influence was clearly very strong."

"When did he die?" asked Julie.

"He died, or rather was killed, in 1970. Not here, although, as you may have noticed, his body is buried at the burial ground."

"Killed?" said Sara, trying to sound innocent.

"Yes, he and his main female partner were killed by another member of their commune, a woman, on their way back from a visit to a place that used to flourish south of Colorado Springs. A place called Drop City."

Sara held her breath.

"Do you know her name?" asked Julie. "The woman who killed them?"

"Yes, I do. Seems she was mentally unstable and was declared to be not competent to stand trial. She was incarcerated in a psychiatric institution near Saguache. Then a few years later she was killed in a fire. She–"

"But what was her name?" interrupted Sara and Julie together.

Pritchard stared at them, surprised at the forcefulness of their question and wondering why it was so important.

"Carr," he said. "Her name was Annie Carr."

Chapter 18

The following morning, they were sitting in the small airport at Durango waiting for the shuttle to fly them back to Denver for the connection to Boston. They had stayed in a small hotel in Durango overnight since by the time they finished at Rocky Mountain View, it was too late to consider returning home.

Pete was lost in a pile of reading material about organic cultivation that Clay had given him, while Sara was staring into space, still processing the exciting information that she now knew her mother's name. Julie was engrossed in texting on her smartphone.

"I hope you're not mentioning any of this to your friends, Julie," said Sara, glancing over Julie's shoulder at the screen.

"Too late for that, Mom," said Julie without taking her eyes from her phone. "I texted the *Washington Post* last night; my friends'll have read all about it in the papers this morning."

"You did what!" cried Sara, looking round in embarrassment as she realized how loudly she'd spoken.

Julie laughed. "Be cool, Mom. I haven't told a soul and I'm not going to. This is just girl stuff." She pointed to her phone. "But, hey, isn't it amazing how much we can get now just by typing a few words into one of these things. A quick search on Matt's laptop and ..." She stopped and smacked her palm against her head.

"Oh my God, I'm so stupid. *We're* so stupid."

Sara frowned. "Why?"

Instead of answering, Julie was frantically typing into her browser's search engine. She scanned the results and clicked on one, then she scrolled down the screen reading an article.

"I don't believe it," she said. "I'm such an idiot."

"Julie, what are you talking about?"

"Google, that's what I'm talking about," replied Julie still shaking her head.

Sara look at her quizzically.

Julie turned to her. "Google, Mom, it was there all the time on Google."

"What was?"

"You're mother's name."

"Really? Where?"

Julie focussed on the phone's screen and read:

"'Durango Herald, September 15th, 1970. Murder Suspect found Not Competent. In a hearing yesterday at the Del Norte courthouse, Judge Lorna McPhee decreed that Annie Carr, the woman suspected of brutally stabbing to death Ty Donnington, the leader of the reclusive community in the hills north of Durango and another woman from the commune, Petra Bozark, was Not Competent to Stand Trial.

"'The hearing was reduced to a farcical level when the defendant, in answer to the judge's questioning, claimed to be nearly five hundred years old. The judge had to forcefully assert her authority to silence the laughter from the members of the community attending...'"

Julie looked up at her mother. "It was all there online, in the newspapers from 1970. Your mother's name, everything. We needn't have wasted our time coming all this way."

Sara smiled at her and took her arm. "It wasn't a waste of time, Julie, we found my grave. If we hadn't come here, we'd never have known about that."

Later that afternoon, as Sara and Julie walked through their front door, they were greeted by an eager Matt running down the stairs clutching a book.

"Hi Mom! Hi Sis!" he cried excitedly. "Where's Pop?"

"He's fetching our bag from the trunk."

"Great!" exclaimed Matt. Then he held up the book. "Look! It arrived this morning."

Sara read the title. *"The Delusional Mind,"* she said. "A gripping plot?"

"Dry as dust," replied Matt, shaking his head. "It's full of psychobabble, but the case studies include one that fits perfectly with what we've found out."

"Does it give the patient's name?" asked Julie, a knowing smile on her face.

"Just her initials. The author says that to maintain patient confidentiality, she has referred to people just by their initials–"

"–And?" interrupted Julie, keen to know exactly what he'd discovered.

"AC!" beamed Matt. "Her initials were AC. And not only that, her daughter was SP. That's gotta be Serena Peace, right?"

He suddenly realised from the satisfied smiles and nods from his mother and sister this was no surprise.

"You've found out, haven't you? What do the initials stand for?"

"Annie Carr," replied Sara. "My mother's name was Annie Carr."

"Annie Carr," echoed Matt. "Wow, that's brilliant!"

"Guess where we found it," taunted Julie smugly.

"At the commune?" said Matt, raising his eyebrows to show his sister that he thought the question stupid.

"And where else?" continued Julie, the smile on her face spreading.

"Fortune cookie?"

"On the Internet, Mr Geek. It was there all the time. Who forgot to check the online newspaper reports about the murder at the motel? Mom told us about the murder and–"

"We forgot! I can't believe it."

He headed for the stairs. "I've got to see it now."

Sara made her way to the kitchen. "Matt, have you had any lunch?"

"No, not yet," he shouted down the stairs. "I got too involved with reading the book."

"OK, let's put some things on a few plates and we'll swap stories," she said as she opened the refrigerator.

As they helped themselves to salad, tomatoes and cheese, Matt said, "OK, you first, Mom. You found your mother's name. That's so cool. What else did you find out about her?"

"Not a lot, really," replied Sara, "but it was definitely the right place, although it had changed beyond recognition since I was there. In fact, there was nothing I recognised for quite a while until we came back from the forest and were shown a couple of very old cabins they decided to keep. When I went into one, there was something about the layout that was very familiar. Then I noticed metal rings attached to the walls in various places. Quite high up."

"What was so special about those?" asked Matt.

"You remember I told you that as a young child, I was tethered? Well, the rings were where they tied the rope. If they wanted me to work on the porch or in the yard just outside, they'd tie the rope to the ring near the main door. I remember that so well. I hated it; it was like being a dog."

"Wow, not good memories, huh!" nodded Matt.

"No, but the really interesting thing was that I found my grave."

"Your what!"

"My grave," laughed Sara. "Or at least a headstone with my name on it. I'm pretty sure there's no one buried there."

"Look," said Julie, showing him the photo on her phone.

Sara explained what Clay Pritchard had told them about the commune practices.

"Wow!" said Matt again, once his mother finished. "That's really weird. Almost as weird as the story Annie Carr told Dr Wright."

"Really?" said Sara. "What does the book say?"

"Well," said Matt, "it's frustratingly short; really thin on detail. As I said, there's a lot of psycho-babble about delusional this and that, but she's kept the story itself to the bare bones. You feel there must be so much more. However, what she does say is really interesting. She says Annie Carr claimed she was hundreds of years old, just like she did in court. She also claimed that she didn't age and was extremely healthy."

Sara gasped. "My mother told me I'd live forever, as I said, and that I'd never be ill, which I'm not."

She paused and looked around the faces of her family. They were all staring back at her.

"You don't think … it could be true, do you?" she said very quietly.

"Well, Dr Wright clearly doesn't," said Matt. "She said she set up various long term tests to prove to Annie Carr that it was all in her head. She was sure that given time she would have been able to cure her, but then Annie was killed, which stopped the whole project. So Wright never knew–"

"Never knew?" interrupted Julie. "Matt, you don't seriously believe it, do you? How can anyone live for hundreds of years? It makes no sense at all."

"Mom's health makes no sense," countered Matt. "Have you ever heard of anyone who has never had anything wrong with them in their lives? Never even a headache! She's never had any dental work, her eyesight's perfect. That's amazing for someone of her age."

"Excuse me!" said Sara in mock indignation. "I am sitting in this room, you know, and I'm only forty-six. I'm not quite ready for the scrapheap!"

"Come on, Mom," said Matt. "You said yourself that you don't understand it. If your mother was telling you the truth about the health stuff, perhaps she was about the age stuff as well."

Julie snorted disdainfully. "I can accept the health thing," she said, "although if you inherited it from your mother, you haven't passed it on. That forest has triggered my hay fever." She sniffed and pulled a face. "But the age thing must have been just a tale, the sort of thing any mother would tell a young child."

"I don't remember telling you things like that," said Sara. "However, I must say I feel our trip was worthwhile. I have discovered my mother's name. It's something I've wondered about for years. Unfortunately, I'd imagine it's a fairly common name, so I doubt we'll be able to find out any more about her background. Added to that, she's dead. So that's it, really, don't you think?"

"I don't know," said Matt, pursing his lips thoughtfully, "it probably is. I'll have a look online to see if there's anything that might lead us back to who Annie Carr was. I wish I had a contact in the FBI, like they do in the movies."

"I can't imagine they'd be very forthcoming," laughed Sara, "and anyway, to continue my nagging, you should be studying for your exams, not sleuthing your ancestors."

"Message received and understood, ma'am," saluted Matt and turned to walk away. Then pausing, he said, "Don't you want to read the book? I think you'd find it interesting."

"Yes, I was going to ask you. Leave it on the table; I'll start it when I've cleared."

By early that evening, Sara had ploughed through the whole of *Delusional Minds,* reading and rereading the chapter on Annie Carr several times. She finally closed the book and looked up. She was sitting on a large sofa in the Farsley den. Pete was sitting in a recliner at the far end, watching golf on the television.

"You know, it's a pity they spoil these fascinating programmes about grass growing with shots of those silly men wandering about hitting little white balls with long sticks," said Sara.

Pete grunted. "They're clubs, and they do versions with large, spiked, round heads for beating wives," he growled without taking his eyes off the screen.

Sara smiled and turned to Julie, who was tapping on her iPad. "I didn't know they did pre-law apps for that thing, Julie."

"I'm checking case law for inheritance. I reckon my grandmother must have been the wife of a count or something at some stage in her hundreds of years, and they would have lived in a huge chateau somewhere in France. I want to kick out the interlopers who are in it now and claim what's rightfully ours. Well, yours, at least."

"So you're coming round to believing it, are you, Sis?" said Matt, loping into the room.

"Yeah," said Julie. "About as much as I believe in the tooth fairy."

"You mean the tooth fairy isn't …?" started Matt, and then laughed at his sister's dismissive toss of her head.

Sara tapped on the book. "You were right about one thing, Matt: it's frustratingly thin on detail, although she does explain in some depth why she thinks Annie Carr is fantasising. She clearly gives no credence to the idea of my mother being as old as she says, even if she does agree her stories are amazing. After all, she's not the first nut who's claimed to have been around when Moses was small, and I doubt she'll be the last."

"I don't think she quite claimed that, Mom," said Matt, "and hey, that's my grandmother you're calling a nut!"

"Explains a lot," commented Julie, looking up from her tapping.

"Your gran too," said Matt. "You know, there could be something in it. I've been looking at a few articles on ageing and DNA. What I found was interesting, even to a non-scientist like me. They say we start to age when our bodies can't repair our cells properly anymore; slowly at first, of course, but then faster as we get older. Suppose there were ways of stopping it, or at least slowing it. Wouldn't you live longer?"

"I suppose you might," mused Sara. "Do you think my mother might have come across some sort of drug?"

"No, not really, since it would have to be a natural drug and why wouldn't it have been discovered before? It's not as if she claims to have gone off into the uncharted depths of the Amazon and found some strange plant. But suppose her genetic structure was different and it held back ageing in some way. That might have made her healthier too."

"Interesting," said Sara, "but why hasn't it been seen before? Why should my mother have been the first?"

"Who says she's the first?" said Matt. "There might have been hundreds like her. Might be, in fact. I mean, they're hardly going to advertise themselves, are they?"

"I suppose not," agreed Sara. "Anyway, genetic or not, having read this dry academic tome, my enthusiasm to learn a little more about my mother has now been whetted. There must be more and I'm hoping Dr Nancy Wright might be willing to reveal it. After all, patient confidentiality isn't too relevant once someone is dead."

She paused and smiled at her son.

"I'm going to get in touch with Dr Wright."

Chapter 19

At seventy-four, Nancy Wright had been semi-retired for several years. However, her reputation in the field of delusional behaviour had increased throughout her career and her opinions were still highly sought after. As much as she wanted to hand over her patients to a younger person, she found it very difficult to let go, especially with the lure of invitations to international conferences all over the world that came with all-expenses-paid trips and business-class luxury. An additional bonus was that her fully retired but very fit and active husband, Chris, now had plenty of time to accompany her, exploring new and exotic golf courses while she attended her meetings.

She still maintained her office in the ageing brownstone on the Upper West Side, despite many overtures from her partners at the main downtown practice to join them. A full-scale renovation to the building some ten years before had brought it up to an acceptable level, and although old demons still lurked in its depths, wreaking occasional havoc with heating, cooling and communications, she loved the place and the location. These days a fully secure intranet link to the main practice gave her no reason to move.

However, being semi-retired, she'd stopped taking on new patients – her list of existing patients was quite long enough. Hence when Sara Farsley telephoned to ask for an appointment, Nancy's secretary initially tried to refer her to the main practice.

"I'm not actually trying to seek Dr Wright's professional help," Sara explained. "I want to talk to her about the book she recently published."

"Would this be a professional discussion?" asked the secretary, ever protective of her boss in these times of cranks looking to freeload or journalists looking for unguarded comments to quote.

Sara thought quickly. "In a manner of speaking, yes. I'm writing a paper on the development of mental health treatment facilities over the last, er, hundred years and I'm looking for first-hand accounts of some remote institutions to compare their approaches with those that were more mainstream. I saw from Dr Wright's book that before working in New York City, she worked in the West back in the seventies. I was hoping she might share some of her knowledge."

She paused, wondering whether her off-the-cuff explanation sounded plausible.

"Why are you writing the paper?" came the reply.

"It's for a part-time masters in health administration I'm following here in Boston. I'm a mature student, married with a family."

"I'll need to ask Dr Wright. Please hold," said the secretary abruptly and the line clicked.

Unbeknown to Sara, improvement in institutional treatment of psychiatric care patients was a cause Nancy Wright had championed for many years, so when she heard her secretary's summary of Sara's request, she immediately agreed to see her.

"Find a convenient spot in the diary, Maureen. Sometime later this week if she can make it."

Sara was relieved when it was the secretary who came back on the line to discuss a time. She didn't wanted to compound her story with more fabrication to Dr Wright herself.

The following Friday, Sara took the train from Boston, arriving at Penn Station at twelve thirty and emerging into the lunchtime crowds. Her appointment was at two thirty so she took the subway to Eighty-sixth Street and found a spot in Central Park to eat the lunch she'd brought with her. She loved New York City and would normally have stayed downtown to immerse herself in the bustle and buzz of the endless stream of people. However, today she wanted to gather her thoughts and remain focussed. She had a feeling her meeting with Nancy Wright might provide answers to the many questions she had about herself and her mother.

Shortly before two fifteen, she made the ten-minute walk from the park to Nancy Wright's office. She was dressed as she would be for her own office in a conservative navy jacket and skirt, with a cream silk blouse. Her large sunglasses concealed her pale grey eyes.

Nancy Wright's secretary asked Sara to sit in the waiting area until the psychiatrist was ready. Not normally nervous about meeting new people, especially at a professional level, Sara found herself fidgeting with her hands as the matronly Maureen quietly scrutinised her from behind her desk. Sara had rarely spoken to a psychiatrist, and only then on social occasions. When she had, she'd wondered whether every word she uttered betrayed her as having some obscure mental disorder. A one-on-one meeting was suddenly a daunting prospect.

The phone on Maureen's desk buzzed. "You can go through now," she said, pointing to the consulting room door.

"Thank you," said Sara, pleased to be removing herself from under the secretary's microscope.

She knocked on the door and went in. The room was a pleasant surprise – she'd expected something austere and formal, not the beiges and soft browns that greeted her. Two large overstuffed and comfortable-looking armchairs on a deep-pile carpet dominated the space, while the psychiatrist's desk was an ancient oak affair at the far end.

Nancy Wright stood to greet Sara.

"Ms Farsley," she said, "I'm Nancy Wright. Please, take a seat,"

"It's Mrs Farsley," replied Sara, taking the offered hand, "but please, call me Sara."

She raised her hand to remove her dark glasses, then changed her mind and simply straightened them.

They sat and Nancy waited while Sara opened her briefcase. To her surprise, all Sara retrieved was a copy of *Delusional Minds* with a number of post-it notes marking various pages.

"Tell me about your research, Sara," smiled Nancy, pushing up her glasses. "You may not know it but you've hit upon a special interest of mine."

Sara gulped silently and looked up at this elderly woman. She wasn't how she had imagined her, although from the dates given in the book, she realised Nancy Wright must be at least well into her

162

sixties, probably older. The psychiatrist's almost completely white hair was drawn back into a tight bun, she wore little make-up and her pale skin had a translucency that reminded Sara of Pete's parents. Her eyes, clearly visible through the unobtrusive rimless spectacles, were soft and smiling, immediately relaxing and reassuring. A professional's eyes, thought Sara, complemented by the gentle smile at the corners of her mouth. Her patients must find their sessions with her a very positive experience.

"Er, to be honest, Dr Wright, I've come here under slightly false pretences. I got the impression from your secretary that you might not be willing to see me so I'm afraid I improvised somewhat."

"You mean you really are seeking professional help and wouldn't take no for an answer?"

"No, it's not that. I'm certainly not asking for your expert services. There's nothing wrong with me; not that I know of," she added with a nervous smile.

"Then what are you asking for?" said Nancy, her smile less reassuring now as she glanced at the door.

"I'm looking for more information regarding one of the sections in your book," replied Sara indicating the copy sitting in her lap. "The one about the institution in Colorado: Sawpine Ridge. You had a patient there whom you described as having lived in a commune in the hills and forests north of Durango. You don't name it, but from the description, I'm almost certain I know it."

"Really?" said Nancy Wright, her voice edged with scepticism.

"Yes," continued Sara. "You see, I grew up in that area, in a commune called Ty'sland. I was there from when I was born, in 1966, until I escaped at the age of thirteen."

"Escaped?" repeated Nancy quietly.

"Yes, I was taken from my mother when I was about four and given to foster parents in the commune. They didn't treat me well; I was more of a slave than anything else."

Sara thought Nancy was looking even warier, and there was something in her eyes, an agitation, as if she couldn't believe what she was hearing.

"Why were you taken from your mother?" asked Nancy.

"She was arrested for murder but found to be not competent to stand trial. At least that's what I was told. Actually, they just said she was nuts. I was never given much detail about her, not even her name. All I was ever told was that she was evil; that she killed the commune's leader and destroyed the commune. Then later they said she'd been killed in a fire where she was held. The members of the commune were jubilant. I remember how they celebrated when they heard; it was awful."

She paused and watched for Nancy's reaction, but now she could read nothing. More than forty years of listening to patients' stories had taught Nancy to remain impassive and she'd quickly hidden whatever inner turmoil she might be feeling.

Sara took a breath and then continued.

"Dr Wright. I'm not a student; I'm a lawyer by profession. I understand evidence and I accept that everything I've just told you is challengeable. I could have read your book, carried out a little research of my own and claimed to be someone I'm not. However, there are a couple of things I hope might persuade you that I am who I say I am. You see, I am convinced the patient you treated at Sawpine Ridge was my mother, the patient you have referred to as AC.

"Also in your account you have only used the initials SP for the daughter AC claimed to have. My name now is Sara Farsley – Farsley is my married name. After I escaped from the commune, I was eventually caught by the police and put into care. A wonderful couple in Boston, whom I now regard as my parents, then fostered me. The Patersons. So before I married, I was Sara Paterson. However, before that, in the commune, I was Serena Peace. That was the name my mother gave me."

Nancy Wright gasped. "How did you find that name? Have you visited the commune? – I believe it still exists. Did they tell you? Why are you doing this?"

"I'm doing it to try to find more information about my mother, Dr Wright. What other motive could I have? However, you are correct. I have visited the commune, or organic farm as it's now called. They didn't mention the name Serena Peace in connection with your patient; I don't think the people who are there now know that she had a daughter. But they did tell me my mother's name, that is, they told me the name of the person responsible for the death of the commune leader back in 1970 was Annie Carr. I'd never known it before. I'd read the account in your book about AC and when they told me that name, I knew she had to be the same person."

"That doesn't really–" started Nancy.

"–Prove anything?" interrupted Sara. "No, I know it doesn't. Even though I found my own grave at the farm, deep in the forest at the old commune burial ground."

"Your own grave?"

"Yes, they placed headstones for people who left or escaped as well as those who really died."

"How bizarre. I didn't know that. Even so, Sara, I'm afraid that everything you've told me you could have found out. It doesn't prove you are the daughter Annie Carr always claimed to have."

Sara nodded. "There's one other point that might be more convincing. The detail about Annie Carr in your book is very limited, which is why I wanted to see you. However, one thing you did describe was her eyes. You said they were very unusual and very striking."

"Yes, they were," said Nancy hesitantly.

Sara reached for her sunglasses and removed them.

Nancy's hand shot to her mouth. "My God!" she exclaimed. "The likeness is uncanny. I was suspicious as soon as you arrived but your rather large glasses hid your features, particularly your eyes."

"You were suspicious? Why?"

Nancy's gaze shifted from Sara as she recalled events from the past. "Something you couldn't possibly be aware of, Sara, since you must have almost no memory of your mother," she said, smiling softly. "It's your voice. The accent is different, but otherwise talking to you is like talking to Annie."

It was Sara's turn to be surprised. "I never imagined," she said as she sat back in her chair. "Was she really like me?"

"Yes, very much so. You are a little taller and your hair is slightly lighter, but your figure and overall facial features are strikingly similar."

She studied Sara's face further as something seemed to occur to her.

"You said you were born in 1966. That would make you …?"

"Forty-six," said Sara.

"You certainly don't look it. You don't look a day older than Annie the last time I saw her, when she must have been, let me see, thirty-four. That was the year before she died. Although in her delusional mind she was, of course, much older."

"Well, I'm certainly not delusional about my age, and while I don't have a birth certificate, I can prove it to within a couple of years," said Sara.

"I'm sure you can, Sara," smiled Nancy. "Tell me, how is your health?"

"Perfect: never a day's illness in my life – the same as Annie Carr. For the limited time you knew her, surely you can agree that part of her story and not consider it part of her delusions."

"No, of course it wasn't. She had the most remarkable health."

"Do you have any photos of her, Dr Wright? Dr Wright, are you OK?"

Nancy had put her head in her hands as Sara was speaking. She nodded and looked up through her fingers. "I'm sorry, Sara, please forgive me. It's just that when you said that – your voice, the tone, everything – it could have been Annie speaking. It suddenly brought back so many memories."

She exhaled, as if to clear her head, then composed herself. "Sorry," she continued. "You asked about photos. Yes, I have many, although I'm not sure I'll show them all to you."

"What do you mean?" asked Sara.

Nancy laughed and stood. "One or two are rather compromising," she said as she walked over to a filing cabinet by the wall opposite her desk and unlocked a drawer. "In fact, we thought them very risqué, although they're probably not by today's standards. At Sawpine Ridge, I kept them locked up in my apartment. Even now, they're in a part of this filing cabinet my secretary can't access."

She retrieved a large brown envelope and returned to her seat. Holding it in her lap, she explained the photo sessions to Sara.

"I haven't looked at them for years," she said as she opened the packet.

She took one out, a head and shoulders shot, and passed it to Sara. "There, that's Annie Carr. My heavens, now that I see her face again, I know there is absolutely no doubt you are her daughter."

Sara took the photo and stared at it in fascination. "My mother," she whispered.

"You could be sisters. Twins almost," said Nancy.

"That's what people are starting to say about my daughter and me," said Sara, not taking her eyes off the face in the picture.

"How old is she, your daughter?"

"She's twenty. Twenty-one in four months."

"Is she …?"

"Like me? Yes, she is, although not in the way you mean. Her eyes are different from mine and she gets her fair share of coughs and colds. May I see the rest of the photos?"

Nancy hesitated for a second and then passed the envelope. "Why not? I was hoping we'd continue taking these and that eventually Annie would have changed sufficiently for her to notice and accept. Perhaps then I could have treated her. However, as you know, she didn't live long enough for the research to run its course."

"Wow!" said Sara flicking through the photos. "Looks like you had some fun."

"Yes," laughed Nancy, "it was hilarious, if a little unprofessional. We were like a couple of silly schoolgirls. Fortunately, I was able to do all the developing and printing myself. No one else has ever seen them. Apart from Annie, you are the first."

"May I keep a couple? Of her face, I mean, although I must say her figure is remarkably like mine."

"Even now?" asked Nancy.

"Yes," smiled Sara, "even now. Nothing is drooping or sagging. It hasn't changed at all, even after having two children."

"Do you get tested? You know, the usual women's things."

"Yes, my doctor is constantly amazed. Everything is as it always has been. Labs, the lot."

"Sara?" Nancy hesitated for a moment. "Would you object to my examining you? I am, of course, a qualified doctor."

"Not at all, if it would help to understand whatever it is that made my mother stay so young, and me."

Nancy nodded. "Although I don't have the medical notes on Annie Carr – they remained at Sawpine Ridge and were lost in the fire – I can remember certain points, and there are the photographs.

I have a small examination room through here," she added, pointing to a door. "You can change into a gown in there."

Half an hour later, they were again sitting in Nancy Wright's main office. Nancy was studying her notes from the physical examination.

"I don't examine many patients these days, Sara, but I must say I have never seen a woman of your age with such a youthful body. It is exactly as Annie's was, although, as I've said, when I knew her, she was younger. And like her, from your external appearance, I would never suspect you've had children."

She stopped, remembering something. "You may recall that in my book I mentioned that Annie claimed to have had a number of children. There were at least five over the centuries she said she'd lived through."

Sara frowned. "Dr Wright, I know you are convinced my mother was delusional; that she somehow researched the lives of the people she claimed to be and had taken on their personas in her mind. However, disregarding all preconceived ideas we have about longevity, given her story and her health, and now considering mine, do you think there might be any possibility she was telling the truth?"

"You mean that she was really over four hundred years old!" Nancy laughed – rather condescendingly, Sara thought.

"No, Sara, I do not. It makes no sense medically; none whatsoever. It contradicts all we know about ageing."

"All we know, yes," agreed Sara, "but what if there is something we don't know, some, I don't know, some genetic factor that could overrule ageing? What about my mother's health and mine? How does our present level of knowledge explain that?"

Nancy nodded. "I must admit it doesn't. However, when you think about it, scientifically or otherwise, there are just too many factors that would need to be explained. No, Sara, there has to be some other explanation, and as far as your mother was concerned, I am completely satisfied she was dangerously delusional."

Sara thought about it. "When my family and I talk about my health and youthful looks, I always say to them that sooner or later I'll suddenly age; that I'll wake up one morning and look much older, like that painting in the Oscar Wilde book, except I'm not claiming to have a pact with the Devil. I've been saying that for over ten years now. However, just suppose it doesn't happen. What would you say if when I'm seventy, say, or eighty, I look exactly as I am now? If that were the case, would you be prepared to reconsider? Remember, I'm not claiming anything about myself like my mother did – I'm not delusional – I'm just as mystified by the whole thing as you are."

Nancy smiled softly. "Sadly, Sara, it's unlikely I'll be around when you're seventy, and certainly not when you're eighty. So I'll never know. However, I am prepared to document it and to leave the file with a colleague, one younger than you are. I must admit it would be very interesting; it's exactly what I'd hoped for with Annie, but for different reasons."

Sara still wasn't prepared to let it go. "You said in your book that my mother's case was different from others; that although you diagnosed her as delusional, her case was unlike any other you'd seen or read about. What did you mean by that?"

"Simply that in most cases the patients' accounts are very calculated and repetitive. They have boundaries they've created, albeit unconsciously since they're deceiving themselves as much as they're deceiving everyone else. They are uncomfortable going outside those boundaries. Hence if you push hard enough, the limits of their accounts become obvious, to the psychiatrist at least; to the patient it's an irritant. These boundaries are the places for detailed discussion, places where the contradictions start to occur.

"In Annie Carr's case, there were never any contradictions and neither did the stories ever seem prepared or become repetitive. If I wanted more detail, I'd always get it, and if I asked for a story again on another occasion, she would tell it to me in different words."

"You mean it would be like me telling you the story of something that happened to Julie, my daughter, when she was small, some tale about something she'd done. If I told you more than once, I might embellish it with detail I'd forgotten the first time, and if there was a third telling, the details might vary again, but never contradict."

"Exactly," agreed Nancy.

"Then if you are prepared to accept what I say as the truth – someone you don't suspect of being delusional – why couldn't you accept what my mother said?"

"Because of the nature of the tale, Sara: it's just too far outside the boundaries of rational thought to be acceptable."

She paused as she considered something, then she continued.

"You know, you shouldn't simply take my word for it. I think you should read the notes of my interviews with your mother. Would you like to do that?"

"Could I really? I'd love to. I think it would give me a great insight into what she was like."

"Of course. Normally I wouldn't dream of releasing patient notes; they are highly confidential. However, in this case, first, your mother has been dead for some thirty-seven years, and second, she was your mother and, given your own circumstances, I think you have a right to know."

She thought for a moment.

"You know, they are quite extensive. No one has ever seen them, not even any of my secretaries over the years, and I think I should prefer to keep it that way, apart from you and me, and perhaps your family. If we work at it together now, it would probably only take an hour or two to photocopy the lot. Shall we do that?"

"Let's get to it," smiled Sara. "I can't wait to read them."

Two hours later, a box of files containing copies of the notes from hundreds of hours of interviews with Annie Carr was sitting on the coffee table in front of Sara and Nancy. Sara reached out and touched the box.

"I can't wait to get home and start on these. I know I've always pushed thoughts of my mother to the back of my mind; it was a natural thing to do – I hardly knew her and the chances of learning more about her seemed beyond reach. Now that's all changed. Whether I find her stories believable or not, I'm sure they will bring her much closer to me."

Nancy shook her head. "I can't believe you've turned up here today; it's brought so much back to me. It's such a tragedy Annie was killed in that fire."

Sara stared through the windows to the trees lining the street outside.

"They never actually found her body, did they?"

"They never identified her body with one hundred per cent certainty, no. However, by a process of elimination, there really wasn't any doubt the body found in her studio was hers. It was where she was known to be heading when she ran back into the building. There was no way she could have escaped that blaze."

She reached out and touched Sara's arm. "I'm sorry, Sara, I wish I could give you hope otherwise." Then she stood. "However, I can give you something else. I've just remembered it."

She walked over to an ornate Chinese cupboard on the far wall of the office and opened the doors. Inside were stacks of papers of various sizes. She leafed through a pile on an upper shelf and removed one sheet.

"I've always intended to have this framed," she said, holding it up.

She was holding a pencil drawing of a child of about four years old.

"Annie didn't just talk about her daughter, about you, she was a very gifted artist and she drew this for me to show me what you looked like. It's you, Sara, as a young child. I want you to have it. Annie wanted me to know what you looked like so that if I went to the commune, I might recognise you. She didn't know you were hidden away."

Sara took the picture and studied it.

"I can't thank you enough, Dr Wright. This is beautiful. I don't know much about art, but I can see that the detail is drawn with incredible skill."

She took a tissue from her bag to wipe her eyes. "You know, it's triggered a memory from the commune – while I don't really remember much about my mother, I think I can remember her sketching."

"Maybe you can, Sara" smiled Nancy, thinking Sara's recall was probably likely to be imagined.

"Did she paint that portrait of you?" asked Sara, pointing to a large framed painting hanging over an unused fireplace on the wall opposite the office windows.

Nancy turned and walked closer to the painting. "She did, yes."

"I know fashions have changed, but that blouse appears to be from another era," said Sara as she stood to join Nancy.

Nancy laughed. "It was interesting. She had been telling me about a period she loved in her life in the eighteen hundreds when she was in Trinidad in the Caribbean. She loved the old colonial fashions and when she painted my portrait, she decided to put me in that blouse. Beautiful, don't you think? If I could find a blouse like that, I'd wear it, fashionable or not."

"Yes," agreed Sara, "it's exquisite. The detail in your face and in the clothing is quite stunning. Like a photograph, but better – it's much more alive than a photo could ever be. Nevertheless, do you think I could take a photograph of it; my new cell phone has a rather good camera."

"Certainly, Sara. I ought to see if I can get it copied. You know, I'm so pleased to have it; I'd never part with it no matter how much I was offered. Almost all of Annie's work was destroyed in the fire. So much was lost that day."

Sara felt as if she were floating as she walked to down the two flights of stairs to the street clutching her file of notes and the tube containing the carefully rolled pencil drawing of herself as a child. From what had started as a day full of trepidation in case Nancy Wright had objected to her questions, she now had a wealth of information about her mother. She couldn't wait to get back to Boston and share it all with her family. She hailed a passing cab and headed for Penn Station.

Had she been more aware of her surroundings and the people in the street, none of whom she noticed at all, she might have wondered why a scruffily dressed young man, partially concealed behind a tree fifty feet away on the far side of the street, was taking photographs of her with a camera equipped with a long lens.

Chapter 20

Marcus Dayton sat behind the sleek, all-glass desk in his minimalist ultra-modern office, his hands steepled to his face, his eyes focussed on the huge monochrome image of his daughter, Emma, on the wall opposite. He was listening with rapt attention to a nervously delivered account from his nerdy researcher Palo Melliff. In front of Dayton, scattered across the desktop, were a dozen large colour photos showing Sara Farsley leaving Nancy Wright's office building and hailing a taxi. Three others showed her emerging from the taxi at Penn station, but after that the crowd had swallowed her up. Although Melliff had frantically searched the huge station for any sign of her, it was as if she had evaporated. He'd hoped his boss's anger at losing this valuable find would be offset by the fact he'd found her at all. Her identity could always be uncovered later in a number of ways.

Marcus Dayton wasn't simply angry; he was furious. This was the breakthrough he'd dreamed about and the idiot had let her slip through his fingers. However, even as he lectured Palo about his ineptness, he had to accept it was down to the nerd's powers of observation that the woman had been noticed at all.

"Tell me again," ordered Dayton, the very slight Central European accent in his voice still present, even after living among English speakers for so long. To Palo it explained a lot: these Krauts, or whatever he was, were all borderline nuts in his opinion, otherwise why would movie directors always use them for the bad guys. Whatever; the bottom line was that, although he found him totally intimidating, from his penetrating, jet-black eyes to his trim but muscular six-foot-five frame, the guy paid well. Really well.

Palo sighed. This would be the fourth run through of the account of his day's work. He was used to it by now – it was his boss's way – but he still couldn't decide if Dayton was slow-witted under all that steely exterior, or whether he really expected some seemingly insignificant detail to reveal itself in retelling the account over and over again.

"Like I said, Mr Dayton, sir," he started, his nasal whine with its harsh New Jersey accent grating on Marcus' nerves, "the shrink's place of work was no secret, so once we'd realised she might know something about what interests you, I checked it out and, according to your instructions, staked out the street to get a handle on her movements. I found she only works in that office part-time, on account of her age, but she has what looks like a battleaxe of a secretary who's there all day, every day. So the best bet to get in there would be at night. I been round the back–"

"Yes, yes, Melliff," interrupted Dayton, "you decided the place is too risky to burgle from the outside."

"Yes, sir, too public."

"Have you tapped into the security cameras inside the building yet?"

"No, sir, it's an old system and not linked to the Internet, so it's more difficult."

Dayton fixed his eyes on Palo with such concentration that Palo, who loved computer games, expected a death ray to spear forth from them and pierce him.

"And then the woman turned up, just like that?"

"Yes sir, just like that, as you say," replied Palo.

"Remarkable," nodded Dayton in satisfaction as he glanced at the warm, gentle amusement in his daughter's eyes as they smiled back at him from the opposite wall, although now he thought he could see a wistfulness, a prescience there too.

"My long wait has been worth it," he said quietly as he absently smoothed the crisp, pure-white, Egyptian-cotton shirtsleeves of his handmade shirt and tugged lightly on the starched cuffs to realign the monogrammed cufflinks.

He refocussed his eyes with distaste at the scruffily dressed Melliff, whose skinny frame was rendered shapeless by baggy jeans and a floppy, grey T-shirt printed with a cartoon of Albert Einstein's face and the words 'Einstein = Mighty Cool Squared'. The fastidious Dayton wondered when the T-shirt had last seen the inside of a washing machine. Nevertheless, he had to admit the shrimpy nerd was bright. It had taken him no time at all to redesign all the search algorithms Dayton's dedicated team of researchers used to scrutinise the Internet for anything that might lead Dayton closer to his goal, while the image comparison routines Melliff had implemented were producing the most remarkable results. Along with all that, the nerd was good on the street. His excellent memory had been triggered instantly when he saw the woman leaving Nancy Wright's office. She was wearing her sunglasses when she went in, but as she left, she'd momentarily removed them to wipe her eyes and in that moment, not only did the nerd link her face with faces he'd discovered just a few days before, but he also managed to shoot a number of frames through the long lens that had Dayton salivating for more.

"You have done well, Melliff," nodded Dayton, "despite your incompetence in losing the woman. You say you have no idea of her identity?"

"No, sir, although I'm certain she went to see the shrink, since, as you know, the upper-floor premises are empty and the street-level offices are accessed through a different door."

"That gives me an idea, Melliff. My secretary can contact the letting agent and I'll rent the floor above this Dr Wright. I'll even set up an office there. That way we'll have legitimate access to the building and at night, once you've gained control of their security cameras, we can have all the time we need to look around Wright's office."

"Won't that be expensive, sir?" said Palo, regretting it immediately as Dayton's eyes bored into him.

"That is no concern of yours, Melliff. Now, while that is set in motion, I want you to run these photographs you have taken against the ones you discovered on the Internet."

Four days later, the deal was signed and a skeleton office set up on the floor above Nancy's consulting rooms. Nancy was concerned when her agent informed her with evident delight she'd struck a good deal with a tenant who wanted to use the space to house a research unit for a company dealing with overseas commercial real estate. The company had paid a year up front and assured the agent there would be only two or three employees, their work entirely Internet-based. There would be no noise and no visitors, apart from their boss.

"I promise you, Dr Wright, you won't know they are there," smiled the agent.

Partly mollified – the offices had been occupied by a small law firm for years until the practice moved following the death of its principal partner – Nancy told the agent she would hope for the best.

The day after moving in, while his very unnerdy assistant, Gloria, distracted the guard by draping herself and her cleavage over the guard's desk, Palo Melliff accessed the security system. He could now control precisely what went onto and, more importantly, stayed on the security discs.

Having established that Dr Wright used her office on a part-time basis, and that her secretary kept very precise hours – locking up and leaving at six on the dot on any day the psychiatrist was not there – Melliff explained to Dayton he considered a Friday evening a good time for their break-in.

"We have to find this woman's name, Melliff," said Dayton, as he paced his office floor, his hands behind his back. "Explain to me again why you do not think she is the actress."

Palo sighed to himself. Here we go again. He had been through his image comparisons over and over with Dayton, who simply refused to believe them.

"As you know, sir," he started, "from the shrink's account about this AC woman in her book – the nut who thought she was hundreds of years old – the only name she gave in recent times was the actress, Dolores di Napoli. This freak thought she was her. So I found a whole load of shots of this di Napoli, enhanced them, and then I did as you instructed and used them as a basis to search the Internet for people with similar features. I got a lot of hits, as you would expect with old black-and-white material, but most of them could be rejected. One that couldn't was of some artist called Mali Whittaker, who turned out to be a dead ringer for the di Napoli woman. As I said to you, Whittaker was probably her daughter."

"Yes, yes, Melliff, we've covered all that. So why do you think the woman at Wright's office is neither of them?"

Palo glanced up at Dayton and thought for the hundredth time that he was certifiable. How could someone of about thirty be the same person as an actress born over a hundred years ago and who died in 1940? He'd raised that objection to his boss several times but Dayton had dismissed it with the toss of a hand.

"Be flexible of thought, Melliff! I want you to disregard time passing and concentrate on the image comparisons," was all he would say by way of explanation.

Melliff scratched his head through his greasy hair. "It's all down to the bone structure, sir. The interocular distances linked with the zygomatic arch positions and nasal bones are excellent places to start when you're trying to determine if someone in two photos is the same person. For di Napoli and Whittaker, the similarity was amazing. If I didn't know that one died in 1940 when the other was twenty, I'd have said they were the same person. Which is why I think they are mother and daughter. For the woman from the shrink's office, while her overall facial features are very similar – which is why I noticed her in the first place – when I looked at all the detailed measurements, there were subtle differences. No, Mr Dayton, sir, she's not the same person as either of the others. But I'd say she's related; perhaps Whittaker's daughter."

Dayton stopped pacing. He had made his decision.

"OK, Melliff, we go in tonight. I'll come to the building at about six o'clock and we'll wait until nine. Get your equipment ready."

Chapter 21

It was past midnight before Sara finally returned home to the Farsley house in Beacon Hill, Boston. Julie was out with friends; Matt was in his room asleep at his desk, his right hand still clutching his computer mouse; while Pete was snoring gently in front of the golf channel, a book on organic gardening open on his lap. Sara quietly made herself a snack before she woke Pete to tell him it was time for bed.

"Hi, Babe," mumbled Pete sleepily as he started from his slumbers. "How'd it go?"

"I'll tell you all about it in the morning," said Sara with a mysterious smile. Then she added, "It went brilliantly, but there's too much to tell right now. We'll have a pow-wow over Saturday brunch."

The following morning, Sara was up before everyone else. Her mind was so full of the notes she'd been reading on the train journey back to Boston that she'd found it hard to sleep, but she'd finally drifted off. Now she wanted to finish scanning through the files before the family emerged, knowing from what she'd seen already that a detailed reading would take some hours. Dr Wright's notes were meticulous and her impeccable but tiny handwriting meant each page was packed with information.

At nine thirty she headed for the stove, knowing the smell of bacon and sausages slowly permeating the house would bring her brood to the kitchen like hounds chasing a scent. She was right. They all arrived within five minutes of each other in varying states of consciousness, Matt in his usual zombie mode.

"Did you make it to your bed or did you remain snuggled up to your books?" Sara asked him.

Matt's reply was a non-committal grunt.

However, copious coffee, together with eggs Benedict, bacon and plump pork sausages on the side saw them all return to an acceptable human form. Sara cleared the plates and placed the box of files on the breakfast counter.

"You'll be pleased to know that we all have some reading to do," she announced, her voice brimming with enthusiasm. "Yesterday was so exciting. There's tons about my mother in these files, and," she added as she flicked open the box's lid and removed a large envelope, "a photograph of her!" She laid it on the counter with a flourish.

"Wow!" exclaimed Julie and Matt together.

"Hey, Mom," added Matt, "she's really beautiful. She's just like you!"

"Flattery will get you everywhere," laughed Sara as she reached over to Matt and kissed him on the cheek.

As they all studied the photo, they kept looking up at Sara to make comparisons.

"You could be sisters," said Julie. "Do you know how old she was when this was taken?"

"It was about three years before the fire, so she will have been thirty-two, according to Annie Carr's date of birth."

"That's a strange way to put it," said Julie, raising her eyebrows. "Are you doubting she was Annie Carr?"

"The notes say she claims to have taken the name from the real Annie Carr when she died in 1964." She paused and ran a hand through her hair. "I don't know what to believe, Julie; it's all rather confusing. The stories she told Dr Wright are incredibly convincing."

"Is this the only photo?" asked Pete.

"No, there were loads; Dr Wright just gave me a couple. She was reluctant to let me take most of them, in fact, initially, to let me see them at all."

"Really?" said Pete. "Why was that?"

Sara laughed and told them about the photo sessions.

"You said 'initially'," said Julie. "Did you see them eventually?"

"Yes," nodded Sara, smiling mysteriously.

"And?"

"Dr Wright was correct. They are really rather private."

"I didn't mean that," said Julie, wrinkling her mouth dismissively. "I meant, did they show you anything else of interest? You'd think if she'd lived through several centuries, she might have a few battle scars."

Sara thought about it. "No, there was nothing like that. Nothing I noticed, anyway. But it's an interesting point. Of course, she doesn't claim to have been a soldier."

Julie laughed. "I didn't mean it literally, Mom, I just thought, you know, you might expect, I don't know… something."

"I agree," said Sara, "perhaps I'll take a magnifying glass to the photos." Then she turned and tapped on the box of files. "Before we dig into this, there's something else Dr Wright gave me which is absolutely fascinating. I'll fetch it for you."

She walked over to the corner of the kitchen where the cardboard tube was leaning against the wall. Opening one end, she carefully pulled out the pencil drawing.

"This," she said, unrolling the drawing and holding it up, "is me as a child of about four. My mother drew it and gave it to Dr Wright."

"Cool!" exclaimed Julie excitedly. She took it and walked over to the fridge where the large stainless steel door had several magnetic ornaments holding up notes. She took four and placed one on each corner of the drawing, then stood back a couple of paces to view it.

"It's brilliant," said Pete quietly as he joined her. "Simply drawn, but with amazing skill." He turned to his wife. "It could also be a drawing of Julie at that age, don't you think, sweetheart?"

"Yes," agreed Sara, "that thought occurred to me too."

"OK," said Matt, returning to the counter and opening the box file. "How do you want to divvy these up?"

"I wondered about that," said Sara. "I scanned through them on the train last night and I think it would be better if we all read everything, just so we can each have the story first hand from my mother; from Annie. I started in detail at the beginning this morning, so I'm about two hours ahead. I suggest, Pete, that you start at the beginning now while Julie and I clear and Matt heads for the shower."

She quashed an emerging objection from Matt with a grimace and a pinch of her nose.

"Whoever's ready next can take the pages Pop's finished with and then pass them on."

"That'll be me," said Julie.

Sara picked up some legal pads and pencils from a side table. "I suggest we each make notes and then we'll compare them once we've all finished. Having skimmed through the whole lot, I can tell you that with Dr Wright's microscopic handwriting, we won't complete the job today."

"But once we have," said Matt, standing up and heading for the door, "we should have a lot of information to compare with stuff from the Internet. It should give us a good handle on whether our grandmother's story is based on any fact."

"You too!" said Julie in surprise. "You're coming round to *accepting* this story?"

"I'm keeping an open mind," replied Matt, shrugging. "Crazy though the story sounds, I suppose scientifically it might be possible, in which case, yeah, why not? Think how cool it would be to have a grandmother who was hundreds of years old. And anyway, you were talking about battle scars over the centuries just now, so you must be accepting it too."

"That's different," said Julie, tossing her head dismissively.

Pete scratched his head and half closed his eyes as an idea occurred to him. "Does she claim to have had any other children apart from you, Sara?"

Sara nodded. "Yes, several, although she says none of them was like her regarding the age and health thing. I was the only one."

Pete nodded. "Interesting," he said, smiling at Sara. "You could have nephews and nieces, well, half-nephews and nieces, several generations removed, all of whom are much older than you."

Matt scribbled something on a scrap of paper. "It wouldn't be difficult for you to be your own great grandmother," he announced.

"They say to be careful what you wish for," laughed Julie, "well, we should be careful who we marry. The potential family relationships are incredibly complicated."

Sunday morning saw Sara and Matt each with their own complete set of notes on Nancy Wright's interviews, while Pete, a meticulous worker, was still engrossed in them. Julie had gone out on a date the previous evening so she'd only covered around half the file.

"I guess the next step is to follow up some of the things we've found on the Internet," said Matt. "I'd like to start in the Caribbean. There's a lot of detail from the interviews and the name of an artist she claimed to have worked with. I'll get on with it now. What are you going to do, Sis?"

"Well," said Julie, "after I've finished going through Dr Wright's notes, I want to look at the beginning of Annie Carr's life, when she claimed she was born in Naples, Italy. Hey, Mom, you could be half-Italian. How cool is that?"

Sara laughed and shrugged her shoulders, Italian style. "Eh!" she exclaimed.

"Annie mentioned the name of her father," continued Julie, "even though she says she never met him. Since she thought she inherited her special genes from him, I'll check out his name to see if it leads anywhere."

She glanced at her mother who was now smiling wryly at them.

"What?"

"Nothing, dear," said Sara innocently.

"Oh, come on, Mom! Something's amusing you. What did I say that's so funny?"

Sara put a hand on Julie's arm. "It's just that yesterday you two were incredulous at the thought that Annie Carr's story might be true and virtually accusing each other of being ridiculous. Today, it's like you've accepted it totally."

"Haven't *you*?" Julie tossed her head defensively.

"Yes, I think I have after reading everything she said to Dr Wright. What surprises me is that Dr Wright doesn't give it any credence at all. She's adamant it's all made up."

"It's probably her professional pride," said Pete looking up from a sheet he was reading. "She's committed herself to a diagnosis and all the causes behind it, and she doesn't want to change it. It's interesting: if these notes were current, I mean, if they had been compiled yesterday from recent interviews, I'd side with Dr Wright. After all, these days it wouldn't be difficult to concoct a story like Annie Carr has produced by trawling the Internet for a few hours picking out people you fancy being and places you'd like to visit. Weird and still delusional perhaps, but easy to set up. However, the interviews aren't current. They took place in the early seventies, when to get information as detailed as all of this would have been incredibly hard. It would have taken, I don't know, an age, and that being the case, you have to ask yourself, why? Why bother? What's it all for?"

He tidied the pile of notes in front of him as he warmed to his theme.

"The point is that Annie Carr appears to have been a free spirit on the fringes of the drug culture in San Francisco; a young woman who had no college education, as far as we know, and who wasn't involved in academia. Anything but, in fact, and yet she would have had to undertake the most meticulous research for all of this. However, I think the really convincing point for me is that she was so young. How in heaven did she get hold of all this stuff in her relatively short life? Yes, she could have completely made it up, as if she were writing a story, but then it would fall apart under scrutiny. According to Dr Wright, it hasn't even come close to doing that. Everything she checked, absolutely everything, has supported the facts as described by Annie."

He sat back and joined his hands behind his head. "As Sherlock Holmes said: when you've eliminated the impossible, whatever remains, however improbable, must be the truth. I can't think of anything more improbable than Annie Carr really being hundreds of years old, but, hey, we used to believe the earth was flat. We certainly don't know everything about life and genetics and so on. I know almost nothing."

Matt nodded. "There is also the added factor of Mom. If you are like Annie Carr, Mom, assuming she is telling the truth, then you could be in for an interesting life that's hardly begun."

Sara looked aghast. "I can't even contemplate it. It's too difficult to imagine. I'm not sure I even want it; it's not natural."

"I'll tell you one thing," said Pete, standing and putting an arm around his wife's shoulder. "It's not something we should advertise. We must agree to keep our thoughts and conclusions very much within these four walls. No discussion with anyone else."

Pete and Sara had a lunch date at the golf club, so after some more reading, they left Matt and Julie in their respective rooms trawling information from the Internet.

When they returned three hours later, they found Matt pacing the living room floor, a pile of printouts in his hands.

"I thought you would never come back," he said by way of greeting. "You should see these."

"Yes, thanks, we had a good lunch," retorted Sara drily, her face deadpan.

Matt grunted. "Well, while you've been enjoying yourselves, your slaves have discovered some interesting material, oh esteemed one," he replied as he bent over in an elaborate bow.

He handed her a colour printout of a portrait.

"What do you think of that?" he beamed triumphantly.

"My heavens, Matt, where did you get this?" said Sara in shock as she scanned the painting.

"Show me," said Pete as he leaned over her shoulder. "Holy Moses!" he exclaimed. He took the print, laid it on a table and masked the hair with his hands.

"This could be you, Sara! Where did you find it, Matt?"

"It's staggering what's buried in the limitless archives of the Internet," said Matt, shrugging nonchalantly. "The painting is by the nineteenth-century painter Michel-Jean Cazabon, who worked in Trinidad in the eighteen thirties and forties. He seems to have had the market of the colonial ladies pretty much to himself, although he is better known for his landscapes of the island. This is a painting of a ... wait for it ... a Mrs Paola Lethrington, who—"

"—That's the name Annie Carr said she went by at that time and on that island!" interrupted Sara. "Paola Lethrington. That's amazing. I mean, who has ever heard of an obscure woman living and working in Trinidad?"

"Exactly," enthused Matt. "And look at this."

He handed his parents another sheet on which were printed two images, one of the portrait Sara was holding and one a copy of one of the photographs of Annie Carr.

"Cool, huh? Well, wait till you see these." He handed them another sheet with the same images, but with the hair and background cropped away, leaving just the faces.

"I masked off the unimportant bits in Photoshop. Paola even has your eyes, Mom. Pale grey. Look at the painting."

"I know. It was one of the first things I noticed," said Sara, unable to keep her eyes off the images. "Did you find anything about her?"

"Not a lot. Apparently she was a seamstress, which is what Annie Carr claimed and which Dr Wright witnessed first hand in Annie–"

"Which, on its own, doesn't mean much," said Pete, his lawyer's mind reducing the fact to minor significance. "Many women can sew."

"Keep your sexist generalizations to the courtroom, Pete Farsley," sniffed Sara.

"I appreciate that, Pop, but it's all grist to the mill," retaliated Matt. "Anyway, I also discovered Paola Lethrington was an artist herself, although I could find no examples of her work. There's nothing in the Port of Spain museum, at least not the online collection."

"So you're proposing popping down to Trinidad, are you?" asked Sara, with a wry smile.

"Not immediately," said Matt in all seriousness, "but I am proposing to go to the Boston Museum of Fine Arts tomorrow to see if they have any art experts who know anything more. After that, I'll check out the better art galleries and shops in town."

"You're going to be busy. I take it you don't have any exams tomorrow."

"You know they don't start for a couple of weeks, Mom, and I'm more than ready. I need a break from all that stuff."

"Where's Julie?" said Sara. "Have you shown her this?"

"Sure. She's in her room chasing up stuff on the original Paola's father."

"Remind me, what was her name in Naples?" asked Pete.

"Paola Santini."

"Yes, of course," he nodded.

Just then, Julie came down to join them.

"Hi Mom. Hi Pop. You've seen that picture, then? Isn't it amazing?"

"Staggering," agreed her father. "Have you found anything?"

"A little, yes, but nothing so impressive," nodded Julie. "I've discovered that Stefano Crispi, the name Annie Carr gave for Paola Santini's father, really did exist and that he was an artist in Naples in the early part of the sixteenth century. I had to dig a long way just to find his name, which is interesting, since again, how would Annie Carr have come up with that information in the seventies? I mean, it was in an obscure reference in some British Museum archive, not the Encyclopaedia Britannica or anything – there was no mention of him in that. Anyway, he existed and, in the end, I found a couple of examples of his work, both portraits. They're beautiful, really amazing. I don't know why he wasn't better known. There's not much about his life though and no association with anyone called Paola Santini."

"Disappointing," said Sara. "Have you printed out his portraits, or shall I come to view them on your computer?"

"I'll print them, Mom. My room's even more of a mess than normal. There are notes and papers lying everywhere."

A few minutes later, they were all gathered around the two printouts. One was of a raven-haired, olive-skinned woman in her early twenties, her almost black eyes capturing the viewer's attention immediately as she seemed to be about to say something. The subject, unknown to any of them, was Stefano Crispi's sister-in-law, Anna, who had married the hapless Gianni in Naples in 1501. The painting was completed in the happier times before Gianni's murder. After Stefano disappeared in 1517, following the discovery of his secret by his profoundly religious wife, Francesca, Anna always kept the painting hidden away.

The other painting was a portrait of a young Renaissance figure with a fringe of tight black ringlets, his high-cut, collarless scarlet tunic over a gold undergarment giving him an almost clerical look. Sara stared at the pale eyes looking back at her.

"I wonder what his story was," she mused.

She put the printout down and picked up the one of the young woman again. There was something about it.

"May I?" asked Pete as he reached over and took it from her. He held it out, not realising he was holding a painting of his wife's great aunt. He turned his head from the painting to Sara and then back again.

"You know," he began, "I–"

"Oh, Pete! Don't be ridiculous! You seem to think every painting or photograph you see at the moment looks like me. I can't be related to every Renaissance woman!"

Chapter 22

Palo Melliff was amazed at how quickly Marcus Dayton picked the lock on the door to Nancy Wright's practice. He'd seen it done in the movies, but that was just the movies where everything was fake. Dayton, with a couple of micro-picks he'd inserted into the keyway, had taken no more than ten seconds. He noticed the satisfied smile on Dayton's face; he must have done this hundreds of times.

Once in, it was Melliff's turn to demonstrate his expertise and override the alarm. He had thirty seconds flat. While lock picking was a mystery to him, alarms were a speciality and he was through with five seconds to go.

As they entered the outer office, Dayton paused to look around, taking note of everything.

"Melliff, check the secretary's diary and computer for a record of our mystery woman. She must have written her name down somewhere. I'll go into the good doctor's consulting room to see if she stores any patient records there."

Dayton had just completed his survey of Nancy Wright's office and picked the lock of the filing cabinet in the corner when he heard Palo come into the room.

"Got it, sir. Her name's Sara Farsley and she lives in Boston. I have her cell number. She's some sort of research student."

"Farsley," replied Dayton thoughtfully as he started to flick through the contents of the filing cabinet. "That sounds like a fairly unusual name; it shouldn't be too difficult to track her down."

"Not a problem, sir, I'll have her address as soon as we get back upstairs."

Dayton nodded as he perused the file labels. "The doctor keeps meticulous notes. Let's see, yes, this looks promising."

He lifted a set of files from a sleeve labelled '*Annie Carr. Interview notes 1970 – 1971. Sawpine Ridge*'.

"Annie Carr – AC. This has to be the woman. Take these, Melliff!" He passed the files to Palo and then turned back to the filing cabinet. "There must be some more," he muttered to himself as he continued checking. "Yes, here they are."

He pulled out the files covering Nancy's remaining interviews with Annie until her departure in 1972.

He was about to open the file to browse its contents when he heard an exclamation from behind him.

"Holy shit! This is unbelievable!"

Dayton turned to see his assistant staring in amazement at the top photograph of a set he'd just removed from an envelope in the file. "This should grab your attention, boss," said Melliff, passing the print to him.

Taking the photograph, Dayton shone his flashlight onto it – it was a head and shoulders shot of Annie and Nancy laughing at the camera. His eyes fell immediately onto Annie's face, the face he'd been studying so carefully over the past month since Palo found the images of Dolores di Napoli. He smiled in satisfaction. This was exactly what he'd hoped for.

Then he remembered Nancy Wright's account of her patient AC in her textbook. This was the woman who was supposed to have perished in the fire at the mental institution. He rubbed his chin thoughtfully as he stared at Annie's picture: he'd faked his own death on many occasions.

"Pass me the rest, Melliff," he said, holding out his hand while continuing to study the photo. When there was no answer, he looked up to see Palo leafing through the other photos, his eyes wide and a lascivious smile on his face.

"Melliff!" snapped Dayton. He saw his pet nerd blush as he hastily stacked the photos and handed them over.

"Think maybe I'll get some sessions with this shrink," Palo leered.

Dayton glanced at the pictures. "I doubt this is part of her normal treatment protocol and anyway, she's an old woman now; she won't look like that anymore."

He nodded towards the papers that Palo had placed on the coffee table when he removed the photos.

"Bring those files," he said. "We'll put them with the others, take them upstairs, copy the lot and then return them. And while we're at it, we'll make copies of these." He waved the photos in his hands.

As he turned to leave, the beam from his flashlight fell on the painting of Nancy hanging over the fireplace. He walked over to it and studied it closely, playing the light on different areas. He frowned, surprised at the quality. He was passionate about fine art, particularly Renaissance works, and with a collection that included a number of old masters, he considered himself something of an expert. The work hanging on the wall in front of him wasn't just some competently painted portrait from one of the many studios around town, it was a masterpiece. The subject was obviously the other woman in the photographs, the psychiatrist, and the signature – Annie Carr!

He stared at the painting, his mind working overtime. Annie Carr's story of being a skilled painter that Wright had described in her book was clearly true. If Annie had used these Victorian fashions in her portrait, she must have had a reason. Could there be paintings from other eras by the same hand?

"Melliff!" he barked. "Does your image comparison software run to comparing paintings, one against the other?"

"Er, no … no, sir, it doesn't," stuttered Palo, surprised by the intensity of the question. "That's a whole nother game."

"See if there's anyone who can do it. When we return these files, bring your camera with you. I want a decent shot of this painting."

"Yes, sir."

Dayton looked again at the portrait. He wondered if a photograph would be good enough. Perhaps he should steal it. He nodded to himself. No need for that tonight; he had free access to the offices and he could return whenever he pleased.

Two hours later, the contents of the files had been carefully copied along with the photographs. Satisfied everything was as they'd found it, Dayton was about to lock up Nancy Wright's offices when

190

he suddenly remembered Sara Farsley. Melliff had said she had been in the offices for more than two hours and that she'd left carrying a box. She probably had a copy of the notes as well. He turned to the armchairs and imagined the two women talking. Wright was a shrink and used to making notes on everyone. He wondered if she had made any on the Farsley woman.

"I think we've overlooked something," he said to Melliff, who was waiting by the office door to reset the alarm.

He opened the filing cabinet again and quickly found what he was looking for.

"'*Sara Farsley*'," he read. He opened the file and saw the notes were the results of a medical examination. He glanced at them and nodded. Very interesting.

"Melliff," he called. "Run upstairs and make a copy of this as well."

Ten minutes later, Nancy Wright's office was locked and secure. Settling into a large armchair in the upstairs office, Marcus Dayton began reading through the files and the long story of Annie Carr's life. However, unlike the doubting psychiatrist, he was prepared to believe every word of it.

Chapter 23

M att checked online with the Boston Museum of Fine Arts for mention of Paola Lethrington and found nothing. However, he knew that behind the world-renowned museum's public collection of works, there must be an extensive archive. Perhaps not all of it was catalogued for Internet searching. Keen to follow up on his findings so far, the next morning he walked the few blocks from the Farsley home to the museum to make enquiries.

Assistant curator for nineteenth-century Art of the Americas, Olivia Kimble, took off her owl-like magnifiers and polished them thoughtfully as she trawled through her mental files.

"Paola Lethrington? You know, that does ring a little bell. Trouble is it's a bit faint."

She smiled thinly at Matt as he stood in front of the information desk at the entrance to the Americas section.

He'd tried the museum's own search points, found nothing, and resorted to the old-fashioned approach: he'd asked somebody. That somebody scratched her head, typed a few words on a keyboard, nodded and lifted a phone. The result, in the form of the conservatively dressed, forty-something Ms Kimble, was now standing before him, slightly irritated that the good-looking Mr Farsley whose name she'd been given wasn't a tad older.

"She was an artist, an amateur I think, in the Caribbean in the nineteenth century," Matt offered. "In Trinidad," he added.

Olivia nodded, distracted as her human hard drive whirled. She was regarded as a world expert on much of the art of the Americas, but even her knowledge was a little thin when it came to the Caribbean.

"Trinidad?" she repeated. Then she nodded as something flagged in her mind. "Yes, of course. The name that comes to mind immediately when Trinidad is mentioned, is Cazabon." She smiled patronisingly.

"Michel-Jean Cazabon?" suggested Matt, thinking that 'immediately' in Ms Kimble's case was a relative term.

"The very one." The corners of Olivia's mouth twitched downwards, her smile collapsing. She was nonplussed that this young man still seemed to be ahead of her.

"He painted at least one portrait of Paola Lethrington in Trinidad," continued Matt. "But it's her paintings we're interested in; we wondered if the museum happened to have any of her work."

"We?" asked Ms Kimble.

"My family and I," replied Matt. "We're fairly sure Paola Lethrington is an ancestor, although her actual name has only recently come to light. It's always been said there was a female artist in our history, in the Caribbean."

He smiled innocently, hoping his ad-libbed embellishment of the Farsley family's genealogy rang true.

He opened the file he was carrying and removed a printout of the Cazabon painting. "I found this in an obscure archive that the British Museum in London, England had a link to," he said, as he handed it to Olivia.

She peered at the print. "Mmm, it appears to be very competently painted," she said, rather condescendingly it seemed to Matt. "Typical of the period."

She handed it back.

"Do you know if you do?" asked Matt.

"Do what?"

"Have any of Paola Lethrington's work."

She studied him with a slight frown, the lenses of her glasses making her eyes disturbingly large.

"No, I'm almost sure we don't," she said after a pause. "However, you're right; she was an artist. It's coming back to me now. Very minor, of course. I doubt there's any of her work here in Boston. If you give me a moment, I'll check."

With that, she turned and marched off through a door, leaving Matt to wonder at her world.

A moment turned into several minutes and several minutes into about fifteen before a triumphant-looking Ms Kimble reemerged from wherever she'd been to check.

"I was right," she announced gleefully across the large room to where Matt was studying a hugely complex painting of Custer's Last Stand. "Nothing here in the museum, and nothing that is known about in Boston. I called a couple of contacts in the more reputable art galleries and they confirmed that. They'd heard of her, though, and both said she was rather good. Underrated even, from the very little they'd seen of her work."

She paused, clasping her hands together protectively across her chest.

"Do you have any other suggestions?" asked Matt, disappointed. "Any ideas as to where I might go next?"

"Of course!" beamed Ms Kimble, as if she'd just been waiting for him to ask. "Here!" She produced a card and offered it to Matt. "There's a wonderful man; don't know why I didn't think of him before. Ryder-Hyde, in New York City. The last word in Caribbean art. He runs a rabbit warren of a shop in The West Village. I've written his address on my card. Be sure to give him my regards."

Not totally convinced he'd exhausted every avenue, Matt spent the rest of the day browsing the art history section of the public library. When that drew another blank, he wandered through three bookshops that specialised in art, with the same result. It was only late in the day, in an antiquarian bookshop where he located a volume on Central American nineteenth-century art, that he even found a passing mention of Paola Lethrington. Frustratingly, there was not a single example of her work.

He arrived back home at seven, tired and hungry, announcing as he walked in that he was off to New York City the following day on the hunt for Paola Lethrington.

"Do you want me to come too?" offered Sara.

"It's fine, Mom, really. I'm a big boy now. I can pass the time on the train chasing up more sources on the Net for the various artists Annie Carr claims to have been."

He paused, feigning a sudden interest in his fingernails. "If I get really bored or run out of steam, I can always study some more for the exams."

Sara harrumphed. "I think maybe you should be doing that anyway, instead of hightailing off to NYC."

"Stop worrying, Mom, I've got the exams covered," he grinned.

Catching the same train as his mother had the week before, Matt arrived the following lunchtime at Penn station and jumped on the subway. By one fifteen, after a short stroll through Greenwich Village, he was standing outside the run-down storefront of Bibliophilia, the bookstore whose name and address Olivia Kimble had scribbled on the back of her card. On each side were several other stores dealing in a variety of old and antique artifacts. At either end of the short street that housed them, yellow cabs, buses and trucks thundered their way through the wider Lower Manhattan streets, but here, time seemed to have stood still. Peeling shop signs were the order of the day, Bibliophilia's worse than most, the remains of its ornate lettering difficult to read owing to decades of attrition from roasting summers, bitter winters and negligible maintenance. The contents of the one window that carried anything comprised a battered set of ancient encyclopaedias, their titles in French, their spines separating glacially but inexorably from their bindings. Otherwise, the shelf on which they stood was a desert of dust. A partition screened the shop interior from easy view from the street, the grime on the windows aiding and abetting it in its task.

Matt pushed open the entrance door and somewhere miles away there was the hint of a bell tinkling, no more really than a slight movement of air. He looked around to take in the shop and was struck by the spectacle of literally thousands of books occupying almost every inch of floor space and every nook and cranny of the countless shelves that disappeared into the gloom. With the boundaries ill-defined, the world of books before him seemed to Matt to be a continuum that defied any attempts by his eyes to discern where it ended. It was an ocean of literature that soared upwards and backwards in apparently limitless profusion.

His visual exploration was interrupted by a cough. He turned to see what appeared to be an elderly bloodhound in a tweed suit propped up in a battered, brown leather armchair by an assorted jumble of threadbare, silk cushions. Next to this slightly disturbing vision was an ancient, wooden desk, its surface largely obscured by numerous piles of untidily stacked books. A huge old-fashioned cash register stood on an adjacent shelf that bowed uncomfortably under the weight of its brass-and-steel burden. The bloodhound, whose few wisps of hair were pure white, looked up at Matt over a pair of gold-rimmed, half-frame spectacles perched on the end of his patrician nose. In his left hand he was holding a slim, leather-bound book, its pages yellowing and delicate; in his right, a large, brass-rimmed magnifying glass.

"May I help you?" The voice was surprisingly rich, the accent British, refined, like a lord lifted from an ancient castle. In those four brief words, it carried an air of confidence, of no-nonsense assurance.

"I sure hope so, sir," said Matt, very much in awe of the man. "I've come all the way from Boston to see you."

The ancient bookseller's eyes, already buried in folds of wrinkles, creased further in amusement.

"Well, I've come all the way from the Cotswolds to be here, but that was a while ago."

"The Cotswolds?" said Matt, his geography failing him and the man's humour passing him by.

"Picturesque spot in the Old Country. Of no import. What's that card you're clutching as if your life depended upon it?"

Matt glanced down at the card and handed it to the man. "Ms Olivia Kimble from the Boston Museum of Fine Arts gave it to me along with your address. She said you might be able to help me."

The bookseller chuckled. "Olivia Kimble. Did she now? It's Dr Olivia Kimble, you know, very eminent lady. You must have interested her. If she sent you here, your inquiry must be an obscure one."

The man suddenly stirred, carefully placed the book he'd been reading on top of one of the smaller piles on the desk and slowly hauled himself to his feet, leaning heavily on the arms of the armchair to do so. As he straightened, Matt was surprised how tall he was. Nestled in the armchair he had seemed small, reduced; but standing he matched Matt's six foot one, a curve in his back evidence that in his youth he must have been even taller.

The man held out his hand. "Forgetting my manners. Ryder-Hyde. How may I help you, young man all the way from Boston?"

Matt shook his hand, noting the firm grip. "Matthew Farsley, Mr Ryder-Hyde. Matt. I'm very pleased to meet you. I'm looking for information on a rather obscure, nineteenth-century artist called Paola Lethrington. She worked in–"

"–Trinidad. Eighteen thirties," interrupted Ryder-Hyde. "Very talented lady, from the little I have seen of her work. You are right, young man; she is certainly obscure. Why are you interested in her?"

Matt smiled. From what Olivia Kimble had told him, he wasn't surprised Ryder-Hyde knew of Paola Lethrington. He trotted out the story about his search for ancestors.

Ryder-Hyde was staring into Matt's eyes, but it seemed to Matt that his mind was elsewhere. The old man grunted and turned to stare at the labyrinth of books that was his world, his left hand rubbing at his chin.

"Yes," he said. "That's the one! Up there! Off you go!"

He pointed a bony finger into the depths of the shelves, and with a couple of flicks of his wrist, indicated to Matt the direction he wanted him to follow.

"About halfway along there. You'll need the ladder. Top shelf."

Matt followed the waving finger and made his way along the narrow lane between two looming towers of shelves. As he walked, motes of dust rose from every surface, tickled gently by the air he was disturbing, air unused to such intrusion. He peered into the gloom for signs of a stepladder and saw to his horror that each aisle had a vertical ladder attached to the top- and bottommost shelves with rollers that allowed it to slide the length of the aisle. Matt's concern as he eyed the mechanism was that his weight would topple the lot.

He heard a chuckle from Ryder-Hyde. "Don't look so worried, young man, those ladders are stronger than they look. Been doing a sterling job for nearly a century."

That's precisely why I *am* worried, thought Matt as he carefully pulled the ladder from the far end of the aisle to the halfway point. To his surprise, the ladder moved fluidly.

"Which shelf, Mr Ryder-Hyde?" he called.

"Top one. About there. Up you go!"

"What am I looking for?"

"Clutterworth's Caribbean Collection. Largish volume. Leather bound. Can't miss it."

Matt gingerly put one foot and then the other on the bottom rung of the ladder, allowing the structure to take his weight. As he climbed, more dust lifted and swirled as he breathed onto the shelves – the books were only a couple of inches from his nose. Suddenly the dust was too much and he sneezed violently, shaking the whole stack. The ladder rolled gently sideways and he grabbed at a shelf. He heard another laugh from below.

"Should have told you to put the brake on. You'll turn the whole thing into a roller coaster if you're not careful," cackled Ryder-Hyde, evidently enjoying the entertainment and not in the least worried.

Matt continued upwards to the top shelf, which was about twelve feet from the ground. Gripping the ladder tightly, he tried to read the titles of the volumes crammed onto the shelves. All were large and leather-bound and all appeared to be collections of art from around the world from the eighteen and nineteen hundreds. Then he saw it, the long words of the title separated with hyphens to makes them fit on the spine. 'Clutter-worth's Carib-bean Collec-tion'. He pulled at the book, but it resisted. He pulled harder and it came free from its companions with a start. Matt took its weight, realizing as he did so that he was holding about ten pounds of book. He struggled not to drop it as the motion of his arm with the weight in his hand set the ladder rolling again, this time faster. The ladder set off along the stack in the direction of the front of the store until it hit the stops in its mechanism at the end of the runners. The jolt spun Matt around and he found himself hanging by his left arm as his right arm flailed into space, his hand still firmly grasping the enormous book. He hung there for a few seconds to regain his equilibrium, convinced the entire stack was about to collapse. However, the old man was right: despite creaking to register its discontent at the assault on its person, the shelving was made of strong stuff and remained intact. Matt clambered down the ladder, relieved to be back on the ground.

He looked up to see Ryder-Hyde sitting in his armchair, wiping his eyes with an enormous spotted handkerchief.

"Most excitement we've had in here for years," he chortled. "Put that tome on the desk; too heavy for me to lift."

Matt looked for a suitable spot and carefully moved several piles of books while Ryder-Hyde looked on in bemusement, as if creating a completely empty space for a book was a novel idea that had never occurred to him.

The bookseller sat forward, opened the book to its first page and read the title. He then turned the page and started to read the introduction. Matt wondered if he was going to make his way slowly through the entire book.

"Fascinating," muttered Ryder-Hyde. "Quite fascinating. Must be forty years since I last looked as this. That's right; I remember now. In the 1970s. Someone came in asking about Cazabon. Didn't buy it, obviously. Your good fortune, heh?"

Matt shook his head in amazement as he watched the bookseller turn to the 'Contents' page and run his finger down it.

"There we are," said Ryder-Hyde, "pages one hundred and twelve to one hundred and fourteen."

Turning several pages at a time, he opened the book to page one hundred and twelve. Matt looked over his shoulder and felt a pang of disappointment. The plates were halftone prints.

"When was the book published, Mr Ryder-Hyde?"

"Nineteen thirties. Why?"

"Are all the prints this quality?"

"Afraid so, young man. All were in those days. Costly business printing plates, even in black and white. Colour was very rare, if that's what you were hoping for. Detail's not too bad, though."

Matt pulled on his bottom lip, not really agreeing but saying nothing as he took in the print on the left side first. It was a portrait that was little more than a sketch, a half-profile of a young woman, her long, dark hair drawn up and hanging in tight ringlets. She was wearing what appeared to be a fine lace blouse – the detail was limited since the artist had vignetted the oval composition. However, it was the eyes and shape of the face that caught his eye. He was immediately convinced he was looking at Annie Carr in nineteenth-century costume.

He looked down at the description. '*Self-Portrait by Mrs Paola Lethrington c.1836. From a private collection*'.

He turned his attention to the print on the opposite page. It was another portrait. This one, of a woman in her forties with a distinctly darker skin, was far more detailed than the sketch of the artist. The caption read 'Portrait of Mrs Maude Duchamp by Mrs Paola Lethrington c.1839'.

Matt turned the page. There was a third print ascribed to Paola Lethrington, a view of sailing boats in a harbour, also detailed and also from a private collection: 'Port of Spain, Trinidad c.1840'.

Matt turned back to the self-portrait and studied it further. After a few moments he glanced at Ryder-Hyde to find the bookseller scrutinising him, shrewd amusement in his eyes.

"Interest you, that one, young man?" he said. "Looked like you'd seen a ghost when your eyes fell on it."

Matt smiled nervously and nodded. "Yes, she's quite like my grandmother as a young woman."

He opened the folder he'd been carrying and pulled out a print of one of the photos of Annie Carr taken by Nancy Wright in the 1970s. "Do you agree?"

Ryder-Hyde took the photo and studied it through his magnifying glass. He then moved his attention to the print in the book.

"Good gracious me!" he exclaimed. "Quite remarkable. Extraordinary. Not much doubt, I should say. Strong genes in your family, eh?"

Matt nodded. "Yes, my mother bears quite a resemblance too."

He pointed to the text under the prints. "Where it says 'From a private collection', do you have any idea where that was?"

"It's fairly unlikely they would have given any detail. Cagey lot in those days. Let's have a look."

He turned back to the introduction and scanned through it. "Mmm, just as I thought, no details. I'm afraid it could have come from anywhere. I know Clutterworth got most of his stuff from collections in the US and wealthy families in the countries or islands he was touring, as well as local museums. That was back in the 1920s and '30s. I also know it took him over ten years to put this book together. Met his son once. Arrogant man. Of course, I was only starting out then. Knew nobody." He sighed as his memories drifted back several decades. "Remarkable, though, that family likeness," he added quietly.

"And you've no way of knowing where the originals of these pictures might be, or even if they still exist?" asked Matt, knowing he was clutching at straws.

"Absolutely none at all, I'm afraid."

Matt chewed his bottom lip. "Mr Ryder-Hyde, I'm sure I couldn't afford to buy this book; it must be priceless. However, would you mind very much if I took photos of the three Paola Lethrington pages with my phone? It has a very good camera."

"With your telephone? Good Lord!" exclaimed Ryder-Hyde, glancing in disbelief to his own huge Bakelite telephone set with its circular dial, sitting precariously on the corner of the desk.

He turned back to Matt. "By all means, young man, go ahead."

He watched in wonder as Matt took out his smartphone and took several shots of each of the three prints. He studied the results and when he was satisfied, he showed the gallery of shots to Ryder-Hyde, enlarging them with his fingers to show the detail.

Ryder-Hyde shook his head. "Quite beyond me, this modern technology. I'm surprised you didn't just talk to the telephone to tell it what to do." He chuckled to himself at the absurdity of the idea.

"Actually ..." started Matt, and then thought better of it.

"One thing," continued Ryder-Hyde, his fingers drumming on the cover of one of the hundreds of books on his desk. "I wouldn't say the book is priceless, although it is worth a bob or two. Can't imagine there are too many copies around. Probably not that many printed in the first place. Don't know how publishers made money in those days."

He paused and puckered his mouth, adding a whole new terrain of creases to the complex hinterland of peaks and valleys already criss-crossing his cheeks.

"I'll make a deal with you, young man. Why don't you take the book with you? Show your family. Bet your mother would love to see it. Is your grandmother still alive? Handsome woman!"

"Er, no, she isn't. But Mr Ryder-Hyde, I can't just take this book."

"Of course you can! You seem like a genuine young man, and you have come all the way from Boston. Honest sort of place. Take it, as long as you promise to look after it. If your family wants to buy it, give me a call and we'll discuss a price. If not, take as many photographs of the prints as you like and then bring it back. All the same to me. Books are to be looked at, to be wondered at; to inform and delight. They don't exist just to sit on some dusty shelf for decades. Might as well not exist at all if that were the case. Off you go now. Delighted to have met you."

He paused and then added wistfully. "Pity about your grandmother."

Chapter 24

The door had hardly opened before Matt was calling out to his family.

"Mom! Pop! Sis! Come here! Take a look at this!"

Sara was in the kitchen dishing up dinner for Matt. He'd called ahead to tell her he would be late, but had given her no inkling of his news.

Matt proudly pulled the large leather-bound volume out of his shoulder bag and placed it carefully on the dining table.

"Wow! Impressive!" exclaimed Julie, rushing into the room. "How did you pay for it?"

"I sold you into white slavery. Can you go pack a bag?"

Sara wiped her hands on a dish towel and walked over to where they were standing.

"Seriously, Matt, a book like this must cost a fortune. Where did you get it?"

Matt laughed at their reaction. "Does it matter what it cost? Don't you want to know what's inside it?"

"Of course we want to know, Matt," nodded Sara, touching the leather carefully, as if it were porcelain and might break. "It's just that ..."

"Don't worry, Mom, I didn't steal it. It's on loan, with an option of buying it if we want it. Just take a look at this print."

He opened the book to the self-portrait sketch of Paola Lethrington and stood back to let the two women see it clearly.

"My heavens!" gasped Sara. "Even though it's not the best of prints – it looks like the sort of print you'd get in a newspaper – it's still incredible. The likeness to Annie Carr, to my mother, is indisputable."

"Here," said Matt, handing his mother the print of the photo of Annie. "I was blown away when I put them side by side. As you say, the quality isn't brilliant, which is disappointing, but the similarity is beyond doubt. Unfortunately, it seems the present location of the original drawing, assuming it still exists, is unknown."

He was about to recount the story of his day when Pete Farsley came in from the utility room where he'd been cleaning his golf shoes and wanted to be brought up to speed. Like the others, he couldn't take his eyes off the print.

"So that's it," said Matt, as he finished telling them about the eccentric Ralph Ryder-Hyde and his bookshop. "I don't know where we go from here. We can't search every bookshop in the US and the Caribbean. Although a trip to Trinidad could be fun."

"Yes," agreed his father. "What we've got so far is all very convincing, even if it does defy logic. However, if we put that little consideration to one side and follow Mr Holmes' improbable, what have we got?"

He held up a hand to count off fingers.

"One. We have a long and very detailed account from a supposedly mentally unstable woman who claimed she was hundreds of years old.

"Two. In support of her claim we have photographs of the two people she said she was in the immediate past that show an incredible similarity to her.

"Three. We now have a print from the 1830s of a self-portrait of another person she claimed to have been, but we know nothing about whom she claimed to have been between that person – Paola Lethrington – and the movie actress."

Julie frowned. "I don't understand."

"It's simple," said her father. "Annie told Dr Wright that she left Trinidad in 1867 and came to the States, but she doesn't seem to have given her any details of what she was called or what she did until she became the actress nearly forty years later. I guess Dr Wright overlooked asking her."

"OK," said Julie.

"Four," continued Pete. "We have cross-referenced some of her account with historical facts and we have found a significant number of points to be true and, perhaps as importantly, nothing that contradicts anything she said. We've even, thanks to Julie, shown the man she claimed to have been her father really did exist and that he was an artist – a brilliant one. There's even a possible family likeness in the subject of one of his paintings, which might be a self-portrait. Also, many of these points are incredibly obscure. It would have been very hard to access them in the days before the existence of the Internet. I really can't imagine how the young Annie Carr would have had the resources.

"And lastly, we have Mom, who we now know with almost total certainty is Annie Carr's daughter and who has the same incredible health that Annie Carr claimed, with some supporting evidence from Dr Wright. In addition, Mom appears to be staying young, just like Annie Carr said she did. Only time will tell on that one, but with every passing year, the case for it will either strengthen, or the whole story will fall apart.

"As you say, Matt, where do we go from here? We know almost certainly that Annie Carr is dead, which is a tragedy. However, there are other questions. Annie thought her father was the same as she was. Is it possible that he is still alive today? It's not beyond the bounds of possibility, assuming he hasn't died in an accident or been killed, although I should assume the statistics for that must increase with time. The trouble is there is just no way of knowing. After all, as Annie pointed out – and it would have been the same for her father – it would have been incredibly dangerous for their secret to be discovered, so they would do everything to cover it up. That would mean changing identities, places where they live, etc., so we are unlikely to get much response from an ad in the newspaper asking for anyone over five hundred years old to contact us in confidence."

Sara laughed. "On the contrary, I think we'd have legions of loonies and weirdos calling us. But you're right, Pete, we can only go so far on this, only compare so many paintings before we are one hundred percent sure, instead of just ninety-nine!"

"I don't know," said Matt. "It would be good to get a definitive answer. I wonder if there is anyone who can compare the work of artists to say whether the same person painted or drew two particular works. A forgery expert, for example."

Pete shook his head. "I'm sure such an animal would couch his opinions in ifs, buts and maybes. Too many variables, I suspect."

Suddenly a thought occurred to him and he grinned at his wife.

"What?" said Sara, immediately suspicious.

"You, Mrs Farsley, are really the centre of what this investigation is all about. Now, when Annie Carr was the focus and Dr Wright was in charge, she had the bright idea of taking photos every year or so to–"

"If you think I'm stripping off to let you produce a whole load of photos of me scantily clad, you can think again, Pete Farsley! And you two can stop leering as well," she replied indignantly, eyeballing Matt and Julie.

"You know, Mom," said Julie, with a wicked smile, "the idea's not without merit."

"Julie, I–"

"I don't mean taking a load of pin-up shots, just some facial pics of you, and some close-ups of your hands and feet … and some full body shots–" she held up a hand as her mother started to object again, "–in a bikini or swimsuit, Mom, not your underwear. They'd be very valuable as a long-term record. We could do it all very scientifically, take the same shots on the same day every year, until I'm so old I look like your grandmother!"

"That I doubt, Julie Farsley," muttered Sara. "However, I can see that given strict rules," she glared at Pete, who held up his hands in innocence, "it might be worthwhile."

"Well, if we want to copy the prints in this book, we need to get a decent camera anyway, so we might as well put it to some good use," said Pete, very pleased with himself.

Sara sighed. "Pete, we just need a camera and a flash, not a full professional photographer's studio. OK?"

Despite the new project, the Farsleys couldn't shake off the negative feeling that they'd reached the end of the road. Matt, in particular, was frustrated and wanted more. So when two days later he got a phone call from Ralph Ryder-Hyde, he thought he'd won the lottery.

"Been doing a bit of sniffing around," said the bookseller after he'd introduced himself formally to Sara and been passed to Matt. "Contacted a few old colleagues in the business I haven't seen for years. Or at least I tried to. Found some of them had died. Terrible shame," he mused absently. "Anyway, not all of them have shuffled off just yet. I found one, Morgan Crabtree. Owns a gallery in Williamsburg, Virginia. Tells me he's got a couple of Lethringtons. Bought them recently. From his description of one, it sounds rather like the self-portrait. That would be interesting, don't you think?"

Matt let out a whoop and punched the air.

"Yes, thought that would make your day, as I believe they say," Matt heard Ryder-Hyde saying when he put the receiver back to his ear. "Now you must tell old Crabtree he's to give you a good price, if you want to buy them. Tell him I insist. He can be a bit of a shark, if I remember rightly, something of a reputation, but genuine enough underneath it all. Get your mother to talk to him. He likes the ladies."

Matt put the phone down and spun on his heels to face his mother, a huge grin on his face. "Is Pop playing golf on Saturday as usual, Mom?"

"Unless a comet strikes the earth, yes, Matt, he is. Why?"

"I think I might be able to persuade him to change his mind," he said, taking hold of his mother in his arms, lifting her off her feet and spinning her around.

"Woohoo!" he yelled.

Chapter 25

Marcus Dayton sat by his all-glass desk, his chair turned towards the floor-to-ceiling windows that looked out onto the stunning fortieth-floor view of Manhattan, but his eyes failed to register it.

He had just read through the entire set of notes he'd copied from Nancy Wright's files for the sixth time, following the same protocol he always adopted with everything he did: the more times you study the facts, the more the small, easily overlooked details come to light.

There was no doubt in his mind that Annie Carr's story was true, no doubt whatsoever. She was born in 1518, of that he was sure. What he was less sure of was whether she died in 1975 as everyone thought. Yes, the evidence was strong: the fire had been severe and she had been last seen at the heart of it. But Annie was resourceful: she had overcome many potentially fatal threats during her more than four hundred and fifty years. She had faked her own death on more than one occasion; why not on this occasion? The problem was that the circumstances didn't quite add up. If Annie had deliberately started the fire as a means of creating chaos at the mental institution, she had succeeded. All she'd needed to do then was wait for the right moment and flee into the forest. She wouldn't have to go back into the burning building; to do so would have been inviting disaster.

Dayton's eyes continued to roam, focusing on nothing while he considered the possibilities, trying to think as Annie would have thought. Yes – suppose it had been planned, her returning to the building? Planned and carefully executed. It was brilliant. If it were thought she'd died, they wouldn't go looking for her, whereas if it were thought she'd escaped, they would have continued their search and hunted her down. They would then have blamed all those deaths in the fire on her, making her chances of escaping the gas chamber minuscule.

He nodded, thinking the plan through, polishing it, refining it, like Annie would have done. It was a good plan; not without risk, but a good plan. The sort of plan he would make. The sort of plan he had made before and would no doubt make again. Annie Carr was like him. A survivor. She had survived for several centuries. He, Marcus Dayton, had survived for many more and yet, apart from just one child, his beloved daughter, Emma, he'd never met anyone else like himself, although he was convinced they must exist. He'd known that for as long as he'd known about himself and he had searched forever, always looking for a sign. He spun his chair round to face the huge photograph of his daughter as he often did when he was looking for inspiration. Her eyes looked back at him, so loving, so young, so full of life and the promise of a future as long as his past. He exhaled slowly and sadly, the emotion rising in his chest. That future had been snatched from her just when their plans were starting to take shape. He held himself responsible for her death; he'd been careless. But he would continue; he had to. It was what he wanted; what Emma would have wanted.

He thought again of Annie Carr. She had to be alive, had to be. She was the closest he'd ever come. It would be too cruel a twist of fate for her to have died so recently.

There was, of course, the Farsley woman, Annie's daughter. There was a chance that she was also like him, quite a good chance if her health was anything to go by – the shrink's medical report indicated the woman had the body and general condition of someone younger than her forty-six years. However, he wanted to be sure, absolutely sure. The Farsley woman could wait, be put on a back burner for a few years. Time would tell. If in twenty years or so she hadn't changed, then that would clinch it. For now, he would concentrate his efforts on finding whether the woman who had been Annie Carr was still alive. With the latest technology at his disposal and the excellent programming skills of his pet nerd, the task shouldn't be too difficult.

He pressed a button on a small console on his desk.

"Tell Melliff to come in."

Two minutes later, Dayton's office door opened and Palo shuffled through. Without being asked, he sat down on one of the transparent plastic, designer chairs facing the desk, keeping his eyes to the ground. He avoided eye contact with his weird boss if he could; those eyes were just too scary.

"Anything more on the Farsley woman?" barked Dayton.

"Nothing new, boss. Like I've told you, she's a lawyer, not a research student. That must have been some sort of ruse to get the shrink to see her. She works for the same law firm as her husband. He's a partner. The firm's founding partner was the Farsley woman's foster father. All very cozy. They live uneventful lives. Two kids, one at college, the other just finishing high school. Both bright, all-American kids without any apparent problems. No criminal records in the family."

"You have photos of the kids?"

"Yes, boss, like I told you."

Jeez, what was wrong with him, thought Palo, we've already been through all this stuff.

"And they don't seem like their mother?"

"On the contrary, they seem very like their mother. Their father too. But if you mean the eyes, no, they don't got her eyes and the girl at least is always sniffing, like she's allergic or something."

Dayton steepled his hands, pushing his index fingers into his lips, which were pursed in thought. He sighed deeply and shifted his focus to Palo.

"I want to change the direction of this investigation, Melliff. You are to keep a watching brief on the Farsley woman but I only want to know if she starts behaving strangely; does anything out of the ordinary. And, of course, I want to know if she goes to see Dr Wright again – your assistant in the office above Wright's can monitor that."

Palo frowned, wondering what was going to be expected of him.

"We are now," continued Dayton, "in the fortunate position of having first-class, high-quality photographs of Annie Carr. Now, since getting those, we have compared them with both di Napoli and Whittaker and found they could all be the same person."

He paused to hold up a hand when he saw Palo about to raise the same objections he had before.

"The photographs of Carr were a breakthrough, Melliff, and they remove the necessity, for the present at least, of continuing to search in the past for whom she might have been."

Palo looked up. Here we go again, he thought, centuries-old women. The man's a fruitcake.

"What I want you to do now, Melliff, is to use the high-quality images you have of Carr and search the Internet, and I mean really search it as only you can, for anyone, anywhere, alive now who matches that face."

"But she's dead boss. The shrink's files say so; the fire reports say so; the coroner said so."

Dayton's eyes narrowed threateningly. "I say differently, Melliff. Those opinions about Carr's death were all based on circumstantial evidence. There was no proof. Her body was never identified beyond question. I think she could well be still alive. If she is, she'll have a different identity. She could live anywhere in the world and, unless she's hitched up with a sugar daddy, she has to work. What do you think that work will be, Melliff?"

Palo nodded. "She's an artist. She'll paint or sculpt, or something like that."

"Right. And these days, artists, like everyone else trying to sell their wares, will have websites. Websites that will have photos of them, information about them, data telling us who they are and where they are. Hell, she's probably on Facebook. She's out there, Melliff. It's your job, you and your team, to find her. If she exists, I want to know. I *have* to know."

Chapter 26

In his excitement over the phone call from Ralph Ryder-Hyde about the two Paola Lethrington paintings, Matt completely overlooked the fact that Williamsburg is some six hundred miles from Boston. It would take around ten hours to drive and slightly longer on the train, since freight trains in the Richmond, Virginia area get priority, slowing down the passenger trains. Even flying would take three to five hours, depending on the connections.

"I've got to see those paintings, Mom. *We've* got to see those paintings. Don't you see? If we can get hold of an original, genuine Paola Lethrington, we could look for an art expert to compare it with an Annie Carr. Wouldn't that be amazing?"

Sara smiled at Matt's enthusiasm. He was Pete all over again: once he was on a mission, nothing would deter him.

"Yes, Matt, it would be amazing, but we can't just drop everything. It's Friday today. It would take most of Saturday to drive and I doubt the dealer would open late on a Saturday–"

"–Come on, Mom, Williamsburg is all about tourists. The weekend? They're bound to be open. Why don't I call the dealer? See what he says? We can share the driving."

"You're seventeen, Matt. You've never driven that far."

"That's why I said 'share', Mom."

Twenty minutes later Matt was back in the kitchen clutching his laptop.

"Mom, we've got to go. Look!"

He pointed to the screen. On it was an image of the same Paola

Lethrington self-portrait sketch they had first seen as a halftone print in the book from Ryder-Hyde. The other was a portrait of a middle-aged black woman in servant's clothes. It appeared to be a very detailed painting.

"The dealer was really friendly once I mentioned Mr Ryder-Hyde. Even took these shots on his phone and sent them as soon as we'd finished talking. He said he bought them both from a private collection – from a family that's had them for generations. There's no record of where they got the sketch from, but for the painting, there's a bill of sale from a no-longer-existing gallery in Port of Spain, Trinidad, dated 1925. The dealer said that because of my connection with Mr Ryder-Hyde and because what he called the provenance of the sketch was unknown, he'd be prepared to sell it for $800. The other one is more expensive. He reckoned $1600."

Sara raised her eyebrows. "That's a lot of car washing, Matt."

"Yeah, Mom, I know. I'll do it every day if you want. Twice a day."

Sara laughed. "And I suppose he's open tomorrow."

"Until six; same on Sunday. Said if he knew we were coming and we were delayed, he'd stay open."

"I'll talk to your father. I don't think he'd be too pleased to miss his golf."

As it turned out, Pete Farsley was more than pleased to miss his golf. One of the three players he'd been lined up with was a local car dealer he couldn't stand. Not only would the man spend the rounds trying to sell cars to anyone within earshot, but he was also known to cheat.

Sara, Pete and Matt set off at five thirty the following morning. Julie had an extra summer class that had been difficult to arrange and Sara wasn't prepared to let her miss it, despite her protests. They made good time, and by just after three in the afternoon they were entering Williamsburg. The Crabtree Gallery was located a stone's throw from the Merchant Square Shopping Center. However, having parked the car, before they entered into negotiations with Morgan Crabtree, a late lunch and shots of coffee were called for.

When his gallery doorbell buzzed, Morgan Crabtree looked up from the large coffee-table book he was studying to make a quick assessment of the potential customers. After years in the business, he reckoned ninety percent of the time he could spot a real customer from a casual tourist within five seconds. The normal giveaway was a bored-looking husband trying to avoid eye contact as he trailed behind an enthusiastic wife. If hubby controlled the purse strings, the most that would likely be sold was a mass-produced print.

The Farsleys clearly didn't fall into that category. All three of them eyeballed him immediately and walked across the gallery floor, more or less ignoring the displays. He'd been expecting them after his call with the young man the previous day, and a follow-up call saying they were on their way. He stood and walked round his desk, extending his hand to Pete.

"Mr Farsley, I believe," he smiled. "I'm Morgan Crabtree."

"Pleased to meet you, Mr Crabtree," said Pete as he shook the proffered hand. "This is my wife, Sara, and my son, Matt, to whom I think you've already spoken."

"I have indeed," beamed Crabtree, resting his clasped hands across his substantial belly. He was a short man, no more than five four, but what he lacked in height, he more than made up for in girth. Pinpoints of light from the spotlights in the gallery ceiling glinted as they reflected from his almost bald, polished crown, dancing as his head bobbed from Matt to Sara and back. Matt smiled to himself, thinking that the white spots on this little man's large blue bow tie should be reflective as well to complete the effect.

"And you've driven down from Boston! My, that is a long way. You must be weary. May I offer you some coffee?"

"That's very kind, Mr Crabtree, but we've just had some along the street," said Sara.

Crabtree ducked his head to one side with a slight smile.

"Then let's get down to business. I believe I have a couple of pieces that will interest you. You're very fortunate; I only picked them up recently, and it's not every day you come across an artist as obscure as Paola Lethrington. I must confess I'd only previously seen her work in rather old books. They are both excellent, in fact I'd go so far as to say that the painting is exceptional. The sketch too, given it's just a sketch, shows remarkable skill. You can tell from the fluidity of the lines, few though they are."

He had slipped into full-on sales mode, as Matt had expected from what Ryder-Hyde told him: talking up the price before the goods were produced.

"Let me fetch them for you. The painting is framed, so we can put it on this easel," he said, pointing to his left. "The sketch I'll put on the magnetic board over here. Better to view it upright rather than lying on a table."

He bustled off to the rear of the gallery as the Farsleys exchanged amused glances. Crabtree was much as they'd imagined from Matt's description of his conversation on the phone: a smooth-talking dealer with hard, calculating eyes behind his ready smile.

They watched as the rotund little man leafed through a vertical stack of framed paintings on the floor at the rear of the gallery until he found what he was looking for and picked it up, a cat-like smile of satisfaction on his face. He carried the painting back to them and, setting it on the easel, stood back with a sigh, his hands once again clasped across his belly.

Matt was surprised at the painting's size – it measured some two and a half feet by one and a half. Having only seen the image Crabtree emailed and the prints in Ryder-Hyde's book, he'd imagined something smaller. Its colours were rich and vibrant, especially in the clothing. The eyes of the black housemaid, which were looking straight at the viewer, had the resigned glaze of servitude, but there was determination and independence in the set of her jaw.

Crabtree adjusted the easel slightly to improve further the light falling onto the painting. "Quite exquisite, don't you think?" he said in the measured tone of confidence he liked to use to demonstrate his unquestionable expertise.

"As I told young Mr Farsley here on the telephone, the provenance of this piece can be traced back to its sale in 1925 in Trinidad. I have the original bill of sale with a detailed description."

"When do you think it was painted, Mr Crabtree?" asked Sara.

"Oh, I don't think, Mrs Farsley; I know," he said, giving Sara his most liquid smile. "It's here on the corner of the painting underneath the signature."

He pointed and Sara bent to look at the tiny numerals: 1845. Above them, equally small, were the initials 'PL'.

"And the sketch?" asked Matt.

"Ah, yes, the sketch," nodded Crabtree. "Here we are."

He opened a drawer in a chest by his desk and lifted out a drawing. Again, it was bigger than Matt had imagined: about half the size of the painting.

Crabtree positioned it on a whiteboard near the easel, securing it in place with four small cloth-covered magnets. They clustered around it, familiar with its lines but thrilled to see it in its original form.

"Gosh, it's so much better than the halftone print," said Sara. "There are faint lines here that don't really show in that at all."

"Yes," nodded Crabtree, "it shows a considerable degree of expertise. It's a pity its provenance isn't known, although the title and date are written on the back."

He turned to Sara. "Tell me, Mrs Farsley, what is it about Paola Lethrington that interests you? Your son mentioned something about searching out your ancestors."

Sara smiled. "That's quite right, Mr Crabtree. With Matt's history studies, we've recently been fired up to try and trace my forebears. They have turned out to be an elusive bunch, although I've always known from what my mother told me that we had artists in the family. She was an artist as well, you know, and although I'm not, I can still draw quite competently. From the rather sketchy details we have so far, with a few gaps, admittedly, I'm fairly convinced Paola Lethrington was a direct ancestor: a several times great grandmother."

"The rest of us are more than just fairly convinced," chimed in Pete. "We've had the benefit of seeing the halftone print of this sketch. If you compare the shape of the face and the features with Sara's, there's a remarkable degree of resemblance. The genes are clearly strong."

Crabtree took hold of the half-frame spectacles dangling from a cord round his neck and put them carefully on his nose. He peered slowly at the drawing and then turned to look at Sara. He cocked his head to one side, adjusting the angle, and then turned again to the drawing.

"You know, that's quite uncanny. I'd certainly agree with you about the resemblance: the subject of this self-portrait could almost be you." He chuckled. "Thank heavens I know the family that sold it to me, or I might think it was a forgery. Of course, I don't know exactly when they acquired it."

"Interesting idea, Mr Crabtree," said Pete. "Why on earth would anyone want to forge a drawing of a very obscure nineteenth-century artist from the ex-British colonies?"

"Precisely, Mr Farsley, precisely. No reason at all," agreed Crabtree.

Sara scratched her head lightly. "Mr Crabtree, you mentioned some prices on the phone to Matt. Could we discuss them further?"

"Delighted, dear lady, delighted," beamed the dealer, all geniality and calculation. "As I mentioned to your son, the sketch is rather less expensive than the painting because of its more obscure provenance, but–"

"– But there's also the fact that the artist herself is very obscure," interrupted Sara, giving Crabtree her most winning smile. "I can't imagine there's a great call for Paola Lethrington's work."

"Of course, of course, I quite agree. Nevertheless, quality work is quality work, and collectors are always on the look out for a different slant; an artist who might have been overlooked."

"Oh dear," said Sara, letting her face move towards crestfallen, "I should hate to see these pieces disappear again onto the walls of some collector, a person who would have no idea or even interest in the artist herself. Just, really, when you come down to it, a purchase as a long-term investment."

"Sadly, that is often the nature of art – collectors are a canny and competitive group. I sympathise with you, Mrs Farsley; both these pieces were painted by your ancestor, and one is an actual self-portrait; they couldn't be more personal. As a sentimental man, I should hate that your family be denied the pleasure of owning them simply over a matter of price."

"You are very kind," said Sara, taking a step towards the little man and touching his arm.

"Quite, quite," said Crabtree, rather flustered by her proximity. "Let me see, I originally thought, well, perhaps ..." He chewed his bottom lip in a display of calculating the best possible price without his having to resort to living on bread and water for several weeks.

"Yes, I'd thought for the painting, that, er, let's say $1800 for the two? Would that be agreeable to you? It's a considerable discount over what I should normally–"

"That would be most agreeable, Mr Crabtree," smiled Sara. "You are very kind; thank you so much. The Farsleys now and in future generations will remain indebted to you."

Pete, Sara and Matt were elated as they walked back to their car, the smile on Sara's face pure self-satisfaction.

"Mom, you're a genius," said Matt, putting an arm around his mother's shoulder. "You had that little man eating out of your hand."

"Don't you believe it," laughed Sara. "He's been in this business for years and knows every trick in the book. He knew exactly what price to pitch his offer. If you'd got him to write down his expected deal price before we even went in there, I'd bet it would have been very close to what we've paid. However, having said that, I'm thrilled with them. We can think about the next step now."

"Which is?" asked Pete.

"To contact some sort of expert who can give us an idea about whether these two gems could have been produced by the same person who drew the portrait of me as a child: my mother."

"You know," added Matt, "there's also the painting of Dr Wright that we know your mother painted, the one you shot on your phone. When I uploaded it to the computer, I could see that it's got amazing detail. Was it large, like this portrait of the servant woman we've just bought?"

Sara nodded. "Yes, it was similar in size, and now that I think of it, it's what was nagging in my brain when I was looking at the portrait in the gallery just now. It was as if I'd seen it before. Annie Carr painted the portrait of Dr Wright wearing nineteenth-century clothes. The two paintings are remarkably similar in style."

"If we can find a suitable expert, do you think Dr Wright would agree to lend us her portrait?" asked Matt.

"I think she might," nodded Sara. "Now that we've got this one, once she's seen it, I think she'd be willing."

Pete clapped his hands. "Well, gang, what now? There's no way we can make the return drive today, even sharing it three ways. I suggest we find a place to stay and celebrate our purchases with some fine food and wine."

"Brilliant idea, honey," said Sara, taking his arm. "We'll just add the price to Matt's car cleaning account."

"Fine by me," grinned Matt, "and tomorrow morning, I'd like to see something of this little piece of historic America before we head north."

"Might even get to blow a bugle," said Pete, miming it with his hand and marching off ahead of them.

Chapter 27

The Farsleys arrived back late on Sunday evening, tired but thrilled with their new acquisitions. The next stage of their quest was for Sara to persuade Nancy Wright to part with her beloved portrait for a few days once Matt had found the name of a forgery expert from Ralph Ryder-Hyde. First thing the following morning, Sara was onto it, catching Nancy Wright at home.

"Oh dear," was Nancy's reply once Sara had explained about the Paola Lethrington paintings, "I hope you're not going to be disappointed."

"Disappointed?" Sara was suddenly worried her request was going to be refused, or worse still that something had happened to the painting.

"Yes, Sara. It seems you have become convinced by your mother's story and now you are talking in very positive terms about Paola Lethrington being a previous persona of your mother's. As you know, while I find the whole matter perplexing, the one explanation I cannot countenance is that your mother's story was true, for all the reasons we've discussed previously. So when I say disappointed, I mean that if the expert is worth his salt, he is going to find differences that prove Annie and Paola were not the same woman. Which will mean, Sara, that the whole theory will come tumbling down."

Sara smiled to herself in relief: she had gone beyond Nancy Wright's resistance to accepting Annie Carr's story.

"What would you say, Dr Wright," she replied quietly, "if the expert finds he can't distinguish the paintings; that in his opinion they were all painted by the same person?"

There was a gentle, slightly superior laugh from the other end of the phone. "Let's worry about that when it happens, shall we, Sara?"

Despite her personal and professional conclusions, Nancy Wright agreed that once they'd found an expert in New York City, Matt could come to her office and take the painting. Perhaps, she thought, this campaign by Sara Farsley will settle matters once and for all and I can close the file on Annie Carr.

"What am I going to tell this expert, Mom?" said Matt when Sara got off the phone from Nancy Wright. "He can't be told what we think to be the truth."

"Certainly he can't, Matt. Actually, I've been thinking and while I don't want to play the age and maturity card, it might be better if I called this person, once you have a name from Mr Ryder-Hyde. I think you'll agree that if a seventeen-year-old youth calls him or turns up in his office, he might be less inclined to take the whole thing seriously. If, on the other hand, you are effectively my messenger and I've assured him his fee will be forthcoming, then he will give it his full attention."

Matt shrugged in acquiescence, but Sara still hadn't answered his question.

"So, what will you tell him?"

"Obviously not the whole truth. I think something along the lines of Annie Carr being an accomplished painter, but delusional and eventually incarcerated in a psychiatric institution. I think we'll leave mention of murder out of it, don't you agree?" Amused at the thought, she raised her eyebrows in question to ensure he understood.

"I'll tell him she was a distant relative rather than my mother and that she appears to have modelled her style of painting on another even more distant relative, or rather, ancestor, who was an obscure nineteenth-century female painter. Hence the association. I'll say that some of the pieces attributed to Paola Lethrington have huge gaps in their timeline and we'd like to know if there's any possibility the delusional Annie Carr painted or perhaps copied any of them earlier in her life. In the case of the self-portrait sketch, we wonder if somehow it got into the hands of the family from whom Morgan Crabtree bought it far more recently than Crabtree thinks. After all, Crabtree only had a bill of sale for the painting, not the sketch."

"But the sketch is shown in the book from the 1920s alongside the others."

"Mmm, well maybe the sketch we have is a copy of the original shown in the book. It would be difficult to say since the quality of the print in the book is relatively poor and anyway, we won't show him the book," smiled Sara conspiratorially. "Remember, we're really just interested in comparing the two big paintings. That's where the details are. The rest are just extras that might help to underscore the case for my mother and Paola being one and the same."

Matt nodded as he thought through the story. "I'll tell Mr Ryder-Hyde the same story, about the paintings, anyway," he said. "I'll call him now."

"Mr Ryder-Hyde? It's Matt. Matt Farsley."

"My dear young man. How are you? And for heaven's sake, you may think that in relation to your tender years I was around before the last Ice Age, but I do have a Christian name, you know. Please, young Matt, it's Ralph." He pronounced his name in the traditional European way as 'Rafe'.

"Thank you, sir," said Matt, puzzled by the pronunciation and continuing with the formality. He had never called any man over the age of fifty anything but 'sir' and he found the concept uncomfortable. "I'm fine," he added.

"Excellent! How did you get on with that old rogue Crabtree? Did he give you a good price?"

"Yes, sir, thanks to you, he did. We, well, my parents, that is, bought both the Paola Lethringtons he had for sale. They're incredible. So much better than any print. The painting, which is of a servant woman, is fantastic. My mom adores it and it'll soon be given pride of place in our living room."

"Jolly good! So that all worked out well. What can I do for you now, or was this just a social call?"

"It was a call to say 'thank you', of course, sir. But, yes, I wanted to ask another favour. Or at least to ask for some information."

"Fire away, young fella."

"Well, you're going to think this rather strange, but we'd really like to consult an art expert about whether any of pieces we've acquired could have been produced by someone other than Paola Lethrington."

"Interesting. Tell me more."

Matt started with the story Sara had decided upon. Having run through it, he added, "We found out about Annie Carr from her psychiatrist, who is a friend of a friend of my mother. Annie Carr died back in the seventies, but she painted a portrait of the psychiatrist that my mother has seen. When Mom saw the Paola Lethrington portrait of the servant woman, she couldn't believe how much it reminded her of the psychiatrist's portrait. Anyway, the psychiatrist, who's getting on in years–"

He heard a loud cough from the other end of the phone and winced as he realised his faux pas.

"I mean, that is–"

"Yes, yes, yes. Another relic. Carry on, young Matt, while I still have the strength to hold this contraption to my ear."

"Sorry. Yes, well, she, the psychiatrist, is willing to lend us the portrait for expert assessment and comparison with the Paola Lethringtons. A little while ago she also gave my mother a drawing by Annie Carr. When my mother put it side by side with the Paola Lethringtons, she thought they were incredibly similar. So there are quite a few interesting comparisons to be made."

"Mmm. Sounds like your Annie Carr might have had the skills to be a good forger. Certainly the sort of thing a forger does, copying an artist's style carefully and faithfully, but for criminal reasons, of course.

"In any event," he continued, "the chap I have in mind for you is thoroughly competent. Shouldn't find it too difficult to separate one from t'other. I'd also like to take a look myself, if I may."

"That's brilliant, er, Rafe, sir," stuttered Matt. "Would you mind finding out when your expert is available?"

"I'll call him now, young Matt, and then call you back. Perhaps when you come over, we could have a spot of afternoon tea."

When Matt arrived at Bibliophilia, he was clutching his portfolio that now included the painting of Nancy Wright he had just picked up from the psychiatrist's office along with the sketch she still had of Annie in sixteenth-century costume. He found Ralph Ryder-Hyde still nestled in his armchair much as he had been on Matt's previous visit; Matt wondered idly if the old man slept there. He carefully unpacked his precious cargo and laid each piece on a table Ryder-Hyde had instructed him to clear. The bookseller announced with a chuckle once it was done that it was the first time in living memory he'd seen so much of the tabletop.

"Has its merits, although heaven only knows where I'd put those books," he said, pointing to the tottering pile Matt had arranged as tidily as he could on a patch of unoccupied floor space beyond the table.

Ryder-Hyde hauled himself to his feet and leaned heavily on the table, grasping a huge magnifying glass in one hand. He pointed to an ancient anglepoise lamp and instructed Matt to plug it in.

During the next fifteen minutes, all Matt heard were grunts, gasps and the odd words of surprise.

"Extraordinary! Remarkable! How very strange!"

Finally, Ryder-Hyde looked up, his shoulders soaring above a head that seemed to have sunk into his chest. With the light playing on his features from a low angle, he looked like a huge and menacing bird of prey disturbed from dismembering a carcass.

However, his words were anything but menacing. "Whoever this woman was, she had a remarkable talent. I'm no forgery expert, but I've seen a painting or two and I know the sort of things the chaps look for, and I for one certainly can't tell them apart. If you hadn't told me they were by two different artists, I'd say they were all by the same person."

Matt said nothing, trying to keep the excitement he felt to himself. As much as he'd like to let Ryder-Hyde know what was going on, he knew he couldn't. He didn't understand it any more than his parents, and it would be foolhardy to tell anyone, no matter how fundamentally honest he felt they were.

"All right, young Matt, here's the name and address of the best New York has to offer, in my humble opinion, that is. He's only a couple of blocks away, as it turns out, and he's agreed to see you immediately once I give him a call. Name's Oliver Scatti. Italian ancestry but his family's been here for a hundred years or more. Nothing scatty about him at all; very serious chap. Knows his stuff."

Oliver Scatti proved to be exactly as Ryder-Hyde described him. He was wearing a rumpled cream linen jacket over an open-necked white shirt and a deep blue silk scarf. A white goatee beard and rimless half-frames gave him a professorial air.

He welcomed Matt and with little preamble he asked Matt to lay out the paintings and drawings – he wasn't really sure how to make small talk with a seventeen-year-old .

Unlike Ryder-Hyde, this man worked in total silence. For the next twenty minutes Matt stood to one side watching as Scatti scrutinised all the pieces. He quickly focussed his attention on the two large portraits, the examination being undertaken through a huge magnifying glass. Then he suddenly stood up straight, spun on his heels and leaned back against the edge of the examination table.

"Ryder-Hyde warned me, you know," he said, his voice rich and deep, the accent revealing a hint of the South. "Called me while you were on your way over here. He said distinguishing the artists for these pieces would be difficult. I didn't believe him – there's always some sort of giveaway, especially when one artist is deliberately copying another. Now, obviously I'll need more time – a couple of days would be ideal, if I can keep the paintings that long. However, I can tell you now from my initial examination that it's a real challenge. If you'd come in here asking a different question, that is, whether all these paintings and drawings are by the same hand, at this stage I'd say they probably are. But that's not what you've asked me."

Scatti paused, scratching his head absently, then continued.

"I should say, in mitigation, that I've never heard of Annie Carr and I am not very familiar with Paola Lethrington's work. From memory, I think I've only ever seen one piece by her before. If you take just the drawings, they are relatively simple in style and therefore it wouldn't be too difficult for a competent artist to copy one sufficiently well to fool most people. However, when we come to the two paintings, they are very detailed, very detailed indeed, which gives a huge number of points for comparison. That's good, of course, since it makes forging them very much more of a challenge."

He suddenly clapped his hands. "May I keep them for a couple of days?"

"Certainly," nodded Matt, then he hesitated and looked around the studio. It was on the first floor of an old building. Although he'd noticed quite substantial locks on the doors on the way in, he wanted reassurance. "This place is secure, isn't it?"

Scatti smiled benignly. "Better than Fort Knox, my boy. State-of-the-art alarms and locks that are simply unpickable. I have that on the highest authority from people on the wrong side of the business! You have no need to worry on that score."

"In that case," said Matt, "I'll wait for your call."

In the end it was three days before Scatti was ready to present his findings. He'd called asking for extra time halfway through the second day and after checking with Nancy Wright, Matt told him to continue. During the call, Scatti would give him no indication of his progress.

When he phoned on the afternoon of the third day to say he was ready, Matt told him he would be at his office the following lunchtime, reminding him he was coming from Boston.

"You really should come too, Mom," said Matt when he told Sara of the arrangement. He knew his mother was champing at the bit over the results. "He's a tad eccentric, as you might expect, but what he's doing is fascinating."

Sara's eyes lit up. "I'd love to, sweetheart. A day out in New York City with a handsome young man sounds perfect."

The train was delayed and it was a little after two in the afternoon when Matt rang on the bell of the entry system to Scatti's studio and introduced his mother through the CCTV camera. After passing through the two highly secure doors that separated the studio from the rest of the world, Matt introduced Sara again and was surprised by the incredulous tone of the expert's response.

"Mrs Farsley, I'm delighted to meet you," said Scatti, unable to take his eyes from Sara's face or hide the astonishment from his voice.

"You look like you've seen a ghost, Mr Scatti," said Sara, intrigued by his reaction.

"Mrs Farsley, I've spent the last three days scrutinising the detail in these drawings and paintings. Now, the paintings are not self-portraits, but two of the drawings are, one by Annie Carr and one by Paola Lethrington. and I must say that apart from the features in the faces of the two being extremely similar to each other, they also bear an amazingly strong resemblance to you. It's really quite remarkable."

Sara laughed. "Not quite as remarkable as you might think, Mr Scatti. You see, the story I gave you over the telephone and the one I'm sure Matt has reiterated wasn't quite correct. The truth, in fact, is that Annie Carr wasn't a distant relative; she was my mother, so it's not so strange that we should look alike."

Scatti nodded. "And Paola Lethrington?"

Sara hesitated rather longer than she intended, enough to raise a question in Scatti's mind. "That's harder to explain, I must admit. She was also a distant relative, as I told you, an ancestor who lived many generations ago. I'm afraid I simply don't know our exact relationship."

Scatti nodded again, not totally convinced by what he was hearing.

Matt looked over to where the various pieces were laid out on the examination table.

"What is your conclusion, Mr Scatti? I mean for these."

Scatti folded his left arm across his body, supporting his right arm at the elbow as he rubbed his chin with his right hand.

"I regret my conclusion is much as it was when you first brought these pieces to me three days ago: I simply cannot tell them apart. Annie Carr, whom you now say was your mother, Mrs Farsley, must have been a remarkable talent to have copied Paola Lethrington's style so completely, so faithfully, without once, in my estimation, ever departing from it. I've never seen anything quite like it. In my defence, I should add that I doubt you would find any other expert who would form a different opinion."

He looked from Sara to Matt and back, noticing the animation in their eyes.

"From your reaction, I sense that is the conclusion you were expecting. Am I right?"

"It's the conclusion we strongly suspected, Mr Scatti, for reasons I'm not really at liberty to explain."

"How enigmatic," smiled Scatti softly, his face relaxing for the first time. Then he frowned. "You know, or, no, perhaps you don't, that there is one further course of action you might be able to take if you want a totally objective assessment of these pieces – my examination has, almost by definition, a degree of subjectivity to it, you understand?"

"There is?" said Sara and Matt together, hardly able to contain their excitement.

"Yes. There's a young man in Britain, remarkably talented, who has taken the art world by storm. Threatening to put the likes of me out of a job. Normally I'd object strongly to his approach, but I have seen the results for myself. They are most extraordinary. You see, he uses a computer to undertake the analysis of paintings. He has written a quite unbelievable program that analyses every nuance of the surface. Not chemically, you understand, no; it's from the brush or pen work – a complete analysis of the style. It can undertake the sort of iterative process that someone like me performs with his eye but with far more detail, together with repetition that no human could maintain."

"So if this expert, with his fancy computer program, forms the opinion that the same person produced all these works you've examined, you would concur, Mr Scatti?"

Scatti coughed, put on the spot by Sara's courtroom tone.

"Er, well, I suppose I should have to. After all, the man's program has never been shown to be wrong."

"What conclusion would you draw from that?" continued Sara.

Scatti exhaled slowly, trying to get his head around the paradox. "It would have to be that we are dealing with some sort of very elaborate forgery." He frowned, shrugged his shoulders and lifted his hands, palms outwards, in an Italian gesture that must have been in his genes. "But why, Mrs Farsley? Why should anyone go to all that trouble over a very minor artist?"

"Why indeed, Mr Scatti?" smiled Sara enigmatically. "However, you must remember, Annie Carr was severely delusional, a psychiatric patient incarcerated in an institution."

"Does he need the original material?" asked Matt, thinking that transporting everything to the UK might be difficult.

"That's the remarkable thing," replied Scatti. "He produces his incredible results from well-taken photographs. Apparently it's what he concentrates his efforts on, knowing how difficult it can be to move priceless paintings around."

"So would photos taken with a camera like this be sufficient?" said Matt, pulling out the professional-level Canon Pete had bought a few days before to start on their series of photos of Sara.

"Yes, I think that would fit the bill."

"I should hope so; it cost a fortune," added Sara ruefully.

Scatti nodded sympathetically. "I've got a rig that goes over this table, if you want to use it. It has good lighting and you'll be able to get just the quality he needs."

"Could you tell us the name of this British expert, Mr Scatti?" asked Matt.

"It would be my pleasure; I'll fetch his contact details. His name is Cedric Fisher."

Chapter 28

Ced Fisher was only half listening once he heard the words 'private work'. For the past two years, he had turned down anything that wasn't connected to a criminal case or an insurance investigation: there simply weren't enough hours in the day for his forensic work, let alone anything else. On top of this, for over a month now, he'd been struggling with a problem he'd encountered in his program's analysis of palette knife strokes. It was tricky, and, although he was almost on top of it, it tended to preoccupy him.

The brilliance of Ced's program had been strongly contributory to unraveling the mystery of John Andrews, the incredibly talented artist working quietly in the Lake District of northern England whose paintings Ced had found to be indistinguishable from the works of long-dead artists from other eras. That John was a fifteenth-century Renaissance artist with all the skills of an old master who was still alive in the 21st century was an explanation too bizarre to believe. Yet Ced's program had stubbornly stuck to its guns, insisting on the matches with a very high degree of confidence – the reality being that all the paintings had been produced by John over the centuries. From utter despair that his program was worthless, once the pieces of the John Andrews puzzle fell into place – thanks to the interpretation of Andrews' DNA by Professor Frank Young – Ced's confidence in his work was completely restored: the program was a work of genius. However, there was a need for total secrecy over the now five-hundred-and-eighty-five-year-old John and his two daughters who shared the rare traits that made the three of them so special – Lily

Saunders, born in Hong Kong in 1885 and now living in New York City; and Phoebe Andrews, now eight. To achieve this, Ced had reconfigured his program in such a way that if any comparison were made of paintings by any two or more of the artists John had been in the past, or of one from the past and a present work by John himself, the outcome would be a falsely erroneous but nevertheless common-sense result: the paintings were by different artists. To achieve this, Ced had hidden certain routines deep within his code in a way he hoped no one would ever discover. It was because of the need for his program to give erroneous results that access to its use was limited to Ced himself and a few other skilled operators working directly for him in the forensic investigation company that employed them: Forefront Forensics. But only Ced had access to the code and the program was never, ever, allowed to be duplicated onto other computers for any reason. However, this situation could only be maintained for so long: sooner or later, the program would have to be allowed into other hands. Ced just hoped he'd blown enough smoke through the code that his deception would continue to remain undetected.

Ced suddenly realised that the earnest young American voice on the other end of his phone had stopped talking. He had little idea of the caller's request and now the caller was expecting some sort of response. Finally, the caller gave up waiting.

"Mr Fisher? Are you still there?"

Ced sighed. "Yes, Mr, er …"

"Farsley. Matt Farsley."

"Yes, Mr Farsley, I'm still here."

"Do you think you would be able to take a look?"

"Take a look?"

"At my paintings and drawings. The ones I want compared."

"Mr Farsley, I'm really sorry, but you must understand I get several requests like this every day. Mostly by email, fortunately, otherwise I'd spend my whole time on the phone."

"Sorry, I should have–"

"It doesn't matter. The point is, I'm so snowed under with my regular work that I simply have no time to undertake any private work, as much as I'd like to. In fact, my bosses insist I stick to crime and insurance work only. So I'm afraid if your request doesn't fit either of those categories, I can't help you."

"Is there no one else on your team …?"

"There are several people, but they are all bound by the same constraints. I'm sorry, Mr Farsley-"

"Could I just pass you on to my mother? I think she could probably explain things better than I can."

"Your mother?"

Before he could respond further, another voice came on the line.

"Hello, Dr Fisher, this is Sara Farsley, Matt's mother. I-"

"It's Mr Fisher, Mrs Farsley, and as I've explained to your son, I'm really very busy, too busy for long phone calls, and there is simply no way I can take on a private examination."

"I appreciate that, Dr, er, Mr Fisher, and I'm sorry to intrude on your valuable time. But before you hang up, could I just explain why this project is so important to me?"

Ced sighed to himself. He might as well let this woman have her say even though it wasn't going to change anything. At least once she'd finished, she'd have less reason to pester him further. His wife, Sally, had for some time been pushing for him to get a secretary to field calls like this. However, since Ced worked mainly from home, the arrangements would be complicated.

"OK, Mrs Farsley, go ahead," he said as he focussed his attention on the code on the screen in front of him.

"Thank you, Mr Fisher, I really am very grateful."

Just get on with it, thought Ced.

Sara got on with it. "You see, I have come into possession of a self-portrait of one of my ancestors, Paola Lethrington, an accomplished artist who lived in the first part of the nineteenth century. It's a drawing and isn't very detailed, I'll admit. Nevertheless, the face shows a quite remarkable resemblance to my mother. Now, my mother was also an artist, a very good one, and since there are gaps in the detailed history of the Lethrington self-portrait, and also since my mother was known to dabble a lot in copying other works, we, my family and I, that is, are strongly suspicious my mother might have actually drawn the Lethrington portrait and made up a whole exotic history about colonial relatives."

Ced stifled a yawn as he concentrated on the lines of code. He pressed the handset to his ear with his shoulder and started typing.

"Now, the really interesting thing is, Mr Fisher, that we've had the self-portrait looked at by an art expert who compared it with a drawing of herself my mother is definitely known to have produced. Two experts, in fact," she added, remembering Ralph Ryder-Hyde, "and, well, they simply can't tell them apart."

She paused, hoping for a reaction from Ced.

"Mr Fisher?"

Ced jolted back to the conversation, realising it was the second time he'd lost the thread.

"Sorry, Mrs, er, Farsley, the line's a bit fuzzy. I missed that last bit."

Sara sighed silently to herself in exasperation and then repeated what she'd just said. This time Ced listened and shrugged. The answer seemed obvious.

"Well, if your experts can't distinguish the pieces, Mrs Farsley, that's perhaps because they were both drawn by your mother."

"I know that sounds like the logical conclusion, Mr Fisher. However, for the Lethrington drawing, although there are gaps in its history, there is still quite convincing evidence that it dates from before my mother was born."

Ced was confused. The story didn't make sense. Either the drawings were by the same person or they weren't. If they weren't, then this woman's mother was just a good copyist. If they were … well, they couldn't be, from what Sara Farsley had told him.

"Sounds like your mother was good enough to fool the experts," he said glibly. "If the works are drawings, I assume they are not very detailed. If a competent copyist puts his or her mind to it, for a work without too much detail, then it's quite conceivable the copy would be good enough to fool even a skilled eye. There are plenty of examples of that happening."

"Which is one of the reasons I've come to you, Mr Fisher. I was told you have a computer program that goes beyond subjective comparison, a program that can distinguish between two works by, say, a forger and the artist they are forging, even when the work isn't very detailed."

Touché, thought Ced.

"I must admit, Mrs Farsley, that my program is pretty successful in such cases, but as I said at the outset, both to you and your son, I'm not in a position to take on such work. I'm really sorry."

"I do understand, Mr Fisher, really I do, but there's a second, more compelling reason I've contacted you. You see, I also have a Lethrington painting of a servant woman that is large and very detailed that was painted almost definitely in the 1840s. The remarkable thing about it is that its style is incredibly similar to a painting that my mother produced in 1970. My experts have also looked at these two paintings and they can't tell them apart with respect to their style."

Ced sighed. "You say 'almost definitely', Mrs Farsley, so I assume you're not one hundred per cent certain. It sounds really like all the drawings and paintings were produced in the modern era by your mother. She was clearly very good. It must be the case if your experts can't distinguish them."

"I know, Mr Fisher, but it's all very difficult to explain. I was wondering if I could just email you copies of the pieces. I have very good, high-resolution images, which I believe are what you normally use. Apart from anything else, they are very enchanting pictures; really beautiful."

Ced looked through the window to the misty rain falling outside. Time for a run, he thought. Then he remembered he was on the phone to the States.

"If you want to email them, it's up to you, Mrs Farsley. I'm afraid I can't guarantee I'll look at them." Ced hoped he was sounding suitably discouraging. He didn't really care how enchanting they were.

"Thank you, Mr Fisher, I'll get on to it right away. I'm really sorry to have disturbed you. Thank you so much for your time."

Ced put the receiver on the cordless cradle and turned back to the dense display of code, but the numbers didn't gel. His mind was still on the conversation he'd just had with the very insistent American woman. There was something she'd said; something that made him think the paintings and drawings she wanted him to look at were worth the effort. What was it? What had she said to trigger that thought? He scratched his head as he sighed in frustration. It would come to him by and by.

Ced and Sally were married in the spring of 2010, just a few months after Ced proposed while they were both up to their knees in mud in a sodden field in the pouring rain. Keen triathletes, they spent every spare minute running, cycling or swimming in all weathers in the Cheshire countryside where they lived.

Everything changed a year after they were married when Sally became pregnant, their daughter, Claudia-Jane, arriving in November 2011. The young parents were ecstatic: they were very much in love and their baby daughter was another level of perfection in their busy but contented lives. Claudia-Jane was named after Claudia Reid, Sally's closest friend and the forensic biochemist whose dogged persistence set the ball rolling in the mystery of John Andrews when she had profiled his DNA and found the results to be a total enigma. Claudia's determination in following a line of inquiry to the bitter end was well known, as was the gushing excitability that was sometimes mistaken for naïvety when the pressure was on. Sally wondered if naming her daughter after her best friend and making that best friend her daughter's godmother had somehow influenced the baby's personality. Certainly Claudia-Jane showed a remarkable interest in everything around her, even at only a few months old, and her attitude to sleep was total resistance in case she might miss something. When she did eventually drop off the slightest noise could disturb her, resulting in both parents tiptoeing around the house and talking in whispers for hours at a time.

When working, Ced was under strict instructions to close his study door and keep quiet, or his shift of looking after the baby would be extended.

Later in the evening, some hours after Sara Farsley's call, when Sally heard a yelp of excitement coming from Ced's study, she knew exactly what was going to happen next. She sighed in exasperation and waited. Within seconds, the speaker of Claudia-Jane's baby monitor sounded with a grunt, then a complaint, then a yowl that quickly transformed into full-on grief.

"Ced, how many times do you need reminding we have a baby in the house?" hissed Sally as she marched into Ced's study carrying the sobbing Claudia-Jane. "Look, she's wide awake. It'll be ages before I get her down again."

Ced wasn't listening. He was pointing to two images on the largest of his monitors, a hi-res screen that showed artwork in staggering detail.

"Look at these, Sal! Look at these drawings!"

Sally sighed. She knew that voice. She'd get no sense out of Ced until he'd explained what was firing him up.

She turned her eyes to the monitor where Sara Farsley's two self-portrait drawings were displayed. Sally was a biochemist with self-confessed limitations in the appreciation of fine art, but having been around Ced and his encyclopaedic knowledge of the subject for several years, she'd become attuned to assessing the many paintings and drawings he regularly showed her.

"They're very competent drawings, hon, and even though the clothing is from different periods, the faces are really quite similar. What's so special about them that you need to announce it to Claudia-Jane?"

When there was no answer, she turned to look at Ced to find him staring in adoration at his daughter, one of her tiny feet in his hand. She was purring quietly to herself, almost asleep again, although Sally knew perfectly well it was a state that was fully reversible in a microsecond.

"Isn't she gorgeous?"

"Yes, so gorgeous that you had to wake her up. You could be in for a long night, marathon man. Now, what's so important about these drawings?"

Ced turned back to the monitor.

"The faces aren't just similar, Sal, they're almost identical. Look!"

He tapped on the keyboard to enlarge the images so that just the faces were displayed.

Sally examined them and nodded. "Yes, I agree. Now they are bigger, there's not much doubt about it: they must be of the same person. Why do you think the clothing is so different?"

Ced laughed. "Forget the clothing, Sal, look at the faces."

Sally frowned. "I am and I've agreed that they are the same person."

Ced shook his head. "Can't you see it, Sal? Look at the features. Who does that face remind you of?"

Sally studied the drawings further, squinted her eyes and tilted her head to one side. Then she gasped. "Oh my God! It's John!" she whispered, ever aware that her daughter was on the edge of sleep. "They're really like John, allowing for the fact they are women and the pictures are just drawings. Ced, you don't think …? Do they have any information with them, dates and so on?"

Ced smiled. "You betcha!" He scrolled down the screen to show the files names and read them out. "Annie Carr. Self-portrait" he said, looking at the left of the two.

"–And Paola Lethrington, also a self-portrait," continued Sally. Her eyes widened. "Paola?"

"Exactly what I thought when I saw the names. I knew when the American woman phoned me earlier that she'd said something significant but I couldn't think what it was. Turned out it was the artist's name: Paola."

Sally pursed her lips. "Paola's not that uncommon a name, hon, and the Paola John is so keen on finding was born in fifteen something or other. This woman is in clothing that looks more nineteenth century; you know, fine lace buttoned up to the throat, hair up in a high bun. It looks sort of colonial – India or somewhere. Do you know where it's from?"

Ced scratched his neck while he thought about it. "What did the woman say?" he muttered. "Yes, I know!" he exclaimed, his voice now louder.

"Ced!"

"Sorry!"

They both stared at the screen. Then Ced glanced back at Sally and Claudia-Jane and chuckled.

"What?"

"Look at her."

Sally looked down at their daughter. Claudia-Jane was now wide awake again and staring intently at the monitor, gurgling quietly.

"God! Not another art expert in the family! I don't think I could cope with two of you!"

"Trinidad," said Ced triumphantly.

"What about it," whispered Sally, still hopeful that Claudia-Jane might doze off.

"She said her ancestor lived in Trinidad; that's where this drawing must have been made."

"Ancestor?"

"Yes, she said one drawing was by her ancestor, Paola Lethrington, while the other was by her mother, Annie Carr."

"But the *other* one has the subject in sixteenth-century dress. Are you sure the names haven't been switched by mistake?"

"I suppose they could have been, but listen, the person is called Paola Lethrington, not Paola whatever-she-was-called in Naples. If she is who we think she might be, then she'd make the drawing in nineteenth-century costume because it was that century."

"What about the one that's by Annie Carr? That's in sixteenth-century costume but you said it was your contact's mother. How does that make sense?"

"Dunno, except, why not? Maybe there was a specific reason."

"If that's the case, it shows a remarkable knowledge of sixteenth-century dress. Look at that bonnet. Even though it's just a drawing, it's amazing. Do you know either of the names, as known artists, I mean?"

Ced shook his head. "No, they don't mean anything. I must admit, I've never heard of them."

"Then they must be beyond obscure, oh font of all fine-art knowledge."

"Mmm," said Ced as he mused on something while he idly rubbed his daughter's foot again. Claudia-Jane was now looking from one parent to the other, wondering how she could capitalise further on this unexpected entertainment. "There was someone in Trinidad … someone known who painted there …" continued Ced. "I know, Cazabon!" he said, the rise in volume of his voice startling Claudia-Jane, whose face wrinkled in protest.

Sally jogged her up and down. "Take no notice of him, sweetheart. Your daddy's just an excitable man."

She turned to Ced. "Who's Cazabon?"

"Nineteenth-century Frenchman. Lived in Trinidad for years. Painted the local gentry as well as bucolic views of the countryside and the coast."

"Do you think they were contemporaries?"

"Could have been. Mmm, if she was, I wonder if she was a member of the local gentry, or the wife of one, and he painted her."

With her free left hand, Sally indicated the keyboard with a flourish. "A job for your friend Mr Google?" she said.

"I suspect it might be a little obscure, even for Mr G's prodigious grey cells," replied Ced as he hit the keys. "However, I can go to places he can only dream about," he added with a self-satisfied grin.

A few seconds later, a list appeared on the screen and Ced ran his eye down it.

"There," he said, moving the cursor and pressing the 'Return' key.

A hi-resolution image materialised on the screen, a portrait in full colour of a woman in nineteenth-century colonial clothing.

"Portrait of Mrs Paola Lethrington by Michel-Jean Cazabon," read Sally. "So they did know each other."

"Sally," whispered Ced, more in awe of what he was seeing than consideration for his daughter. "Look at the eyes!"

"Wow!" agreed Sally, "With those pale grey eyes and the resemblance in the face, this has got to mean something."

Ced smiled as his hands blurred over the keyboard. "The two images the American woman sent me are good quality. I'll set up a comparison routine while we get this little bundle back to sleep in her cot. Hang on, I've just remembered, she also sent me images of two paintings of other people, one she thinks Paola produced and one her mother. I happened to click on the drawings first and I was so gobsmacked by them that I forgot all about the paintings. Let's have a look at them."

He pulled up the images of the paintings of Nancy Wright and of the servant woman.

"Wow! They're good and I'd agree that they are pretty similar in style. I'll get the program to compare all four and for good measure, I'll throw in the Cazabon. Not that I think he painted the others, but it's important to eliminate him using the program as well as my eyes."

Fifteen minutes later, all was quiet on the Claudia-Jane front. Ced and Sally had returned to Ced's study and Ced was scrutinising the comparison results on one of his smaller monitors.

"Not much doubt about that, Sal; the figures couldn't be any more definite, given that we're dealing with drawings as well as paintings."

Sally fixed her eyes on the images on the large screen as she computed the information. "Tell me again what the American woman said about them, hon," she said.

"Well, for the drawings, she said the one by Paola Lethrington is her mother's alleged ancestor, while the one in the Renaissance clothing is her mother, whom she said was called Annie Carr," replied Ced as he clicked on and enlarged various parts of the images. "Their quality would support that. The Paola Lethrington has some foxing and the paper looks to be discoloured, while the other one looks definitely more modern. It's in excellent condition: no foxing and no fading or smearing."

Sally turned to Ced. "Do you really think that this Paola is the Paola that John has talked about, the one from Naples?"

Ced nodded. "Well, given we have two indistinguishable drawings and two indistinguishable paintings that were apparently produced over a hundred years apart, and given we have the same face also in the painting by Cazabon, and the same very unusual eyes that not only John has, but also Lily and Phoebe, yes, I think it's pretty definite."

Sally suddenly gasped, her hand going to her mouth. "Oh my God, Ced! This American woman – what did you say her name was?"

"Farsley. Sara Farsley."

"She told you that the woman, Annie Carr, was her mother. If Annie Carr and Paola are the same person, and they are also the Paola from Naples, then Sara Farsley would be John's granddaughter. I wonder if she's the same as he is, you know, different, with the same rare alleles in her DNA and same exceptional health."

"Difficult to say," mused Ced. "She was hardly likely to tell me. If she was born recently, maybe she doesn't even know – about her mother, I mean, although she'd have to be aware her health was special."

"There's nothing to say she was born recently, hon, although it would seem she's only just become aware of Paola Lethrington's work."

"It's possible," agreed Ced. "Whatever, it's an amazing finding, and to think I almost rejected her out of hand. If she hadn't mentioned the name Paola, there wouldn't have been a nagging question in my mind and I wouldn't even have looked at any of the stuff she sent."

"I'm amazed that the name Paola didn't immediately have bells belting out a refrain in your ears, hon."

Ced shrugged. "I don't spend my days thinking about John Andrews' ancestors, or rather his daughters." He pulled a face. "You know what I mean; it's all still rather confusing. Anyway, I think we should call John immediately."

Sally raised her eyebrows. "Really?"

"Yes, why not?"

"It's one o'clock in the morning, hon. I think if John's been waiting for nearly five hundred years for news of his daughter, he won't mind if we leave it until breakfast time."

Chapter 29

Palo Melliff sat in the darkened room he'd chosen over all the smart, glass-walled goldfish bowls he'd been offered once Dayton had realised his value.

"I need to concentrate, boss. I can't do that in a room full of light with stuff going on outside. Gimme a cupboard somewhere with good AC and good connections."

In front of him were three large monitors, each, apparently, with a life of its own. Images and text scrolled and flashed ceaselessly across them – cascades of dancing data with no obvious human input. An untrained eye might have noticed the blur above the keyboard from Palo's hands as a constant stream of typed commands fed the bank of computers in the corner of the room, but it wouldn't be able to follow. Neither would the weird, staccato movements of Palo's eyes mean much – a casual observer could be forgiven for thinking the man was having some sort of fit. In reality, Palo had long abandoned the use of a mouse or trackpad: time spent using either was time away from the keyboard. In their place he used a combination of eye movements, picked up by microlens cameras mounted in his nerdy, black-rimmed glasses, and voice instructions muttered quietly and continuously into the microphone attached to his jaw.

It was a sophisticated skill to operate one screen with Palo's set-up; to have three screens with three sets of independent instructions feeding three computers required a level of concentration few could match. Yet once settled in his comfortable leather recliner, Palo could maintain his activities for hours on end. Or until he was interrupted, when everything was likely to degenerate into chaos as images cartwheeled across the screen. No wonder he was getting fed up with the frequent calls from Dayton demanding progress reports.

"Look, boss, I don' wanna be rude or nothin' but each time you call me, it sets me back fifteen minutes. This is a fine-tuned system I got here. Let me keep it sweet. I swear, as soon as there's somethin', anythin' at all, I'll call yuh."

An increasingly impatient Marcus Dayton closed his phone and drummed his fingers on his glass desk. What was taking the nerd so long? It had been nearly two days since he'd set him the task of searching the world's databases for any indication of someone with Annie Carr's features, features that were shown in perfect detail in the photos he'd copied from Nancy Wright's files.

It would appear from the results of Melliff's searches so far, or rather the lack of them, that Annie Carr, assuming she was still alive, was being very careful. If she was working somewhere in the world, making her living as an artist, she kept a very low profile. Dayton stared out of the window at the New York City skyline: so modern; so recent in terms of his lifetime; so different. He didn't like it, but it suited his purposes. She had to be out there.

Two hours later, his phone buzzed. It was Melliff.

"Yes."

"Boss, Mr Dayton, sir, I got somethin'. It's not much, but it's a possibility. Do you wanna come see?"

Dayton hated the room Palo worked in – he couldn't tolerate the flashing images on the computer screen or the smell of stale pizza and cheap coffee.

"Can you feed something through to me, or bring me some printouts?"

A sigh from the other end. Palo had been expecting it.

"OK, boss. Oh, Mr Dayton, sir?"

"What is it?"

"Do you speak Spanish?"

"Spanish? Of course I do. Why?"

"Well, there's a lot of Spanish in this stuff."

"Where's it from?"

"Rio mainly. Rio de Janeiro."

"Then it's more likely to be Portuguese, Melliff."

"Really? Why?"

"Because that's what's spoken in Brazil."

"Not Spanish? It's just I had this girlfriend once. She was from South America somewhere, Colombia, I think. She spoke Spanish."

"That's right, Melliff. In most South American countries apart from Brazil they speak Spanish."

"And they don't in Brazil?"

"No, Melliff, they don't."

"That's pretty dumb."

"That's just the way it is, Melliff. It's their problem, not yours. Anyway, I also speak Portuguese, so let's drop this stupid discussion. Just bring me your results."

He paused and then added, "Melliff?"

"Sir?"

"You had a girlfriend?"

If a click could register disdain, then it was the click Dayton heard through his phone as Palo disconnected.

"OK, sir, here's what I got," announced Palo as he pushed open Dayton's office door. Dayton's secretary had long since ceased trying to stop him so she could announce him; it seemed her normally very demanding and pernickety boss accepted the nerd's eccentricities.

Palo dumped a sheaf of printouts on Dayton's desk.

"I sent you an image too. Do you want to put it on the big screen?"

Dayton clicked his mouse a few times and an image appeared on a massive monitor on the wall opposite next to the large photograph of his daughter. He stood and walked over to it, rubbing his chin thoughtfully.

"Is this it?"

"That's the best one, Mr Dayton, sir, yes. There're others, but they're not as clear or as full face."

Dayton stared at the fuzzy image on the screen. It was clearly a huge enlargement from a poor-quality shot. It showed a woman's face in a crowd with several other people. She was smiling, coyly it seemed, and the others were looking at her, possibly congratulating her on something. It was a full-face shot, although her long hair partly obscured her face. As did the dark glasses.

"She's wearing sunglasses, Melliff. What use is this?"

Palo smiled. "It gets better, boss." He wanted to keep Dayton dangling; show him just how good he was.

Dayton scowled at him. "I'm waiting."

"OK," said Palo, walking over to Dayton's desk and clicking on his mouse. "Here's a couple of others I've enhanced."

The next image showed just the woman's face, enlarged even further, but distinctly clearer.

"I put it through a few iterations to sharpen it up. It's somethin' I been working on. Good, huh?"

Dayton nodded, his impatience mollified. "Impressive, Melliff, impressive."

"Yeah, well, I checked this one against the shots of Carr for all the facial characteristics and it fits pretty good. Once I done that, I took off the dark glasses and some of the hair."

"You did what?"

"I got this little routine to remove stuff and for the computer to come up with the best likelihood of what's underneath, although obviously I've fudged the colour of the eyes. Here's the result."

He clicked the mouse again and suddenly Annie Carr was on the screen in front of them.

Dayton walked up to the screen and touched it.

"I knew it," he said softly.

He turned to Palo. "I thought you said what you'd found wasn't much."

Palo shrugged. "It could be better and the other thing is that it's five years old. This shot was taken at some art exhibition in Rio in 2007. I got nothing since."

"Did you get a name for this woman?"

Palo grinned. "Sure did, boss."

Ignoring the menacing look on Dayton's face, he walked over to the desk and picked up the sheaf of printouts. He leafed through them and pulled one out.

"Here's a blow-up of a poster that was in one of the shots."

Dayton took the sheet and read from it, translating as he did. "'Portraits from the Countryside. A Collection of the Work of Cassie

Gomes.' Cassie Gomes, Melliff? Have you found out anything about her?"

Palo looked down at his feet and sucked at his teeth, his mouth puckering. "That's the frustrating part, boss, Mr Dayton, sir. Apart from this, which was a newspaper article that was repeated in a few other papers, there's nothin'. She must keep an incredibly low profile."

"I can't believe there's nothing else at all. She's an artist. She's got to display her work; sell it somewhere. Did the report show any of the pieces from this exhibition?"

"There was only one that showed any detail. It was a painting of some kid."

"Show me."

Palo leafed through the printouts again and pulled out the picture.

"Can't do much with that, I'm afraid, sir," he muttered apologetically.

Dayton stared at the painting. It was similar in style to the painting of Nancy Wright, but the subject was so different, it was difficult to be sure.

"I still got the computers churning through just about every database in the world I can access, and that includes quite a few I shouldn't, if you know what I mean. There's a lot out there to go through, but if there's anything else, I'm sure I'll unearth it."

"Keep trying, Melliff, keep trying. Meanwhile, I have a contact on the ground in Rio who might conduct his investigations in a more old-fashioned way but he also gets results."

Fifteen minutes later, Marcus Dayton was on the phone to Eduardo Antônio Correia, an ex-police officer who had worked in the Rio police department's extensive drug investigation division. Marcus' business activities extended worldwide, his South American links a complex web of legitimate business interlaced with layer upon layer of a more shadowy nature. Before he'd been forced out of the police under a cloud of suspicion several years before, Correia had provided Dayton with useful and timely information on a number of occasions, information that had resulted in several human obstacles to deals he was trying to close disappearing without trace. Dayton had not forgotten the favours and still used Correia's new persona as a private detective and occasional enforcer when his skills were needed.

"So Eduardo, you think you can find this woman?"

Dayton was speaking Portuguese as fluently as any Brazilian, but not using the coarse dialect that was Correia's habitual tongue.

There was a rough laugh from the other end of the phone.

"Marcus, this is Eduardo Antônio Correia you are speaking to, not some rookie with the brains of a donkey. You'd better think of something else for me to do as well, or my afternoon is going to be very quiet. If you had just given me the name of Gomes, that would be a problem. It's a common name. But Cassie Gomes, that can't be so common. I'll be in touch with you after lunch."

"I knew I could rely on you, Eduardo."

"No problem, my friend."

Dayton could picture the evil smile spreading under Correia's large moustache, a smile that had distracted the attentions of many unwitting suspects from the cold, sunken eyes boring through them.

Dayton sat back in his chair and focussed on the image still displayed on the huge screen opposite. Cassie Gomes, he thought, a confident smile forming slowly on his lips. I wonder what you've been up to these past thirty-seven years and how long you've been gracing the streets of Rio. You must have a protector to have maintained such a low profile for so long.

Chapter 30

"John, hi, it's Ced. How are you?"

"Ced! Lola and I were just talking about you over dinner last night. How's that gorgeous little bundle, Claudia-Jane, and, of course, the lovely Sally?"

"Both amazing, John. I tell you, I thought triathlons were fun, but fatherhood knocks them sideways. It's such a joy. I want to absorb and remember every minute."

"That's terrific, Ced. I knew you and Sally would be wonderful parents. Now, what can I do for you at eight o'clock in the morning? Of course, you've probably been up for hours with a baby in the house."

"Actually, it depends on how long she's insisted on staying awake the previous night. At the moment, both she and Sal are still sound asleep. Sorry, is it too early for you? It's just that I have some news I couldn't wait to tell you."

"News?" replied John, amusement in his voice.

"Yes. Oh, no, not that sort of news. There's only one Fisher offspring for the time being. John, look, I've just sent you an email with three image files. Could you open the one called 'Cazabon' first?"

"Now you've introduced me to the wonders of the digital age, I can do that easily, yes. Let me just wander through to the computer."

There was a pause, then Ced heard the tapping of some keys.

"Ok, Let's have a look. I …"

There was a stunned silence.

"Ced!" gasped John. "Where did you get this?"

"I got it from a rather obscure archive in the British Museum. It's a portrait painted by a chap called Michel-Jean Cazabon around 1839. The subject is a Mrs Paola Lethrington."

"Paola? 1839? What's the location? It looks tropical."

"It's Trinidad in the West Indies. Cazabon lived there, did local scenery and portraits of the colonial wives."

"Why are you looking at it? Is it part of a case you're doing?"

"No, it isn't. I found it after I'd looked at the two drawings in the second file, the one called 'drawings'. They were sent to me by an American lady who called me yesterday. Take a look at that file now. I've put the two drawings together, side by side in the same file, to make them easier to compare."

There was another pause while John opened the second attachment.

"They're just drawings, John," continued Ced, "but the features are good. Don't you think, in fact, that the features are remarkably similar?"

There was no immediate reply.

"John?"

"Yes, Ced, yes. Sorry. I'm quite stunned. These drawings are remarkable. You can't see much about the eyes, unfortunately, not like the eyes in the painting, but the features – they appear to be drawings of the same woman. They don't look like Cazabon's hand, though."

Ced laughed. "Who needs my program when there are eyes like yours, John?"

"The clothing is interesting," continued John, ignoring the flattery. "In one drawing, the dress is very similar to the dress in the Cazabon, which makes me think it was possibly contemporary. That drawing looks old as well – I think there's some foxing. In the other one, the dress, the hairstyle and the bonnet are straight out of sixteenth-century Naples. However, despite that, the drawing looks more modern."

Another pause as his mind processed the information.

"Ced, are we–?"

"I think you've got it, John. I've run them through the program. They were drawn by the same person, but as you astutely observe, they certainly weren't produced at the same time. Now the older one is labelled as being a self-portrait by Mrs Paola Lethrington, who is clearly the same woman as in the Cazabon. The other is a self-portrait by someone called Annie Carr. That's the one I would agree could be quite modern."

"Ced, this could be Paola. My Paola. The features, the hair, the skin tones, all the detail in the Cazabon painting – she could easily be of Mediterranean origin. In fact, she could be Francesca's … Let me look again; I didn't think of Francesca. Yes, I'm right. She's Paola, Ced. She has to be. Where did you get these?"

"As I said, they're from an American lady who called me yesterday from the US. She said she wanted the two drawings and the two paintings in the third file compared. Take a look at those. They're not self-portraits but they are very detailed paintings, and the program can't distinguish the styles."

He paused to wait for John to open the paintings file.

"Incredible," whispered John. "There's no doubt, is there, Ced?"

"None at all. To think I told her I couldn't help since I don't do private work. Fortunately, she wouldn't take no for an answer and she insisted on emailing me the images. To be honest, I wasn't even going to look at them, but something she'd said on the phone puzzled me, although I couldn't think what it was. When I saw the file names and one included the name Paola, I realised that was it, so I opened the images."

"Where was she from?"

"I don't think she said."

"What time did she call?"

"Er, it was around lunchtime, one to one thirty, something like that."

"Mmm, that would be around eight in the morning in New York but only five on the West Coast. Chances are she's East Coast. Do you have her number?"

"No, I don't; it didn't register on the caller display. I can always reply to her email. Do you want me to do that?"

"No, I don't think you should immediately. I need to think this through. Anyway, there's no hurry; it's still the middle of the night in the States. Ced, did she say why she wanted them compared?"

"Oh gosh, I forgot that bit. Annie Carr, the name of the woman who produced the modern work. She was her mother."

"Her mother! Did she say anything …? No, of course she wouldn't. What was her name, Ced?"

"Farsley. Her name was Sara Farsley."

While Claudia-Jane was enjoying her morning feed from Sally, Ced recounted his conversation with John Andrews.

"I'm not quite sure how to play it, Sal. I'm still wondering how much Sara Farsley knows. I wonder, in fact, if she does suspect something about her mother and the story she told me was just spin." He was absently rubbing his daughter's tiny foot as he spoke.

"Statistically, it's incredibly unlikely, but I suppose there's a possibility she's the same as her mother," mused Sally. "After all, John has managed to defy what you'd expect from the numbers and produce five offspring with the same characteristics he has."

"Five?"

"Yes: Lily, Phoebe and Paola, plus the two sons who were killed centuries ago. I think their names were Henri and Michel."

"Yes, of course. I'd forgotten about them. God, it must be so hard for John at times; I don't know how he copes with it all. He's had so many wives, children, grandchildren and so on. Apart from remembering them all, most of them are long gone while he just carries on. So many ghosts."

"I asked him about it when I was first pregnant and we were up in the Lakes visiting them. You were off charging around the hills. He said that when he first started to notice he was different – when his friends and relations were getting old and dying while he wasn't – he found it very hard. But he eventually learned to accept just how different he was, that it's the way life is for him. And now there's the added bonus of having Lily around and, possibly, Paola, if this person really is Paola."

"I wonder how he deals with the generation stuff," added Ced. "I mean, you know what our parents are like: the music we listen to; the way we treat Claudia-Jane; the way we dress, talk etc – it's all a bit different from their day. As for our grandparents, those that are still around can find it even harder to understand us. John's older than all of them and yet, at the same time, he's younger. In a few years, he'll effectively be younger than we are, in that we'll overtake him."

Sally smiled. "Yeah, it's mind-boggling. I suppose it helps that he's a fairly conservative sort. I mean, I doubt he's ever got caught up with the extremes of any generation."

"The notion of extreme varies a lot depending on where you are in history. He might have thought Mozart was radical when he appeared on the scene?"

"I wonder if he met him?"

Ced thought about it. "I can't remember where John was in the 1780s. Or who he was."

Sally laughed. "I wonder if he does. I sometimes can't remember what I was doing last week."

"Anyway," sighed Ced, "all this doesn't solve my problem about what to say to this Sara Farsley if I write back to her. However, I'll wait for John's call to see if he's decided how he'd like to play it."

When John called back at three that afternoon, Ced could still hear the excitement in his voice.

"I had to wait until it was morning in New York before I could tell Lily the news," he explained. "She's incredibly excited by it, as I am. Have you heard any more from Sara Farsley?"

"Nothing so far. I–" Ced paused as his computer pinged with an incoming email. "Just a sec; this could be something."

As Ced scanned through the incoming email, he could almost feel John leaning eagerly over his shoulder to read it.

He laughed. "Well, this lady's certainly persistent. It's another email from Mrs Farsley, John. She's asking if I've had a chance to look at the images yet and if I haven't, to implore me – her words – to do so. She's nothing if not pushy. Hey, there's a phone number and an address. She must be in her office -- yes, it's from a different email address – so her business address and contact details have been automatically added."

"And?"

"She's a lawyer; there's a website address for the practice she works for. I wonder if it has a photo."

"Where does she work, Ced?"

"Boston," replied Ced as he typed on his keyboard. "Her office is in the centre of Boston. And yes, there's a photo."

"Really!" John was itching for more information. "What's it like? What's the address? I want to see her."

"Hang on, John, let's have a look. Mmm."

"What, Ced?"

"Well, there's a group happy snappy of her along with her colleagues, but it's a full body shot so there's not too much detail. I can't really see her eye colour … except that it's probably quite pale."

"Can't you enhance the image?"

"No. It's low res. As soon as you start enlarging it, it'll pixellate."

"Stop keeping me in suspense, Ced. What's the site address?"

"Oh, sorry."

As Ced recited the url, he heard John tapping on the keys of his computer.

There was a pause.

"You're right, Ced, not too much detail and no other individual images in the biographies. How irritating. I wonder how old she is; she certainly looks no more than about thirty."

"Yes, you're right. Actually, that's an interesting point, John. Her son spoke to me first yesterday, before Mrs Farsley came on the line. He sounded pretty adult. At least late teens, I'd say."

"Ced, I've got it. In her biography. It says she graduated from Boston University School of Law in 1988. If we assume she was in her early twenties, that would make her mid-forties now. Mmm, she certainly doesn't look it. However, we need to meet her. I've already discussed this with Lily and she's raring to go. Fortunately I didn't know where Sara Farsley lived when we spoke or she'd be on her way now. I'll tell her to hang on. I'm going over there Ced, on the first available flight. I've really got to talk face to face with this lady. She must have the key to finding Paola."

"What do you suggest about my reply to her email? I've got to say something or she'll just keep pestering me."

"It would be better if she didn't know I was coming in advance. I somehow feel I need to see her before revealing anything about myself or Lily. Can we stall her?"

"Let's think. I could say I've had a quick look at the images and that they appear interesting. I'll add that I'm prepared to bend the rules and run the comparisons but she'll have to wait a couple of weeks before I get round to it; that I have too many urgent cases for hers to jump the queue. What will you do – just turn up at her house?"

"No. Now we have an office address, it would be easier to see her there. I'll make an appointment; she'll think I'm just another client. However, before we get to that stage, there's a certain man in Whitehall I'd better inform."

Ced laughed. "Ah, yes, the inscrutable Mr Digby Smith."

Chapter 31

Eduardo Antônio Correia's confidence in his own abilities proved somewhat unjustified. Rather than a few well-placed phone calls and a couple of hours including lunch, it took him nearly two days to unearth information about Cassie Gomes. That she was so elusive puzzled him; it was as if she didn't exist. She was on none of the usual databases; she didn't have a driver's license or health card; and he couldn't find a bank account in her name.

It was getting frustrating and he was running out of people to contact. Marcus Dayton had given him details of the art exhibition from five years before and having tracked down the location from the newspaper that covered it, he made his way there. Five years was a long time, but he was getting desperate.

The exhibition had been held in a large room above a cafe frequented by painters in the Rua Paschoal Carlos Magno in the hilly artists' quarter of Santa Teresa. The area was an untidy collection of winding, cobblestoned streets bordered with an eccentric mixture of crumbling mansions, smaller colonial-style houses and more modern, soulless apartment blocks. Adventurous clusters of bougainvillea took advantage of the support offered by the looms of overhead power cables that interrupted the postcard-perfect views of Sugarloaf mountain to the south and the Centro commercial district to the north. Tourists flocked there to soak up the atmosphere, even though the tram had stopped working. Only five kilometres from Correia's upmarket apartment in Ipanema with its panoramic view over the Lagoa Rodrigo de Freitas, Santa Teresa was a world apart and Correia hated it.

The cafe owner, surly and unshaven and wearing an ancient, black, V-neck pullover over a grubby vest in deference to the cooler, winter temperatures, remembered the name Cassie Gomes well enough, but he wasn't about to tell someone who had 'cop' written all over him.

He eyed Correia suspiciously as the ex-cop spun him a story about why he was looking for Cassie.

His reply was grudgingly given. "We have a lot of exhibitions here. It's what the room's for. There's one nearly every week. How do you expect me to remember one from so long ago?" he snarled, not attempting to hide his disdain. He remembered the cop's name now. Correia. He'd been unceremoniously slung out of the police, only his personal connections saving him from being prosecuted. The man was an arrogant fool. There were plenty of corrupt policemen; only the stupid ones got caught.

"I don't expect you to remember the exhibition. It's the artist, Cassie Gomes, I'm looking for," replied Correia, well aware the cafe owner was lying to him. Unfortunately, he was no longer in a position to apply some of the more persuasive techniques he'd perfected while with the police.

"Cathy Gomes?" repeated Nando, deliberately getting the name wrong.

"*Cassie* Gomes," corrected Correia.

The cafe owner shrugged. "Doesn't mean a thing," he lied.

Correia sighed in frustration. He was about to leave when his phone beeped. He looked at it and saw there was a message from Marcus Dayton with three attached files: the enhanced image of Cassie that Palo Melliff had produced and two more images Palo had found of paintings from the exhibition. Correia had contacted Marcus Dayton that morning to declare his frustration and to ask for the supporting images to be sent.

"Perhaps this will jog your memory," he said, holding up the phone to show the cafe owner. "She's an attractive young woman, surely you couldn't forget that face." His voice was heavy with sarcasm.

Once again, Nando just shrugged. Correia checked the other two images on his phone. The first was the one in the newspaper and the other … he paused … the other looked very familiar. He looked up from his phone and scratched his ear, trying to think where … then he smiled. Nando, who was still standing in front of him, wondered what this ex-cop had suddenly found so amusing.

Correia pushed past him and walked two paces to a wall hung with posters and paintings. There, for all the world to see, was the original of the second image Dayton had sent.

Correia bent forward to look at the signature. "C. Gomes," he read out loud. "That would be Cassie's brother Carlo, would it?"

"Who wants to know?" Nando's sneer was even more disdainful now. He didn't appreciate being caught out.

"Believe me," replied Correia, fixing his cold eyes on the man, "you don't want to know."

Nando was no coward – he'd crossed paths with more than his fair share of bullies, crooks and strutting cops – but there was something about this smartly dressed, corrupt ex-cop that said it was in his best interests to tell him something. It didn't have to be everything, but it needed to be true and it needed to be enough to send him on his way.

He stared into Correia's eyes for a long moment, deciding what to say. His stare was calmly and ominously returned with none of the underlying threat diminished.

"She went north," he said finally.

"Where north?"

The cafe owner scowled.

"Where?" insisted Correia.

"São Luís."

"Christ, that's nearly three thousand clicks away. Are you sure?"

Nando's eyebrows flickered upwards. That was the information. The ex-cop could take it or leave it.

"When did she go?"

Nando sighed, walked to the bar and picked up a glass to polish it.

Correia followed him menacingly.

"When?" he repeated insistently.

"Soon after the exhibition. I don't remember exactly. Never saw her again."

"Jesus!" muttered Correia. "São Luís."

Still polishing the glass, Nando walked towards Correia, his eyes moving slowly from his handiwork to Correia's face. He seemed to be deciding where exactly he was going to thrust the glass.

"Get out of my cafe. Get out and don't come back."

Correia looked over at the wall display and smiled arrogantly.

"Nice painting," he said, as he turned to leave.

"Marcus, it's Eduardo."

"Christ, you've taken your time. You'd better have good news."

Correia squeezed the mobile phone in anger. He didn't appreciate being spoken to like that, even if it was Dayton.

"She's in São Luís. It's–"

"I know where it is. Are you on the way there?"

"Jeez, Marcus. I only just found out. It's late. I'll get a flight first thing in the morning. There won't be any more tonight."

"Are you sure?"

"Quite sure. I'll go in the morning."

Cassie Gomes was just letting herself into her small apartment on the Rua do Egito in the historical centre of São Luís when her cell phone rang. It wasn't the usual tone; it was one she had reserved for one specific reason. It was to tell her that something very serious had happened. Even if she couldn't answer it, she would know immediately to be extra alert.

She pressed the connect button. "Rodrigo," she said quietly.

The voice at the other end was heavy, serious.

"Cassie, we have a problem. Nando called."

"Nando from the cafe?"

"Yes. Someone was asking about you. Someone very unfriendly. He remembered him: he's an ex-cop. If he's involved, it's serious. Nando said he's very sorry but he had to tell this guy where you are. He said he had his family to think about, his business. I think this is it, Cassie, what you said would happen eventually."

Cassie sighed. "Yes. It had to happen one day."

"I know, Cassie. I guess I just didn't want it to. Listen. I don't think this guy's going to hang around. He might even be driving up now, although I doubt it. He'll probably take the morning flight. So you need to be flying in the other direction at the same time. OK?"

"OK, Rodrigo. Thanks. What then?"

"As it happens, I have an out for you."

"What sort of out?"

"I have a dead American woman."

"Really? How did she die?"

"Road accident. Riding a scooter. Came off it in a back street. Listen, Cassie, she's perfect."

"How so?"

"She's twenty-nine, quite a Latin complexion, black hair. Could be you."

"Except I'm fifty-two."

"You and I both know that isn't true, Cassie, even if the rest of the world doesn't."

"Won't someone miss her?"

"I've checked her out. She's here alone. Travelling. She'll just disappear. I'll get the body moved out to the slums. She'll be a Jane Doe. She could easily be Brazilian. She'll be just another unidentified body."

Cassie hesitated. "Seems a rough way to go. Can't we do something more respectful with the body?"

"She's dead Cassie. Whatever we do with the body, her folks in the States are going to go through the same enquiries. Embassy, last known contacts etc."

"But no closure."

"No. Listen Cassie, it's your call, but I don't have any other options at the moment."

Cassie hesitated some more.

"Rodrigo, you know how appreciative I am, but I do want to help her parents, in the event that they care. Once I've moved on, gone to the States, probably, got in on her passport, couldn't you arrange for some of her documentation to be found somewhere near the body? At least the parents will have something. Where does she come from?"

"Somewhere in the mid-West. Ohio, I think."

"OK, wherever I go, I'll keep well away from there."

"Where will you go?"

"I don't know. East Coast, possibly. What's her name, Rodrigo?"

"It was Tripley. Naomi Tripley."

Cassie ended the call and stared out of the window. She'd known for a few years it was time to move on; in many ways, she'd stayed too long. The problem was she liked Brazil and she particularly liked São Luís, despite its sticky, tropical monsoon climate and extensive poverty. She'd chosen to rent some upstairs rooms in a two-storey row of tired shops and apartments that were long past their prime, if they'd ever had one. She far preferred the bustle and energy in the narrow streets of the old town over the smarter but sterile high-rise apartment blocks mushrooming next to the beaches of white sand a few kilometres away in Ponta d'Areia. She smiled as she thought of Senhor Rocha, her landlord. He was a sweet old man who loved artists and who treated her like a daughter. He'd be shocked when she suddenly disappeared, as would the good friends she'd made while working quietly as just another artist in a small community of artists. She'd forgotten to ask Rodrigo how he was going to explain her disappearance. Another road accident, probably. He had good connections; it could be arranged.

Rodrigo Barros first met Cassie just a few months after she arrived in Rio in 1980. She was a mess at the time, still beating herself up over waiting too long to return for Serena.

Their first encounter could hardly have been less likely to forge a friendship. Rodrigo was a young cop, bright and still very keen, and recently transferred to Rio from São Paolo. At the time there was a big campaign on illegal immigration. He'd stopped Cassie in the street outside a bar late one evening on a routine search, taken one look at her ID and arrested her. Cassie was stunned. She couldn't believe he'd seen through her ID; the papers were genuine, she thought, and she'd made herself look very like the photo. What Cassie didn't know was that Rodrigo was the officer in São Paolo to whom the real Cassie Gomes had reported her ID stolen. Or at least that was what she claimed. In fact, the São Paolo Cassie was no more the real one than the young woman now sitting across the desk from a bemused Rodrigo in the interview room. He wondered just how many Cassie Gomeses there were.

Cassie looked into the young policeman's eyes, trying to read him as he examined her ID. He looked up.

"So, Cassie Gomes, where are you from?"

"Rio."

He smiled. "Born and bred?"

Shit, thought Cassie. While her language skills were good, her Portuguese was still not perfect. He must have picked up an accent.

"Yes."

"Well, I'm from São Paolo, where we speak Portuguese properly, and your accent doesn't sound too good to me. So I'll ask you again, where are you from?"

"I told you – Rio. My mother was American and insisted I spoke English to her. It accounts for the accent."

Rodrigo laughed and nodded.

"I can believe you are American; you have a certain way about you. But you're no more from Rio than I am. How did you get these papers?"

Cassie ran her hands through her hair, wondering how to play this.

"Let's cut the crap, Cassie, or whatever your name is. Unfortunately for you, before I was posted here, I was in São Paolo, and guess what? I stopped a young woman one evening who looked very like you, no papers, who claimed she was Cassie Gomes and that her papers had been stolen. Small world, eh?"

Cassie said nothing. He seemed to like to talk so if she let him, there might be an opening.

Rodrigo puckered his mouth in thought as something occurred to him. "So, you speak English. Anything else?"

"What do you mean?"

"I mean do you speak any other languages?"

Cassie couldn't help smiling. More than you could imagine, she thought.

"Yes, as it happens I do. How about Spanish, French, German and Italian?"

"Fluently?" asked Rodrigo, trying not to appear impressed.

"Better than my Portuguese, all of them," said Cassie ruefully.

He laughed.

"OK, Cassie Gomes. You want to remain Cassie Gomes?"

"It's the only name I have at the moment. Are you offering me some sort of deal?"

"You're a clever young woman, Cassie; I can see you could be useful to me. I suspect you have a problem you don't want to tell me about, but whatever it is, I'll find out, eventually. Do you want to be useful to me?"

"Do I have a choice? What about the other Cassie Gomes? São Paolo isn't that far away."

"She was a lying little whore and a drug addict. She OD'd just a week after I saw her. She's dead. When I made more enquiries, it turned out she'd stolen her ID, just like you stole it from her."

"I didn't steal it; I bought it," said Cassie defiantly, knowing there was no more point in lying.

Rodrigo smiled at his victory. "Tell me, Miss Gomes, when you're not hanging around outside bars, what do you do? Don't tell me you're an actress – that means only one thing around here. It would be very disappointing."

"I'm an artist – a painter and a sculptress. And I wasn't hanging around outside that bar for no reason. I was meeting someone, a potential client who will now be long gone."

"A client?" Rodrigo raised an eyebrow.

"God, you're all the same. He wanted his portrait painted!"

Rodrigo stood and handed Cassie her papers. "I'll be in touch, Cassie Gomes. For now, you can go."

A week later, Rodrigo surprised Cassie by arriving one evening at the small apartment she'd rented. In answer to her unspoken question as he stood at the door, he simply shrugged and said, "I'm a policeman, of course I know where you live. Now, I want you to come with me."

"Where are we going?"

"To the police station. I'm arresting you."

"What! I thought you said we had a deal!"

"We have. Don't worry, Cassie, the charges won't stick. I need you to be American this evening. Can you do that?"

"American?"

"Yes, you are a young American who's just been arrested for, what, overstaying your visa. That's not too serious is it? I'm going to put you in a cell with another young American. She's got a lot she wants to tell me; she just doesn't realise it yet. Now I want you to befriend her in the cell; talk to her. You see, the dumb policeman who arrested you – that's me – he missed the fact that you are up to your eyes in drug dealing. He just thought you were a stupid girl who'd overstayed. I need some information about her, Cassie, something I can use to help lift the mask from her eyes."

"Why should she talk to me? She'll think I'm a cop if I start asking her a lot of questions."

Rodrigo laughed. "Cassie, if there's one thing you're not, it's a cop. Look, there's no one on this force who could speak fluent enough English, American English, that is, to convince anyone they are American. But you …"

The subterfuge worked well. The young girl turned out to be scared witless about the possibility of spending the rest of her life in prison. Within five minutes of Cassie being thrown into the cell and responding with histrionics and threats to the door that had just been slammed in her face, the girl was telling her a long tale of woe, some of it true. Cassie spent twelve hours locked up with her, extracting enough information for Rodrigo's squad to make some significant raids and arrests. The girl was very relieved to be deported in return for her information. Her only regret was not being able to help the compatriot she'd left behind in the cell.

As time went by, Rodrigo called upon Cassie to play similar roles – sometimes she was an American, sometimes French, sometimes English; it depended on whom Rodrigo had arrested. For her part, Cassie was happy to comply; this serious young man was her protector and potentially very useful to her. He became her friend, her confidant, but never more. She was initially puzzled by this, but then she discovered he'd had a childhood sweetheart, Maria, in São Paolo whom he'd planned to marry. Then one evening, when Maria was returning home from the evening classes she attended, she had been mugged in a dark street and left dying. The devastated Rodrigo swore there would never be anyone else. But he couldn't stay in São Paolo; he needed a fresh start. It was Cassie's good fortune he was transferred to Rio.

By the mid-1990s, Rodrigo was becoming increasingly puzzled by Cassie's looks; she didn't seem to have changed in all the time he'd known her. Cassie wondered how she could tell him. Their relationship was such that she felt she could trust him to keep her secret, but first she needed him to believe it. The opportunity arose when she found a painting by Paola Lethrington on display in a small gallery that specialised in South and Central American nineteenth-century art, a painting she had produced in Trinidad over one hundred and sixty years before of one of Cazabon's daughters.

To Cassie's surprise, Rodrigo accepted her story without reservation. His reaction was one of fascination rather than disbelief. The more information she gave him, the more he just nodded.

"How incredible, Cassie, and how terribly sad your young daughter who was the same as you has been lost."

Ever practical, he knew Cassie would one day need his help with a new ID. They discussed it often, but Cassie loved Rio and her life there. She wanted to put off changing for as long as possible.

In 2001, when the Internet was taking hold, it was Rodrigo who pointed out its potential threat to Cassie.

"These search programs are getting more and more sophisticated every year, Cassie. If they carry on like this, they will soon have access to huge amounts of information. Anyone sitting anywhere in the world will be able to find out anything."

"What's your point?"

"My point is that you have a remarkable secret and one that must remain a secret, as you well know. But in the future, if anyone wants to look for you, for whatever reason, I think the Internet is going to make it easier to find you. I think you should make an effort to avoid getting onto this Internet for as long as you can; it could be dangerous for you. This will of course only protect you so much. I can foresee that before long someone clever will compare your paintings from when you were Paola Lethrington with those you're producing now as Cassie Gomes."

"Why should they want to do that?"

"I don't know, Cassie, perhaps just because they can. I have a feeling of foreboding about it. I think you need to try to cover your

tracks as much as possible. Naturally, I shall help you in every way I can. Before long, of course, you are going to have to change your identity again like you have so many times in the past. You can't remain Cassie Gomes forever."

Chapter 32

The blue telephone on Digby Smith's oak desk jumped into life, its ring tone as distinctive as its colour. Truth be told, it didn't need a separate ring tone, not the line in his office: its number was known to only one person, a person who would reveal the number to no one.

Smith looked up from the file he was reading, the only words stamped on the plain jacket being 'Top Secret', in red ink. A handwritten file reference, also in red, was below them. He closed the file and placed it neatly on the desktop before lifting the receiver.

"John. Good morning. How are you? Nothing wrong, I trust?"

For John and those close to him who knew of his secret, Digby Smith was a character straight out of fiction. Professor Frank Young, the brilliant and eccentric genetics researcher who, with the assistance of Claudia Reid, unravelled the mystery of John's DNA, had been very concerned over John's future and potential threats to his life. Using his contacts in Whitehall's more secret corridors he found a solution in the enigmatic Digby Smith, a man who seemed to have influence everywhere while maintaining a staggering anonymity. Lola, John's wife, described him as so forgettable that when he came into a room, it was really as if he had just left. On a more practical level, she also referred to him as John's get-out-of-jail card, a Mr Fixit who could provide new identities as well as protection for them all in return for exclusive accounts from John and Lily of their long and complex lives. Exactly whom he worked for and what else filled his clandestine days was a mystery to John, but the plain fact of the matter was that he was John's lifeline to a secure future.

The call was unexpected: John Andrews seldom phoned him and Digby was as close as he came to being surprised.

"On the contrary, Digby, everything is absolutely fine. Couldn't be better, in fact."

As Digby waited quietly for the reason for the call, he could hear a very faint electronic buzz in the background from the line's sophisticated scrambler: in the extremely unlikely event of the call being intercepted, all that would be heard would be earsplitting whistles.

"I had a call earlier from Ced. He had some amazing news, in fact, the very best of news, if what I suspect is true. But before taking it any further, I know it's important to inform you."

"Beyond question, John. I am here to act entirely in your interests, as you know. So tell me, what is this news?"

"Ced has uncovered evidence that my daughter, Paola, from Naples, might be still alive and living in the United States."

"Really? If it's true, it would indeed be exciting. Tell me more."

"He was contacted yesterday by a woman called Sara Farsley, who is a lawyer in Boston. She asked him to carry out a comparison of two portraits, both drawings and both labelled as self-portraits. She told him that one portrait was of an ancestor of hers and the other of her mother, whom she called Annie Carr. Ced turned her down but she emailed copies of the drawings anyway. When he saw that the name of the supposed ancestor was Paola Lethrington and then noticed the similarity of the features of the subjects in the two drawings, he carried out a comparison using his program and found they are both by the same hand. They were produced over a hundred years apart, almost definitely, and they are by the same artist. Not only that, she also sent images of two very detailed paintings, one by Paola Lethrington and one by Annie Carr, and they too are indistinguishable. I can't believe it, Digby."

"Remarkable, John. Has Cedric had any further contact with this Sara Farsley?"

"No, I told him to stall her, even though she's pestering him for a result. You see, Ced followed up with some searching and found a portrait in oils of Paola Lethrington by another artist, painted in Trinidad in 1839. I've seen a detailed, hi-res copy. The eyes are very telling: they are the same pale shade of grey as mine, Lily's and Phoebe's. The shape of the face also shows a distinct family resemblance, both to me and to Paola's mother, Francesca."

"I see. Do you know anything else about Ms Farsley?"

"Only that she is Mrs Farsley, seemingly in her mid-forties but from a not-very-detailed photograph on her law practice's website looks around thirty. She has a son to whom Ced also spoke and who, according to Ced, sounded at least in his late teens. Now, obviously I want to visit Sara Farsley, see her close up, talk to her, but initially without revealing anything about myself. I've told Lily in New York and she can't wait to get in touch."

Smith sighed quietly to himself. He never failed to be staggered by the reckless way people are prepared to charge into situations without the least precaution.

"John, I'm very pleased you urged caution in Cedric; you need to do the same with Lily. It would be foolhardy for anyone to make any contact before I make a few discreet enquiries."

"I thought you'd say that, Digby, but assuming that Sara Farsley turns out to be above suspicion, I intend to fly to New York in the next twenty-four hours, so that once you have cleared her–"

"–If I clear her–"

"–Of course. If or when, I'll be in a position to visit her in Boston at the first opportunity. You realise, Digby, that if she is this Annie Carr's daughter, and Annie Carr is Paola, Sara Farsley would be my granddaughter."

"Yes, of course she would. I presume that from what you have seen so far from the photograph, you suspect that she could be the same as you; that she could have inherited your traits."

"It's a distinct possibility, yes."

"But of course, she may not have, and even if she has, if she is genuinely in her mid-forties, she might not yet be fully aware that she is different."

"If she's in contact with her mother she will be."

"That raises an interesting point. If she is in contact with her mother, whether or not she has inherited your traits, why would she want a self-portrait that her mother has produced compared with another self-portrait of her mother from another era?"

"Maybe she's finding it hard to believe her mother."

"Which would imply that she has not inherited your traits, or, perhaps, that she is not in contact with her."

"Possibly."

"Fascinating. OK, John, firstly, I'll arrange the ticket for you. I suggest an afternoon flight from Manchester; there's plenty of choice. That will give you time to get down there without having to leave at the crack of dawn. I'll send a car, of course."

"Thank you, Digby, wonderful service, as always. Actually, it's less than two hours from here to Manchester airport. A late morning flight would be fine."

"I'll see what's available. The second point, John, is please do nothing by way of contacting this Sara Farsley until I give you the all clear. I know you think I'm paranoid but it's my job to be so. You'll agree it's in your best interests, I'm sure."

Your government's, too, thought John. During the past three years, via Digby Smith, he had given a select band of researchers details of daily life, extinct Italian and French dialects and first-hand accounts of encounters with various artists and others over the past five hundred years that were beyond their wildest dreams. He was fully aware that no government would trade such commodities without expecting something in return from the privileged few recipients, their unbending loyalty and support being just the beginning.

Four hours later, Digby Smith was facing a dilemma. His contact in the US had proved remarkably efficient: he had checked out Sara Farsley and discovered that she was a respected lawyer with a reputation for incisive delivery in the courtroom. Otherwise, she led an uneventful life. Her background had been traced to her foster parents and before that to her early days in the commune. None of this worried Digby Smith, although the word 'commune' caused his mouth to twitch slightly in distaste. What concerned him was that in the notes from the social worker who dealt with Sara at the time of her fostering, it was stated that Sara's mother was dead. Significantly, he thought, no name was given for the mother, only for the child: Serena Peace.

Yet now, it would appear that Sara Farsley knew the name of her mother. Digby decided he needed to know more about Annie Carr and asked his contact to dig further. In the meantime, his dilemma was whether to tell John that Sara's mother was apparently dead. If it were true, he would be bitterly disappointed. But was it true? Being familiar with the very complex details of John's long life, Digby knew that from time to time it had been convenient for him to be thought of as dead as a part of assuming a new identity. If Annie Carr was truly Paola Santini, John's daughter from Naples, she would be only around ninety years younger than John and she would inevitably have honed her survival skills: reports of her death could not necessarily be believed.

And what of Sara Farsley? From the information he had, she seemed to be genuinely in her forties. Why was she only now surfacing with questions about her mother? Digby decided he needed more answers about Sara as well, but on the face of it, there appeared to be no reason why John could not go ahead and meet the woman who might well be his granddaughter. He didn't want to bias the meeting so he wouldn't tell John that Paola might be dead; there was insufficient information as yet to confirm it. However, he wanted John to proceed with caution, to play his hand very carefully.

He pondered the question well into the night, wondering whether to have minders quietly following John and Lily once they arrived in Boston to visit Sara Farsley. In the end he decided against it: both John's and Lily's antennae were to be relied on, even in the potentially emotional situation of a meeting with John's previously unknown granddaughter. There was, however, one little prop he thought it worth them using.

"Digby. Good morning. I hope you're calling with good news."

It was eight the following morning; John was packed and waiting for the car to arrive to take him to the airport. He wanted Lola to go with him to meet Sara and to learn what she knew about her mother, about Paola. Unfortunately, much as Lola wanted to be with him, she wasn't able to leave their young daughters, Sophie and Phoebe, at short notice. She stood holding John's hand expectantly as he spoke to Digby Smith.

"So far so good, John. The information I've been able to glean on Sara Farsley gives me nothing to indicate that you shouldn't go ahead and meet her. However, since there are still unanswered questions about her background, I think it better to err on the side of caution."

John frowned, wondering what was coming. Lola felt him tense and her face darkened. She liked Digby Smith but she found his Whitehall reserve frustrating and his secrecy maddening. She waited, hoping there was no bad news.

Unaware of the tension he'd created, Digby Smith continued.

"Firstly, John, while I don't expect you to record your meeting, I should very much appreciate it if you could let me have, as close as possible, a verbatim record. Both you and Lily have excellent memories for detail so I don't think it should be a problem."

"Of course, Digby, we can do that," replied John cautiously.

"Secondly, I've been thinking about the dynamics of the meeting. Now, both you and Lily have very pale grey eyes – it's something of a characteristic – and although plenty of other people have pale grey eyes, yours are particularly striking. If Sara Farsley is your granddaughter and, in addition, she shares your very special traits, I should assume she would have pale grey eyes as well. I was imagining the situation when you meet. She would be bound to notice your eyes immediately; she may even be looking for them."

"That's a very good point, Digby." John was nodding absently, while Lola continued frowning at him, wanting to know what constraints Digby was putting in place.

"The point is, John, there are still unanswered questions over Mrs Farsley. You could call them lingering doubts, although doubts is possibly rather strong. I should hate for you not to be in the best position when you meet her, not to have the upper hand. After all, we don't know what she knows or suspects. When you turn up at her office with Lily as supposedly new clients, you don't want her to think you are otherwise, not immediately, anyway. What I'm proposing is that when you meet her, it would be best in the first instance to maintain your anonymity."

John glanced at Lola. For the first time in the conversation, she saw there was a twinkle in his eye. She tilted her head in question.

"I know Lily is in the habit of wearing rather large dark glasses, Digby," said John, "but they are not really me. Are you suggesting I get out my box of whiskers and make-up?"

"Nothing so complex, John," replied Digby, not responding to John's lightness, even if he was aware of it. "What I have in mind is that both of you wear coloured contact lenses; dark brown, I should suggest. That way, Mrs Farsley is less likely to be alerted. I've taken the liberty of leaving packets of them for you and Lily with the driver, although he, of course, has no idea what he's passing over to you."

"Of course, Digby, that's an excellent idea. In fact, Lily mentioned to me a while ago that she sometimes wears coloured lenses simply to avoid questions about her having Asian features but pale eyes. It's pretty unusual."

"Precisely, John. I'm glad we've sorted that out. Your driver should be along shortly. Have a safe flight and I'll be in touch very soon."

John rang off and turned to his wife, smiling in amusement as he did.

"I take it that was Mr Whitehall just being his usual cloak-and-dagger self?" said Lola.

"Yes," replied John, kissing her on the forehead.

"What is it, John? You're looking distracted."

"Nothing, really. It's just that Digby is still being cautious about Sara. 'Unanswered questions' is how he put it. I wonder what he means."

"Oh, you know Digby, John; until he's put her through his own third degree, he won't be happy."

Chapter 33

"**M**arcus, I think I got her."

"What do you mean, you think? Either you have her or you don't!" Dayton was yelling down the phone in frustration.

"Hey, Marcus, don't yell, it's not polite. I'm doing well here. Now listen, I don't actually have her in my hands, so to speak, but I am in her apartment in São Luís. All I gotta do now is sit tight and she'll come home. What do you want me to do with her then?"

"You're in her apartment? Are you sure?"

"Absolutely, Marcus. There are photos of her around the place; she looks just the same as in the ones you sent me. When were those black and whites taken? She hasn't aged much."

Dayton ignored the question.

"Is there a camera on your phone, Eduardo?"

"Marcus, please…"

"I want you to take some shots of those photos and send them to me now. What else is there in the apartment? Any paintings?"

"Yeah, quite a few. Do you want photos of some of those as well?"

"Yes. Choose some portraits, if there are any. The larger the better. Are they framed?"

"Er, yeah, some of them."

"Right, while you are waiting, make some preparations. I'm going to need to see some of those actual paintings, not just photographs of them. I want you to make a selection of what seem to be the most detailed; cut them out of the frames if necessary. Then roll them up and wrap them. They can come with Cassie Gomes once we've got her. Have you got that, Eduardo?"

"Yes … Sure."

"What is it Eduardo? You sound distracted."

"Just some noise on the stairs. It's nothing."

"OK. Now, I think I should get down there myself. We're going to need to get Gomes out of the country and into the US. My private jet is the obvious way, so I'll make the arrangements. How long …? Eduardo, are you still there?"

Marcus took the phone from his ear and looked at the screen. Call ended. He dialled again and waited while the phone rang. Nothing. He tried again. This time he just got an unobtainable signal. A third attempt resulted in an automated message in Portuguese telling him the number was out of service.

"What the hell's going on? Doris!" he yelled to his secretary. "Get Melliff in here now!"

The most senior of the four police officers put Correia's phone, minus the battery and SIM card, on the coffee table in front of where two of his colleagues were holding Correia by the arms.

"What are you doing here, Senhor?"

"I'm a friend of Ms Gomes."

"Your name?"

"Ernesto Cruz."

"Papers?"

"Let go of me and I'll show you."

The police officer nodded to his colleagues who slackened their grip. Correia shrugged away their arms and reached into his jacket pocket.

"There," he said, producing his fake ID.

The police officer took it and studied it. Then he took some folded papers from his uniform pocket, unfolded them and held them against the ID card.

He sighed.

"Senhor Correia, I am arresting you for burglary, possession of false identity papers and attempting to pervert the course of justice."

As Correia started to object, the police officer held up the documents to show him. They contained a colour photocopy of Correia's genuine ID and a copy of his cancelled police warrant card.

"What are you doing here, Senhor Correia?"

"I do not wish to say anything until I have spoken to my attorney."

The police officer gave him a thin smile.

"That could take a while, Senhor. You know how unreliable communications can be out here in the sticks." He looked pointedly at the dismantled cell phone on the table.

Five long days later, the same senior police officer walked into the cell where Correia was being held and handed him a bag containing the pieces of the dismantled phone. "You are free to go. By that I mean you go straight to the airport and leave São Luís. You are not welcome here."

Correia snatched the bag and slipped it into his pocket. As he stood, the police officer put up his hand. "Before you go, I think you should see these."

Correia frowned. "What's this? A car wreck?"

"Exactly. The poor victim, as you can see, is a woman who was driving alone at night. She was, it seems, driving too fast; she was in a hurry to reach a friend who needed her help. She died instantly when her car hit the tree."

"Why are you showing me these?"

"The victim was the woman in whose apartment you were apprehended. Her name was Cassie Gomes."

Correia snatched the photos to take a better look. The victim's head was badly injured, having hit the windscreen very hard in the impact. She had not been wearing a seat belt. He could tell nothing from the battered and bloodied face, although the overall shape and size of the body appeared similar to Gomes' in the photos he'd seen.

He handed the photos back.

"She has been positively identified?"

"Beyond any doubt. The victim was Cassie Gomes."

Marcus Dayton threw his phone across the room in temper. The incompetent fool! If Correia had gone to São Luís when Dayton told him to, he might have intercepted Cassie Gomes before she left. He didn't believe the story about the car crash for one moment. It was all too convenient. However, whether it was true or not, he knew he would gain nothing by trying to pull strings in Rio. Doors would just slam in his face. Officially, Cassie Gomes was dead and that was that. Worse, the leads to her were now useless and he would have to start again. With luck, she would continue to make a living as an artist; it seemed her habit and perhaps all she could do. He would have to wait until whoever Cassie Gomes became appeared somewhere online. But it might take years...

His eyes fell on the file in front of him on his desk. He was no longer prepared to wait years. He wanted to move now. He smiled and nodded to himself. There was an alternative that was ninety-five per cent certain. More, probably. He would refocus his efforts on Sara Farsley.

Chapter 34

John sat in a quiet corner of the British Airways business class lounge at Manchester airport and took his new smartphone from his pocket. From being a techno-dinosaur, with the combined help of Ced and Lily's tuition – and a helping hand from his two young daughters when he got stuck – he now embraced the brave new world of communications with something approaching confidence, although there was still a slight residual awe.

He tapped on Lily's name and put the phone to his ear. After a few seconds of swishing, whooshing and what sounded like waves breaking – he always imagined the signals swimming their way through the Atlantic rather than bouncing their way through the atmosphere above it – there was a click, one ring and then Lily's voice.

"Papa! I was about to call you. I couldn't sleep I was so excited. Have you got any more news?"

John laughed. "And I was worried I was going to wake you, Lei-li."

Lei-li was Lily's original name, the one that John, as Stephen Waters, and his wife, Mei-ling, had given her when she was born in Hong Kong in 1885. John still used it whenever he was talking in private to Lily.

"It's just after seven in the morning, Papa; I'm always up by now. You know how I love the mornings for working; they are my most creative time."

"Of course. Lei-li. Well, do you think you'll be able to drag yourself away from your work this afternoon? I have a little task for you."

"You've found out where this Sara Farsley lives? Is she here in New York City? Do you want me to go visit her? I can go this morning."

"Lei-li, slow down! I do know where she lives, yes, but no, I don't want you to go and visit her. The task I have for you this afternoon is to pop along to JFK."

"Oh, sure," she replied somewhat flatly. "You want me to meet someone? Who?"

"Me, Lei-li. I'll be arriving on the BA flight that lands at around three thirty. I'm about to board it now. Allowing for the endless queues at US immigration, I hope to be through by five thirty."

"Papa! That's fantastic! I'll be there. Oh, I can't wait! So you must have found out more about Sara. Can you tell me?"

"I'd rather not talk about it on the phone, Lei-li, but yes, there is more."

"At least tell me where we'll be going, where we're going to find her."

"Boston, Lei-li, we're going to Boston."

Immigration procedures at JFK at the time of John's arrival were even slower than normal, so it was almost six in the evening before he finally emerged to be greeted by Lily's enthusiastic hugs.

"I'm thinking of getting Digby Smith to get me a new nationality," said John ruefully as they joined the taxi queue. "Apparently, if you're Dutch, South Korean or Mexican, you can join the fast track scheme. Whatever happened to the 'special relationship'?"

"South Korean should do it," laughed Lily. "No one would suspect a thing. Actually, I think the Canadians get the privilege as well."

John shook his head. "We live in strange times, Lei-li. It doesn't seem so long ago that I used to write out my own passport in whatever name I chose. Not so now. Thank heavens we have Digby Smith."

Settling in their taxi, Lily gave the taxi driver the address and then attempted to exchange a few words. She sat back, satisfied.

"What was that about, Lei-li?"

"Just checking. Like most New York taxi drivers these days, he doesn't appear to speak any known language apart from major street addresses, so we should be ok to talk, as long as we do it sotto voce."

She turned in her seat to face her father, her eyes sparkling in expectation. "Ok, tell me all. What have you found out?"

John smiled and squeezed her hands. "Not a huge amount more than I told you before. Our friend–" he glanced at the back of the driver's head, but the man was humming along to some atonal Eastern music on his radio, apparently oblivious of them. "Our friend in London has checked up on Sara. She's a lawyer, a successful one, apparently, and a mom. She's forty-six years old but from her firm's website looks younger."

"Url?" said Lily as she pulled her phone from her bag.

"What?"

"What's the website address, Papa?"

John thought for a moment. "I can't remember. Google Paterson and Associates in Boston. There's a group photo."

Lily called up the site and enlarged the photo as much as she could.

"Mmm, can't see a lot of detail, but if this is anything to go by, she doesn't look forty-six."

She clicked around the site. "How frustrating – they don't have any more photos with the biographies. What about the name she gave for her mother?"

"Annie Carr? I looked her up and could find nothing at all, so if she's working as an artist, either she's very secretive or she's using another name."

"You didn't find any Annie Carrs?" said Lily in surprise. She tapped onto her phone again.

"Yes, of course I found some, but none that seemed to make any sense in the context of anything we know."

"Which isn't a great deal," frowned Lily as she stared absently at the passing scenery. "How do you think we should play this?"

John rubbed his chin thoughtfully "I've been musing about that on the plane. I suggest we make an appointment to see our lawyer friend in her office. Given that you and I are regarded as contemporaries by most people, we can pose as man and wife, or if you prefer, as brother and sister."

"Brother and sister! I don't think so!" said Lily, raising her eyebrows in amusement. Then she pursed her lips into a bow and squeezed her eyes shut.

"I Chin-ee, mister."

Relaxing her face, she touched John's arm. "I think I'd better be your wife. Sara Farsley's not a divorce lawyer, by any chance?"

"That was a short marriage," laughed John. "No, she specialises in criminal law."

"So are we looking for her to represent us? What have we done? Or are you the criminal and I'm just the loving wife, supporting you for better or for worse?"

"Well, whatever ruse we use to get through the door, I don't suppose we'll need to go very far with it. One look at her will tell us plenty."

"Only if we think she's like us. Suppose she's not. Suppose she is Paola's daughter but doesn't share our longevity."

"Or she's neither," added John. "I've thought of that, but there must be some connection otherwise why would she have the paintings and drawings? And anyway, Digby's given her a tentative all clear."

"We've got to have some story, even if it's only to get past her secretary," said Lily, frowning in thought as she considered a few scenarios. Then, smiling, she turned to John. "How's your father getting on in that retirement home?"

"What?"

"The one that had the fire. He was accused of arson, which might well be true but since he went a bit gaga, he can hardly be held responsible."

John nodded. "We're looking for representation for him. He's being unfairly treated and the authorities aren't listening. Ok, that should be enough. Let's hope we don't have to ad lib too much."

Lily suddenly lifted her wrist to check her watch. "Damn, I forgot the time. We need to make an appointment. It'll be too late now. I'll have to call first thing in the morning, but I doubt we'll get one tomorrow."

"The day after will do," yawned John. "I'll need twenty-four hours to get over my jet lag."

When Lily called the office of Paterson and Associates the following morning, she was disappointed to find that Sara Farsley was busy for the next two days. However, she managed to get a slot for them for early the day after, a Friday.

"The appointment's at nine fifteen, Papa," she told John when he emerged from his room, still groggy with the time difference. "We'll have to go tomorrow afternoon and stay in a hotel for the night. It's a four-hour train ride, or if you want, we can drive."

"The train sounds more relaxing, Lei-li, let's do that."

They had intended to spend the rest of the day at Lily's studio where she wanted to show John her latest work, but neither of them was really in the mood to concentrate on the paintings, brilliant though they were. John remained restless, distracted, the anticipation of meeting Sara at the forefront of his mind, and with that, the possibility that Paola might finally be within reach.

At four, Lily suggested they go for a walk. She wanted to show John the progress with the Highline, the old, elevated rail line in south-west Manhattan that had been developed over the past few years as a so-called linear park. An unusual walk above some of Manhattan's older districts, it was somewhere Lily now enjoyed going for a pleasant stroll that made a change from Central Park. The fresh air was good, but neither of them could get their minds off the coming meeting in Boston and they passed most of the walk discussing what they might say in the first five minutes or so in Sara Farsley's office.

At eight thirty on Friday morning, John and Lily left their hotel in downtown Boston, having arrived in the city early the previous evening. With time on their hands, they parked themselves in a coffee bar a block away from the offices of Paterson and Associates and watched as the occupants of the many nearby offices scuttled through the busy streets to work. Lily looked over her coffee at her father, the man from whom she had been violently snatched in 1905 following a murderous attack on the junk on which they were fleeing

Hong Kong, the man she didn't then see for over a hundred years. Yet now, miraculously, here he was sitting with her in Boston where they both hoped they might be about to extend their unique family further.

"Nervous?" smiled John, as he saw Lily staring at him.

She nodded. "Nervous but excited. If what we think is true, this could be quite a day."

"Good morning, how may I help?"

The middle-aged receptionist looked up from her computer monitor at the reception counter of Paterson and Associates. John and Lily approached the desk and John said, "Mr and, er, Mrs John Andrews. We have an appointment with Sara Farsley."

"Certainly, Mr and Mrs Andrews. Sara is expecting you. If you'd like to take a seat, I'll let her know you're here." She pointed to a pair of brown leather sofas to the right of the entrance.

As they sat, John saw Lily was staring at him, a half-smile in the corners of her mouth.

"What?"

She pursued her lips. "You were speaking with an American accent, Papa. I didn't know you were that suggestible."

"I'm not," retorted John. "I didn't realise. You must remember that I lived in this country for nearly thirty-five years. I was an Italian immigrant brought up here; I had to have an American accent."

Lily laughed. "Well, you'd better make up your mind which one you're going to use with Sara Farsley. Perhaps-a you wanna be Italiano, Babbo." She gave an exaggerated shrug.

"I think I'll revert to British English, thank you," said John, with mock petulance. "And while I think of it, you'd better remember not to call me Papa, or Babbo, in there."

Lily put her hands together on one side of her face, tilted her head into them and fluttered her eyelashes.

"I just can't help it, my dear husband, what with you being so much older than I am, an' all."

They were interrupted in their banter by a voice to one side of them.

"Mr and Mrs Andrews? Good morning, I'm Sara Farsley."

Chapter 35

John's and Lily's heads both shot round to see Sara Farsley standing next to them. Their eyes focussed straight onto Sara's and instantly they both felt any lingering doubts evaporate.

For John, it was as if the centuries had peeled away before his eyes: this attractive young woman standing in front of him, a light, slightly quizzical smile on her face, was the image of his beloved daughter, Gianna, born to his wife, Beth, on the last day of 1548. Gianna, who died a frail old woman eighty years later, holding her youthful-looking father's hand on her deathbed and calling him Babbo.

"Is everything all right, Mr Andrews? You look as if you've seen a ghost." Sara was wondering if her potential new client needed medical attention.

John stood and held out his hand, which Sara took.

"I, er, yes, I'm fine, thank you, Mrs Farsley. I apologise; it was just … you reminded me of someone." The corners of his mouth twitched in a nervous smile, but his mind was still distracted, filled with memories of Gianna.

Sara broadened her smile, trying to soften the moment. "You know, I felt the same when I saw you. How strange."

She turned to Lily. "Mrs Andrews, I apologise. I'm pleased to meet you. Perhaps you'd both like to come through to my office where we can talk. Would you like some coffee? Tea?"

Brandy? thought Lily, as she chewed her lip in an attempt to contain her emotions.

Sara settled them on a sofa on one side of her office while she sat on another sofa facing them.

"My secretary said you were coming from New York City. Surely you didn't travel down this morning?"

"No," said Lily as she coughed, trying to find her voice. "We, er, we arrived yesterday evening. We came by train and stayed in a hotel overnight."

"Are you staying long? Do you have relatives in Boston?"

"Yes, I think we do," said John mysteriously.

Sara frowned, somewhat puzzled by his answer. She was about to ask him what he meant when her secretary knocked on the door and walked in with a tray of coffee that she placed on a low table between the sofas.

As the door closed behind the secretary, Sara looked up from where she was pouring the coffee.

"I'm intrigued, Mr and Mrs Andrews, as to why you have come all the way to Boston to seek my counsel. Are there no lawyers in New York anymore?" She smiled at them as she raised her eyebrows in question.

John looked confused and Lily stepped in. She laughed lightly at Sara's comment. "I'm sure there are plenty, Mrs Farsley. It's just that you are more conveniently placed."

"Really? How so?"

"It's my … John's, er, father, you see. The problem is with him. He's in a retirement home not far from Boston and they are accusing him of things."

"Things?"

"There was a fire. People were injured. They think he started it."

Lily couldn't believe how unconvincing she sounded. She glanced round to her father to see his eyes fixed on Sara Farsley.

Sara picked up a legal pad and a pen. "Has he been formally charged? If you could give me some reference. Perhaps there are some papers you've been given?"

When there was no reply, Sara glanced up at Lily from her pad to see her looking expectantly at John. Sara turned her head to him. "Mr Andrews?"

John sat back, folded his arms and sighed deeply. He had made a decision.

"Mrs Farsley. I'm sorry. I should imagine you are puzzled by our behaviour and by our not-very-convincing performance. As you so astutely say, why would we come all the way to Boston for legal advice when lawyers are falling over themselves in New York?"

"But I thought …" Sara started to reply but the words dried up. She was feeling uneasy and wondering if she should make an excuse to call in Pete. She moved to the edge of her seat.

"The fact is Mrs Farsley," continued John, "we haven't come here today for your legal advice. We've come on another matter entirely, a personal matter."

"I'm afraid I don't handle family law," said Sara, starting to stand. "Would it help if–?"

John held up his hand.

"Please, Mrs Farsley, it's you we want to talk to. If you could just hear us out."

Sara slowly sat back down. "Go on, Mr Andrews. What sort of personal matter? Is it to do with Matt or Julie, my children?"

John shook his head. "No, certainly not."

He leaned over to retrieve the briefcase he'd brought with him and clicked it open. He looked up at Sara.

"A few days ago you called a friend of ours in England about some paintings and drawings that you wanted compared. I have copies here."

He pulled out printouts of the two self-portraits and the paintings and held them up.

Sara was stunned. Who were these people? Had Ced Fisher made his comparisons against company policy and these two were trying to sack him for breaking the rules? That was ridiculous. Surely they wouldn't fly all the way from England. Maybe they were employees from a US branch of the company.

"Mr Andrews, who are you? Is Mr Fisher in some sort of trouble? Because I really don't think–"

"Trouble?" echoed John, genuinely surprised at the suggestion. "No, of course not. Why should he be in trouble?"

"So you don't work for the same company that he works for?"

"Heavens no. I'm an artist, I work for myself, in England. Lily works in New York. She's an artist as well."

Sara glanced at Lily who smiled back in agreement.

"That must be difficult," said Sara, frowning.

"Difficult?" said John.

"Well, I don't know, if you work in England and your wife in New York. Isn't that a little …?" Her voice trailed away. She shouldn't pry.

John shook his head. "Oh, yes, I mean, no, it's not difficult. You see, Lily isn't my wife. We just thought it would be easier to say she was."

"Mr Andrews, please, you're really not making a lot of sense."

"I'm sorry, Mrs Farsley. Let's start again. These drawings. You told Ced Fisher that one of them was a self-portrait by your mother and that her name was Annie Carr. The other, you said, was a self-portrait of an ancestor of yours, Paola Lethrington. Is that correct?"

Sara stared at the two images and nodded hesitantly. "Yes, it is."

"You asked Ced if he could compare them to see if they were drawn by the same person. Why would you do that, given they seem to be from different periods? This Lethrington portrait appears to be far older than the other one."

Sara was now distinctly uneasy. She desperately wanted Pete to be in the room with her.

"Mr Andrews, may I ask if Ced Fisher knows you're here? If he does, is he in agreement with these questions?"

John nodded. "Yes. Ced is perfectly aware of our trip and he knows what we are asking."

Sara paused to think, recalling the story she'd rehearsed for Ced Fisher.

"OK, then I'll answer your question. It's actually quite simple, Mr Andrews. You see, my mother was an artist, a very good one, and she was also accomplished at copying other people's work. She always told me that being an artist ran in the family; that she had ancestors who were brilliant artists. I doubted it since I'm certainly not gifted that way. Anyway, she had an old drawing that she said had been in the family for years, although I'd never seen it before. It was a self-portrait by a nineteenth-century artist called Paola Lethrington, whom my mother claimed was an ancestor who lived in Trinidad in the Caribbean. I must admit it all seemed very fanciful, but I didn't really pay it any mind. She also had a self-portrait she'd drawn in pencil, putting herself in very old costume, like something out of

Renaissance Europe. Recently, my son, Matt, got interested in the family history and the whole subject of the drawings came up. Now, Matt is a bit of an artist and when he studied the two drawings, firstly, he was very impressed by their quality and, secondly, he thought their style and execution was so similar that they could have been drawn by the same person."

"Fascinating," nodded John. "Your son has a good eye."

"Yes, well, I got to thinking about it and I thought that if they were produced by the same person – my mother, that is – maybe the whole exotic family history of a mysterious artist in the Caribbean was made up–"

John's words suddenly registered.

"What do you mean by 'your son has a good eye'? Has Mr Fisher compared them? Are they by the same artist?"

John nodded gently. "Yes, Mrs Farsley, they are."

Sara put a hand to her mouth. "My God, then it's true."

"True?" said John and Lily together.

Sara stared at them as if their presence in front of her was a total surprise.

"Er, yes, true," she said, trying to regain her composure. "True that my mother drew them both, true that she just invented the family history," she said, hoping it sounded convincing.

Neither John nor Lily said anything. They knew Sara was making it up; what they didn't yet know was how much she knew about herself, and about her mother.

John felt it was time for the big question.

"Mrs Farsley, what I don't understand about what you've just told us is why you haven't simply asked your mother."

There was a gasp from beside him as Lily grabbed his arm.

"Oh, God! No! You said 'your mother was'; you used the past tense. Your mother's–"

"Dead, Mrs Andrews?" said Sara quietly. "Yes, she's dead. She died many years ago, in 1975, when I was quite young."

Sara was surprised by the strength of the reaction from her two visitors. They both visibly paled as they stared at her in shock.

"Dead?" John's whispered question was almost inaudible as he shook his head in disbelief. "It can't be true, not now, not with all this."

He gestured towards the printouts lying on the coffee table. "How? How did she die?"

"In a fire. It was in Colorado. She was locked up in a psychiatric institution and there was a fire. No one knows how it started, but it was said to be arson. She was trying to rescue her paintings."

"Were you there with her?" asked John. Then he realised the absurdity of the question. "No, of course you couldn't have been. Why was she locked up; I don't understand?"

Sara still felt distinctly uneasy. Who were these people? She attempted to take the lead. "Well, I don't understand why you should be so interested in my mother."

Lily leaned forward to her. "Mrs Farsley," she said, as she regained her composure. "You said just then that your mother died in 1975, when you were quite young. How old were you?"

"I ... I was nine, but I hadn't seen my mother since I was four. I didn't even know her name at the time. I only found that out recently, when Matt, and Julie, my daughter, started digging around the Internet. Listen, can you please tell me what this is all about?"

Lily nodded. "Of course, we need to lay everything on the table." She turned to John. "Do you agree, Papa? Shall I explain?"

As John nodded, he noticed Sara's puzzled expression. Papa?

Lily turned back to Sara. "Mrs Farsley, it's difficult to know where to start. Maybe it would be better if I told you something about yourself that I think is true, rather than ask what might sound like rather personal questions."

Sara waited, saying nothing.

"If you were nine in 1975, that means you were born in 1966, which would make you now forty-six, or perhaps forty-five, depending on the month you were born."

"Forty-six," agreed Sara.

Lily smiled to herself. With every piece of information, she became more and more convinced about Sara Farsley.

"OK. Mrs Farsley, may I tell you something about yourself that I think will be true? About your health. Am I right in thinking that it's, well, remarkable? That you enjoy the most amazing health; that you are never ill and never have been?"

Sara was shocked. "How do you know–?"

"–What about your mother? Do you know if she was the same?"

"Yes, I believe–"

"–And your eyes, they are the same as your mother's? The same very pale grey?"

"I think so, yes, but I don't really remember my mother's eyes," replied Sara in an almost inaudible whisper. "Why are my eyes significant?"

Lily put up her hand. "Please, another point first. You don't look forty-six, Mrs Farsley; you don't look any more than about thirty. Does that puzzle you?"

Sara nodded, her face suddenly fearful. "Yes, it does. I don't understand it. At first, around ten years ago, I thought it was great; I wasn't showing all the early signs of middle age descending on me like so many of my friends. They were all starting to, you know, apply more creams, hit the gym harder, some even starting to think about nips and tucks, Botox and the like. All the usual stuff that the modern American woman is pressured into thinking is important, bombarded by companies who are really only interested in their profit line. Don't get me started. I'm always lecturing my friends about growing old gracefully and all I get is sneers. They are increasingly convinced I have found the secret of staying young; that I've got some secret formula I won't give them. It all gets quite heated at times."

She paused. Then shaking her head, she said, "Why am I telling you all this?"

Lily laughed, surprising Sara. "But Mrs Farsley, you have!"

"Have what?"

"The secret of staying young. You've not so much found it, but you certainly have it. You just don't understand it."

"What do you mean? How do you know all this?"

"Mrs Farsley, look at me. How old do you think I am?"

Sara swallowed hard, the significance of Lily's words sending a cold chill down her spine. She looked from Lily to John and then back again as she remembered Annie Carr's story in Nancy Wright's notes. She shook her head, unable to speak.

Lily smiled, seeing the confusion in Sara's eyes.

"Well, Mrs Farsley, my friends who've known me for quite a long time think I'm fifty-two."

"You can't be! Not with skin and a figure like that," exclaimed

Sara. Then the pieces fell further into place. "Are you saying …? Are you–?"

"–Just like you?"

"Yes, just like me," said Sara quietly.

"So if I hadn't told you I was fifty-two, how old would you say I was?"

Sara shrugged. "I don't know, late twenties, early thirties? It's hard to say precisely."

"Just like you, in fact. That's what people who don't know you think you are. Around thirty. Am I right?"

"So, are you saying that you are the same as I am?" said Sara. Then a light switched on in her head. "Is your health the same? Are you also never ill?"

"Exactly so. I have never had a day's illness in my life."

"So if you're fifty-two and still look–"

"I'm not fifty-two," smiled Lily softly. "I am, in fact, much older."

"Older?" Sara was incredulous. "How old are you?"

Lily glanced at John. This was an important moment. He nodded his head a fraction to tell her to continue.

"Look, I don't know how much you suspect and how much you know, about yourself and your mother, I mean," said Lily, opening her hands as if to help her story. "So I don't know just how strange, how crazy, in fact, what I'm about to say is going to seem."

Sara said nothing.

"You asked how old I am, Mrs Farsley. Well, I was born in 1885. I'm a hundred and twenty-seven years old but I haven't aged one jot since I was around thirty."

Lily paused, watching for Sara's reaction.

"You don't seem over-surprised by that statement. Aren't you thinking I'm nuts; that you're going to have to find some way of getting me out of here?"

"Oh, I'm surprised all right. In fact I'm stunned. It's just that, well, my mother said something similar. I don't remember very much about what she said to me, I was too young, but one thing that stuck in my mind was she said we would both live forever. She told her psychiatrist the same thing; that she was hundreds of years old, although Dr Wright never believed her. She still doesn't but I'd come round to thinking it might be true."

She paused.

"How do you two fit into all this?"

John sighed deeply, wanting this woman sitting opposite him to understand everything. He leaned forward.

"Mrs Farsley. Please, may I call you Sara? With what I'm about to say, I don't think you'll think it, what, inappropriate?"

Sara moved her eyes to him.

John smiled at her. "I'd like you to explain to us, in a moment, why your mother was telling her history to a psychiatrist, what she was doing locked up. But firstly, let me tell you how we fit into your life."

He paused to take a deep breath. "We introduced ourselves as husband and wife. However, as I said just now, that isn't true. Then you heard Lily call me papa, which she does because I am indeed her father."

He paused, allowing Sara time to make the connections.

She frowned. "So are you saying that you are very old as well? Are you also very healthy?"

John nodded. "Yes, Sara, I am. From what we've pieced together, we're sure now that not only was your mother telling the truth when she told her story to the psychiatrist, but also that she too was my daughter, Lily's half-sister. However, while Lily was born in 1885, as she said, your mother, who's original name wasn't Annie Carr, was born in 1518."

Sara stared at John in disbelief, and then wondered at herself. Here was a man sitting opposite her intimating that he was hundreds of years old, and she was accepting it. Not laughing in derision or yelling for help but accepting it, just like she was starting to accept the story her mother had told Nancy Wright. She shook her head. This couldn't possibly be right. Where had they got this information from?

"How could you know that? Have you seen Dr Wright's notes? I thought they were confidential. She certainly didn't put all that information in her book."

"I know it, Sara, because it's true. Your mother's name in Naples, where she was born, was Paola Santini. I never met her because I'd been forced to flee Naples months before she was born. I didn't even know her mother was pregnant."

He frowned. "I don't know anything about a book. Has Dr Wright written a book about your mother?"

"A chapter in a book, yes, but she didn't mention her name. I've only recently found that out, as I said, but not initially from Dr Wright, although she confirmed it."

She sat back in her chair and ran her hands through her hair. This was unreal, but everything agreed perfectly with what she'd read in Nancy Wright's notes and with Matt and Julie's research. However, it still made no sense.

"Mr ... um, should I call you John? Or are you suggesting Grandpa?"

John laughed. "I think John would be better."

"John, how much do you know about my mother? You say she was born in 1518 ..." She paused. "Did I really just say that?" She shook her head and continued. "You say she was born in 1518. What happened to her after that?"

"I, we, know nothing about her at all after that except that she fled Naples at the age of about sixty, much as I had to, owing to being in danger from the Church. They thought she was in league with the Devil. But where she went and what she did, I have simply no idea. The first indication I had that she might have survived all this time was when Ced saw the drawings you sent and recognised her features. Then he found a more detailed portrait of her when she was Paola Lethrington by a French artist."

"The Cazabon picture," said Sara. "Yes, I've seen it."

"Exactly," said John. "When I saw that, I could see how much like her mother and me she was. I'd always hoped and prayed that she might be alive, so you can see why it is a desperate shock and disappointment to discover that she died so recently."

Sara steepled her hands to her face as she sat forward in her chair. Her mind was a whirlwind of conflict, the lawyer in her screaming 'Challenge this; it can't be true!'

"John, as you know, I'm a lawyer. I deal in facts. You must realise that this conversation is surreal, like something out of a movie. I need to ask you a couple of questions."

"Of course," nodded John.

"If you are my mother's father, you must have been born even longer ago than 1518. When was that? Hundreds more years earlier?

My mother told Dr Wright that her name was Paola Santini, just like you said. What was your name at the time?"

"Stefano Crispi," he said. "I was Stefano Crispi during my time in Naples. It was the first name I took after I fled my original life. I was born in the early fourteen hundreds, 1427 to be precise, in San Sepolcro in Italy. My original name was Luca di Stefano."

Sara took a breath. "I've never heard of Luca di Stefano, but that other name, Stefano Crispi, is the name my mother told Dr Wright was her father's. Matt found a painting by him on the Internet. Of course, that's why you looked familiar. It must have been a self-portrait. The face in that painting, it's very much like yours."

John laughed. "Perhaps that's because it was my face. I painted a number of self-portraits and I know that at least one still exists in an art museum in Italy. However, there's something in your voice, Sara, that tells me that you're still not completely convinced by us."

"Well, you must admit; it's all rather weird. There was something else you said … I know, my eyes, and my mother's eyes, you implied they were important, significant, the colour, that is. You and your … Lily … don't have the pale grey eyes you described."

"Actually," smiled Lily, "we do. It's just that we didn't want to distract the conversation by showing them, so we both put in coloured contacts. Look."

She put her fingers to her eyes and removed the plastic lenses. "Go on, Papa," she said, turning to John.

"I'll be pleased to be rid of them," said John, as he discarded his own set.

As John and Lily looked up at Sara and she saw their eyes were the same as hers, all her lingering doubts vanished. She leaned forward to take Lily's hands with her left hand and then John's in her right.

"Is it really true? Are you really my grandfather and aunt? But you have Asian features, Lily …"

"I was born in Hong Kong. My mother was Chinese," explained Lily. "I think this is all new to you, Sara," she added. "How long have you suspected you might be different?"

"Well," sighed Sara, "as I said, the ageing thing has bugged me for a while, but it was only recently, when we saw Dr Wright's book and then she gave me copies of her notes, that I began to wonder. That's why I wanted Mr Fisher to use his program to check the paintings and drawings."

John leaned forward. "Could you tell us about this Dr Wright and what led to your mother being treated by her?"

Sara nodded. "Of course. I'll give you the abridged version. Then, I should introduce you to my husband, Pete. After that, we'll go to my home where you can look through the notes for yourself. There are some photographs of my mother amongst them that I'm sure you'd love to see."

Chapter 36

Palo Melliff nodded in impatience as he listened to his boss issuing his latest instructions. He was already way ahead of him: he knew exactly what to do and, unlike his boss, he knew exactly how to do it.

"Is that clear, Melliff?" Dayton was pacing his office. "I want you to set up an automatic screen and search for any new image of Carr, Gomes, whatever her name is – and I mean any new image – that appears on any database anywhere in the world. I know it might take time, years perhaps, but when you find it, I need to know. Whether it's today, tomorrow, next year or in ten years time, the program must alert you. Then you must alert me. Immediately."

He paused as a thought struck him.

"We couldn't get access to immigration records, could we? You know, those cameras in arrivals halls that pick up everyone as they exit with their luggage?"

Palo looked up at him and laughed. "Do you know how many airports there are in the world, Mr Dayton, sir? Sorry, there's no way of getting into those systems. Apart from anything else, they don't put them online. If they are linked to somewhere, it's within a closed loop that's very well secured."

Dayton was sceptical. "Not like you to turn down a challenge, Melliff. Surely if they are on some sort of intranet, it must be accessible somehow."

Palo shrugged. "I could get into some of the minor ones in places where they're not so savvy, you know, like in some tin pot African state, but if you think I could get into the JFK system, boss, or something like that … well, I'm flattered, but … we're not in the movies."

Resigned to the limits of what even his brilliant pet nerd could achieve, Dayton abandoned the idea and moved on.

"Right, Melliff, while that's going on in the background, I want to refocus attention on Sara Farsley. Have the assistants who have been keeping an eye on her noticed anything of interest?"

"Not really, sir, no. She's been carrying on pretty much as usual. She hasn't been back to the shrink's place. The only thing out of the ordinary was that she finished early at her office last Friday, mid-morning in fact. Left with her husband and another couple of people, a man and a woman. They all went to the Farsleys' place, stayed there for a few hours and then the couple left."

"Do you know who they were, Melliff, this couple? There are photos of them, presumably?"

"Just the woman, sir. There was only one girl trailing them at the time, the one who followed them from the office. Mr Farsley dropped them all outside the house and went to park the car. They were in the street for just a few seconds, so she only got a couple of shots and they weren't so great. It was one of those bright days, you know, everyone was wearing sunglasses. I'd say from the shape of the woman's face that she was oriental, Chinese perhaps."

"Chinese?"

"Yeah, about thirty, slim, attractive. Similar to Sara Farsley, in a way, except Farsley's older."

He opened a file that was resting in his lap and took out a slightly blurred, half-profile shot of Lily in large dark glasses arriving at the Farsley house.

Dayton took the photograph from Palo.

"Yes, I'd agree; she looks oriental," he reflected as he took in what he could of Lily's features and luxuriant black hair. "I'd say she's an attractive woman. Do you know who she is?"

"No, sir, Mr Dayton. Do you want me to find out?"

"I don't think it's necessary, not at this point, Melliff. What about the man?"

"Didn't get a shot of him, Mr Dayton, sir. The girl was worried about being spotted. Like I said, they were only there for a few seconds."

"Replace her, Melliff. She's obviously incompetent. She's not paid to mess things up. Did she say what he looked like?"

"Dark glasses as well, sir. She reckoned he was in his thirties, like the woman. Quite tall, slim, black hair."

"How long were they there?"

Palo consulted his file. "Left at ten thirteen in the evening."

"No photos from when they left?"

"No, sir. Mr Farsley must have gone out the back entrance of the house to fetch the car. Drew up unexpectedly outside. There was a lot of hugging, apparently, but both the visitors had their backs to my girl. Then they got in the car and left. She didn't get sight of their faces."

Dayton banged his fist on the desk. "Definitely replace her, Melliff. This is intolerable. Put more people on the surveillance. Teams with two at the minimum. You have to cover the angles."

He stared again at the photo of Lily. "Doesn't your magic routine help? The one that removes glasses and hair?"

Palo pulled another photo out of the folder and handed it to his boss. "Not a lot in this case, sir. It's too much of a profile shot. All it really confirms is that she's oriental."

Dayton frowned at the image and then glared at Palo who shrank into his chair. "Anything else?"

"No, sir."

"Right, Melliff. Back to Sara Farsley. I want to know everything about her daily life: what her schedule is – when she goes to work, to the gym, to her girlfriends' houses, whom she meets. Everything, Melliff, everything. When she's at home, I want to know when there's no one else there. OK? I particularly want to know when I can reliably find her alone. Actually, Melliff, just to cover all the bases, so we don't get any surprises, you'd better get the same information on the whole family. I want to know where each of them is at any given time and where they are likely to be an hour or so after any given time. Are we clear?"

"Shouldn't be a problem, boss, Mr Dayton, sir. I might have to pull a couple of people out of the shrink's place. Just leave one girl there."

"I don't think Dr Wright is of any great importance or use to us now, but if that couple shows up again, I want them recorded properly. OK, Melliff, get to it!"

"Yessir!" said Palo, shooting a mocking salute at Dayton as he slouched out of the office.

Dayton watched him go. He wasn't pleased. It was unlike Melliff to employ sloppy assistants. He had to accept that he'd stretched his nerd's resources at short notice. He doubted that the unknown couple was important; the Farsleys would have lots of friends. This could have been something social that had been arranged for months; visitors in town. He looked again at the photographs of Lily. The quality was too poor for any meaningful analysis. Damn the dark glasses; they blocked everything. Even when the computer removed them, there wasn't much more. All that could be said was that she was young, attractive, oriental and of a similar build to Sara Farsley. Was that significant? Was there something about her face? He shrugged. He was reading too much into it. If she showed up again, Melliff could get better shots. Otherwise, he would forget her. It was Sara Farsley who was his goal. He wanted to arrange her abduction and get her to the house in Italy. The sooner the better. She would be in no danger, as long as she didn't resist. She just needed to serve his purpose and she would be released. Eventually.

Dayton stared through the doorway after Melliff. The next part of his plan would not involve him directly – Melliff might be prepared to mine data, steal it, adjust it and extract whatever was useful from it, but the average eighty-year-old with a walker could probably get the better of him physically. No, in the real world, Dayton needed the right sort of muscle.

He pressed the button on his console for his secretary. "Doris, call Rodney Heston, please. Tell him I need to see him here as soon as possible."

An hour later, a muscle-packed man almost as tall as Dayton himself appeared at the office door, escorted by Doris. "Mr Heston's here, Mr Dayton," she announced.

Among the strange assortment of characters her boss did business with, she far preferred the Rodney Heston type. He might be larger than the average truck and probably about as intelligent, she thought, but at least he's polite and courteous. Not like the computer crowd, most of whom looked and behaved as if they'd just crawled out of some sewer. Courtesy went a long way in Doris' book.

For Rodney, looks were deceptive. While he wouldn't have been comfortable gracing the halls of academia, he was no dummy. However, he was happy to keep that to himself. He was streetwise, reliable and immensely strong, the latter an asset he had no qualms about using when necessary. He worked with a small group of similar men who hired themselves to the rich and unscrupulous. They had no name, no office and certainly no website. They were known to just the few who could afford them and were prepared to use them, but that was enough.

His relationship with Marcus Dayton went back several years and involved a number of what Dayton called housekeeping assignments. As with Correia in Rio, most of these centred around persuading an awkward opponent in a business transaction that it wasn't in his best interests to continue with the venture.

"Come in, Rodney. Sit, please," said Dayton. "Thank you for coming at short notice. How are you?"

"As ever, thank you, Mr Dayton. How can I help you?"

Dayton smiled thinly. Small talk was not Rodney Heston's strongpoint.

"It's a fairly straightforward matter, Rodney. I need someone escorted from their home to an address in Italy. Much of the transportation will occur using my own jet; it's the smooth carriage from the point of origin to the aircraft that will need your particular skills. It will, however, require a certain sensitivity. Under no circumstances do I want the subject harmed in any way. She is to be treated with kid gloves."

"Not a problem, Mr Dayton," replied Heston without hesitation. "Just tell me who, when and where."

"The details are in here," said Dayton, handing him a file. "Now, there's one aspect of this particular assignment that differs, apart from the need to protect the subject."

Heston's face registered nothing even though he suspected he knew what was coming. Dayton was a hands-on man.

"I want to be there at the point of collection, in fact, I want to pick up the subject myself."

Heston sighed. "Forgive me, Mr Dayton, but is that wise?"

"Wise or not, Rodney, this lady represents my future and I feel it's important for our relationship."

"You're the boss, Mr Dayton. I have no doubt we can make it work."

After Rodney Heston left, Dayton sat back in his chair and looked up at the huge photograph of his late daughter, Emma, her eyes as always reassuring and encouraging.

"Not long now, my sweetheart," he said. "We'll create the brothers and sisters you never had."

Chapter 37

After Pete Farsley had been introduced to Sara's two visitors and once he'd stopped shaking his head in disbelief, the four of them drove the short distance to the Farsleys's house in Beacon Hill, Boston. Julie was out with friends but Matt was home, having finished the last of his exams that morning. Sara phoned ahead and told him to stay put.

"Matt, sweetheart, you are simply not going to believe who I'm bringing home for lunch. Do you think you could call Julie and without worrying her or alerting her friends about anything, persuade her to drop what she's doing and come home? She'll never forgive me if she misses this. But on no account is anyone else to be involved."

"I think I get the message, Mom. I'll call her now. Putting two and two together, I can't wait for you to get back."

On the short drive over, Sara explained to John and Lily how it was because of Matt and Julie's persistence that she had told them the story of her childhood and then how Matt had started unearthing material from the Internet.

Matt was waiting for them with the front door open. Aware that it would be better for the introductions to be made inside rather than in the street, even if it did appear to be deserted, he stood back as the car drew up and allowed his mother to show John and Lily straight into the hallway.

An amused smile on his face, John took Matt's hand and greeted him. "Hello Matt; I believe you are my great-grandson. This is my daughter, Lily, your great-aunt."

"W-what do I call you, sir?" was all Matt managed to stutter.

John laughed. "Certainly not 'sir', that's for sure. I think, Matt, given how bizarre this all must seem to you, it would be easier to call us by our names: John and Lily. Better to keep the relationships in the background, just in case anyone overhears any conversations we have."

"John it is, then, sir," said Matt, not quite sure why everyone immediately burst out laughing.

For several minutes after this introduction, Matt was speechless, much to Sara's amusement. As they all moved into the Farsley's large and comfortable living room, he hovered by the door, unable to take his eyes off either of the guests.

"I'll fetch the photographs of Annie Carr," said Sara.

"While you do that, sweetheart, we'll go into the dining room," added Pete. "I'll show John and Lily the paintings."

Ten minutes later, John stood back from the Paola Lethrington painting of the serving woman and the large printout of Annie Carr's portrait of Nancy Wright that were laid out on the table in Sara Farsley's dining room, his right hand pulling thoughtfully at his chin.

"Well?" said Sara.

"Come on, Papa, tell us what you think," added Lily.

John turned to them. "They are brilliant. I agree completely with Ced's program: the link between Annie Carr and Paola Lethrington is confirmed."

He sighed, still coming to terms with the news that Annie Carr was dead. "There's no doubt that Annie was my Paola. If only we'd known she was here in the States, Lei-li. When I think of all the time I lived here in the first part of the twentieth century, and all the time you've lived here..."

Lily took his hand. "I know, Papa; it's tragic, but at least we've found Sara, which is a bonus we never even dreamed of."

Sara held up the envelope of photos. "You still haven't seen these, John. Let's go and sit in the living room; we can spread them out on the coffee table."

John and Lily were completely absorbed in examining the photos of Annie Carr from her sessions with Nancy Wright when there was the sound of a door slamming from the rear of the house followed by rapidly approaching footsteps.

"Mom, I–" Julie stopped at the living room door as she rapidly took in the faces turning to look at her.

"Julie," said Sara as she stood to take her daughter's arm. "Come and sit down. I'll introduce you and explain everything."

Julie was in awe. "I think I know already, Mom. It's all true, isn't it? Everything we've suspected from the paintings, drawings and stuff about Annie Carr. Everything in Dr Wright's notes that Annie Carr told her, it's all true." Her voice was little more than a whisper as her eyes darted from John to Lily and back.

Sara nodded. "Yes, Julie, it is. What we didn't anticipate was that all that information would lead us to these two wonderful people."

She introduced John and Lily and then spent the next few minutes explaining who they were. As she finished, to her surprise, Julie burst into tears.

"Julie, whatever's wrong? This is such a happy occasion."

"I know, Mom; I get that, but what's bugged me since we started thinking the story of Annie Carr might be true and that it applies to you as well is that I'm not like you. I'm going to grow old while you remain the same. You're not going to change, Mom, while I become an old lady."

Sara nodded, her eyes also moist. "I've had the same thoughts and I've tried to put them to one side. It's too awful to think that I won't be part of the normal order of things; that Pop and Matt and you will … well …"

She turned to her grandfather, whose existence had been unknown to her until that morning. "How do you deal with this, John?"

John leaned forward and took her hand, smiling gently at her.

"You're quite right, Sara, and you too, Julie. It's the hardest thing. All I can do is tell you about the children I've had over the centuries and how we coped with it all. For me, they are all very much alive in my mind, even those who lived over five hundred years ago. It will be the same eventually for you, Sara. One of the features of this strange condition is a really acute memory – events from the distant past are just as strong for me as things that happened yesterday. I think Lei-li – Lily – will agree. What also help are family likenesses. When I first saw you this morning, Sara, I was staggered by how like my daughter Gianna you are. She lived in Florence in the sixteenth century and she lives on in you."

He turned to Julie.

"And you, Julie, it's amazing. My other daughter from that time, Sofia, Gianna's elder sister, had a daughter, Chiara, who was so like you. If you were to dress in the fashions of sixteenth-century Venice, it would be hard to tell you apart. I'll paint your portrait and we'll use that clothing and a hairstyle that was very popular then."

Julie had moved from the sofa to her preferred position of sitting on the floor. She sniffed and wiped her eyes with a tissue. "That would be amazing. Wow! This is all going to take some getting used to. I can't wait to hear all your stories. Yours too, Lily." Then her bottom lip trembled again. "But I wish I was like you all."

Pete put an arm around Julie's shoulder and squeezed her gently.

"John, when we were trying to get to grips with the idea that Sara might be like we thought her mother was, we realised there was a need to keep everything under wraps; that we can't really advertise what we know. In fact, that we can't tell anyone."

"Yes, Pete," said John, "you're absolutely correct. I can tell you from bitter experience that the fewer people who know about us, the better. The negative part about how we are – Lei-li, Sara and I, and, of course, my other daughter, Phoebe – is that there are people out there who want to be the same. That's understandable, but there are some who would stop at nothing to try and find out what it is that makes us tick. Of course, in the past, there have been religious fanatics who thought I was in league with the Devil. As you know, Sara's mother, Annie, when she was Paola, suffered the same problems."

"Wow!" said Matt, who was still turning over in his head just how old John was and wondering why he wasn't incredibly fragile, why his skin wasn't like the crazed glaze on a piece of antique porcelain. "I can't wait to hear all the details."

John turned to him. "I'll gladly tell you, Matt, but first, there's someone I need to run certain things by. You see, we're fortunate in having a person, I can't say who right at this moment, but he's someone who is looking after our best interests. It's complicated and I need to get his take on how we go forward. Believe me, he has made an enormous difference to my peace of mind. Lei-li's too."

"That's good to know," said Pete. "It's something that's certainly been worrying me."

"Can I ask something?" said Julie. "Why is it that you keep calling Lily Lei-li? I realise there must be a Chinese connection. Could you tell us about that, at least?"

John laughed. "Certainly, Julie, there's no reason not to." He turned to Lily. "Why don't you explain, Lei-li? Tell Julie all about Hong Kong."

For the following three hours, John and Lily explained some of the details of their past lives to the enthralled Farsley family. For Sara, Matt's words of a few weeks before about her life only just beginning echoed in her head as she wondered what the future might hold. John was careful not to broach more recent events regarding his abduction in 2009 and the failed attempts at experimenting on him at the secret research laboratory of Peterson Biotech. Nor did he tell them about Claudia Reid's results and Professor Frank Young's subsequent research. He knew that before the Farsleys were told of this, there were formalities Digby Smith would want to organise in his own arcane way, arrangements that John felt sure Smith would try to keep from the US authorities. John knew it would be wrong to anticipate how Smith might want to play it. He also knew that he couldn't discuss any of it over the phone: a face-to-face discussion was required.

Around six o'clock, Sara announced that she was the poorest of granddaughters in that they must all be starving and she'd offered little more than a few soft drinks. As she headed for the kitchen with Pete in tow, she stopped and turned to him. "Whatever did we start with the revelations at your birthday dinner, Pete? Can you believe just what a strange person you married?"

"Strange? Maybe, but also exotic, beautiful and wonderful," said Pete taking her in his arms. "I always said there was no one in the world like you, and I was right."

Over a rapidly prepared dinner around the kitchen table and glasses of inky-purple Sagrantino, a much-coveted Umbrian wine Pete had recently discovered through a specialist-wine-merchant golfing buddy, talk turned to the future.

"John, as a family, we've always wanted to discover more about Europe, Italy in particular," said Pete. "Have you ever revisited some of these places from your past?"

"Actually," replied John, "I haven't been to continental Europe since the early seventies and that trip was only very brief. I'd intended for it to be longer but circumstances changed and I returned to England. Before that, apart from the Normandy beaches in World War II, the last time I was there was back in the 1870s. I've been saying to Lola for ages that I'd love to go back and show her some of the places I've told her so much about."

Pete's eyes flitted from John to Lily and back again. "Normandy beaches? World War II? 1870s?" he echoed, shaking his head. Then he nodded thoughtfully, an idea forming in his head. "I know you'll think what I'm going to say is a little crazy, given we've only all known each other for a few hours, but hey, this whole thing is crazy. I can still hardly believe I'm having these conversations."

John looked at him quizzically, an amused glint in his eye.

"Well," Pete continued, "what I was thinking was that once you've sorted out matters with your mysterious friend, maybe we could all set off on our own version of the Grand Tours of two hundred years ago, with you, John, as our guide. What do you think?"

John smiled. He was already warming to Pete's earnestness, seeing in him a man who wholeheartedly embraced anything he took on.

"Actually, Pete, I think it's a great idea; there's nothing crazy about it at all. However, I shouldn't recommend going just yet – it's mid-summer and the heat in Italy can be fierce. I think the autumn would be a better time. What I do think would be a good idea right now is for you all to come to England as soon as possible and meet my family. We can all get to know each other in the relaxed surroundings of the Lake District and then make our plans. How about that?"

Pete glanced at Sara and saw the excitement in her eyes. "Thank you, John, that would be amazing," he said.

"I can't wait to meet Lola, John," added Sara, "and, of course, your girls. Gosh! Imagine going to all the places you've lived in and finding art works created by you. I assume that some will still be there?"

John laughed. "Most of the paintings are in art museums – we can make a start in the National Gallery in London, or even the Met in New York. As for frescos, there might still be some here and there from the early days. Certainly 'The Awakening' that I painted with Piero has now been unearthed and is on public display. Ced Fisher has been urging me to go with him to see it. Perhaps he'll agree to come on a Grand Tour as well. What he doesn't know about art isn't worth knowing."

"I don't think he knew about Paola Lethrington," reflected Matt, to everyone's amusement.

"Nor did I, Matt," smiled John. "She was pretty obscure."

They compared schedules and, after considering Pete and Sara's work constraints, agreed the trip to England could start in a month's time.

"Lola will be thrilled," said John. "She really wanted to come with me; she's itching to meet you all. As for the girls, they'll be very excited to find they have new cousins. However, first things first. I'll fly back to England very soon and meet up with our contact."

He looked around to see Pete frowning.

"Something wrong, Pete?"

Pete started from his reverie. "Uh, no, not at all. I was just wondering. Is your place in the Lake District far from St Andrews?"

"Pete!" said Sara. "We can't turn this into a grand tour of golf courses."

John laughed. "I'm not a golfer but I'm sure that a couple of rounds in Britain's best might be possible. St Andrews isn't that close but Lytham is no distance at all. I'll talk to my contact."

Sara scowled at him in mock castigation. "I can see that I'm going to have to keep a tight rein on you two."

"Talk to Lola," laughed Lily. "She's a force to be reckoned with."

"I shall," replied Sara, not taking her eyes off John. "I can see that she and I are going to be the best of friends."

Chapter 38

Three weeks later, the plans for the trip to England were taking shape. Full of excitement, Lily called Sara to say she had arranged all the flights for them and that she was coming over to Boston the next day to go through the final details before she and the entire Farsley crew flew out the following week.

"How was your visit from our secretive friend?" she asked Sara with a giggle – John had returned to Boston with Digby Smith a week after his first meeting with the Farsleys.

"It was something else," laughed Sara. "That guy is every grey British civil servant you see in the movies rolled into one. Pete had been determined to make a case for approaching the US government about future plans for me, but your man Smith was adamant. He explained that I would offer no value to them, as he put it, since I have no past to tell them about – he conveniently forgot to mention that my DNA might prove interesting to them. He said that both your past and John's were effectively the property of the British government and what he called a state secret. He also said that if Pete chose to approach the FBI or anyone, the Brits would just deny it all and Pete would be written off as a crank. Worse still, they would wash their hands of me, making my future a problem. Once he'd detailed the benefits of what he could offer us, Pete had little choice but agree. But it was all very cloak and dagger; you should see the forms we had to sign."

"I can imagine," replied Lily. "Actually, Sara, we shouldn't really discuss it on the phone."

"Why, do you think the NSA is tapping our line?" said Sara.

"I doubt it, but you can't be too careful."

"OK, Mata Hari, enough said. What time are you arriving tomorrow? I can't wait, Lily, this is all so exciting. We're going to England!"

Sara had spent the past week ensuring everything was in order for their trip: passports up to date, clothes ready, presents for their new family bought. She couldn't wait to meet John's two young daughters, Sophie and Phoebe, who were, in fact, her aunts. As for Lola, she knew instinctively she'd be a soul-mate.

At her office, Sara had been able to delay some of her cases and pass on others to colleagues, all of whom were mystified by her sudden desire to rush off to England. Pete was winding up his current commitments and would be ready by the weekend.

Lily was arriving on an early train from Penn Station that arrived shortly after eleven. Sara's plan was to finish a few chores upstairs before she got out the maps and documents to go through with Lily. She knew that maps were not her strong suit – nor were they Lily's – but she wanted to try and gain some insight into where they were going in and around the fascinating-sounding Lake District of England.

Although Matt and Pete had already studied every map they could find, their cursory explanations were too rushed for Sara; Julie's were little better. Sara felt she would make more headway with Lily, as long as Matt and Julie were out of the house so they wouldn't interrupt. Since she also wanted just to sit down with Lily and chat, she hatched a plan to occupy her offspring.

However, Matt and Julie had other ideas. What they didn't want to do at this point was miss time with Lily, so they both objected strongly when Sara told them their tasks for the morning.

"That's crazy, Mom, not a good use of time," argued Matt. "Mine, that is. Julie could easily do all that stuff in no more time than it will take us both. What's the point in me going?"

"He's right, Mom," said Julie, her comment gaining surprised sideways glances from both Sara and Matt. Was Julie actually volunteering for something? Then she continued and they realised magnanimity was not her motivation. "Except that the opposite is the much better option. Matt has his bike and could cover all this ground in a flash. There's no need for me to go at all."

"Yeah, like I'm going to go and exchange Mom's underwear. No way!" said Matt.

Julie curled her lips and pulled a face at Matt.

Sara laughed at them. "That's why I want both of you to go – there are chores for each of you. Matt's right, Julie, I don't expect him to go wandering around the ladies' lingerie department, and Matt, you're the one to go check with the phone company about our roaming plans in Britain. The idiot I spoke to was quoting me numbers that sounded like it would cost around the annual budget of some Third-World country just to send a text."

"Who do you want to text? We'll be on vacation."

"I might want to text you. You're not going to be walking alongside me holding my hand for the whole time, surely?"

"With your sense of direction, I might need to, Mom."

"Very funny," said Sara, raising her eyebrows imperiously.

"Come on, Mom," said Matt, warming to his theme, "no guessing now, which one's your right hand? Hold it up!"

"It's the one I beat you with," she said, accidentally holding up her left hand.

"I rest my case," laughed Matt, ducking.

She had finally packed them off, both still complaining and now arguing over the rules of a competition for who was going to be back first.

"Out of here! Now!" ordered Sara as she shut the street door on them.

She checked the time. Lily's train wouldn't be arriving at South Station for another forty-five minutes. Since it was a glorious day, she would probably walk through the sun-dappled Boston streets to the Farsley house. There was time to finish the chores.

When the doorbell rang some forty minutes later, Sara again checked her watch. She frowned. She wasn't expecting anyone else. Maybe Lily's train had arrived early and she'd caught a cab after all. She ran lightly down the stairs and pulled open the door. "Lil– oh, hello, can I help you?"

"I do hope so," said the smiling, middle-aged woman standing in front of her.

Marcus Dayton had made his plans carefully. Following Rodney Heston's evaluation of the streets and alleyways around the Farsleys' house, he'd decided to slip quietly through the rear gate – the lock was child's play – and from there through the yard to the rear door that led into the kitchen. He'd already been in twice on other days when he knew no one was home, noting the position of all obstacles and potential hazards to his progress. On those occasions, he even carefully ascended and descended the three flights of stairs checking for the most silent route. He didn't want to be announced by errant floorboards creaking.

With only a narrow window of opportunity, the timing for the operation needed to be perfect. From Melliff's watchers he knew that Sara Farsley was seldom at home alone, her normal weekday routine being to set off to work and return with her husband. The weekends, therefore, offered the better option – the husband normally played golf and while the son and daughter were often at home, there was a chance they would both go out, leaving their mother alone. This is exactly what had happened today and the watchers reported it within two minutes of Matt and Julie leaving. Another five minutes of following both of them into town confirmed they would be gone for a while. It took a further fifteen minutes for Dayton to get into place behind the house while Heston parked the black van a hundred yards along the street at the front.

Dayton was about to go in when he received a text telling him to hold: the daughter had left the department store and appeared to be heading home. Five impatient minutes later – he felt exposed in the lane behind the house – the good news arrived. Julie had bumped into a couple of girlfriends and was now settled in a Starbucks with them. The watcher sitting at an adjacent table reckoned they would be involved in girl-talk for some time.

Dayton texted back. 'What about the boy?' He smiled at the reply. Matt was tenth in a slow-moving line in the phone shop and at the present rate of progress it would be at least half an hour until he was through. When he finally left the shop, he would find that both tyres on his bike were flat.

A final exchange of texts, this time to a watcher in the street, confirmed all was quiet – no kids, dog walkers or other pedestrians, and no traffic. Dayton took his picks and quietly opened the gate.

There would be just two people involved in the overpowering of Sara Farsley: Dayton himself and a middle-aged woman called Edith. Once Dayton was in position in the kitchen, he would send a text to everyone to confirm it was a 'go' and Edith would ring the bell to the house. At the same moment, Heston would start the engine and begin rolling the van slowly along the street.

The use of the innocuous-looking Edith was a masterstroke that was Heston's idea. She would appear slightly flustered when Sara opened the door, immediately soliciting sympathy and putting Sara completely off her guard. Edith carried a syringe hidden in her right hand, ready to plunge it into one of Sara's veins as soon as Dayton had grabbed hold of her from behind.

On reaching the kitchen, Dayton listened to the noises from the house. He could hear Sara moving about upstairs singing quietly to herself. It was essential to Dayton that Sara would seem simply to evaporate. There could be no disturbance; it must appear that she'd gone out and failed to return.

He punched a key for a pre-written text and almost immediately his phone vibrated with the answer: 'Clear' – the street was still quiet. They were ready. He moved to the foot of the stairs, listened again, then slunk back towards the kitchen door – when Sara came downstairs to answer the front door bell, she would be most unlikely to look towards the kitchen.

He looked down to the cell phone still in his hand, hit another key and the message 'Go' was on the way. Ten seconds later the doorbell rang and he heard the sound of Sara running lightly to the landing and down the stairs. As she opened the door, he heard her say, "Lil– oh, hello, can I help you?"

"I do hope so," said the smiling, middle-aged woman standing in front of her.

Dayton started to move forward.

Palo Melliff was where he preferred to be – in his darkened, air-conditioned room in Marcus Dayton's Manhattan offices surrounded by his computer monitors, the servers humming sweetly to him from the racks on the far wall. He was bored with all the street activity he'd had to organise recently with his watchers and he was pleased that he'd been able to delegate much of the work and supervision to Gloria, his principle assistant. Gloria enjoyed the work and was good at it – she got on with people far better than Palo did. He knew he was people-skill-challenged but it didn't bother him.

He was sitting in his leather recliner, keyboard on his lap, his hands flying across the keys as he quietly issued instructions into the microphone attached to his headset. His eyes flashed across the screens as he seamlessly shifted the target for his data input from one computer to the next.

He was aware that the task set him by Dayton – to monitor the world's networks for any indication of artwork by or images of the woman who had been Cassie Gomes – was probably going to be long term. If she was savvy, and it seemed she was, she would try to avoid getting herself online at all. Try but probably fail. She might have a friend on Facebook, for example, who put up a harmless photo of a gathering that included her. Palo was trying to access as many accounts on all the social networks as he could. It wasn't straightforward – there were millions of them for a start – but it was amazing how ignorant of simple security most people were. Although his coverage wasn't total, it was improving exponentially. He was confident that should an image with Gomes' face in it be posted, there was an increasingly good chance it would come to his attention.

This and all the other search algorithms required a huge amount of automation, routines that looked after themselves but which would alert him whenever they discovered anything that fitted within the parameters he'd set. Palo's problem was he had to accept that tightening those parameters to the limits he'd prefer meant potentially missing a hit. He had, therefore, to keep the limits relatively loose, which meant checking a massive amount of potential hits. When he wasn't checking data, he was constantly refining his search algorithms: a man in his element as thousands of lines of code flashed before his eyes, all to the sound of the other passion in his life filling his ears with complex harmonies. Bach. Palo loved Bach. It was his inspiration, his joy. For Palo, Bach was the ultimate programmer: creator of the most wonderful code that translated into infinite refrains of exquisite pleasure.

When the hit happened, it took Palo completely by surprise. He'd expected a simple alert – a ping and the flash of a link. However, this particular hit was so strong that several of his algorithms found it almost simultaneously. Coinciding with a crescendo in one of his favourite fugues, the series of alarms resonated with an insistence that saw Palo's hands momentarily cease in their perpetual flight across the keyboard. The room suddenly lit up as all three of his large monitors flashed up the same image, one that was steadily refining and sharpening as the many sub-routines completed their work.

Palo stared in awe at the face on the screens. He knew that face almost better than his own; he'd seen it in so many guises over the past few weeks that its sudden appearance, so large and so vivid, was like a moment of divine revelation. The first images he'd seen had been grainy images from the past, and then there were the far better black-and-white shots from the seventies. Now, here it was again, a shot so clear that having found it, Palo needed none of his programs to confirm its identity – his own eyes were more than capable of leaving him in no doubt. He pressed a key and the source flashed up next to one of the images. He read the information, shook his head in disbelief and reached for his cell phone.

As Marcus Dayton took a step towards Sara Farsley, he realised he was still holding his phone. Needing both hands free, he was about to slip it into his pocket when it started to vibrate. He glanced down at the screen, wondering in irritation if the scene outside had suddenly changed. When he read the brief message, his eyes widened.

'URGENT! Found Gomes'.

For a brief moment, he froze in his steps, totally unprepared, a mixture of shock and elation suddenly coursing through him. Then he made his decision. He looked across the twenty feet from where he stood to Edith on the doorstep. He could see from the angle of her arm that she had the syringe poised in her hand. Although her eyes were firmly fixed on Sara's, the smile still on her face, Dayton knew one part of her vision would be watching him. He shook his head slightly and backed quickly into the kitchen, lifting his phone to his eyes again as he did. He had one more pre-programmed message to send, this one tied in with an automatic voice message.

Edith knew it was coming but still it sounded deafening through the concealed earpiece in her left ear. 'Abort!'

Edith was a professional, prepared for instant action and reaction. Expect the unexpected was her default position in any operation; things could change in a microsecond and her reaction and response were crucial.

There was only a slight pause between her initial reply to Sara and what she said next, the delay masked by the distraction of her left hand running through her hair in apparent confusion.

"Yes," she continued, the smile still fixed on her face. "I do hope so. I'm looking for a friend of mine, Mrs Lorna Whitely. I appear to have made a mistake with the address."

Sara nodded; she knew Lorna Whiteley. "Right number, wrong street," she smiled, stepping through the door and pointing past a black van that seemed to be hovering. "Go down to the end and turn left, then go along to Brookton. It's the next street. You'll find her there."

"Thank you so much, my dear," said Edith. She was perfectly aware that Sara knew Lorna Whitely – she had done her homework and set up this contingency plan. She slipped the syringe back into its holder in her pocket. "I'm so sorry to have bothered you. My good fortune that you know her."

She turned and walked off in the direction of the black van. As she drew level, she turned as if to wave, but Sara had gone back into the house and closed the door.

Edith yanked open the passenger door, slamming it after her as she settled fuming into the seat. She turned to Heston. "What the hell happened?"

"Search me," shrugged Heston. "All I could see were the messages flying around. Damned amateur. I should never have agreed to letting him be part of it. We could all have been compromised."

"What are you waiting for?" growled Edith, still fuming. "Let's get out of here."

Chapter 39

Nancy Wright picked up the notes she'd been working on, tapped them together on the desktop and placed them in their folder. Then she walked over to the filing cabinet, pulled open a drawer and deposited the folder into its sleeve.

As she pushed the drawer back into place, she sighed in satisfaction. She might only be part-time these days but it had been a busy week getting everything shipshape. Now all patients and their records were up to date; nothing outstanding. She was ready for the break in Cape Cod with her family she took at this time every year. It had been a family tradition from when the girls were small. Each year was the same and yet different, as her two girls had grown from youngsters racing and tumbling around the clapboard house and the sandy shore of the lake – the 'pond' as it was called – to gangly, awkward teenagers who never seemed to know quite where their limbs ended and the world started. Then in no time at all they were graceful but shy young college girls with assorted boyfriends in tow, and now they were confident women with husbands and children of their own. Nancy and Chris had loved every moment, loved watching their grandchildren splashing in the warm water, loved the games of cards, the barbecues, the laughter and the reminiscences.

She looked up from her empty desktop and her eye fell, as always, on the portrait that Annie Carr had painted of her so many years ago. My, but she looked young. More and more it was like looking at a painting of either one of her two daughters. The strange thing was that while Connie was normally regarded as the image of Chris, Maddie was a reincarnation of Nancy. Yet the face in the painting, if you looked at it in one light, was Maddie, without question, and yet in another, it was Connie. However, above all, it was Nancy, changed over the years – she had been just thirty-two then and now she was seventy-four – but still unmistakably Nancy.

Her eyes roamed wistfully over the detail as she thought of Annie. She had been such a talent in so many ways. Not just her skills as an artist, which were profound – if only those skills could have been recognised, channelled – but also her talent as a storyteller. Nancy had no qualms about her rejection of Annie's tales of being hundreds of years old – the woman was a classic delusional case and, combined with her violent, unpredictable and dangerous outbursts, incarceration was the only option at the time to protect society from her. However, she did regret not believing Annie about her daughter. At the time, it was just another story and the members of the commune had clearly conspired to lie about her for whatever reason. It was so sad, thought Nancy, that Annie died in that dreadful, unnecessary fire, not ever seeing her daughter again. Serendipitously – thanks for the most part to Nancy writing her book of case studies – Sara, as Nancy now knew Annie's daughter, at least now had the benefit of Nancy's copious notes on her mother. She had the photographs too, or some of them! Nancy smiled. She would have to dispose of the other, more compromising photographs before long; she didn't really want them discovered by her daughters after she was gone, or worse still, deposited in some library along with the rest of her files to be ridiculed by some as-yet-unborn researcher years in the future, incredulous at her bizarre methods of treatment.

The following morning, Nancy and Chris set off early from their apartment in New York City's Upper West Side. The traffic was light and they made good time, covering the two hundred and fifty miles to the Hawesley holiday cottage in a little less than four and a half hours. Their daughters, together with their own families, had arrived the night before – Connie from New Haven and Maddie from Providence, Rhode Island. As Nancy and Chris carried their bags into the cottage – with six bedrooms and baths, Nancy had always laughed at the realtor's description, but the term had stuck – they were greeted by Jack, Connie's husband, with the news that Connie and Maddie had driven into Falmouth to shop.

"Bob's on the beach trying to prevent the kids from drowning each other while I'm doing some chores here," he added. "There must have been quite a storm; a good number of the light bulbs are out."

"I'll give you a hand with that as soon as I've dropped the bags," volunteered Chris.

Nancy walked over to the screen doors and onto the large balcony. From there she could see beyond the small garden below to the beach. Three of her grandchildren were dancing and splashing in the water, while the eldest, Bob junior, was doing his best to remain aloof from his younger, irritating siblings and cousins as he tried, without a great deal of success, to master his father's latest toy: an inflatable paddleboard.

Leaving her unpacking, Nancy made her way down the outside steps to the garden and crept up to the children, who were too engrossed in their games to notice her coming. Suddenly the youngest grandchild, Charlotte, looked up from where she was methodically filling a small plastic bucket with sand using a tiny teaspoon from her favourite doll's tea set. The furrows of concentration on her forehead evaporated as her face lit up with the pleasure of seeing her grandmother.

"Gwammie!" she squealed, throwing out her arms, "I making lunch for my dollies."

Nancy scooped her up from the sand, careful not to knock over the half-filled bucket – destroying half-an-hour's intensive labour could well have resulted in a serious meltdown, despite the child's joy at seeing her grandmother.

"My, you're getting to be a big girl, young Charlotte. You're so like your mommy was when she was your age."

"Did she come here?" asked Charlotte, her tiny fingers playing inquisitively with Nancy's grey hair.

"She did, my darling. This very same spot. She loved making lunch for her dolls, just like you are."

There was a splash as Bob junior fell off the paddleboard for the tenth time.

"Bob's trying to ride the puddle bore, but he's not very good," declared Charlotte.

As Nancy was greeting the other grandchildren, she heard a shout from the house.

"Mom! Hi! We're back!"

Connie was leaning over the upstairs balcony railings waving at Nancy.

"Hi, sweetheart, I'll be up in a moment," called Nancy.

The grandchildren were soon reabsorbed in their games and Nancy walked quietly away, laughing as she watched Bob helping an unappreciative Bob junior in the water: he wanted to master the board without parental help.

"Hi, Mom!" cried Connie again as Nancy walked into the kitchen, turning from the fridge where she was stacking packets to give her mother a hug. "Mad's just getting the rest of the food."

Two minutes later, Maddie staggered into the kitchen under the weight of several bags of provisions. Nancy rushed to her assistance. "Couldn't you make two journeys, Maddie?" she laughed, "or do you just enjoy juggling eggs?"

"No pwarbrem, Marmy," said Maddie, speaking New Jersey. She loved accents, and as ever, she would be treating the family to her full repertoire during the course of the week. Connie had always tried to convince her mother there must be some hitherto undiagnosed condition she could research while at the same time having her clearly insane younger sister locked up.

The shopping put to rest, the three of them sat down to a pot of tea.

"How was Falmouth?" asked Nancy. "Buzzing with tourists?"

"Not too overrun," said Connie, "and there're a few new stores. Hey, that reminds me. There's a new art gallery, well, it's always been a gallery, I think, but it's got a new owner. And guess what, there's a painting in the window, bigger than all the others and sitting on an easel, that's very like that one you have in your office. You know, the one painted by that patient of yours?"

"Annie Carr's painting?" Nancy was shocked.

"That's the one," replied Connie. "It's been a long time since I saw it, but from what I remember, it's really very like it. I mean, although it's clearly not you, it's of a woman in her thirties, like

319

yours, and the features are really quite similar. I thought for a moment that you'd sold your painting, but then I noticed that the one in the window has modern clothing, whereas I think your Annie Carr dressed you in nineteenth-century clothes, didn't she?"

"Sold it! I'd never sell it! I treasure that painting above any other I own. Whatever makes you think I would sell it?" Nancy was aghast at the thought. "Heavens," she added, "I was looking at it only last evening as I left the office. I could see both of you in that picture. It's truly brilliant."

Connie laughed at her mother's intensity. "I told Mad that you couldn't've. But she reckoned it was so like yours that if you hadn't sold it, someone must have stolen it and put it on sale down here."

"What are you talking about, Connie?"

"Well, lady," chimed in Maddie, now a New York City detective, "it's like this. There's a new kid in town, opened a gallery on Main Street. Got this pic in the window. Dead ringer for yours."

"Maddie, talk sense, for heaven's sake!" Nancy was becoming exasperated.

"Mom, don't worry, it's not your painting," said Connie, reaching out to touch her mother's arm in reassurance, "but the artist certainly paints in the same sort of style."

"Where is it, this gallery?"

"As Maddie said, it's on Main Street, Tipley's or Tripley's; something like that. I'm sure it was different the last time we were down. It's got some really amazing paintings on show, mainly coastal scenes from the Cape. Plus some portraits. And there, right in the middle, pride of place, really, is this painting like yours. Mom? You OK?"

Nancy sat back in her chair, her eyes haunted as she tried to understand what she was hearing. She realised her heart was beating wildly. Annie's portrait of her wasn't just any painting; it was in a league of its own. She had never seen another remotely like it. So how could there be a painting so similar in the window of a gallery in Falmouth? What could it mean? She had to see it. She put a hand to her forehead.

"Yes," she said, her voice distracted and distant, "I'm fine. I think I'd better go take a look at this painting."

She stood up.

"You're going now?" asked Maddie. "It's lunchtime, Mom, the kids'll be up soon."

Nancy turned to her, as if wondering who she was. "Er, actually, I'm not very hungry. Your father cooked me an enormous breakfast. You know what he's like when we go anywhere. I think he's convinced all the shops here will have sold out of food and that we're going to starve." She turned and started towards the door. "Yes, I think I'll go now."

She smiled in reassurance at her two puzzled daughters. "I won't be long."

The drive into Falmouth took fifteen minutes and Nancy cruised for another five to find a parking spot. It was the height of summer and the town was benefiting from a long hot spell. The restaurants were packed.

Still in a daze, Nancy locked the car with her key fob and then remembered she hadn't asked the girls where on Main Street the new gallery was located. She walked east along the road, checking the shops on both sides. Two hundred yards along, she saw it. She knew the premises; it had been a gallery for many years. It must have changed hands. She looked up at the sign as she approached. The name was in an ornamental script – cornflower blue on a white background – the words stating simply 'Tripley Gallery'.

As Nancy got closer, what immediately caught her attention was the large painting displayed on an old wooden easel in the centre of the window. The girls were right; it was really very like the portrait of her, except that the clothing was modern and the features different enough for it to be of someone else. But the style …

She rubbed her hands together; they felt clammy and cold. She thought she really should sit down. She shook her head, wild thoughts flashing across her mind. She pushed her glasses up the bridge of her nose and peered through the window. There were no customers in the shop, just someone at the back sitting at a desk. Taking a few deep breaths, she straightened, took another look at the painting in front of her, then pushed open the gallery door.

The woman sitting at the rear of the gallery stood as Nancy entered and walked around her desk. She was about fifty years old; her hair was drawn back in a bun and a cashmere cardigan was draped over her shoulders. A pair of reading glasses dangled from a cord round her neck. Walking towards Nancy, she smiled and said, "Hello, can I help?"

Nancy stared at her as if the words were in a language she didn't understand.

"Are you feeling all right, ma'am?" asked the woman. "Would you like to sit down?"

The words finally filtered into Nancy's consciousness.

"The portrait," she said. "The one in the window."

The woman nodded. "Beautiful isn't it? It was one of the first Naomi did when she took the gallery."

"Naomi?"

"Naomi Tripley, the artist."

"So you're not the artist?"

"Me?" the woman laughed dismissively. "Dear me, no. I just mind the store when Naomi's busy."

"Is she … is she your daughter?"

The woman looked at Nancy askance.

"My daughter? Heavens, no! I just work for her. I saw her setting up here a couple of months ago and I offered my services."

"How long has the portrait – the one in the window – how long has it been there?" stuttered Nancy.

The woman thought about it. "As I said, Naomi painted it soon after she moved in here, so it must have been there on display for almost two months. It's not actually for sale. Naomi said she painted it to show people what she could do. Said that once she'd finished it, she couldn't bear to part with it."

"Two months?"

"More or less, yes."

Nancy frowned in confusion, her eyes moving slowly around the gallery, not focusing on any one thing. She took a deep breath. "Is she here? The artist? Naomi Tripley? Is she here?"

The woman shook her head. "No, she's not in today. She's out painting some more coastal views. They're proving incredibly popular, selling wonderfully well." She smiled as if expecting Nancy to add her name to the list of customers.

"Which part of the coast has she gone to?" asked Nancy.

"She's up at Marconi Beach today. There's a good easterly

blowing so the water's lively. She has a lovely spot up there and the rangers allow her to walk along the restricted paths to get to it. She can work there without being interrupted."

Cape Cod projects out into the Atlantic Ocean for some thirty-five miles before turning sharply north for another twenty or so, the northernmost tip curling to the west in an enormous claw at Provincetown. Halfway up the northerly projection, on the wild eastern side that bears the brunt of many of the storms the Atlantic slings at the US seaboard, is Marconi Beach, the place from where its namesake made the first transatlantic radio transmissions. The windswept beach is a little over fifty miles from Falmouth's location in the southwest of the Cape. Nancy drove the distance at a risky pace, given the density of traffic and ever-present traffic cops, in exactly an hour.

Pulling into the large car park set back on the sandy cliffs above the beach, Nancy was surprised to see so many cars and so few people. In the mid-afternoon, they were all still on the beach, some forty feet below the level of the car park. She hurried towards the wooden steps that descended to the beach and stopped to look along the clifftop in both directions. The paths along the sandcliffs were restricted to help protect the terrain from even more erosion than it already suffered at the hand of nature. To the north, about three hundred yards away, she could see a single figure, standing by what appeared to be an easel. It had to be Naomi Tripley. Nancy started to walk along the path when she was stopped in her tracks by an officious shout.

"Ma'am, that's a restricted path! You can't go along there!"

Nancy turned to see a woman in a ranger's uniform standing at the top of the steps, her hands on her hips. She retraced her steps until she was face-to-face with the serious-looking young woman.

"I'm sorry, I didn't know it was restricted. I–"

"That's why we put up all these notices, ma'am. To tell folks. All you gotta do is read them."

"Sorry, yes, I was in a hurry. You see, I really have to speak with that lady along there. The artist."

"Why would that be?"

"It's, well …" What could she say? That she thought she might be someone who is nearly five hundred years old? "It's really rather personal," she offered quietly. Then she lifted her chin. "It's very important; I simply have to see her."

"Doesn't she have a cell? Couldn't you call her?"

"I don't know if she does and anyway, I don't have her number."

The ranger eyed the old woman in front of her. She reminded her of her grandmother, especially in the earnest way she was pleading her case.

"OK, ma'am. It's against the rules but I can't see that one more person's gonna do much harm. After all, the chief lets the artist go out there. Mind, that's probably got something to do with the fact that he's got a coupla very nice paintings hanging on his wall now."

"Thank you, ranger. Thank you very much," said Nancy as she turned and hurried back to the path.

"Go careful, now," the ranger called after her.

Nancy waved an arm.

The wind was blowing from slightly north of east with the result that Naomi didn't hear Nancy coming and, since she was facing up the coast, she didn't see her either. The three hundred yards seemed like three miles to Nancy as she hurried along, but finally she was just a few feet away. She stopped, wondering what to say. At that moment, one of the hundreds of huge gulls patrolling the shore flew a few feet above Nancy's head and let out a piercing screech.

Naomi turned, distracted by the noise, and her eyes fell on Nancy. She tilted her head in surprise, not expecting to be disturbed. Concerned initially by the woman's apparent agitation, she studied her carefully, slowly taking in her age and her face. She frowned slightly and suddenly she knew. A gentle smile spread slowly across her face.

She took off her large-brimmed hat and tossed her hair. "Hello, Dr Wright, you look like you've seen a ghost," she said, her eyes sparkling.

When she saw the reaction in her ex-psychiatrist, she turned quickly to grab her folding chair and hurried the few paces to where Nancy was standing, her mouth gulping air.

Naomi took her arm and guided her into the chair. "Sit down, Dr Wright, before you fall down. I'll get you some water."

Nancy took the water gratefully, not taking her eyes off Naomi.

"Annie," she finally stuttered. "How is it possible?"

"I'm Naomi these days, Dr Wright, but yes, what you're thinking is correct. Annie didn't die in the fire, although her identity changed soon after."

She knelt on a tuft of grass next to Nancy and took her hands. "Are you feeling all right?"

Nancy nodded quickly as she pulled a tissue from her pocket. "Yes, thank you, I am, but Annie, I–"

She sobbed into the tissue. Naomi continued smiling at her and waited until she'd regained her composure. Then she said, "Do you believe my story now, Dr Wright?"

Nancy nodded even harder, smiling, then sobbing. "Yes, Annie, yes, I do. I believed it from the moment I saw the portrait in your gallery window. My girls told me about it when we arrived today, Chris and I. I went into town to see it immediately."

Naomi laughed. "Then perhaps I can finally call you Nancy, like you suggested all those years ago. I was going to look you up, but I had a kind of feeling about the portrait; that you might just see it and wonder. I remembered you saying that you came to Cape Cod."

"Wonder? I nearly fell over in the street. Oh, Annie, how did you escape the fire? It was so intense; I saw the damage for myself. How did you get out?"

"I was rescued by one of the other women – her name was Olive. Without her, I would have died, for sure. She saw me go back in – I was desperate to rescue more of my work but I was quickly overcome by smoke and the next thing I knew was when I woke up in the woods about a mile from Sawpine. Olive had carried me there. She was in a bad way, coughing a lot. I knew I couldn't stay with her, grateful as I was; she was making too much noise and anyway, she was in need of medical attention."

Nancy nodded. "Yes, she was soon recaptured. You were the only one who escaped. They never positively identified your body, of course. How could they? They thought one of the bodies in the library was you and that someone else, Lepri I think her name was–"

"–Cheryl Lepri. Yes, I remember her well. I think she was around the library when the fire started."

"Then the body they thought was yours must have been hers,"

said Nancy. "What happened then, Annie? Where did you go?"

Naomi sighed. "It's a long story, Dr Wr– Nancy. I left the country, went to Mexico and finally ended up in Brazil, where I remained until very recently. I would have stayed there too but someone dangerous found out about me. I was more or less forced to leave."

She squeezed Nancy's hands with both of hers. "So can you accept I wasn't delusional and certainly not insane? That it was something of an act? I hope you're not thinking of turning me in, since although I was telling the truth when I said I killed Ty Donnington, I was also telling the truth when I said it was in self-defence."

Nancy shook her head. "The thought hasn't crossed my mind, Annie. Anyway, who'd believe me? Annie Carr would be, what, seventy-two by now. If I tried to convince anyone you are seventy-two, *I'd* be locked up for being delusional."

A shadow passed across her face.

"However, I am in shock, Annie, to think I've based an entire career on the assumption that I was right in my diagnosis of you. You even featured, albeit anonymously, as a special case study in a textbook I wrote. I never considered for one moment that your story could be true, not for one moment." She wrung her hands together. "My God, if it hadn't been for the fire, in which you nearly died, my narrow, inflexible thinking might have had you still locked up. I wonder how many other patients have been telling me the truth?"

Naomi shrugged. "They all tell you what they believe to be the truth, Nancy. However, I doubt there are any others like me, so I shouldn't worry about how you've diagnosed them. As for the institution, I can tell you my escape plans were pretty far along when the fire happened, so I wouldn't have been there much longer. And you can hardly blame yourself for the fire."

Nancy looked away. "Nevertheless, it's hard to realise just how wrong I've been, how inflexible."

"Mine was a very difficult story to swallow; I haven't come across many people who were willing to accept it without reservation."

Nancy shook her head in wonder. "So you really were all those people, Annie – the actress, the painter in Trinidad? It's hard to understand."

Suddenly she remembered. "Oh, heavens, Annie, your daughter, I–"

Naomi nodded and interrupted her. "Yes, Serena. That's a regret I really do have. Hardly a day goes by without my thinking of her. Thinking about what could have been if only I'd gone back sooner. I did go back, you know, to the commune. In 1980. I went back with a new identity for both of us. I was going to rescue her, take her out of the country. We were going to be together. That's when I found out she was dead; that she had been killed just the previous year in the woods. That old witch Zelda told me. If only I hadn't waited so long."

It was Nancy's turn to take Naomi's hands.

"Annie," she smiled, her eyes radiating her delight. "Annie. I have the most incredible thing to tell you. The woman, Zelda, was lying to you. When she told you Serena was dead, she was lying. Serena also escaped, in 1979. She's alive, Annie, alive! I've met her."

Naomi sat back on her heels, unable to believe what she was hearing.

"Oh my God!" she said as she clasped her hands to her face. "Alive? Where? You've met her?"

"Yes, I have. She came to see me. She somehow found out about the book I'd written and sought me out. She recognised you from my description in the book. She didn't know your name, Annie. Those people in the commune wouldn't even tell her that."

Naomi nodded. "I know. Zelda told me with so much glee." She shook her head. "I have no regrets about what happened to her that night."

The briefest of shadows passed across Nancy's face as she wondered what Naomi meant by the remark. Then it was gone and she squeezed Naomi's hands again. "Annie, I had a very long conversation with Sara. I've just realised–"

"Sara?"

"That's Serena's name now. Sara Farsley. She's married with two lovely children. Well, they're adults really. I examined her, medically, I mean. I wouldn't believe it at the time, even with all the evidence screaming at me. Annie, what you told me, what you believed to be true about her when she was tiny, I think it's true. I think she's the same as you. You should see her; she's forty-six and she looks … well, she looks just like you do."

"Where is she? Where does she live?"

"She's not far away; she lives in Boston. That's just a couple of hours away. We could see her today! I'll call my husband. He'll take us. Shall we do that?"

Naomi took Nancy's hands and helped her to her feet. Then she threw her arms around her and they hugged each other. The years fell away and they were back in 1970 again, laughing about taking each other's photographs. Naomi held Nancy out at arm's length. "Oh, Nancy, I can't believe this has happened. I think it's the happiest day of my long, long life. Let's do it. I'll put all this stuff together and we'll do it." Suddenly she remembered Nancy's age. She frowned. "Are you feeling all right? Just now, you looked rather–"

"Old?" interrupted Nancy.

"I was going to say pale."

Nancy laughed. "I may be getting on, Annie – oh, heavens, I'm going to have to get used to calling you Naomi – anyway, I may be getting on but I'm still pretty fit."

They gathered Naomi's gear and hurried back along the path. Nancy took out her cell phone to call Chris, expressing surprise she'd got a signal. Naomi laughed. "Think about where we are; this spot is where telecommunications all started. If we can't get a signal here, there's no hope!"

As she watched Nancy punch the speed dial, a thought crossed her mind. She put her hand on Nancy's. "Before you connect, how much does your husband know about Annie Carr and Serena?"

Nancy hit the red button to cancel the call. "Well, whenever I've discussed you – Annie Carr, that is – with him over the years, it's always been from the point of view that you were delusional and, of course, dead. I haven't spoken to him about Sara – Serena. So he doesn't know much."

Naomi nodded. "Look, I know today has been a shock and you've only just reversed a position you've held for years, but now you do understand and accept the truth, I also need you to accept the need for, well, secrecy. About me, I mean. I've lived a long time, Nancy, and I've had some narrow escapes, believe me. I am very reluctant to let more people know about me than need to know. What I'm saying, asking really, is does your husband have to know? You see, if he comes to Boston with us, you're going to have to explain, which will be kind of difficult, don't you think?"

Nancy stared at the ocean. "Yes, you're right, of course. I didn't really think it through. But you can't just turn up at Sara's house unannounced; I have to go with you. Let me think about it for a moment. I'll need to tell my family something."

Naomi looked at her watch. "Listen, Boston is actually about three hours away, more possibly, depending on the traffic, and you've driven a long way today already. I assume you've come from New York?"

Nancy nodded.

"Then it's too far to go today. Let's go tomorrow when you're fresh. I can take us in my car. We just need a story for your family."

"You're the one whose good at stories, Annie – sorry, Naomi."

Naomi smiled softly, but there was a distance in her eyes.

"Ah, but mine were all true."

Chapter 40

Naomi collected Nancy from the cottage at nine the following morning. They'd stopped in a diner for coffee on the way back to Falmouth the previous afternoon to agree on the story that Nancy later repeated to her family. She told them she'd been amazed to discover Naomi was the daughter of one of her patients from more than twenty years ago, a woman now sadly in the final stages of palliative care in a hospice in Boston. When Naomi mentioned she visited her mother twice a week and was going the following day, Nancy said she'd asked if she could go with her to see her old patient one last time.

Chris immediately suggested he drive them but Nancy said no: he'd done enough driving already and anyway, Naomi was returning the same day. They would be back by late afternoon.

"You did call ahead like you said you would?" asked Naomi once they were on their way.

"Yes," replied Nancy. "I spoke with Sara to check she'd be there. Obviously I told her nothing, just that I needed to see her. She seemed quite distracted. She and her family are off on a trip to England in a couple of days. We're lucky to have caught her."

"I hope this doesn't affect their plans," said Naomi. "I'd suggest waiting until they return but I really don't think I can. Is that terribly selfish of me?"

"Hardly," smiled Nancy, touching her arm. She kept turning to look at Naomi's face as they were driving, still unable to believe what her eyes were telling her.

"Perhaps I'll go with them, if they'll have me," mused Naomi. "Although I can't go quite yet; I've got two urgent commissions I've promised to finish and I need the money. I didn't leave Brazil with much; just enough to set up the gallery."

"I'm sure that situation will change once you've become better known on the Cape, Annie – whoops, there I go again."

As they drove from the Cape onto the main freeway to Boston, Nancy was turning the years over in her head. There was an unanswered question about the events back in 1970 that had always puzzled her.

"Heavens," she started, trying not to sound like the interviewing psychiatrist. "That whole business in the motel seems so long ago, Naomi, back when you were Annie. Do you still think about that day?"

Naomi shrugged lightly. "Not really. As you say, it was a long time ago."

"I often wonder what happened to the other man in your party. Seth was his name, wasn't it?"

Naomi didn't change the expression on her face as she thought of Seth Short, although there was an almost imperceptible hardening of her eyes. She had needed to lose him in order to carry out her and Petra's half-baked plan to escape.

She'd intended just to leave him stranded in Del Norte but he wouldn't get out of the truck. Annie sighed, deciding she'd have to resort to desperate measures.

As they drove out of Del Norte, she told him she needed to pee. As she expected, he took a track into the woods – she knew what he was thinking from the stupid look on his face. She walked away from the van into a clump of trees and squatted down, waiting. Sure enough, she heard him creeping up behind her. She timed her blow to perfection: as he reached out to grab her, she swung her arm round, the rock in her hand connecting squarely with his head. With little more than a grunt, he fell to the ground. In an instant she was on him, delivering three more crushing blows to his head. Then she grabbed a spade from the truck and dug a deep hole for his body, wanting to be sure it wouldn't be found.

"He must have decided to move on," said Naomi distantly. "Why is he on your mind?"

"It was just that I heard they found a body in the woods outside Del Norte in the late '80s, no more than a skeleton really, with its skull crushed. They never identified it. The pathologist reckoned it had been there the best part of twenty years."

She turned to Naomi in time to see her glance at her. There was a steely hard look in her eyes she had never seen before, a coldness that made Nancy think of all the people Naomi, as Annie, had admitted killing over the centuries during those long-ago interviews.

Naomi shrugged. "Maybe it was him, who knows? The last I saw of him was when he stormed off down the road in Del Norte after the row with Ty."

Nancy said nothing more. What could be gained by it? However, she knew in her heart she didn't believe this woman sitting next to her, the woman she thought she'd got to know very well but who was now, suddenly, a stranger. Annie had always told her that her killing Ty was self-defence. Now she wondered.

Sensing the atmosphere had cooled, Naomi changed the subject and started telling Nancy about her time in Rio. Nancy knew Rio from a number of conferences she'd attended there; and she had also visited São Luís.

"It's amazing we didn't bump into each other," said Naomi.

"That would have been a bit of shock for both of us," smiled Nancy. They both laughed as they reminisced further. Seth Short was soon forgotten.

Arriving in Boston, they parked as close as they could to the Farsleys' house, walking the last two blocks. As Naomi locked the car, she turned to Nancy and took both her hands.

"Nancy, I can't believe this is happening. Is my Serena really here? God, my heart's racing. I don't know how long I'll be able to remain in the street while you prepare Serena ... Sara ... for the shock we are going to deliver."

"Just give me a few minutes, Naomi. As we've agreed, if we're both standing there when she opens the door and she sees your eyes, she'll, I don't know, I–"

"–I could put on my dark glasses," said Naomi.

"She's really only expecting me," replied Nancy, "Let's stick to what we've planned."

Naomi sighed impatiently to herself. She'd only agreed to hang back in deference to Nancy's age and obvious agitation. She turned to walk a couple of reluctant lengths of the street while her ex-psychiatrist walked up to the Farsleys' door and rang the bell.

When Julie answered, Nancy introduced herself. "I think your mother's expecting me," she said.

"Yes," smiled Julie, "she told me. Please, come in."

"Dr Wright!" exclaimed Sara as she approached them along the hallway. "Sorry, I was in the kitchen. How lovely to see you. I must admit I'm intrigued to know what's prompted your visit. Your conversation was very enigmatic. Let's go into the sitting room. Would you like some tea or coffee?"

Nancy was about to answer when Lily emerged from the kitchen. "Hello," she said, offering her hand. "Are you Dr Wright? Sara's told me all about you. I'm Lily Saunders."

Nancy's mouth opened in surprise as Lily's eyes and features registered.

"I– You're–" she stuttered. She felt her legs start to buckle. "Sara, I–"

Sara stepped quickly forward to take her arm and guided her into the sitting room.

"I think you'd better sit down, Dr Wright."

As she slumped into an armchair, Nancy looked again at Lily, who was standing by the door.

"I do apologise," whispered Nancy, "you must think me so rude. Sara, we really need to talk. There's someone–"

"Don't worry, Dr Wright," smiled Sara. "I can explain everything."

"No. Yes. I'm sure you can." Then she shook her head. "No, you can't. You don't understand. It's not, er, Lily, it's well ..." She put her hands together over her mouth, shaking her head. "Oh dear, this is all so complicated."

She looked up at Lily and Sara.

"How about that tea?" suggested Sara.

"I'll fetch it," said Lily, heading for the kitchen.

"Yes," said Nancy, "thank you. Sara, we must talk. I–"

She was interrupted by the sound of the doorbell.

Sara looked round in exasperation. "Julie, could you?"

"OK, Mom," said Julie, who'd been hovering at the doorway, puzzled by the psychiatrist's behaviour.

She walked down the hall to the front door and opened it.

"Hello," said Naomi. "You must be Julie. I've come to see your mother."

Julie stood frozen to the spot. It wasn't just her eyes, it was her whole face. A slightly different version of her mother was standing in front of her. She turned her head to the sitting room and thought about Nancy Wright and the notes from the interviews. Then she remembered the photographs.

"Are you? ... I mean ... they said ... Oh my God!" She clasped her hands to her face. "You're my ..."

Naomi smiled. "Yes, Julie, I am. May I come in?"

"God! Wow! Sorry, yes." said Julie through her hands, immediately forgetting to move.

"This day is about to get really weird," she continued. "What's your name? Are you still Annie Carr?"

Naomi laughed quietly. "No, not for a long time. I'm Naomi Tripley now."

"Naomi Tripley," repeated Julie. "This is all amazing," she said and threw her arms around Naomi, nearly knocking her off her feet.

"Oh God, I'm sorry," she said. "I just had to hug you. I forgot. You're–"

"Old?" laughed Naomi. "Don't worry. I won't break."

Julie took her hand and walked her into the sitting room.

"Mom," she said, "there's someone to see you."

As she started to turn her head towards her daughter, Sara saw the reaction on Nancy's face was a cross between a smile and panic. "Naomi," she heard Nancy say, "I haven't ..."

"Sorry, Dr Wright, I just couldn't wait," said Naomi, chewing her lip to control the emotion she could feel starting to burst within her.

Nancy nodded as she lifted her glasses to brushed at her eyes with the backs of her fingers.

"Sara," she said. "This is Naomi Tripley, but she used to be–"

"Annie Carr," whispered Sara as she stood to face Naomi. She shook her head in total disbelief, then stretched out her arms. "My Mom," she choked as she took a step forward to take Naomi in her embrace.

A few moments later, Pete came in carrying a tray of cups, tea, coffee and milk. "Damn, forgot the sugar," he muttered. He looked up to see Julie leaning against the doorway, her eyes still wide with disbelief.

"Julie, what's up, honey?" He turned his head to the room to see his wife and Naomi hugging each other and stroking each other's faces and hair. Sara caught his eye. "Pete. Oh, Pete."

Pete stood looking helpless, not quite working it all out.

"Pete," said Sara again.

Naomi turned her face to Pete and smiled through her tears.

Pete looked around quickly for somewhere to put the tray before he dropped it. "My God. You're ... Does Lily know? No, she can't, she didn't say anything."

"Lily?" said Naomi, tilting her head in question.

"Does Lily know what?" said Lily as she walked into the room.

It was Naomi's turn to be shocked. She felt her mouth working as she turned to Nancy. "Dr Wright?"

Nancy was shaking her head. "I didn't know, Annie," she said.

"Annie!" exclaimed Lily. "Of course, you must be. I don't believe it." She reached out and put her hands on Naomi's shoulders. "You're Annie, which means you're Paola!" Then she saw the hesitation on Naomi's face.

"I'm Lily. I'm your sister!"

Naomi gasped. "My sister! I haven't got a ... but why shouldn't I have?" She took Lily's hands in hers. "Are you ...? How old ...? But you're Chinese."

Lily laughed. "Half Chinese. I'm a lot younger than you are, Annie, Paola – what do I call you?"

"Naomi, I'm Naomi now."

"Naomi. Wow! So many names. Just like me. I'm a lot younger than you are, Naomi, but I've got a pretty good start on everyone else here." She smiled. "I was born in Hong Kong in the eighteen eighties."

Naomi's eyes widened. "Does that mean your father – our father – is he still alive?"

"Very much so. Oh God, I can't wait to tell him. He'd always thought you were alive as well, so when we found out about the fire, I can't tell you, he was …" She shook her head. Then she continued excitedly, "Oh Naomi, this is amazing."

She turned to Sara and put out her arm to gather the three of them together. "How ever has all this happened?"

The front door to the house suddenly slammed and Matt rushed breathlessly into the room.

"Mom, I–"

They all burst out laughing at the look of utter bewilderment on his face as his eyes flicked from Sara to Lily and then fell on Naomi.

"Matt," said Sara, holding out her hand. "Come and meet your grandmother."

Half an hour later, Lily had called John in England to tell him the news. After the initial shock, he had gleefully spoken to Naomi. Lola was in the room with him, shaking her head as he broke into a Neapolitan dialect she had no hope of understanding. At the other end of the line, Naomi responded in the same tongue, laughing as she did.

"Are you testing me?" she chided him, amazed that the words still flowed as freely as if she still spoke the dialect every day. "Are you …Tata?" she added softly, using the dialect form for 'Daddy'.

"No, my carissima Paola, not at all. It's just that I've waited so long for this day. We've never met but I've felt your presence all these years. It's only right we should talk to each other in our own language."

The travel plans were delayed slightly while John flew immediately over to Boston for a joyful and emotional meeting with the daughter who'd been lost to him for nearly five hundred years. He insisted she join them on their trip, which she was thrilled to agree to – out of nowhere, she suddenly had a family.

There was only one minor problem.

"I'm sorry but I really have to finish these two paintings," Naomi explained to John. "I can't let the clients down; they both need their portraits for big family celebrations that are set in stone. They're absolutely relying on me."

John wanted to delay the trip to England, to help his daughter finish the paintings, but once Naomi realised that Sara and Pete had limited time available from their law practice, she insisted they all go ahead as planned. She would fly over as soon as she could.

"It will only be two weeks at the outside. I'll be over in no time and we can be together as one big family. I've never been to England; I can't wait."

Epilogue

Ten days later, Naomi was close to finishing the two paintings she had promised to her clients. Once her father and Lily left with the Farsleys, she worked with a purpose and intensity she had not felt for some years. Despite her thoughts constantly straying to the family waiting for her in England, she found the portraits flowing from her brushes, the likenesses of her subjects among her best work. She wished John, her tata, could be with her, admiring her skills and coaching her to improve further. She smiled to herself contentedly as she thought of a more secure future than she'd ever known. John had explained briefly about the enigmatic Digby Smith. Meeting him would be one of the first appointments once she reached England after she'd met her new stepmother, Lola – who was over four hundred and fifty years her junior – and her two half-sisters, Sophie and Phoebe. As they did for Lily, the two young girls would think she was yet another long-lost cousin until they were older.

Naomi was working in the studio at the rear of the gallery, her assistant, Mary, out front and under strict instructions not to disturb her. She was therefore surprised and somewhat annoyed when Mary put her head round the door.

"Naomi, I'm really sorry; I tried to resist but the gentleman is very insistent. I really don't think he's going to leave until he's spoken to you."

Naomi looked round. What part of 'do not disturb' didn't Mary understand?

She frowned. Mary was trying to mouth something to her. She put down her brush, wiped her hands on a cloth and walked over to the studio door, cocking her head in question.

"He's a very strange man," whispered Mary behind her hand. "He's really given me the creeps." She pulled a face of distaste, the corners of her mouth almost reaching her chin.

"I'll get rid of him," sighed Naomi, "but stay with me. I don't like 'creepy'."

She walked into the gallery to see a very tall, well-built man in his mid-thirties bending to peer at a display of her seascapes.

"Hello," she said. "I'm Naomi Tripley. My assistant said you wanted to speak with me."

Marcus Dayton stood up straight and turned to face her.

"Ms Tripley. I'm delighted," he smiled.

Naomi felt a chill touch her spine: although this man's smile carried a mask of sincerity, there was a coldness behind it he couldn't hide. She looked into his piercing eyes. They were emotionless pinpoints, like two black holes absorbing the very essence of life from the room.

"I read about your gallery in an article in an online newspaper," he said.

Naomi cursed silently. She'd been reluctant to give the interview but the young reporter had been very gushing and keen. She'd worried about the photograph the girl had insisted on taking, but thinking the whole thing was only for a local paper, she felt it couldn't do much harm. She hadn't realised the article would go online.

Dayton was still talking. "I love coastal scenes," he enthused, "so I was very keen to see more of your work. Now I have, I'm even more impressed. I'd very much like to buy this large work over here, if I may, but really I want to talk to you about commissioning a series of others."

Naomi listened to the words knowing she should be pleased by the proposition. However, she had spun many stories herself over the course of hundreds of years; there was a tone to his voice that she immediately recognized, a tone that didn't ring true.

"Certainly you may buy that seascape," she heard herself saying, not taking her eyes off his. "That's why it's there. Mary can sort that out for you immediately. As for future commissions, I'm afraid they will have to wait a while. I'm about to depart on a trip to England. It could take several weeks. I hope there's no urgency." She managed a thin smile.

"None at all, Ms Tripley," came the silky, almost condescending reply. "None at all. I can return in a couple of months when we can discuss it further."

"Good," said Naomi. "That's good. Thank you, Mr …?"

"Creed," replied Dayton. "Charles Creed." He held out his hand. Naomi shook it, shuddering slightly to herself. She could feel a latent power that disturbed her.

"Then I'll see you in a couple of months, Mr Creed. I look forward to it," she said, realising her words sounded no more sincere than those of the man facing her.

She returned to her studio and stared blankly at the almost-completed portrait on her easel. She had lost her concentration. Five minutes later, Mary came through again to find Naomi gazing out of the window.

"He's gone," she said. "Bought the painting; paid cash."

She paused, then added, "Sorry, Naomi; I really didn't know how to deal with him. He was kind of weird, don't you think?"

Naomi looked down at the paintbrush she was holding and nodded absently, her reply as much to herself as to Mary.

"He had the dust of centuries about him."

Acknowledgements

As with my first novel, Rare Traits, this second book in the trilogy could not have been completed without the help and encouragement of many people.

First and foremost, I could not have continued down my novel-writing journey without the constant support and encouragement of my wife, Gail. She is always there as a sounding board for ideas, a reviewer of drafts and an enthusiastic supporter of the project. This book is dedicated to her, with love.

Much of Delusional Traits is set in the United States. I thought I knew the place and the people quite well, but without the critical eyes of a number of American friends, I should not have been able to extricate myself from the huge number of semantic, geographic, linguistic and cultural holes that I managed to dig for myself in the first draft. My grateful thanks are therefore due to Anne Mensini, Sanford Foster, and Wendy Bearns, all three of whom put me straight on innumerable matters, as well as raising many salient points about the plot.

Also in the US, thanks are due to Gail's Bostonian cousins whose rented 'cottage' by the pond I borrowed for the text. Thanks also to Janey for the trip to Marconi Beach; it made all the difference.

Thanks for an early edit, and for very positive comments, are also due to my son-in-law, Simon O'Reilly – the fastest copy editor in the East!

A number of people have kindly read through the book in draft form and all were very positive in their comments. Thanks go to Cedric Harben; my sister, Jill Pemberton; Sarah Barnes; my daughter, Lea Woodward; my step-daughter, Zoe O'Reilly; and Jill Harrison.

Jill Harrison also wore her art historian's hat once again as she read it. Thanks, Jill, for our discussions and your input.

Two other friends volunteered to use their professional experience to proof-read and copy edit printed versions. Luci de Nordwall-Cornish provided me with a duly and brilliantly marked up script in record time; thank you, Luci. Then Janette Lesser applied skills honed many moons ago when working for a well known publisher and proved that none of those skills has lost its edge over the decades. Thank you, Janette, for the huge amount of time and effort you put into the task, and thank heavens for your amazing eagle eye! Thanks as well to Danny Lesser for duly scanning all the marked-up pages in Tel Aviv and sending them to me. A truly international operation.

My thanks are also due to Paula Svensen for her professional copy-editing services. As an American who has lived in Colorado, Paula was a great find and a pleasure to work with. Your many, many suggestions have made a huge difference to the final product.

I used the ideas behind the cover of Rare Traits to create the cover design for Delusional Traits, which was a fascinating venture. Thanks to Derek Murphy, who put together the cover for Rare Traits, for generously pointing me in the right direction for stock images, and to my son-in-law, Jonathan Woodward, for casting his designer and illustrator's professional eye over my efforts and helping me polish them.

I should like to thank my cousin Peg Cooke for agreeing to becoming a country doctor, while I'm sure that my good friend the late Julian Critchley would have been delighted to be a colonial governor. I have, once again, use the names of my five grandchildren (at time of writing): Lily, Phoebe, Frank, Digby and Mali. Grandchild number six, Samson Woodward, came along too late for inclusion, but I suspect his name might pop up in book three. To them all I say that I hope that if one day you read this book, you will be amused, even though your namesakes in the book are in no way meant to be like you.

When Rare Traits was self-published, I had no idea how it might be received. I have been thrilled by all the positive comments and encouragement, as well as the many reviews on Amazon from complete strangers. I'm delighted to have shared my characters with you and I hope that you find this offering as enjoyable.

Finally, I should like to thank the characters in the book who all came to life for me as they appeared. Good or evil, I enjoyed my time with you all and I look forward to meeting you again in Murderous Traits.

David George Clarke

If you enjoyed this book and you haven't yet read Rare Traits, then now is the time. As with Delusional Traits, Rare Traits is available on Amazon as an ebook and a paperback.

The third, and probably final part of the Rare Traits Trilogy, Murderous Traits, should be published by the end of 2014.

You can find details of my books together with other book related news on my website at www.davidgeorgeclarke.com If you would like to write to me directly to share your views and comments on either or both of the parts of the trilogy published so far (as of December 2013), send me an email at david@davidgeorgeclarke.com. I always reply.

Do you have kids or grandchildren, a favourite godson or goddaughter, a class of kids you teach or support in some way? My wife, Gail Clarke, is an author and illustrator. She has published three beautifully illustrated children's books that are available through Amazon's print-on-demand arm at CreateSpace. They are written in rhyme that children from 4-8 years-old just love reading or having read to them. Her three books are:

Patrick's Birthday Message
Searching for Skye - An Arctic Tern Adventure
Cosmos the Curious Whale

You can find more details at Gail's website:
www.gailclarkeauthor.com

David George Clarke
December 2013

Facebook: David George Clarke - Author
Twitter: @dgclarke_author